Meet t
Long, T
absol

D0428017

Meet Simon Hart: He's gruff and gorgeous…and not about to let his guard down and fall for a headstrong socialite, no matter how enticingly innocent she might be. But this lady has always secretly loved Simon, and now this Long, Tall Texan is about to become her beloved….

"Nobody tops Diana Palmer…I love her stories."
—*New York Times* Bestselling Author
Jayne Ann Krentz

And introducing Callaghan Hart:

His eyes were bold on her body, as if he knew exactly what was under her clothing.

The thought of Callaghan Hart's mouth on her lips made Tess's breath catch in her throat.

She'd always been a little afraid of her big, brooding boss. But lately at night she lay wondering how it would feel if he kissed her. She'd thought about it a *lot,* to her shame.

Callaghan was mature, experienced, confident—all the things Tess wasn't. She knew she couldn't handle an affair with him. She was equally sure he wouldn't have any amorous interest in a novice like her.

She'd *been* sure, Tess amended.

Because Callaghan was looking at her now in a way he'd never looked at her before....

DIANA PALMER

THE HART BROTHERS
SIMON & CALLAGHAN

ISBN 0-373-77088-X

THE HART BROTHERS: SIMON & CALLAGHAN

This edition published by arrangement with Harlequin Books S.A.

www.HQNBooks.com

Printed in U.S.A.

Classic "Long, Tall Texans" titles
from Diana Palmer and HQN Books

LONG, TALL TEXANS: EMMETT & REGAN
LONG, TALL TEXANS: BURKE & COLTRAIN
THE HART BROTHERS: REY & LEO
THE HART BROTHERS: SIMON & CALLAGHAN

and watch for Diana Palmer's new hardcover

BEFORE SUNRISE

available in bookstores now!

CONTENTS

BELOVED 11

CALLAGHAN'S BRIDE 187

To Debbie and the staff at Books Galore,
in Watkinsville, GA.
and to all my wonderful readers there and in Athens.

BELOVED

Prologue

Simon Hart sat alone in the second row of the seats reserved for family. He wasn't really kin to John Beck, but the two had been best friends since college. John had been his only real friend. Now he was dead, and there *she* sat like a dark angel, her titian hair veiled in black, pretending to mourn the husband she'd cast off like a worn coat after only a month of marriage.

He crossed his long legs, shifting uncomfortably against the pew. He had an ache where his left arm ended just at the elbow. The sleeve was pinned, because he hated the prosthesis that disguised his handicap. He was handsome enough even with only one arm—he had thick, wavy black hair on a leonine head, with dark eyebrows and pale gray eyes. He was tall and well built, a dynamo of a man; former state attorney general of Texas and a nationally known trial lawyer, in addition to being one of the owners of the Hart Ranch Properties, which were worth millions. He and his brothers were as famous in cattle circles as Simon was in legal circles. He was filthy rich and looked it. But the money didn't make up for the loneliness. His wife had died in the accident that took his arm. It had happened just after Tira's marriage to John Beck.

Tira had nursed him in the hospital, and gossip had run rampant. Simon was alluded to as the cause of the divorce. Stupid idea, he thought angrily, because he wouldn't have had Tira on a bun with ketchup. Only a week after the divorce, she was seen everywhere with playboy Charles Percy, who was still her closest companion. He was probably her lover, as well, Simon thought with suppressed fury. He liked Percy no better than he liked Tira. Strange that Percy hadn't come to the funeral, but perhaps he did have some sense of decency, however small.

Simon wondered if Tira realized how he really felt about her. He had to be pleasant to her; anything else would have invited comment. But secretly, he despised her for what she'd done to John. Tira was cold inside—selfish and cold and unfeeling. Otherwise, how could she have turned John out after a month of marriage, and then let him go to work on a dangerous oil rig in the North Atlantic in an attempt to forget her? John had died there this week, in a tragic accident, having drowned in the freezing, churning waters before he could be rescued. Simon couldn't help thinking that John wanted to die. The letters he'd had from his friend were full of his misery, his loneliness, his isolation from love and happiness.

He glared in her direction, wondering how John's father could bear to sit beside her like that, holding her slender hand as if he felt as sorry for her as he felt for himself at the loss of his son, his only child. Putting on a show for the public, he concluded irritably. He was pretending, to keep people from gossiping.

Simon stared at the closed casket and winced. It was like the end of an era for him. First he'd lost Melia, his wife, and his arm; now he'd lost John, too. He had wealth and success, but no one to share it with. He wondered if Tira felt any guilt for what she'd done to John. He couldn't imagine that she did. She was always flamboyant, vivacious, outgoing and mercurial. Simon had watched her without her knowing it, hating himself for what he felt when he looked at her. She was tall, beautiful, with long, glorious red-gold hair that went to her waist, pale green eyes and a figure right out of a fashion magazine. She could have been a model, but she was surprisingly shy for a pretty woman.

Simon had already been married when they met, and it had been at his prompting that John had taken Tira out for the first time. He'd thought they were compatible, both rich and pleasant people. It had seemed a marriage made in heaven; until the quick divorce. Simon would never have admitted that he threw Tira together with John to get her out of his own circle and out of the reach of temptation. He told himself that she was everything he despised in a woman, the sort of person he could never care for. It worked, sometimes. Except for the ache he felt every time he saw her; an ache that wasn't completely physical....

When the funeral service was over, Tira went out with John's father holding her elbow. The older man smiled sympathetically at Simon. Tira didn't look at him. She was really crying; he could see it even through the veil

Good, Simon thought with cold vengeance. *Good, I'm glad it's hurt you. You killed him, after all!*

He didn't look her way as he got into his black limousine and drove himself back to the office. He wasn't going to the graveside service. He'd had all of Tira's pathetic charade that he could stand. He wouldn't think about those tears in her tragic eyes, or the genuine sadness in her white face. He wouldn't think about her guilt or his own anger. It was better to put it all in the past and let it lie, forgotten. If he could. If he *could*....

Chapter One

The numbered lot of Hereford cattle at this San Antonio auction had been a real steal at the price, but Tira Beck had let it go without a murmur to the man beside her. She wouldn't ever have admitted that she didn't need to add to her substantial Montana cattle herd, which was managed by her foreman, since she lived in Texas. She'd only wanted to attend the auction because she knew Simon Hart was going to be there. Usually his four brothers in Jacobsville, Texas, handled cattle sales. But Simon, like Tira, lived in San Antonio where the auction was being held, so it seemed natural to let him make the bids.

He wasn't a rancher anymore. He was still tall and well built, with broad shoulders and a leonine head topped by thick black wavy hair. But the empty sleeve on his left side attested to the fact that his days of working cattle were pretty much over. It didn't affect his ability to make a living, at least. He was a former state attorney general and a nationally famous trial attorney who could pick and choose high-profile cases. He made a substantial wage. His voice was still his best asset, a deep velvety one that projected well in a courtroom. In addition to that was a dangerously deceptive manner that lulled witnesses into a false sense of security before he cut them to pieces on the stand. He had a verbal killer instinct, and he used it to good effect.

Tira, on the other hand, lived a hectic life doing charity work and was independently wealthy. She was a divorcée who had very little to do with men except on a platonic basis. There weren't many friends, either. Simon Hart and Charles Percy were the lot, and Charles was hopelessly in love with his brother's wife. She was the only person who knew that. Many people thought that she and Charles were lovers, which amused them both. She had her own secrets to keep. It suited her purposes to keep Simon in the dark about her emotional state.

"That was a hell of an anemic bid you made," Simon remarked as the next lot of cattle were led into the sale ring. "What's wrong with you today?"

"My heart's not in it," she replied. "I haven't had a lot to do with the Montana ranch since Dad died. I've given some thought to selling the property. I'll never live there again."

"You'll never sell. You have too many attachments to the ranch. Besides, you've got a good manager in place up there," he said pointedly.

She shrugged, pushing away a wisp of glorious hair that had escaped from the elegant French twist at her nape. "So I have."

"But you'd rather swan around San Antonio with Charles Percy," he murmured, his chiseled mouth twisting into a mocking smile.

She glanced at him with lovely green eyes and hid a carefully concealed hope that he might be jealous. But his expression gave no hint of his feelings. Neither did those pale gray eyes under thick black eyebrows. It was the same old story. The wreck eight years ago that had cost him his arm had also cost him his beloved wife, Melia. Despite their differences, no one had doubted his love for her. He hadn't been serious about a woman since her death, although he escorted his share of sophisticated women to local social events.

"What's the matter?" he asked when his sharp eyes caught her disappointment.

She shrugged in her elegant black pantsuit. "Oh, nothing. I just thought that you might like to stand up and threaten to kill Charles if he came near me again." She glanced at his shocked face and chuckled. "I'm kidding!" she chided.

His gaze cut into hers for a second and then they moved back to the sale ring. "You're in an odd mood today."

She sighed, returning her attention to the program in her beautifully manicured hands. "I've been in an odd mood for years. Not that I ever expect you to notice."

He closed his own program with a snap and glared down at her. "That's another thing that annoys me, those throwaway remarks you make. If you want to say something to me, just come out and say it."

Typically blunt, she thought. She looked straight at him and she made a gesture of utter futility with one hand. "Why bother?" she asked. Her eyes searched his and for the first time, a hint of the pain she felt was visible. She averted her gaze and stood up. "I've done all the bidding I came to do. I'll see you around, Simon."

She picked up her long black leather coat and folded it over her arm as she made her way out of the row and up the aisle to the exit. Eyes followed her, and not only because she was one of only a handful of women present. Tira was beautiful, although she never paid the least attention to her appearance except with a critical scrutiny. She wasn't vain.

Behind her, Simon sat scowling silently as she walked away. Her behavior piqued his curiousity. She was even more remote lately and hardly the same flamboyant, cheerful, friendly woman who'd been his secret solace since the accident that had cost Melia her life. His wife had been his whole heart, until that last night when she betrayed a secret that destroyed his pride and his love for her.

Fool that he was, he'd believed that Melia married him for love. In fact, she'd married him for money and kept a lover in the background. Her stark confession about her long-standing affair and the abortion of his child had shocked and wounded him. She'd even laughed at his consternation. Surely he didn't think she wanted a child? It would have ruined her figure and her social life. Besides, she'd added with calculating cruelty, she hadn't even been certain that it was Simon's, since she'd been with her lover during the same period of time.

The truth had cut like a knife into his pride. He'd taken his eyes off the road as they argued, and hit a patch of black ice on that winter evening. The car had gone off the road into a gulley and Melia, who had always refused to wear a seat belt because they were uncomfortable to her, had been thrown into the windshield headfirst. She'd died instantly. Simon had been luckier, but the airbag on his side of the car hadn't deployed, and the impact of the crash had driven the metal of the door right into his left arm. Amputation had been necessary to save his life.

He remembered that Tira had come to him in the hospital as soon as she'd heard about the wreck. She'd been in the process of divorcing John Beck, her husband, and her presence at Simon's side had started some malicious rumors about infidelity.

Tira never spoke of her brief marriage. She never spoke of John. Simon had already been married when they'd met for the first time, and it had been Simon who played matchmaker with John for her. John was his best friend and very wealthy, like Tira herself, and they seemed to have much in common. But the marriage had been over in less than a month.

He'd never questioned why, except that it seemed unlike Tira to throw in the towel so soon. Her lack of commitment to her marriage and her cavalier attitude about the divorce had made him uneasy. In fact, it had kept him from letting her come closer after he was widowed. She'd turned out to be shallow, and he wasn't risking his heart on a woman like that, even if she was a knockout to look at. As he knew firsthand, there was more to a marriage than having a beautiful wife.

John Beck, like Tira, had never said anything about the marriage. But John had avoided Simon ever since the divorce, and once when he'd had too much to drink at a party they'd both attended, he'd blurted out that Simon had destroyed his life, without explaining how.

The two men had been friends for several years until John had married Tira. Not too long after the divorce, John had moved out of Texas entirely and a year later that tragic oil rig accident had claimed his life. Tira had seemed devastated by John's death and, for a time, she went into seclusion. When she came back into society, she was a changed woman. The vivacious, happy Tira of earlier days had become a dignified, elegant matron who seemed to have lost her fighting spirit. She went back to college and finished her degree in art. But three years after graduation, she seemed to have done little with her degree. Not that she skimped on charity work or political fund-raising. She was a tireless worker.

Simon wondered sometimes if she didn't work to keep from thinking.

Perhaps she blamed herself for John's death and couldn't admit it. The loss of his former friend had hurt Simon, too. He and Tira had become casual friends, but nothing more, he made sure of it. Despite her attractions, he wasn't getting caught by such a shallow woman. But if their lukewarm friendship had been satisfying once, in the past year, she'd become restless. She was forever mentioning Charles Percy to him and watching his reactions with strange, curious eyes. It made him uncomfortable, like that crack she'd made about kindling jealousy in him.

That remark hit him on the raw. Did she really think he could ever want a woman of her sort, who could discard a man she professed to love after only one month of marriage and then parade around openly with a philanderer like Charles Percy? He laughed coldly to himself. That really would be the day. His heart was safely encased in ice. Everyone thought he mourned Melia—no one knew how badly she'd hurt him, or that her memory disgusted him. It served as some protection against women like Tira. It kept him safe from any emotional involvement.

Unaware of Simon's hostile thoughts, Tira went to her silver Jaguar and climbed in behind the wheel. She paused there for a few minutes, with her head against the cold steering wheel. When was she ever going to learn that Simon didn't want her? It was like throwing herself at a stone wall, and it had to stop. Finally she admitted that nothing was going to change their shallow relationship. It was time she made a move to put herself out of Simon's orbit for good. Tearing her emotions to pieces wasn't going to help, and every time she saw him, she died a little more. All these years she'd waited and hoped and suffered, just to be around him occasionally. She'd lived too long on crumbs; she had to find some sort of life for herself without Simon, no matter how badly it hurt.

Her first step was to sell the Montana property. She put it on the market without a qualm, and her manager pooled his resources with a friend to buy it. With the ranch gone, she had no more reason to go to cattle auctions.

She moved out of her apartment that was only a couple of blocks from Simon's, too, and bought an elegant house on the outskirts of town on the Floresville Road. It was very Spanish, with graceful arches and black wrought-iron scrollwork on the fences that enclosed it. There was a cobblestone patio complete with a fountain and a nearby sitting area with a large goldfish pond and a waterfall cascading into it. The place was sheer magic. She thought she'd never seen anything quite so beautiful.

"It's the sort of house that needs a family," the real estate agent had remarked.

Tira hadn't said a word.

She remembered the conversation as she looked around the empty living room that had yet to be furnished. There would never be a family now. There would only be Tira, putting one foot in front of the other and living like a zombie in a world that no longer contained Simon, or hope.

It took her several weeks to have the house decorated and furnished. She chose every fabric, every color, every design herself. And when the house was finished, it echoed her own personality. Her real personality, that was, not the face she showed to the world.

No one who was acquainted with her would recognize her from the decor. The living room was done in soft white with a pastel blue, patterned wallpaper. The carpet was gray. The furniture was Victorian, rosewood chairs and a velvet-covered sofa. The other rooms were equally antique. The master bedroom boasted a four-poster bed in cherrywood, with huge ball legs and a headboard and footboard resplendant with hand-carved floral motifs. The curtains were Priscillas, the center panels of rose patterns with faint pink and blue coloring. The rest of the house followed the same subdued elegance of style and color. It denoted a person who was introverted, sensitive and old-fashioned. Which, under the flamboyant camouflage, Tira really was.

If there was a flaw, and it was a small one, it was the mouse who lived in the kitchen. Once the house was finished, and she'd moved in, she noticed him her first night in residence, sitting brazenly on a cabinet clutching a piece of cracker that she'd missed when she was cleaning up.

She bought traps and set them, hoping that the evil things would do their horrible work correctly and that she wouldn't be left nursing a wounded mouse. But the wily creature avoided the traps. She tried a cage and bait. That didn't work, either. Either the mouse was like those in that cartoon she'd loved, altered by some secret lab and made intelligent, or he was a figment of her imagination and she was going mad.

She laughed almost hysterically at the thought that Simon had finally, after all those years, driven her crazy.

Despite the mouse, she loved her new home. But even though she led a hectic life, there were still the lonely nights to get through. The walls began to close around her, despite the fact that she involved herself in charity work committees and was a tireless worker for political action fund-raisers. She worked long hours, and pushed herself unnecessarily hard. But she had no outside interests and too much money to work a daily job. What she needed was something interesting to do at home, to keep her mind occupied at night, when she was alone. But what?

It was a rainy Monday morning. She'd gone to the market for fresh vegetables and wasn't really watching where she was walking when she turned a corner and went right into the path of Corrigan Hart and his new wife, Dorothy.

"Good Lord," she gasped, catching her breath. "What are you two doing in San Antonio?"

Corrigan grinned. "Buying cattle," he said, drawing a radiant Dorothy closer. "Which reminds me, I didn't see you at the auction this time. I was standing in for Simon," he added. "For some reason, he's gone off sales lately."

"So have I, coincidentally," Tira remarked with a cool smile. It stung to think that Simon had given up those auctions that he loved so much to avoid her, but that was most certainly the reason. "I sold the Montana property."

Corrigan scowled. "But you loved the ranch. It was your last link with your father."

That was true, and it had made her sad for a time. She twisted the shopping basket in her hands. "I'd gotten into a rut," she said. "I wanted to change my life."

"So I noticed," Corrigan said quietly. "We went by your apartment to say hello. You weren't there."

"I moved." She colored a little at his probing glance. "I've bought a house across town."

Corrigan's eyes narrowed. "Someplace where you won't see Simon occasionally," he said gently.

The color in her cheeks intensified. "Where I won't see Simon at all, if you want the truth," she said bluntly. "I've given up all my connections with the past. There won't be any more accidental meetings with him. I've decided that I'm tired of eating my heart out for a man who doesn't want me. So I've stopped."

Corrigan looked surprised. Dorie eyed the other woman with quiet sympathy.

"In the long run, that's probably the best thing you could have done," Dorie said quietly. "You're still young and very pretty," she added with a smile. "And the world is full of men."

"Of course it is," Tira replied. She returned Dorie's smile. "I'm glad things worked out for you two, and I'm very sorry I almost split you up," she added sincerely. "Believe me, it was unintentional."

"Tira, I know that," Dorie replied, remembering how a chance remark of Tira's in a local boutique had sent Dorie running scared from Corrigan. That was all in the past, now. "Corrigan explained everything to me. I was uncertain of him then, that's all it really was. I'm not anymore." She hesitated. "I'm sorry about you and Simon."

Tira's face tautened. "You can't make people love you," she said with a poignant sadness in her eyes. She shrugged fatalistically. "He has a life that suits him. I'm trying to find one for myself."

"Why don't you do a collection of sculptures and have a show?" Corrigan suggested.

She chuckled. "I haven't done sculpture in three years. Anyway, I'm not good enough for that."

"You certainly are, and you've got an art degree. Use it."

She considered that. After a minute, she smiled. "Well, I do enjoy sculpting. I used to sell some of it occasionally."

"See?" Corrigan said. "An idea presents itself." He paused. "Of course, there's always a course in biscuit-making…?"

Knowing his other three brothers' absolute mania for that particular bread, she held up both hands. "You can tell Leo and Cag and Rey that I have no plans to become a biscuit chef."

"I'll pass the message along. But Dorie's dying for a replacement," he added with a grin at his wife. "They'd chain her to the stove if I didn't intervene." He eyed Tira. "They like you."

"God forbid," she said with a mock shudder. "For years, people will be talking about how they arranged your marriage."

"They meant well," Dorie defended them.

"Baloney," Tira returned. "They had to have their biscuits. Fatal error, Dorie, telling them you could bake."

"It worked out well, though, don't you think?" she asked with a radiant smile at her husband.

"It did, indeed."

Tira fielded a few more comments about her withdrawal from the social scene, and then they were on their way to the checkout stand. She deliberately held back until they left, to avoid any more conversation. They were a lovely couple, and she was fond of Corrigan, but he reminded her too much of Simon.

* * *

In the following weeks, she signed up for a refresher sculpting course at her local community college, a course for no credit since she already had a degree. In no time, she was sculpting recognizable busts.

"You've got a gift for this," her instructor murmured as he walked around a fired head of her favorite movie star. "There's money in this sort of thing, you know. Big money."

She almost groaned aloud. How could she tell this dear man that she had too much money already? She only smiled and thanked him for the compliment.

But he put her sculpture in a showing of his students' work. It was seen by a local art gallery owner, who tracked Tira down and offered her an exclusive showing. She tried to dissuade him, but the offer was all too flattering to turn down. She agreed, with the proviso that the proceeds would go to an outreach program from the local hospital that worked in indigent neighborhoods.

After that, there was no stopping her. She spent hours at the task, building the strength in her hands and attuning her focus to more detailed pieces.

It wasn't until she finished one of Simon that she even realized she'd been sculpting him. She stared at it with contained fury and was just about to bring both fists down on top of it when the doorbell rang.

Irritated at the interruption, she tossed a cloth over the work in progress and went to answer it, wiping the clay from her hands on the way. Her hair was in a neat bun, to keep it from becoming clotted with clay, but her pink smock was liberally smeared with it. She looked a total mess, without makeup, even without shoes, wearing faded jeans and a knit top.

She opened the door without questioning who her visitor might be, and froze in place when Simon came into view on the porch. She noticed that he was wearing the prosthesis he hated so much, and she noted with interest that the hand at the end of it looked amazingly real.

She lifted her eyes to his, but her face wasn't welcoming. She didn't open the door to admit him. She didn't even smile.

"What do you want?" she asked.

He scowled. That was new. He'd visited Tira's apartment infrequently in the past, and he'd always been greeted with warmth and even delight. This was a cold reception indeed.

"I came to see how you were," he replied quietly. "You've been conspicuous by your absence around town lately."

"I sold the ranch," she said flatly.

He nodded. "Corrigan told me." He looked around at the front yard and the porch of the house. "This is nice. Did you really need a whole house?"

She ignored the question. "What do you want?" she asked again.

He noted her clay-smeared hands, and the smock she was wearing. "Laying bricks, are you?" he mused.

She didn't smile, as she might have once. "I'm sculpting."

"Yes, I remember that you took courses in college. You were quite good."

"I'm also quite busy," she said pointedly.

His eyebrow arched. "No invitation to have coffee?"

She hardened her resolve, despite the frantic beat of her heart. "I don't have time to entertain. I'm getting ready for an exhibit."

"At Bob Henderson's gallery," he said knowledgeably. "Yes, I know. I have part ownership in it." He held up his hand when she started to speak angrily. "I had no idea that he'd seen any of your work. I didn't suggest the showing. But I'd like to see what you've done. I do have a vested interest."

That put a new complexion on things. But she still didn't want him in her house. She'd never rid herself of the memory of him in it. Her reluctant expression told him that whatever she was feeling, it wasn't pleasure.

He sighed. "Tira, what's wrong?" he asked.

She stared at the cloth in her hands instead of at him. "Why does anything have to be wrong?"

"Are you kidding?" He drew in a heavy breath and wondered why he should suddenly feel guilty. "You've sold the ranch, moved house and given up any committees that would bring you into contact with me…."

She looked up in carefully arranged surprise. "Oh, heavens, it wasn't because of you," she lied convincingly. "I was in a rut, that's all. I decided that I needed to turn my life around. And I have."

His eyes glittered down at her. "Did turning it around include keeping me out of it?"

Her expression was unreadable. "I suppose it did. I was never able to get past my marriage. The memories were killing me, and you were a constant reminder."

His heavy eyebrows lifted. "Why should the memories bother you?" he asked with visible sarcasm. "You didn't give a damn about John. You divorced him a month after the wedding and never seemed to care if you saw him again or not. Barely a week later, you were keeping company with Charles Percy."

The bitterness in his voice opened her eyes to something she'd never seen. Why, he blamed her for John's death. She didn't seem to breathe as she looked up into those narrow, cold, accusing eyes. It had been three years since John's death and she'd never known that Simon felt this way.

Her hands on the cloth stilled. It was the last straw. She'd loved this big, formidable man since the first time she'd seen him. There had never been anyone else in her heart, despite the fact that she'd let him push her into marrying John. And now, years too late, she discovered the reason that Simon had never let her come close to him. It was the last reason she'd ever have guessed.

She let out a harsh breath. "Well," she said with forced lightness, "the things we learn about people we thought we knew!" She tucked the smeared cloth into a front pocket of her equally smeared smock. "So I killed John. Is that what you think, Simon?"

The frontal assault was unexpected. His guard was down and he didn't think before he spoke. "You played at marriage," he accused quietly. "He loved you, but you had nothing to give him. A month of marriage and you were having divorce papers served to him. You let him go without a word when he decided to work on oil rigs, despite the danger of it. You didn't even try to stop him. Funny, but I never realized what a shallow, cold woman you were until then. Everything you are is on the outside," he continued, blind to her white, drawn face. "Glorious hair, a pretty face, sparkling eyes, pretty figure…and nothing under it all. Not even a spark of compassion or love for anyone except yourself."

She wasn't breathing normally. Dear God, she thought, don't let me faint at his feet! She swallowed once, then twice, trying to absorb the horror of what he was saying to her.

"You never said a word," she said in a haunted tone. "In all these years."

"I didn't think it needed saying," he said simply. "We've been friends, of a sort. I hope we still are." He smiled, but it didn't reach his eyes. "As long as you realize that you'll never be allowed within striking distance of my heart. I'm not a masochist, even if John was."

Later, when she was alone, she was going to die. She knew it. But right now, pride spared her any further hurt.

She went past him, very calmly, and opened the front door, letting in a scent of dead leaves and cool October breeze. She didn't speak. She didn't look at him. She just stood there.

He walked past her, hesitating on the doorstep. His narrow eyes scanned what he could see of her face, and its whiteness shocked him. He wondered why she looked so torn up, when he was only speaking the truth.

Before he could say a thing, she closed the door, threw the dead bolt and put on the chain latch. She walked back toward her studio, vaguely aware that he was trying to call her back.

The next morning, the housekeeper she'd hired, Mrs. Lester, found her sprawled across her bed with a loaded pistol in her hands and an empty whiskey bottle lying on its side on the stained gray carpet. Mrs. Lester quickly looked in the bathroom and found an empty bottle that had contained tranquilizers. She jerked up the telephone and dialed the emergency services number with trembling hands. When the ambulance came screaming up to the front of the house, Tira still hadn't moved at all.

Chapter Two

It took all of that day for Tira to come out of the stupor and discover where she was. It was a very nice hospital room, but she didn't remember how she'd gotten there. She was foggy and disoriented and very sick to her stomach.

Dr. Ron Gaines, an old family friend, came in the door ahead of a nurse in neat white slacks and a multicolored blouse with many pockets.

"Get her vitals," the doctor directed.

"Yes, sir."

While her temperature and blood pressure and pulse rate were taken, Dr. Gaines leaned against the wall quietly making notations on her chart. The nurse reported her findings, he charted them and he motioned her out of the room.

He moved to the bed and sat down in the chair beside Tira. "If anyone had asked me two weeks ago, I'd have said that you were the most levelheaded woman I knew. You've worked tirelessly for charities here, you've spearheaded fund drives… Good God, what's the matter with you?"

"I had a bad blow," she confessed in a subdued tone. "It was unexpected and I did something stupid. I got drunk."

"Don't hand me that! Your housekeeper found a loaded pistol in your hand."

"Oh, that." She started to tell him about the mouse, the one she'd tried unsuccessfully to catch for weeks. Last night, with half a bottle of whiskey in her, shooting the varmint had seemed perfectly logical. But her dizzy mind was slow to focus. "Well, you see—" she began.

He sighed heavily and cut her off. "Tira, if it wasn't a suicide attempt, I'm not a doctor. Tell me the truth."

She blinked. "I wouldn't try to kill myself!" she said, outraged. She took a slow breath. "I was just a little depressed, that's all. I found out yesterday that Simon holds me responsible for John's death."

There was a long, shocked pause. "He doesn't know why the marriage broke up?"

She shook her head.

"Why didn't you tell him, for God's sake?" he exclaimed.

"It isn't the sort of thing you tell a man about his best friend. I never dreamed that he blamed me. We've been friends. He never wanted it to be anything except friendship, and I assumed it was because of the way he felt about Melia. Apparently I've been five kinds of an idiot." She looked up at him. "Six, if you count last night," she added, flushing.

"I'm glad you agree that it was stupid."

She frowned. "Did you pump my stomach?"

"Yes."

"No wonder I feel so empty," she said. "Why did you do that?" she asked. "I only had whiskey on an empty stomach!"

"Your housekeeper found an empty tranquilizer bottle in the bathroom," he said sternly.

"Oh, that," she murmured. "The bottle was empty.

I never throw anything away. That prescription was years old. It's one Dr. James gave me to get me through final exams in college three years ago. I was a nervous wreck!" She gave him another unblinking stare. "But you listen here, I'm not suicidal. I'm the least suicidal person I know. But everybody has a breaking point and I reached mine. So I got drunk. I never touch alcohol. Maybe that's why it hit me so hard."

He took her hand in his and held it gently. While he was trying to find the words, the door suddenly swung open and a wild-eyed Simon Hart entered the room. He looked as if he'd been in an accident, his face was so white. He stared at Tira without speaking.

It wasn't his fault, really, but she hated him for what she'd done to herself. Her eyes told him so. There was no welcome in them, no affection, no coquettishness. She looked at him as if she wished she had a weapon in her hands.

"You get out of my room!" she raged at him, sitting straight up in bed.

The doctor's eyebrows shot straight up. Tira had never raised her voice to Simon before. Her face was flaming red, like her wealth of hair, and her green eyes were shooting bolts of lightning in Simon's direction.

"Tira," Simon began uncertainly.

"Get out!" she repeated, ashamed of being accused of a suicide attempt in the first place. It was bad enough that she'd lost control of herself enough to get drunk. She glared at Simon as if he was the cause of it all—which he was. "Out!" she repeated, when he didn't move, gesturing wildly with her arm.

He wouldn't go, and she burst into tears of frustrated fury. Dr. Gaines got between Simon and Tira and hit the Call button. "Get in here, stat," he said into the intercom, following the order with instructions for a narcotic. He glanced toward Simon, standing frozen in the doorway. "Out," he said without preamble. "I'll speak to you in a few minutes."

Simon moved aside to let the scurrying nurse into the room with a hypodermic. He could hear Tira's sobs even through the door. He moved a little way down the hall, to where his brother Corrigan was standing.

It had been Corrigan whom the housekeeper called when she discovered Tira. And he'd called Simon and told him only that Tira had been taken to the hospital in a bad way. He had no knowledge of what had pushed Tira over the edge or he might have thought twice about telling his older brother at all.

"I heard her. What happened?" Corrigan asked, jerking his head toward the room.

"I don't know," Simon said huskily. He leaned back against the wall beside his brother. His empty sleeve drew curious glances from a passerby, but he ignored it. "She saw me and started yelling." He broke off. His eyes were filled with torment. "I've never seen her like this."

"Nobody has," Corrigan said flatly. "I never figured a woman like Tira for a suicide."

Simon gaped at him. "A *what?*"

"What would you call combining alcohol and tranquilizers?" Corrigan demanded. "Good God, Mrs. Lester said she had a loaded pistol in her hands!"

"A *pistol...?*" Simon closed his eyes on a shudder and ran a hand over his drawn face. He couldn't bear to think about what might have happened. He was certain that he'd prompted her actions. He couldn't forget, even now, the look on her face when he'd almost flatly accused her of killing John. She hadn't said a word to defend herself. She'd gone quiet; dangerously quiet. He should never have left her alone. Worse, he should never have said anything to her. He'd thought her a strong, self-centered woman who wouldn't feel criticism. Now, almost too late, he knew better.

"I went to see her yesterday," Simon confessed in a haunted tone. "She'd made some crazy remark at the last cattle auction about trying to make me jealous. She said she was only teasing, but it hit me the wrong way. I told her that she wasn't the sort of woman I could be jealous about. Then, yesterday, I told her how I felt about her careless attitude toward the divorce only a month after she married John, and letting him go off to get himself killed on an oil rig." His broad shoulders rose and fell defeatedly. "I shouldn't have said it, but I was angry that she'd tried to make me jealous, as if she thought I might actually feel attracted to her." He sighed. "I thought she was so hard that nothing I said would faze her."

"And I thought I used to be blind," Corrigan said.

Simon glanced at him, scowling. "What do you mean?"

Corrigan looked at his brother and tried to speak. Finally he just smiled faintly and turned away. "Forget it."

The door to Tira's room opened a minute later and Dr. Gaines came out. He spotted the two men down the hall and joined them.

"Don't go back in there," he told Simon flatly. "She's too close to the edge already. She doesn't need you to push her the rest of the way."

"I didn't do a damned thing," Simon shot back, and now he looked dangerous, "except walk in the door!"

Dr. Gaines' lips thinned. He glanced at Corrigan, who only shrugged and shook his head.

"I'm going to try to get her to go to a friend of mine,

a therapist. She could use some counseling," Gaines added.

"She's not a nutcase," Simon said, affronted.

Dr. Gaines looked into that cold, unaware face and frowned. "You were state attorney general for four years," he said. "You're still a well-known trial lawyer, an intelligent man. How can you be this stupid?"

"Will someone just tell me what's going on?" Simon demanded.

Dr. Gaines looked at Corrigan, who held out a hand, palm up, inviting the doctor to do the dirty work.

"She'll kill us both if she finds out we told him," Gaines remarked to Corrigan.

"It's better than letting her die."

"Amen." He looked at Simon, who was torn between puzzlement and fury. "Simon, she's been in love with you for years," Dr. Gaines said in a hushed, reluctant tone. "I tried to get her to give up the ranch and all that fund-raising mania years ago, because they were only a way for her to keep near you. She wore herself out at it, hoping against hope that if you were in close contact, you might begin to feel something for her, but I knew that wasn't going to happen. All I had to do was see you together to realize she didn't have a chance. Am I right?" he asked Corrigan, who nodded.

Simon leaned back against the wall. He felt as if someone had put a knife right through him. He couldn't even speak.

"What you said to her was a kindness, although I don't imagine you see it that way now," Dr. Gaines continued doggedly. "She had to be made to see that she couldn't go on living a lie, and the changes in her life recently are proof that she's realized how you feel about her. She'll accept it, in time, and get on with her life. It will be the very best thing for her. She's trying to be all things to all people, until she was worn to a nub. She's been headed for a nervous breakdown for weeks, the way she's pushed herself, with this one-woman art show added to the load she was already carrying. But she'll be all right." He put a sympathetic hand on Simon's good arm. "It's not your fault. She's levelheaded about everything except you. But if you want to help her, for old time's sake, stay away from her. She's got enough on her plate right now."

He nodded politely to Corrigan and went on down the hall.

Simon still hadn't moved, or spoken. He was pale and drawn, half crazy from the doctor's revelation.

Corrigan got on the other side of him and took his arm, drawing him along. "We'll get a cup of coffee somewhere on the way back to your office," he told his older brother.

Simon allowed himself to be pulled out the door. He wasn't sure he remembered how to walk. He felt shattered.

Minutes later, he was sitting in a small café with his brother, drinking strong coffee.

"She tried to kill herself over me," Simon said finally.

"She missed. She won't try again. They'll make sure of it." He leaned forward. "Simon, she's been overextending for years, you know that. No one woman could have done as much as she has without risking her health, if not her sanity. If it hadn't been what you said to her, it would have been something else...maybe even this showing at the gallery that she was working night and day to get ready for."

Simon forced himself to breathe normally. He still

couldn't quite believe it all. He sipped his coffee and stared into space.

"Did you know how she felt?" he asked Corrigan.

"She didn't tell me, if that's what you mean," his brother said. "But it was fairly obvious, the way she talked about you. I felt sorry for her. We all knew how much you loved Melia, that you've never let yourself get close to another woman since the wreck. Tira had to know that there was no hope in that direction."

The coffee in Simon's cup sloshed a little as he put it down. "It seems so clear now," he remarked absently. "She was always around, even when there didn't seem a reason for it. She worked on committees for organizations I belonged to, she did charity work for businesses where I was a trustee." He shook his head. "But I never noticed."

"I know."

He looked up. "John knew," he said suddenly.

Corrigan hesitated. Then he nodded.

Simon sucked in a harsh breath. "Good God, I broke up their marriage!"

"Maybe. I don't know. Tira never talks about John." His eyes narrowed thoughtfully. "But haven't you ever noticed that she and John's father are still friends? He doesn't blame her for his son's death. Shouldn't he, if it was all Tira's fault?"

Simon didn't want to think about it. He was sick to his stomach. "I pushed her at John," he recalled.

"I remember. They seemed to have a lot in common."

"They had me in common." Simon laughed bitterly. "She loved *me*..." He took a long sip of coffee and burned his mouth. The pain was welcome; it took his mind off his conscience.

"She can't ever know that we told you that," Corrigan said firmly, looking as formidable as his brother. "She's entitled to salvage a little of her pride. The newspapers got hold of the story, Simon. It's in the morning edition. The headline's really something—local socialite in suicide attempt. She's going to have hell living it down. I don't imagine they'll let her see a newspaper, but someone will tell her, just the same." His voice was harsh. "Some people love rubbing salt in wounds."

Simon rested his forehead against his one hand. He was so drained that he could barely function. It had been the worst day of his life; in some ways, worse than the wreck that had cost him everything.

For years, Tira's eyes had warmed at his approach, her mouth had smiled her welcome. She'd become radiant just because he was near her, and he hadn't known how she felt, with all those blatant signs.

Now, this morning, she'd looked at him with such hatred that he still felt sick from the violence of it. Her eyes had flashed fire, her face had burned with rage. He'd never seen her like that.

Corrigan searched his brother's worn face. "Don't take it so hard, Simon. None of this is your fault. She put too much pressure on herself and now she's paying the consequences. She'll be all right."

"She loved me," he said again, speaking the words harshly, as if he still couldn't believe them.

"You can't make people love you back," his brother replied. "Funny, Dorie and I saw her in the grocery store a few weeks ago, and she said that same thing. She had no illusions about the way you felt, regardless of how it looks."

Simon's eyes burned with anguish. "You don't know what I said to her, though. I accused her of killing John, of being so unconcerned about his happiness that she let him go into a dangerous job that he didn't have the experience to handle." His face twisted. "I said that she was shallow and cold and selfish, that I had nothing but contempt for her and that I'd never let a woman like her get close to me…." His eyes closed. "Dear God, how it must have hurt her to hear that from me."

Corrigan let out a savage breath. "Why didn't you just load the gun for her?"

"Didn't I?" the older man asked with tortured eyes.

Corrigan backed off. "Well, it's water under the bridge now. She's safely out of your life and she'll learn to get along on her own, with a little help. You can go back to your law practice and consider yourself off the endangered species list."

Simon didn't say another word. He stared into his coffee with sightless eyes until it grew cold.

Tira slept for the rest of the day. When she opened her eyes, the room was empty. There was a faint light from the wall and she felt pleasantly drowsy.

The night nurse came in, smiling, to check her vital signs. She was given another dose of medicine. Minutes later, without having dared remember the state she was in that morning, she went back to sleep.

When she woke up, a tall, blond, handsome man with dark eyes was sitting by the bed, looking quite devastating in white slacks and a red pullover knit shirt.

"Charles," she mumbled, and smiled. "How nice of you to come!"

"Who'll I talk to if you kill yourself, you idiot?" he muttered, glowering at her. "What a stupid thing to do."

She pushed herself up on an elbow, and pushed the

mass of red-gold hair out of her eyes. She made a rough sound in her throat. "I wasn't trying to commit suicide!" she grumbled. "I got drunk and Mrs. Lester found an old empty prescription bottle and went ballistic." She shifted sleepily and yawned. "Well, I can't blame her, I guess. I still had the pistol in my hand and there was a hole in the wall..."

"Pistol!?"

"Calm down," she said, grimacing. "My head hurts. Yes, a pistol." She grinned at him a little sheepishly. "I was going to shoot the mouse."

His eyes widened. "Excuse me?"

"There's a mouse," she said. "I've set traps and put out bait, and he just keeps coming back into my kitchen. After a couple of drinks, I remembered a scene in *True Grit*, where John Wayne shot a rat, and when I got halfway through the whiskey bottle, it seemed perfectly logical that I should do that to my mouse." She chuckled a little weakly. "You had to be there," she added helplessly.

"I suppose so." He searched her bloodshot eyes. "All those charity events, anybody calls and asks you to help, and you work day and night to organize things. You're everybody's helper. Now you're working on a collection of sculpture and still trying to keep up with your social obligations. I'm surprised you didn't fall out weeks ago. I tried to tell you. You know I did."

She nodded and sighed. "I know. I just didn't realize how hard I was working."

"You never do. You need to get married and have kids. That would keep you busy."

She lifted both eyebrows. "Are you offering to sacrifice yourself?"

He chuckled. "Maybe it would be the best thing for

both of us," he said wistfully. "We're in love with people who don't want us. At least we like each other."

"Yes. But marriage should be more than that."

He shrugged. "Just a thought." He leaned over and patted her hand. "Get well. There's a society ball next week and you have to go with me. She's going to be there."

Tira knew who *she* was—his sister-in-law, the woman that Percy would have died to marry. She'd never noticed him, despite his blazing good looks, before she married his half brother. In fact, she seemed to actually dislike him, and Charles's half brother was twenty years her senior, a stiff-necked stuffed shirt whom nobody in their circle had any use for. The marriage was a complete mystery.

"I don't have a dress."

"Buy one," he instructed.

She hesitated.

"I'll protect you from him," he said after a minute, having realized that Simon would most likely be in attendance. "I swear on my glorious red Mark VIII that I won't leave your side for an instant all evening."

She gave him a wary glance. His mania about that car was well-known. He wouldn't even entrust it to a car wash. He washed and waxed it lovingly, inch by inch, and called it "Big Red."

"Well, if you're willing to swear on your car," she agreed.

He grinned. "You can ride in it."

"I'm honored!"

"I brought you some flowers," he added. "One of the nurses volunteered to put them in a vase for you."

She gave him a cursory appraisal and smiled. "The way you look, I'm not surprised. Women fall over each other to get to you."

"Not the one I wanted," he said sadly. "And now it's too late."

She slid her hand into his and pressed it gently. "I'm sorry."

"So am I." He shrugged. "Isn't it a damned shame? I mean, look what they're missing!"

She knew he was talking about Simon and the woman Charles wanted, and she grinned in spite of herself. "It's their loss. I'd love to go to the ball with you. He'll let me out of here today. Like to take me home?"

"Sure!"

But when the doctor came into the room, he was reluctant to let her leave.

She was sitting on the side of the bed. She gave him a long, wise look. "I wasn't lying," she said. "Suicide was the very last thing on my mind."

"With a loaded pistol, which had been fired."

She pursed her lips. "Didn't anyone notice where the shot landed? At a round hole in the baseboard?"

He frowned.

"The mouse!" she said. "I've been after him for weeks! Don't you watch old John Wayne movies? It was in *True Grit!*"

All at once, realization dawned in his eyes. "The rat writ."

"Exactly!"

He burst out laughing. "You were going to shoot the mouse?"

"I'm a good shot," she protested. "Well, when I'm sober. I won't miss him next time!"

"Get a trap."

"He's too wily," she protested. "I've tried traps and baits."

"Buy a cat."

"I'm allergic to fur," she confessed miserably.

"How about those electronic things you plug into the wall?"

She shook her head. "Tried it. He bit the electrical cord in half."

"Didn't it kill him?"

Her eyebrows arched. "No. Actually he seemed even healthier afterward. I'll bet he'd enjoy arsenic. Nope, I have to shoot him."

The doctor and Charles looked at each other. Then they both chuckled.

The doctor did see her alone later, for a few minutes while Charles was bringing the car around to the hospital entrance. "Just one more thing," he said gently. "Regardless of what Simon said, you didn't kill John. Nobody, no woman, could have stopped what happened. He should never have married you in the first place."

"Simon kept throwing us together," she said. "He thought we made the perfect couple," she added bitterly.

"Simon never knew," he said. "I'm sure John didn't tell him, and you kept your own silence."

She averted her eyes. "John was the best friend Simon had in the world. If he'd wanted Simon to know, he'd have told him. That being the case, I never felt that I had the right." She looked at him. "I still don't. And you're not to tell him, either. He deserves to have a few unshattered illusions. His life hasn't been a bed of roses so far. He's missing an arm, and he's still mourning Melia."

"God knows why," Dr. Gaines added, because he'd known all about the elegant Mrs. Hart, things that even Tira didn't know.

"He loved her," she said simply. "There's no accounting for taste, is there?"

He smiled gently. "I guess not."

"You know, you really are a nice man, Dr. Gaines," she added.

He chuckled. "That's what my wife says all the time."

"She's right," she agreed.

"Don't you have family?"

She shook her head. "My father died of a heart attack, and my mother died even before he did. She had cancer. It was hard to watch, especially for Dad. He loved her too much."

"You can't love people too much."

She looked up at him with such sadness that her face seemed to radiate it. "Yes, you can," she said solemnly. "But I'm going to learn how to stop."

Charles pulled up at the curb and Dr. Gaines waved them off.

"Look at him," Charles said with a grin. "He's drooling! He wants my car." He stepped down on the accelerator. "Everybody wants my car. But it's mine. Mine!"

"Charles, you're getting obsessed with this automobile," she cautioned.

"I am not!" He glanced at her. "Careful, you'll get fingerprints on the window. And I do hope you wiped your shoes before you got in."

She didn't know whether to laugh or cry.

"I'm kidding!" he exclaimed.

She let out a sigh of relief. "And Dr. Gaines wanted *me* to have therapy," she murmured.

He threw her a glare. "I do not need therapy. Men love their cars. One guy even wrote a song about how much he loved his truck."

She glanced around the luxurious interior of the pretty car, leather coated with a wood-grained dash, and nodded. "Well, I could love Big Red," she had to confess. She leaned back against the padded headrest and closed her eyes.

He patted the dash. "Hear that, guy? You're getting to her!"

She opened one eye. "I'm calling the therapist the minute we get to my house."

He lifted both blond eyebrows. "Does he like cars?"

"I give up!"

When she arrived home, she was met at the door by a hovering, worried Mrs. Lester.

"It was an old, empty prescription bottle!" Tira told the kindly older woman. "And the pistol wasn't for me, it was for that mouse we can't catch in the kitchen!"

"The mouse?"

"Well, we can't trap him or drive him out, can we?" she queried.

The housekeeper blushed all the way to her white hairline and wrung her hands in the apron. "It was the way it looked..."

Tira went forward and hugged her. "You're a doll and I love you. But I was only drunk."

"You never drink," Mrs. Lester stated.

"I was driven to it," she replied.

Mrs. Lester looked at Charles. "By him?" she asked with a twinkle in her dark eyes. "You shouldn't let him hang around here so much, if he's driving you to drink."

"See?" he murmured, leaning down. "She wants my car, that's why she wants me to leave. She can't stand having to look at it day after day. She's obsessed with jealousy, eaten up with envy..."

"What's he talking about?" Mrs. Lester asked curiously.

"He thinks you want his car."

Mrs. Lester scoffed. "That long red fast flashy thing?" She sniffed. "Imagine me, riding around in something like that!"

Charles grinned. "Want to?" he asked, raising and lowering his eyebrows.

She chuckled. "You bet I do! But I'm much too old for sports cars, dear. Tira's just right."

"Yes, she is. And she needs coddling."

"I'll fatten her up and see that she gets her rest. I knew I should never have let her talk me into that vacation. The first time I leave her in a month, and look what happens! And the newspapers…!" She stopped so suddenly that she almost bit her tongue through.

Tira froze in place. "What newspapers?"

Mrs. Lester made a face and exchanged a helpless glance with Charles.

"You, uh, made the headlines," he said reluctantly.

She groaned. "Oh, for heaven's sake, there goes my one-woman show!"

"No, it doesn't," Charles replied. "I spoke to Bob this morning before I came after you. He said that the phone's rung off the hook all morning with queries about the show. He figures you'll make a fortune from the publicity."

"I don't need—"

"Yes, but the outreach program does," he reminded her. He grinned. "They'll be able to buy a new van!"

She smiled, but her heart wasn't in it. She didn't want to be notorious, whether or not she deserved to.

"Cheer up," he said. "It'll be old news tomorrow. Just don't answer the phone for a day or two. It will blow over as soon as some new tragedy catches the editorial eye."

"I guess you're right."

"Next Saturday," he reminded her. "I'll pick you up at six."

"Where will you be until then?" she asked, surprised, because he often came by for coffee in the afternoon.

"Memphis," he said with a sigh. "A business deal that I have to conduct personally. I'll be out of town for a week. Bad timing, too."

"I'll be fine," she assured him. "Mrs. Lester's right here."

"I guess so. I do worry about you." He smiled sheepishly. "I don't have any family, either. You're sort of the only relative I have, even though you aren't."

"Same here."

He searched her eyes. "Two of a kind, aren't we? We loved not wisely, and too well."

"As you said, it's their loss," she said stubbornly. "Have a safe trip. Are you taking Big Red?"

He shook his head. "They won't let me take him on the plane," he said. "Walters is going to stand guard over him in the garage with a shotgun while I'm gone, though. Maybe he won't pine."

She burst out laughing. "I'm glad I have you for a friend," she said sincerely.

He took her hand and held it gently. "That works both ways. Take care. I'll phone you sometime during the week, just to make sure you're okay. If you need me…"

"I have your mobile number," she assured him. "But I'll be fine."

"See you next week, then."

"Thanks for the ride home," she said.

He shrugged and flashed her a white smile. "My pleasure."

She watched him drive away with sad eyes. She was going to have to live down the bad publicity without telling her side of the story. Well, what did it matter, she reasoned. It could, after all, have been worse.

Chapter Three

The week passed slowly until the charity ball on Saturday evening. It was to be a lavish one, hosted by the Carlisles, a founding family in the area and large supporters of the local hospital's charity work. Their huge brick mansion was just south of the perimeter of San Antonio, set in a grove of mesquite and pecan trees with its own duck pond and a huge formal garden. Tira had always loved coming to the house in the past for these gatherings, but she knew that Simon would be on the guest list. It was going to be hard facing him again after what had happened. It was going to be difficult appearing in public at all.

She did plan to go down with all flags flying, however, having poured her exquisite figure into a sleeveless, long black velvet evening gown with lace appliqués in entrancing places and a lace-up bodice that left little gaps from her diaphragm to her breasts. Her hair was in an elegant French twist with a diamond clip that matched her dangling earrings and delicate waterfall diamond necklace. She looked wealthy and sophisticated and Charles gave her a wicked grin when she came through to the living room with a black velvet and jewel wrap over one bare shoulder. It was November and the weather was unseasonably warm, so the wrap was just right.

Charles dressed up nicely, she thought, studying him. His tuxedo played up his extreme good looks and his fairness.

"Don't we make a pair?" he mused, glancing in the hall mirror at them. "Pity it isn't the right one."

"We'll both survive the evening," she assured him.

"Only if we drink hard enough," he said with graveyard humor. Then he noticed her expression and grimaced. "Sorry," he said genuinely.

"No need to apologize," she replied with a wry smile. "I did something stupid and had the misfortune to be found doing it. I'll survive all the gossip. But whatever you do, don't leave me alone with Simon, okay?"

"Count on it. What are friends for?"

She smiled at him. "To get us through rough times," she said, and was suddenly very grateful that she had a friend as good as Charles.

Charles chided her gently for her growing and obvious nervousness as he drove rapidly down the road that led to the Carlisle estate. "Don't worry so. You're old news," he reminded her. "There's the local political scandal to latch onto now."

"What political scandal?" she asked. "And how do you know about it when you've been out of town?"

"Because our lieutenant governor has been participating in a conference on the problems of inner cities in Memphis. I sat next to him on the flight home," he said smugly. Keeping his eyes on the road, he leaned toward her. "It seems that the attorney general intervened in a criminal case for a friend. The criminal he got paroled was serving time for armed robbery, but when he got out, he went right home and killed his ex-wife for testifying against him and is now back in prison. But the wheels of political change are going to roll over the governor's fair-haired boy."

"Oh, my goodness," she burst out. "But he was only doing a kindness. How could he know…?"

"He couldn't, and he isn't really to blame, but the opposition party is going to use it to crucify him. I understand his resignation is forthcoming momentarily."

"What a shame," Tira said honestly. "He's done a wonderful job. I met him at one of the charity benefits earlier this year and thought how lucky we were to have elected someone so capable to the position! Now, if he resigns, I guess the governor will have to temporarily appoint someone to finish his term."

"No doubt he will."

"Maybe he'll slide out of it. Lots of politicians do."

"Not this time, I'm afraid," Charles said. "He's made some bitter enemies since he took office. They'll love the opportunity to settle the score."

She recalled that Simon had antagonized plenty of people when he held the office of state attorney general. But it would have taken more than a scandal to unseat him. He had a clever habit of turning weapons against their wielders.

She closed her eyes and ground her teeth as she realized how pitiful she was about him, still. Everything reminded her of Simon. She hadn't wanted to come tonight, either, but the alternative was to stay home and let the whole city know what a coward she was. She had to hold her head up high and pretend that everything was fine, when her whole world was lying in shards around her feet.

She hadn't tried to kill herself, but one particularly lurid newspaper account said she had, and added that it had been over former attorney general Simon Hart, who'd rejected her. It was in a newspaper published by a relative of Jill Sinclair, a woman who'd been a rival of Tira's for Simon during the past few years. Tira had been even more humiliated at that particular story, but when she'd phoned the reporter who wrote it, he denied any knowledge of Jill Sinclair. Still, she was certain dear Jill had a hand in it.

Tira shuddered, realizing that Simon must have seen the story, too. He'd know what a fool she'd been over him, which was just one more humiliation. Living that down wasn't going to be easy. But she did have Charles beside her. And he had his own ordeal to face, because his sister-in-law would certainly be present.

A valet came to park the car for Charles, who was torn between escorting Tira inside or accompanying the elegantly dressed young man assigned to the car placement to make sure he didn't put a scratch on Big Red.

"Go ahead," Tira said with amused resignation. "I'll wait on the steps for you."

"You're such a doll," he murmured and made a kissing motion toward her. "How many women in the world would understand a man's passion for his car? Here, son, I'll just ride down with you to the parking lot."

The valet seemed torn between shock and indignation.

"He's in love with it!" Tira called to the young man. "He can't help himself. Just humor him!"

The valet broke into a wide grin and climbed under the steering wheel.

It was unfortunate that while she was waiting on the wide porch for Charles to return, Simon and his date got out of his elegant town car at the steps and let the valet drive it off. He looked devastating, as usual. He was wearing the prosthesis, she noticed, and wondered at how much he seemed to use it these days. Just after the wreck, he wouldn't be caught dead wearing an artificial arm.

The woman with him was Jill Sinclair herself, a socialite, twice divorced and wealthy, with short black hair and dark eyes and a figure that drew plenty of interest. It would, Tira thought wickedly, considering that her red sequined dress must have been sprayed on and the paint ran out at midthigh. Advertising must pay, she mused, because Simon certainly seemed pleased as he smiled down at the small woman and held her elbow as they climbed up the steps.

He didn't see Tira until they were almost at the top. When he did, he seemed to jerk, as if the sight of her was unexpected.

She didn't let anything of her feelings show, despite the pain of seeing him now when her whole life had been laid bare in the press. She did her best not to let her embarrassment show, either. She smiled carelessly and nodded politely at the couple and deliberately turned away in the direction where Charles and the valet were just coming into view.

"Why, how brave she is," Jill Sinclair purred to Simon, just loud enough for Tira to hear her. "I'd never have had the nerve to face all these people after that humiliating story in the—Simon!"

Her voice died completely. Tira didn't look toward them. Her face was flaming and she knew her accelerated heartbeat was making her shake visibly. She and Jill had never liked each other, but the woman seemed to be looking for a way to hurt her. She was obviously exuding her power since she'd finally managed to get

Simon to notice her and take her out. God knew, she'd been after him for years. Tira's fall from grace had obviously benefitted her.

Charles bounded up the steps and took Tira's arm. "Sorry about that," he said sheepishly.

"You love your car," she replied with a warm smile. "I understand."

"You're one in a million," he mused. His hand fell to grasp hers, and when she looked inside the open doors she knew why. His half brother was there, and so was his sister-in-law, looking unhappy.

"Gene," he called to his older half brother. "Nice to see you." He shook the other man's hand. Gene was tall and severe looking with thinning gray hair. The woman beside him was tiny and blond and lovely, but she had the most tragic brown eyes Tira had ever seen.

"Hello, Nessa," Charles said to the woman, his face guarded, a polite smile on his lips.

"Hello, Charles, Tira," Nessa replied in her soft, sweet voice. "You both look very nice. Isn't this a good turnout?" she added nervously. "They'll make a lot of money at five hundred dollars a couple."

"Yes," Tira agreed with a broad smile. "The hospital outreach program will probably be able to afford two vans and the services of another nurse!"

"For indigents," Gene Marlowe said huffily, "who won't pay a penny of their own health care."

The other three people looked at him as if he'd gone mad. He glared at them, reddening. "I have to see Todd Groves about a contract we're pursuing. If you'll excuse me? Nessa, don't just stand there! Come along."

Nessa ground her teeth together as Gene took her arm roughly. Charles looked as if he might attack his own brother right there. Tira caught his hand and tugged.

"I'm starving," she told him quickly, exchanging speaking glances with a suddenly relieved Nessa. "Feed me!"

Charles hesitated for an instant, during which Gene dragged Nessa away toward a group of men.

"Damn him!" Charles bit off, his normally pleasant face contorted and threatening.

Tira shook his hand gently. "You're broadcasting," she murmured, bumping deliberately against his side to distract him. "Come on, before you cause her any more trouble than she's already got."

He let out a weary sigh. "Why did she marry him?" he groaned. "*Why?*"

"Whatever the reason doesn't matter much now. Let's go."

She pulled until he let her lead him to the long buffet table, where expensive nibbles and champagne were elegantly arranged.

"This is going to eat up all the profits," Tira murmured worriedly, noting the crystal flutes that were provided for the champagne, and the fact that caviar was furnished as well.

Charles leaned toward her. "It's grocery store caviar, and the champagne is the sort they deliver in big round metal tractor trucks..."

"Charles!" She couldn't repress a giggle at the insinuation, and just as she felt her face going red from glee, she looked up and saw Simon's pale eyes glittering at her from across the room. She averted her eyes to the table and didn't look in that direction again. His expression had been far different from the one he'd worn when he'd seen her in the hospital. Now it was indignant and outraged, as if he blamed her for the publicity that made him look guilty, too.

* * *

Charles did waltz divinely. Tira found herself on the floor with him time after time. People noticed her, and there were some obvious whispers, which probably concerned her "suicide attempt." She was uncomfortable at first, but then she realized that the opinion of most of these people didn't matter to her. She knew the truth about what had happened and so did Charles. If the others wanted to believe her to be so weak and helpless that she'd die rather than face up to her failures, let them.

"Doesn't it worry you, being seen with such a notorious woman?" she chided when they were standing again at the buffet table with more champagne.

"Notorious women are fascinating," he returned, and smiled. His eyes lifted to his half brother and Nessa and his jaw clenched. The two of them were going out the door and Nessa looked as if she were crying.

"You can't," she said, catching his arm when he looked as if he might follow them.

"She should leave him."

"She'll have to make that decision for herself."

He glanced down at her with worried eyes. "She isn't like you. She isn't independent and spirited. She's shy and gentle and people take advantage of her."

"And you want to protect her. I understand. But you can't, not tonight."

He made a rough sound in his throat. "Damn it!"

She leaned against him affectionately for an instant. "I'm sorry. I really am."

His arm slipped around her shoulders. "One day," he promised himself.

She nodded. "One day."

"Why, Charles, how handsome you look!" Jill Sinclair's high-pitched, grating voice turned them around. "Are you enjoying yourself?"

"I'm having a great time," Charles said through his teeth. "How about you?"

"Oh, Simon is just the most wonderful escort," she sighed and glanced at Tira with half-closed eyes. "We've been everywhere together lately. There are *so* many charity dos this time of year. And how are you, Tira? I was so sorry to hear about your near tragedy!" She was almost purring, enjoying Tira's stiff posture and cold face. She raised her voice, drawing attention from the couples hovering near the buffet table. "Isn't it a pity that the newspapers made such a big thing of your suicide attempt? I mean, the humiliation of having your feelings made public must be awful. And for the gossips to say that you wanted to die just because Simon couldn't love you back…why he was just shattered that you made him look like a coldhearted villain in the eyes of his friends. God knows, it isn't his fault that he doesn't love you!"

Tira was too shaken by the unexpected attack to reply. Charles wasn't.

"Why, you prissy little cat," Charles said with cold venom, making Jill actually catch her breath in surprise at the unexpected verbal jab. "Why don't you go sharpen your claws on the curtains?"

He took Tira's arm and led her away. She was so shocked and outraged that she couldn't even manage words. She wanted to empty the punch bowl over the woman, but that was hardly the sort of thing to do at a benefit ball. Her proud spirit had all but been broken by recent events. She was still licking her wounds.

Simon was talking to a man near the door that Charles was urging her toward. He paused in midsentence and looked at Tira's white face with curious concern.

Before he could speak, Charles did. "Never mind adding your two cents worth. Your girlfriend said it all for you."

Charles prodded her forward and Tira didn't look Simon's way. She was barely able to see where she was going at all. Until Jill's piece of mischief, she'd actually thought she could get through the evening unscathed.

"That cat!" Charles muttered as they made their way to the bottom of the steps.

"The world is full of them," she breathed. "And how they love to claw you when you're down!"

None of the valets were anywhere in sight. Charles grumbled. "I'll have to go fetch the car. Stay right here. Will you be all right?"

"I'm fine, now that we're outside," she said.

He gave her a last, worried glance, and went around the house to the parking area.

She drew her wrap closer, because the air was chilly. Once, she'd have made Jill pay dearly for her nasty comments, but not anymore. Now, her proud spirit was dulled and she'd actually walked away from a fight. It wasn't like her. Charles obviously knew that, or he wouldn't have rushed her out the door so quickly.

She heard footsteps behind her and her heart jumped, because she knew the very sound of Simon's feet. Her eyes closed as she wished him in China—anywhere but here!

"What did she say to you?" he asked shortly.

She wouldn't turn; she wouldn't look at him. She couldn't bear to look at him. The humiliation of having him know how she felt about him was so horrible that it suffocated her. All those years of hiding it from him, cocooning her love in secrecy. And now he knew, the whole world knew. And worst of all, she loved him still. Just being near him was agony.

"I said, what did she say to you?" he repeated, moving directly in front of her so that she had to look at him.

She lifted her eyes to his black tie and no further. Her voice was choked, and stiff with wounded pride. "Go and ask her."

There was a rough sigh and she saw his good hand go irritably into the pocket of his trousers. "This isn't like you," he said after a minute. "You don't run and you don't cry, regardless of what people say to you. You fight back. Why are you leaving?"

She lifted tired eyes to his and hated the sudden jolt of her heart at the sight of his beloved face. She clenched every muscle in her body to keep from sobbing out her rage and hurt. "I don't care what anyone thinks of me," she said huskily, "least of all your malicious girlfriend. Yes, I've spent most of my life fighting, one way or another, but I'm tired. I'm tired of everything."

Her lack of animation disturbed him, along with the defeat in her voice, the cool poise. "You can't be worried about what the newspapers said," he said, his voice deep and slow and oddly tender.

"Can't I? Why not? They believed every word." She inclined her head toward the ballroom.

His features were unusually solemn. "I know you better than they do."

She searched his pale eyes in the dim light from the house. Her heart clenched. "You don't know me at all, Simon," she said with painful realization. "You never did."

He seemed to stiffen. "I thought I did. Until you divorced John."

Her heart stilled at the reference. "And until he died." Defeat was in every line of her elegant body. "Yes, I know, I'm a murderess."

His face went taut. "I didn't say that!"

"You might as well have!" she shot back, raising her voice, not caring if the whole world heard her. "If Melia had died in a similar manner, I'd never have believed you guilty of her death! I'd have known you well enough to be certain that you had no part in anything that would cause another human being harm. But then, I had a mad infatuation for you that I couldn't cure." She saw his sudden stillness. "Don't pretend that you didn't read all about it in the paper, Simon. Yes, it's true, why shouldn't I admit it? I was obsessed with you, desperate to be with you, in any way that I could. It didn't even matter that you only tolerated me. I could have lived on crumbs for the rest of my life—" Her voice broke. She shifted on trembling legs and laughed with pure self-contempt. "What a fool I was! What a silly fool. I'm twenty-eight years old and I've only just realized how stupid I am!"

He frowned. "Tira..."

She moved back a step, her green eyes blazing with ruptured pride. "Jill told me what you said, that you blame me for making you look like a villain in public with my so-called suicide attempt, as well as for John's death. Well, go ahead, hate me! I don't give a damn anymore!" she spat, out of control and not caring. "I'm not even surprised to see you with Jill, Simon. She's as opinionated and narrow-minded as you are, and she knows how to put the knife in, too. I daresay you're a match made in heaven!"

His face clenched visibly. "And you don't care that I'm with another woman tonight, instead of with you?"

he chided, hitting back as hard as he could, with a mocking smile on his lips.

Her face went absolutely white. But if it killed her, he'd never hear from her how she did care. She smiled deliberately. "No," she agreed softly. "Actually I don't. All this notoriety accomplished one good thing. It made me see how I'd wasted the past few miserable years mooning over you! You did me a favor when you told me what you really thought of me. I'm free of you at last, Simon," she lied with deliberation. "And I've never been quite so happy in all my life!"

And with that parting shot, she turned and walked slowly to the driveway where Charles was pulling up in front of the house, leaving Simon rigidly in place with an expression of shock that delighted her wounded pride.

After what she'd said, she didn't expect Simon to follow her, and he didn't. When Charles had installed her in the passenger seat, she caught just a glimpse of Simon's straight back rapidly returning to the house. She even knew the posture. He was furious. Good! Let him be furious. She was not going to care. She wasn't!

"Take it easy," Charles said softly. "You'll burst something."

"I know how you felt earlier," she returned, leaning her hot forehead against the glass of the window. "Damn him! And damn her, too!"

"What did he say to you?"

"He wanted to know what she said, and then he gave me his opinion of my character again. But this time, he didn't know he'd hit me where it hurt. I made sure of it."

Charles let out a long breath. "Why can't we love to order?" he asked philosophically.

"I don't know. If you ever find out, you can tell me." She stared out the dark window at the flat landscape passing by. Her heart felt as if it might break all over again.

"He's an idiot."

"So is Jill. So is Gene. We're all idiots. Maybe we're certifiable and we can become a circus act."

They drove in silence until they reached her house. He turned off the engine and stared at her worriedly. She was pale and she looked so miserable that he hurt for her.

"Go inside and change your clothes and pack a suitcase," he said suddenly.

"What?"

"We'll fly down to Nassau for a long weekend. It's just Saturday. We'll take a three-day vacation. I have a friend who owns a villa there. He and his wife love company. We'll eat conch chowder and play at the casino and lay on the beach. How about it?"

She brightened. "Could we?"

"We could. You need a break and so do I. Be a gambler."

It sounded like fun. She hadn't been happy in such a long time. "Okay," she said.

"Okay." He grinned. "Maybe we'll cheer up in foreign parts. Don't take too long. I'll run home and change and make a few phone calls. I should be back within an hour."

"Great!"

It was great. The brief holiday made Tira feel as if she had a new lease on life. Charles was wonderful, undemanding company, much more like a beloved brother than a boyfriend. They padded all over Nassau, down West Bay Street to the docks and out on the pier to look at the ships in port, and all the way to the shopping district and the vast straw markets. Nassau was the most exciting, cosmopolitan city in the world to Tira. She never tired of going there. Just now, it was a godsend. She hated the memory of Jill's taunting words and Simon's angry accusations. It was good to have a breathing space from them, and the publicity.

They stretched their stay to five days instead of three and returned to San Antonio refreshed and rested, although Charles had confessed that he did miss his car. He proved it by rushing home as soon as the limousine he'd hired to meet them at the airport delivered Tira at her house.

"I'll phone you in the morning. We might have a game of tennis Saturday, if you're up to it," he said.

"I will be. Thanks, Charles. Thanks so much!"

He chuckled. "I enjoyed it. So long."

She watched the limousine pull away and walked slowly up to her front door. She hated homecomings. She had nothing here but Mrs. Lester and an otherwise empty house, and her work. It was cold compensation.

Mrs. Lester greeted her with enthusiasm. "I'm so glad you're home!" she said. "The phone rang off the hook the day after you left and didn't stop until three days ago." She shook her head. "I can't imagine why those newspaper people wanted to drag the whole subject up again, but I guess the shooting downtown Tuesday afternoon gave them something new to go after."

"What shooting?"

"Well, that man the attorney general had paroled—you remember?—was in court to be arraigned and he went right over the table toward the judge and almost killed him. They managed to pull him away and he grabbed the bailiff's gun. They had to shoot him! It's been on all the television stations. They had the most awful photographs of it!"

Tira actually gasped. "For heaven's sake!"

"Mr. Hart was right in the middle of it, too. He had a case and was waiting for it to be called when the prisoner got loose."

"Simon? Was he…hurt?" Tira had to ask.

"No. He was the one who pulled the man off the judge. The man had that bailiff's gun leveled right at him, they said, when a deputy sheriff shot the man. It was a close call for Mr. Hart. A real close call. But you'd never think it worried him to hear him talk on television. He was as cold as ice."

She sat down on the edge of the sofa and thanked God for Simon's life. She wished that they were still friends, even distant ones, so that she could phone him and tell him so. But there was a wall between them now.

"Mr. Hart wondered why you hadn't gotten in touch with him, afterward," Mrs. Lester said, hesitating.

Tira glanced at her breathlessly. "He called?"

She nodded and then grimaced. "He wanted to know if you heard about the shooting and if you'd been concerned. I had to tell him that you were away, and didn't know a thing, and when he asked where, he got that out of me, too. I hope it was all right that I told him."

Simon would think she went on a lover's holiday with Charles. Well, why shouldn't he? He believed she was a murderess and a flighty, shallow flirt and suicidal. Let him think whatever else he liked. She couldn't be any worse in his eyes than she already was.

"Give a dog a bad name," she murmured.

"What?" Mrs. Lester asked.

She dragged her mind back to the subject at hand. "Yes, of course, it's perfectly all right that you told him, Mrs. Lester," Tira said quietly. "I had a wonderful time in Nassau."

"Did you good, I expect, and Mr. Percy is a nice man."

"A very nice man," Tira agreed. She got to her feet. "I'm tired. I think I'll lie down for a while, so don't fix anything to eat for another hour or so, will you?"

"Certainly, dear. You just rest. I'll have some coffee and sandwiches ready when you want them."

Would she ever want them? Tira wondered as she went slowly toward her bedroom. She was empty and cold and sick at heart. But that seemed to be her normal condition. At least for now.

Chapter Four

It was raining the day Tira began taking her sculptures to Bob Henderson's "Illuminations" art gallery for her showing. She was so gloomy she hardly felt the mist on her face. Christmas was only two weeks away and she was miserable and lonely. Only months before, she'd have phoned Simon and asked him to meet her for lunch in town, or she'd have shown up at some committee meeting or benefit conference at which he was present, just to feed her hungry heart on the sight of him. Now, she had nothing. Only Charles and his infrequent, undemanding company. Charles was a sweetheart, but it was like having a brother over for coffee.

She carried the last box carefully in the back door, which Lillian Day, the gallery's manager was holding open for her.

"That's the last of them, Lillian," Tira told her, smiling as she surveyed the cluttered storage room. She shook her head. "I can't believe I did all those myself."

"It's a lot of work," Lillian agreed, smiling back. She bent to open one of the boxes and frowned slightly at what was inside. "Did you mean to include this?" she asked, indicating a bust of Simon that was painfully lifelike.

Tira's face closed up. "Yes, I meant to," she said curtly. "I don't want it."

Lillian wisely didn't say another word. "I'll place it with the others, then. The catalogs have been printed and they're perfect, I checked them myself. Everything's ready, including the caterer for the snack buffet and the media coverage. We're doing a Christmas motif for the buffet."

Media coverage. Tira ground her teeth. The last thing in the world she wanted to see now was a reporter.

Lillian, sensitive to moods, glanced at her reassuringly. "Don't worry. These were handpicked, by me," she added. "They won't ask any embarrassing questions, and anything they write for print will be about the show. Period."

Tira relaxed. "What would I do without you?" she asked, and meant it.

Lillian grinned. "Don't even think about trying. We're very glad to have your exhibit here."

Tira had worried about Simon's reaction to the showing, since he was a partner in Bob Henderson's gallery. They hadn't spoken since before his close call in the courtroom and she half expected him to cancel her exhibit. But he hadn't. Perhaps Mrs. Lester had been mistaken and he hadn't been angry that Tira hadn't phoned to check on him. Just because she hadn't called, it didn't mean that she hadn't worried. She'd had a few sleepless nights thinking about what could have happened to him. Despite her best efforts, her feelings for him hadn't changed. She was just as much in love with him now as she had been. She was only better at concealing it.

The night of the exhibit arrived. She was all nerves, and she was secretly glad that Charles would be by her side. Not that she expected Simon to show up, with the media present. He wouldn't want to give them any more ammunition to embarrass him with. But Charles would be a comfort to her.

Fate stepped in, however, to rob her of his presence. Charles phoned at the last minute, audibly upset, to tell her he couldn't go with her to the show.

"I'm more sorry than I can tell you, but Gene's had a heart attack," he said curtly.

"Oh, Charles, I'm so sorry!"

"No need to be. You know there's no love lost between us. But he's my half brother, just the same, and there's no one else to look after him. Nessa is in shock herself. I can't let her cope alone."

"How is he?"

"Stabilized, for the moment. I'm on my way to the hospital. Nessa's with him and he's giving her hell, as usual, even flat on his back," he said curtly.

"If there's anything I can do..."

"Thanks for your support. I'm sorry you have to go on your own. But it's unlikely that Simon will be there, you know," he added gently. "Just stick close to Lillian. She'll look out for you."

She smiled to herself. "I know she will. Let me know how it goes."

"Of course I will. See you."

He hung up. She stared at the phone blankly as she replaced the receiver. She looked good, she reasoned. Her black dress was a straight sheath, ankle length, with spaghetti straps and a diamond necklace and earrings to set it off. It was a perfect foil for her pale, flawless complexion and her red-gold hair, done in a complicated topknot with tendrils just brushing her neck. From her austere getup, she looked more like a widow in mourning than a woman looking forward to

Christmas, and she felt insecure and nervous. It would be the first time she'd appeared alone in public since the scandal and she was still uncomfortable around most people.

Well, she comforted herself as she went outside and climbed into her Jaguar, at least she didn't have to add Simon to her other complications tonight.

The gallery was packed full of interested customers, some of whom had probably only come for curiosity's sake. It wasn't hard to discern people who could afford the four-figure price tags on the sculptures from those who couldn't. Tira pretended not to notice. She took a flute of expensive champagne and downed half of it before she went with Lillian to mingle with the guests.

It didn't help that the first two people she saw were Simon and Jill.

"Oh, God," she ground out through her teeth, only too aware of the reporters and their sudden interest in him. "Why did he have to come?!"

Lillian took her arm gently. "Don't let him know that it bothers you. Smile, girl! We'll get through this."

"Do you think so?"

She plastered a cool smile to her lips as Simon pulled Jill along with him and came to a halt just in front of the two women.

"Nice crowd," he told Tira, his eyes slowly going over her exquisite figure in the close-fitting dress with unusual interest.

"A few art fans and a lot of rubberneckers, hadn't you noticed?" Tira said, sipping more champagne. Her fingers trembled a little and she held the flute with both hands, something Simon's keen eyes picked up on at once.

"Nice of you to come by," Lillian said quietly.

He glanced at her. "It would have been noticeable if I hadn't, considering that I own half the gallery." His attention turned back to Tira and his silvery eyes narrowed. "All alone? Where's your fair-haired shadow?"

She knew he meant Charles. She smiled lazily. "He couldn't make it."

"On the first night of your first exhibition?" he chided.

She drew in a sharp breath. "His half brother had a heart attack, if you must know," she said through her teeth. "He's at the hospital."

Simon's eyes flickered strangely. "And you have to be here, instead of at his side. Pity."

"He doesn't need comforting. Nessa does."

Jill, dressed in red again with a sprig of holly secured with a diamond clip in her black hair, moved closer to Simon. "We just stopped in for a peek at your work," she said, almost purring as she looked up at the tall man beside her. "We're on our way to the opera."

Tira averted her eyes. She loved opera. Many times in the past, Simon had escorted her during the season. It hurt to remember how she'd looked forward to those chaste evenings with him.

"I don't suppose you go anymore?" Simon asked coldly.

She shrugged. "Don't have time," she said tightly.

"I noticed. You couldn't even be bothered to phone and check on me when that lunatic went wild in the courtroom."

Tira wouldn't look at him. "You can't hurt someone who's steel right through," she said.

"And you were out of the country when it happened."

She lifted her eyes to his hard face. "Yes. I was in Nassau with Charles, having a lovely time!"

His eyes seemed to blaze up at her.

Before the confrontation could escalate, Lillian diplomatically got between them. "Have you had time to look around?" she asked Simon.

"Oh, we've seen most everything," Jill answered for him. "Even the bust of Simon that Tira did. I was surprised that she was willing to sell it," she added in an innocent tone. "I wouldn't part with something so personal, Simon being such an old friend and all. But I guess under the circumstances, it was too painful a reminder of…things, wasn't it, dear?" she asked Tira.

Tira's hand automatically drew back, with the remainder of the champagne, but before she could toss it, Simon caught her wrist with his good hand.

"No catfights," he said through his teeth. "Jill, wait for me at the door, will you?"

"If you say so. My, she does look violent, doesn't she?" Jill chided, but she walked away quickly just the same.

"Get a grip on yourself!" Simon shot at Tira under his breath. "Don't you see the reporters staring at you?"

"I don't give a damn about the reporters," she flashed at him. "If she comes near me again, I swear I'll empty the punch bowl over her vicious little head!"

He let go of her wrist and something kindled in his pale eyes as he looked at her animated face. "That's more like you," he said in a deep, soft tone.

Tira flushed, aware that Lillian was quietly deserting her, stranding her with Simon.

"Why did you come?" she asked furiously.

"So the gossips wouldn't have a field day speculating about why I didn't," he explained. "It wouldn't have done either of us much good, considering what's been in print already."

She lifted her face, staring at him with cold eyes at the reference to things she only wanted to forget. "You've done your duty," she said. "You might as well go. And take the Wicked Witch of the West with you," she added spitefully.

"Jealous?" he asked in a sensuous tone.

Her face hardened. "I once asked you the same question. You can give yourself the same answer that you gave me. Like hell I'm jealous!"

He was watching her curiously, his eyes acutely alive in a strangely taciturn face. "You've lost weight," he remarked. "And you look more like a widow than a celebrity tonight. Why wear black?"

"I've decided that you were right. I should have mourned my husband. So now I'm in mourning," she said icily and with an arctic smile. "I expect to be in mourning for him until I die, and I'll never look at a man again. Doesn't that make you happy?"

He frowned slightly. "Tira…"

"Tira!"

The sound of a familiar voice turned them both around. Harry Beck, Tira's father-in-law, came forward, smiling, to embrace Tira. He turned to shake Simon's hand. "Great to see you both!" he said enthusiastically. "Dollface, you've outdone yourself," he told Tira, nodding toward two nearby sculptures. "I always knew you were talented, but this is sheer genius!"

Simon looked puzzled by Harry's honest enthusiasm for Tira's work, by his lack of hostility. She'd killed his only son, didn't he care?

"I'm glad to see you, Simon," Harry added with a smile. "It's been a long time."

"Simon was just leaving. Weren't you?" Tira added meaningfully.

"Someone's motioning to you," Harry noted, indicating Lillian frantically waving from across the room.

"It's Lillian. Will you excuse me?" Tira asked, smiling at Harry. "I won't be a minute." Simon, she ignored entirely.

The two men watched her go.

"I'm glad to see her looking so much better," Harry said on a sigh, shoving his hands into his pockets. "I've been worried since she went to the hospital."

"Do you really care what happens to her?" Simon asked curiously.

Harry was surprised. "Why wouldn't I be? She was my daughter-in-law. I've always been fond of her."

"She divorced John a month after they married and let him go off to work on a drill rig in the ocean," Simon returned. "He died there."

Harry stared at him blankly. "But that wasn't her fault."

"Wasn't it?"

"Why are you so bitter?" Harry wanted to know. "For God's sake, you can't think she didn't try to change him? He should have told her the truth before he married her, not let her find it out that way!"

Simon was puzzled. "Find what out?"

Jill glared at Simon, but he made a motion for her to wait another minute and turned back to Harry. "Find what out?" he repeated curtly.

"That John was homosexual, of course," Harry said, puzzled.

The blood drained out of Simon's face. He stared down at the older man with dawning comprehension.

"She didn't tell you?" Harry asked gently. He sighed and shook his head. "That's like her, though. She wanted to preserve your illusions about John, even if it meant sacrificing your respect for her. She couldn't tell you, I guess. I can't blame her. If he'd only been able to accept what he was…but he couldn't. He tried so hard to be what he thought I wanted. And he never seemed to understand that I'd have loved him regardless of how he saw his place in the world."

Simon turned away, his eyes finding Tira across the room. She wouldn't meet his gaze. She turned her back. He felt the pain right through his body.

"Dear God!" he growled when he realized what he'd done.

"Don't look like that," Harry said gently. "John made his own choice. It was nobody's fault. Maybe it was mine. I should have seen that he was distraught and done something."

Simon let out a breath. He was sick right to his soul. What a fool he'd been.

"She should have told you," Harry was saying. "You're a grown man. You don't need to be protected from the truth. She was always like that, even with John, trying to protect him. She'd have gone on with the marriage if he hadn't insisted on a divorce."

"I thought…she got the divorce."

"He got it, in her name, and cited mental cruelty." He shrugged. "I don't think he considered how it might look to an outsider. It made things worse for him. He only did it to save her reputation. He thought it would hurt her publicly if he made it look like she was at fault." He glanced at Simon. "That was right after your wreck and she was trying to take care of you. He thought it might appear as if she was having an affair with you and he found out. It might have damaged both of you in the public eye."

His teeth clenched. "I never touched her."

"Neither did John," Harry murmured heavily. "He couldn't. He cried in my arms about it, just before he saw an attorney. He wanted to love her. He did, in his way. But it wasn't in a conventional way at all."

Simon pushed back a strand of dark, wavy hair that had fallen on his brow. He was sweating because the gallery was overheated.

"Are you all right?" Harry asked with concern.

"I'm fine." He wasn't. He'd never be all right again. He glanced toward Tira with anguish in every line of his face. But she wouldn't even look at him.

Jill, sensing some problem, came back to join him, sliding her hand into his arm. "Aren't you ready? We'll miss the curtain."

"I'm ready," he said. He looked down at her and realized that here was one more strike against him. He was giving aid and comfort to Tira's worst enemy in the city. He'd done it deliberately, of course, to make her even more uncomfortable. But that was before he knew the whole truth. Now he felt guilty.

"Hello. I'm Jill Sinclair. Have we met?" she asked Harry, smiling.

"No, we haven't. I'm—"

"We have to go," Simon said abruptly. He didn't want to add any more weapons to Jill's already full arsenal by letting Harry tell her about John, too. "See you, Harry."

"Sure. Good night."

"Who was that?" Jill asked Simon as they went toward the door.

"An old friend. Just a minute. There's something I have to do."

"Simon...!"

"I won't be a minute," he promised, and caught one of the gallery's salespeople alone long enough to make a request. She seemed puzzled, but she agreed. He went back to Jill and escorted her out of the gallery, casting one last regretful look toward Tira, who was speaking to a group of socialites at the back of the gallery.

"Half the works are sold already," Jill murmured. "I guess she'll make a fortune."

"She's donating it all to charity," he replied absently.

"She can afford to. It will certainly help her image and, God knows, she needs that right now."

He glanced at her. "That isn't why."

She shrugged. "Whatever you say, darling. *Brrrr*, I'm cold! Christmas is week after next, too." She peered up at him. "I hope you got me something pretty."

"I wouldn't count on it. I probably won't be in town for Christmas," he said not quite truthfully.

She sighed. "Oh, well, I might go and spend the holidays with my aunt in Connecticut. I do love snow!"

She was welcome to all she could find of it, he thought. His heart already felt as if he were buried in snow and ice. He knew that Harry's revelation would keep him awake all night.

Tira watched Simon leave with Jill. She was glad he'd gone. Perhaps now she could enjoy her show.

Lillian was giving her strange looks and when Harry came to say goodbye, he looked rather odd, too.

"What's wrong?" she asked Harry.

He started to speak and thought better of it. Let Simon tell her what he wanted her to know. He was tired of talking about the past; it was too painful.

He smiled. "It's a great show, kiddo, you'll make a mint."

"Thanks, Harry. I had fun doing it. Keep in touch, won't you?"

He leaned forward and kissed her cheek. "You know I will. How's Charlie?"

"His brother-in-law had a heart attack. He's not doing well."

"I'm really sorry. Always liked Charlie. Still do."

"I'll tell him you asked about him," she promised.

He smiled at her. "You do that. Keep well."

"You, too."

By the end of the evening, Tira was calmer, despite the painful memory of her argument with Simon's and Jill's catty remarks. She could just picture the two of them in Simon's lavish apartment, sprawled all over each other in an ardent tangle. It made her sick. Simon had never kissed her, never touched her in anything but an impersonal way. She'd lived like a religious recluse for part of her life and she had nothing to show for her reticence except a broken heart and shattered pride.

"What a great haul," Lillian enthused, breaking into her thoughts. "You sold three-fourths of them. The rest we'll keep on display for a few weeks and see how they do."

"I'm delighted," Tira said, and meant it. "It's all going to benefit the outreach program at St. Mark's."

"They'll be very happy with it, I'm sure."

Tira was walking around the gallery with the manager. Most of the crowd had left and a few stragglers were making their way to the door. She noticed the bust of Simon had a Sold sign on it, and her heart jumped.

"Who bought it?" Tira asked curtly. "It wasn't Jill Sinclair, was it?"

"No," Lillian assured her. "I'm not sure who bought it, but I can check, if you like."

"No, that's not necessary," Tira said, clamping down hard on her curiosity. "I don't care who bought it. I only wanted it out of my sight. I don't care if I never see Simon Hart again!"

Lillian sighed worriedly, but she smiled when Tira glanced toward her and offered coffee.

Simon watched the late-night news broadcast from his easy chair, nursing a whiskey sour, his second in half an hour. He'd taken Jill home and adroitly avoided her coquettish invitation to stay the night. After what he'd learned from Harry Beck, he had to be by himself to think things out.

There was a brief mention of Tira's showing at the gallery and how much money had been raised for charity. He held his breath, but nothing was said about her suicide attempt. He only hoped the newspapers would be equally willing to put the matter aside.

He sipped his drink and remembered unwillingly all the horrible things he'd thought about and said to Tira over John. How she must have suffered through that mockery of a marriage, and how horrible if she'd loved John. She must have had her illusions shattered. She was the injured party. But Simon had taken John's side and punished her as if she was guilty for John's death. He'd deliberately put her out of his life, forbidding her to come close, even to touch him.

He closed his eyes in anguish. She would never let him near her again, no matter how he apologized. He'd said too much, done too much. She'd loved him, and he'd savaged her. And it had all been for nothing. She'd been innocent.

He finished his drink with dead eyes. Regrets seemed to pile up in the loneliness of the night. He glanced toward the Christmas tree his enthusiastic housekeeper had set up by the window, and dreaded the whole holiday season. He'd spend Christmas alone. Tira, at least, would have the despised Charles Percy for company.

He wondered why she didn't marry the damned man. They seemed to live in each other's pockets. He remembered that Charles had always been her champion, bolstering her up, protecting her. Charles had been her friend when Simon had turned his back on her, so how could he blame her for preferring the younger man?

He put his glass down and got to his feet. He felt every year of his age. He was almost forty and he had nothing to show for his own life. The child he might have had was gone, along with Melia, who'd never loved him. He'd lived on illusions of love for a long time, when the reality of love had ached for him and he'd turned his back.

If he'd let Tira love him…

He groaned aloud. He might as well put that hope to rest right now. She'd hate him forever and he had only himself to blame. Perhaps he deserved her hatred. God knew, he'd hurt her enough.

He went to bed, to lie awake all night with the memory of Tira's wounded eyes and drawn face to haunt him.

Chapter Five

Simon was not in a good mood the next morning when he went into work. Mrs. Mackey, his middle-aged secretary, stopped him at the door of his office with an urgent message to call the governor's office as soon as he came in. He knew what it was about and he groaned inwardly. He didn't want to be attorney general, but he knew for a fact that Wally was going to offer it to him. Wallace Bingley was a hard man to refuse, and he was a very popular governor as well as a friend. Both Simon and Tira had been actively involved in his gubernatorial campaign.

"All right, Mrs. Mack," he murmured, smiling as he used her nickname, "get him for me."

She grinned, because she knew, too, what was going on.

Minutes later, the call was put through to his office.

"Hi, Wally," Simon said. "What can I do for you?"

"You know the answer to that already," came the wry response. "Will you or won't you?"

"I'd like a week or so to think about it," Simon said seriously. "It's a part of my life I hadn't planned to take up again. I don't like living in a goldfish bowl and I hear it's open season on attorneys general in Texas."

Wallace chuckled. "You don't have as many political enemies as he does, and you're craftier, too. All right, think about it. Take the rest of the month. But two weeks is all you've got. After the holidays, his resignation takes effect, and I have to appoint someone."

"I promise to let you know by then," Simon assured him.

"Now, to better things. Are you coming to the Starks's Christmas party?"

"I'd have liked to, but my brothers are throwing a party down in Jacobsville and I more or less promised to show up."

"Speaking of the 'fearsome four,' how are they?"

"Desperate." Simon chuckled. "Corrigan phoned day before yesterday and announced that Dorie thinks she's pregnant. If she is, the boys are going to have to find a new victim to make biscuits for them."

"Why don't they hire a cook?"

"They can't keep one. You know why," Simon replied dryly.

"I guess I do. He hasn't changed."

"He never will," Simon agreed, referring to his brother Leopold, who was mischievous and sometimes outrageous in his treatment of housekeepers. Unlike the other two of the three remaining Hart bachelor brothers, Callaghan and Reynard, Leopold was a live wire.

"How's Tira?" Wallace asked unexpectedly. "I hear her showing was a huge success."

The mention of it was uncomfortable. It reminded him all too vividly of the mistakes he'd made with Tira. "I suppose she's fine," Simon said through his teeth.

"Er, well, sorry, I forgot. The publicity must have been hard on both of you. Not that anybody takes it seriously. It certainly won't hurt your political chances, if that's why you're hesitating to accept the position."

"It wasn't. I'll talk to you soon, Wally, and thanks for the offer."

"I hope you'll accept. I could use you."

"I'll let you know."

He said goodbye and hung up, glaring out the window as he recalled what he'd learned about Tira so unexpectedly. It hurt him to talk about her now. It would take a long time for her to forgive him, if she ever did.

If only there was some way that he could talk to her, persuade her to listen to him. He'd tried phoning from home early this very morning. As soon as she'd heard his voice, she'd hung up, and the answering machine had been turned on when he tried again. There was no point in leaving a message. She was determined to wipe him right out of her life, apparently. He felt so disheartened he didn't know what to try next.

And then he remembered Sherry Walker, a mutual friend of his and Tira's in the past who loved opera and had season tickets in the aisle right next to his, in the dress circle. He knew that Sherry had broken a leg skiing just recently and had said that she wasn't leaving the house until it healed completely. Perhaps, he told himself, there was a way to get Tira to talk to him after all.

The letdown after the showing made Tira miserable. She had nothing to do just now, with the holiday season in full swing, and she had no one to buy a present for except Mrs. Lester and Charles. She went from store to colorfully decorated store and watched mothers and fathers with their children and choked on her own pain. She wouldn't have children or the big family she'd always craved. She'd live and die alone.

As she stood at a toy store window, watching the

electric train sets flashing around a display of papier mâché mountains and small buildings, she wondered what it would be like to have children to buy those trains for.

A lone, salty tear ran down her cold-flushed cheek and even as she caught it on her knuckles, she felt a sudden pervasive warmth at her back.

Her heart jumped even before she looked up. She always knew when Simon was anywhere nearby. It was a sort of unwanted radar and just lately it was more painful than ever.

"Nice, aren't they?" he asked quietly. "When I was a boy, my father bought my brothers and me a set of 'O' scale Lionel trains. We used to sit and run them by the hour in the dark, with all the little buildings lighted, and imagine little people living there." He turned, resplendant in a charcoal gray cashmere overcoat over his navy blue suit. His white shirt was spotless, like the patterned navy-and-white tie he wore with it. He looked devastating. And he was still wearing the hated prosthesis.

"Isn't this a little out of your way?" she asked tautly.

"I like toy stores. Apparently so do you." He searched what he could see of her averted face. Her glorious hair was in a long braid today and she was wearing a green silk pantsuit several shades darker than her eyes under her long black leather coat.

"Toys are for children," she said coldly.

He frowned slightly. "Don't you like children?"

She clenched her teeth and stared at the train. "What would be the point?" she asked. "I won't have any. If you'll excuse me..."

He moved in front of her, blocking the way. "Doesn't Charles want a family?"

It was a pointed question, and probably taunting. Charles's brother was still in the hospital and no better, and from what Charles had been told, he might not get better. There was a lot of damage to Gene's heart. Charles would be taking care of Nessa, whom he loved, but Simon knew nothing about that.

"I've never asked Charles how he feels about children," she said carelessly.

"Shouldn't you? It's an issue that needs to be resolved before two people make a firm commitment to each other."

Was he deliberately trying to lacerate her feelings? She wouldn't put it past him now. "Simon, none of this is any of your business," she said in a choked tone. "Now will you please let me go?" she asked on a nervous laugh. "I have shopping to do."

His good hand reached out to lightly touch her shoulder, but she jerked back from him as if he had a communicable disease.

"Don't!" she said sharply. "Don't ever do that!"

He withdrew his hand, scowling down at her. She was white in the face and barely able to breathe from the look of her.

"Just…leave me alone, okay?" She choked, and darted past him and into the thick of the holiday crowd on the sidewalk. She couldn't bear to let her weakness for him show. Every time he touched her, she felt vibrations all the way to her toes and she couldn't hide it. Fortunately she was away before he noticed that it wasn't revulsion that had torn her from his side. She was spared a little of her pride.

Simon watched her go with welling sadness. It could have been so different, he thought, if he'd been less judgmental, if he'd ever bothered to ask her side of her brief marriage. But he hadn't. He'd condemned her on the spot, and kept pushing her away for years. How could he expect to get back on any sort of friendly footing with her easily? It was going to take a long time, and from what he'd just seen, his was an uphill climb all the way. He went back to his office so dejected that Mrs. Mack asked if he needed some aspirin.

Tira brushed off the chance meeting with Simon as a coincidence and was cheered by an unexpected call from an old friend, who offered her a ticket to *Turandot*, her favorite opera, the next evening.

She accepted with pure pleasure. It would do her good to get out of the house and do something she enjoyed.

She put on a pretty black designer dress with diamanté straps and covered it with her flashy velvet wrap. She didn't look half bad for an old girl, she told her reflection in the mirror. But then, she had nobody to dress up for, so what did it matter?

She hired a cab to take her downtown because finding a parking space for the visiting opera performance would be a nightmare. She stepped out of the cab into a crowd of other music lovers and some of her painful loneliness drifted away in the excitement of the performance.

The seat she'd been given was in the dress circle. She remembered so many nights being here with Simon, but his reserved seat, thank God, was empty. If she'd thought there was a chance of his being here, she'd never have come. But she knew that Simon had taken Jill to see this performance already. It was unlikely that he'd want to sit through it again.

There was a drumroll. The theater went dark. The

curtain started to rise. The orchestra began to play the overture. She relaxed with her small evening bag in her lap and smiled as she anticipated a joyful experience.

And then everything went suddenly wrong. There was a movement to her left and when she turned her head, there was Simon, dashing in dark evening clothes, sitting down right beside her.

He gave her a deliberately careless glance and a curt nod and then turned his attention back to the stage.

Tira's hands clenched on the evening bag. Simon's shoulder brushed against hers as he shifted in his seat and she felt the touch as if it were fire all the way down her body. It had never been so bad before. She'd walked with him, talked with him, shared seats at benefits and auctions and operas and plays with him, and even though his presence had been a bittersweet delight, it had never been so physically painful to her in the past. She wanted to turn and find his mouth with her lips, she wanted to press her body to his and feel his cheek against her own. The longing so was poignant that she shivered with it.

"Cold?" he whispered.

She clenched her jaw. "Not at all," she muttered, sliding further into her velvet wrap.

His good arm went, unobtrusively, over the back of her seat and rested there. She froze in place, barely daring to move, to breathe. It was just like the afternoon in front of the toy store. Did he know that it was torture for her to be close to him? Probably he did. He'd found a new way to get to her, to make her pay for all the terrible things he thought she'd done. She closed her eyes and groaned silently.

The opera, beautiful as it was, was forgotten. She was so miserable that she sat stiffly and heard none of it. All she could think about was how to escape.

She started to get up and Simon's big hand caught her shoulder a little too firmly.

"Stay where you are," he said gruffly.

She hesitated, but only for an instant. She was desperate to escape now. "I have to go to the necessary room, if you don't mind," she bit off near his ear.

"Oh."

He sighed heavily and moved his arm, turning to allow her to get past him. She apologized all the way down the row. Once she made it to the aisle, she felt safe. She didn't look back as she made her way gracefully and quickly to the back of the theater and into the lobby.

It was easy to dart out the door and hail a cab. This time of night, they were always a few of them cruising nearby. She climbed into the first one that stopped, gave him her address, and sat back with a relieved sigh. She'd done it. She was safe.

She went home more miserable than ever, changed into her nightgown and a silky white robe and let her hair down with a long sigh. She couldn't blame her friend, Sherry, for the fiasco. How could anyone have known that Simon would decide to see the opera a second time on this particular night? But it was a cruel blow of fate. Tira had looked forward to a performance that Simon's presence had ruined for her.

She made coffee, despite the late hour, and was sitting down in the living room to drink it when the doorbell rang.

It might be Charles, she decided. She hadn't heard from him today, and he could have stopped by to tell her about Gene. She went to the front door and opened it without thinking.

Simon was standing there with a furious expression on his face.

She tried to close the door, but one big well-shod foot was inside it before she could even move. He let himself in and closed the door behind him.

"Well, come in, then," she said curtly, her green eyes sparkling with bad temper as she pulled her robe closer around her.

He stared at her with open curiosity. He'd never seen her in night clothing before. The white robe emphasized her creamy skin, and the lace of her gown came barely high enough to cover the soft mounds of her breasts. With her red-gold hair loose in a glorious tangle around her shoulders, she was a picture to take a man's breath away.

"Why did you run?" he asked softly.

Her face colored gently. "I wasn't expecting you to be there," she said, and it came out almost as an accusation. "You've already seen the performance once."

"Yes, with Jill," he added deliberately, watching her face closely.

She averted her eyes. He looked so good in an evening jacket, she thought miserably. His dark, wavy hair was faintly damp, as if the threatening clouds had let some rain fall. His pale gray eyes were watchful, disturbing. He'd never looked at her this way before, like a predator with its prey. It made her nervous.

"Do you want some coffee?" she asked to break the tense silence.

"If you don't put arsenic in it."

She glanced at him. "Don't tempt me."

She led him into the kitchen, got down a cup and poured a cup of coffee for him. She didn't offer cream and sugar, because she knew he took neither.

He turned a chair around and straddled it before he picked up the cup and sipped the hot coffee, staring at her disconcertingly over the rim.

With open curiosity, she glanced at the prosthesis hand, which was resting on the back of the chair.

"Something wrong?" he asked.

She shrugged and picked up her own cup. "You used to hate that." She indicated the artificial arm.

"I hate pity even more," he said flatly. "It looks real enough to keep people from staring."

"Yes," she said. "It does look real."

He sipped coffee. "Even if it doesn't feel it," he murmured dryly. He glanced up at her face and saw it color from the faint insinuation in his deep voice. "Amazing, that you can still blush, at your age," he remarked.

It wouldn't have been if he knew how totally innocent she still was at her advanced age, but she wasn't sharing her most closely guarded secret with the enemy. He thought she and Charles were lovers, and she was content to let him. But that insinuation about why he used the prosthesis was embarrassing and infuriating. She hated being jealous. She had to conceal it from him.

"I don't care how it feels, or to whom," she said stiffly. "In fact, I have no interest whatsoever in your personal life. Not anymore."

He drew in a long breath and let it out. "Yes, I know." He finished his coffee in two swallows. "I miss you," he said simply. "Nothing is the same."

Her heart jumped but she kept her eyes down so that he wouldn't see how much pleasure the statement gave her. "We were friends. I'm sure you have plenty of others. Including Jill."

His intake of breath was audible. "I didn't realize how much you and Jill disliked each other."

"What difference does it make?" She glanced at him with a mocking smile. "I'm not part of your life."

"You were," he returned solemnly. "I didn't realize how much a part of it you were, until it was too late."

"Some things are better left alone," she said evasively. "More coffee?"

He shook his head. "It keeps me awake. Wally called and offered me the attorney general's post," he said. "I've got two weeks to think about it."

"You were a good attorney general," she recalled. "You got a lot of excellent legislation through the general assembly."

He smiled faintly, studying his coffee cup. "I lived in a goldfish bowl. I didn't like it."

"You have to take the bad with the good."

He looked at her closely. "Tell me what happened the night they took you to the hospital."

She shrugged. "I got drunk and passed out."

"And the pistol?"

"The mouse." She nodded toward the refrigerator. "He's under there, I can hear him. He can't be trapped and he's brazen. I got drunk and decided to take him out like John Wayne, with a six-shooter. I missed."

He chuckled softly. "I thought it was something like that. You're not suicidal."

"You're the only person who thinks so. Even Dr. Gaines didn't believe me. He wanted me to have therapy," she scoffed.

"The newspapers had a field day. I guess Jill helped feed the fire."

She glanced up, surprised. "You knew?"

"Not until she commented on it, when it was too late to do anything. For what it's worth," he added quietly, "I don't know many people who believed the accounts in her cousin's paper."

She leaned back in her chair and stared at him levelly. "That I did it for love of you?" she drawled with a poisonous smile. "You hurt my feelings when you accused me of killing my husband," she said flatly. "I was already overworked and depressed and I did something stupid. But I hope you don't believe that I sit around nights crying in my beer because of unrequited passion for you!"

Her tone hit him on the raw. He got slowly to his feet and his eyes narrowed as he stared down at her.

She felt at a distinct disadvantage. She'd only seen Simon lose his temper once. She'd never forgotten and she didn't want to repeat the experience.

"It's late," she said quickly. "I'd like to go to bed."

"Would you really?" His pale gaze slid over her body as he said it, his voice so sensuous that it made her bare toes curl up on the spotless linoleum floor.

She didn't trust that look. She started past him and found one of her hands suddenly trapped by his big one. He moved in, easing her hand up onto the silky fabric of his vest, inside it against the silky warmth of his body under the thin cotton shirt. She could feel the springy hair under it as well, and the hard beat of his heart as his breath whispered out at her temple, stirring her hair. She'd never been so close to him. It was as if her senses, numb for years, all came to life at once and exploded in a shattering rush of physical sensation. It frightened her and she pushed at his chest.

"Simon, let go!" she said huskily, all in a rush.

He didn't. He couldn't. The feel of her in his arms exceeded his wildest imaginings. She was soft and warm and she smelled of flowers. He drank in the scent and felt her begin to tremble. It went right to his head. His hand left hers and slid into her hair at her nape, clenching, so that she was helpless against him. He fought for control. He mustn't do this. It was too soon. Far too soon.

His breath came quickly. She could hear it, feel it. His cheek brushed against hers roughly, as if he wanted to feel the very texture of her skin there. He had a faint growth of beard and it rasped a little, but it was more sensual than uncomfortable.

Her heart raced as wildly as his. She wanted to draw back, to run, but that merciless hand wasn't unclenching. If anything, it had an even tighter grip on her long hair.

She wasn't protesting anymore. He felt her yield and his body clenched. His cheek drew slowly against hers. She felt his mouth at the corner of her own, felt his breath as his lips parted.

"Don't..." The little cry was all but inaudible.

"It's too late," he said roughly. "Years too late. God, Tira, turn your mouth against mine!"

She heard the soft, gruff command with a sense of total unreality. Her cold hands pressed against his shirtfront, but it was, as he said, already too late.

He moved his head just a fraction of an inch, and his hard, hot mouth moved completely onto hers, parting her lips as it explored, settled, demanded. There was a faint hesitation, almost of shock, as sensual electricity flashed between them. He felt her mouth tremble, tasted it, savored it, devoured it.

He groaned as his mouth began to part her lips insistently. Then his arm was around her, the one with the prosthesis holding her waist firmly while the good one lifted and traced patterns from her cheek down to her soft, pulsing throat. He could hear the tortured sound of his own breath echoed by her own.

She whimpered as she felt the full force of his mouth, felt the kiss she'd dreamed of for so many years suddenly becoming reality. He tasted of coffee. His lips were hard and demanding on her mouth, sensual, insistent. She didn't protest. She clung to him, savoring the most ecstatic few seconds of her life as if she never expected to feel anything so powerful again.

Her response puzzled him, because it wasn't that of an experienced woman. She permitted him to kiss her, clung to him closely, even seemed to enjoy his rough ardor; but she gave nothing back. It was almost as if she didn't know how…

He drew back slowly. His pale, fierce eyes looked down into hers with pure sensual arrogance and more than a little curiosity.

This was a Simon she'd never seen, never known, a sensual man with expert knowledge of women that was evident even in such a relatively chaste encounter. She was afraid of him because she had no defense against that kind of ardor, and fear made her push at his chest.

He put her away from him abruptly and his arms fell to his sides. She moved back, her eyes like saucers in a flushed, feverish face, until she was leaning against the counter.

Simon watched her hungrily, his eyes on the noticeable signs of her arousal in her body under the thin silk gown, in her swollen mouth and the faint redness on her cheek where his own had rubbed against it with his faint growth of beard. He'd never dreamed that he and Tira would kindle such fires together. In all their years of careless friendship, he'd never really approached her physically until tonight. He felt as if he were drowning in uncharted waters.

Tira went slowly to the back door and opened it, unnaturally calm. She still looked gloriously beautiful, even more so because she was emotionally aroused.

He took the hint, but he paused at the open door to stare down at her averted face. She was very flustered for a woman who had a lover. He found himself bristling with sudden and unexpected jealousy of the most important man in her life.

"Lucky Charles," he said gruffly. "Is that what he gets?"

Her eyes flashed at him. "You get out of here!" she managed to say through her tight throat. She pulled her robe tight against her throat. "Go. Just, please, go!"

He walked past her, hesitating on the doorstep, but she closed the door after him and locked it. She went back through the kitchen and down the hall to her bedroom before she dared let the tears flow. She was too shaken to try to delve into his motives for that hungry kiss. But she knew it had to be some new sort of revenge for his friend John. Well, it wouldn't work! He was never going to hurt her again, she vowed. She only wished she hadn't been stupid enough to let him touch her in the first place.

Simon stood outside by his car in the misting rain, letting the coolness push away the flaring heat of his body. He shuddered as he leaned his forehead against the cold roof of the car and thanked God he'd managed to get out of there before he did something even more stupid than he already had.

Tira had submitted. He could have had her. He was barely able to draw back at all. What a revelation that had been, that a woman he'd known for years should be able to arouse such instant, sweeping passion in him. Even Melia hadn't had such a profound effect on him, in the days when he'd thought he loved her.

He hadn't meant to touch her. But her body, her exquisite body, in that thin robe and gown had driven him right over the edge. He still had the taste of her soft, sweet lips on his mouth, he could still feel her pressed completely to him. It was killing him!

He clenched his hand and forced himself to breathe slowly until he began to relax. At least she hadn't seen him helpless like this. If she knew how vulnerable he was, she might feel like a little revenge. He couldn't blame her, but his pride wouldn't stand it. She might decide to seduce him and then keep him dangling. That would be the cruelest blow of all, when he knew she was Charles Percy's lover. He had sick visions of Tira telling him everything Simon had done to her and laughing about how easily she'd knocked him off balance. Charles was Tira's lover. Her lover. God, the thought of it made him sick!

He could see why Charles couldn't keep away from her. It made him bitter to realize that he could probably have cut Charles out years ago if he hadn't been so blind and prejudiced. Tira could have been his. But instead, she was Charles's, and she could only hate Simon now for the treatment he'd dealt out to her. He couldn't imagine her still loving him, even if he had taunted her with it to salvage what was left of his pride.

He got into his car finally and drove away in a roar of fury. Damn her for making him lose his head, he thought, refusing to remember that he'd started the whole damned thing. And damn him for letting her do it!

Chapter Six

After consuming far more whiskey than he should have the night before, Simon awoke with vivid memories of Tira in his arms and groaned heavily. He'd blown it, all over again. He didn't know how he was going to smooth things over this time. Jill called and invited herself to lunch with him, fishing for clues to his unusual bad humor. He mumbled something about going to the opera and having an argument with Tira, but offered no details at all. She asked him if he'd expected Tira to be there, and he brushed off further questions, pleading work.

Jill was livid at the thought that Tira was cutting in on her territory, just when things were going so well. She phoned the house and was told by Mrs. Lester that Tira had gone shopping. The rest was easy....

Tira, still smoldering from the betrayal of her weak body the night before, treated herself to lunch at a small sandwich shop downtown. Fate seemed to be against her, she thought with cold resignation, when Jill Sinclair walked into the shop and made a beeline for her just as she was working on dessert and a second cup of coffee.

"Well, how are you doing?" Jill asked with an innocent smile. "Just sandwiches? Poor you! Simon's taking me to Chez Paul for crepes and cherries jubilee."

"Then why are you here?" Tira asked, not disposed to be friendly toward her worst enemy.

Jill's perfect eyebrows arched. "Why, I was shopping next door for a new diamond tennis bracelet and I spotted you in here," she lied. "I thought a word to the wise, you know," she added, glancing around with the wariness of a veteran intelligence agent before she leaned down to whisper, "Simon was very vexed to have found you sitting next to him at the opera last night. You really should be more careful about engineering these little 'accidental' meetings and chasing after him, dear. He's in a vicious mood today!"

"Good!" Tira said with barely controlled rage. She glared at the other woman. "Would you like to have coffee with me, Jill?" She asked, and drew back the hand that was holding the cup of lukewarm coffee. "Let me introduce you to Miss Cup!"

Jill barely stepped back in time as the coffee cup flew through the air and hit the floor inches in front of her. Her eyes were wide open, and her mouth joined them. She hadn't expected her worst enemy to fight back.

"My, my, aren't I the clumsy one!" Tira said sweetly. "I dropped Miss Cup and spilled my coffee!"

Jill swallowed, hard. "I'll just be off," she said quickly.

"Oh, look," Tira added, lifting the plastic coffeepot the waitress had left on her table with a whimsical smile. "Mr. Coffeepot's coming after Miss Cup!"

Jill actually ran. If Tira hadn't been so miserable, she might have laughed at the sight. As it was, she apologized profusely to the waitress about the spilled coffee and left a tip big enough to excuse the extra work she'd made for the woman.

But it didn't really cheer her up. She went back home and started sculpting a new piece for the gallery.

It wasn't necessary work, but it gave her something to do so that she wouldn't spend the day remembering Simon's hard kisses or thinking about how good Jill would look buried up to her armpits in stinging nettles.

The next day she was asked to serve on a committee to oversee Christmas festivities for a local children's shelter. It was a committee that Simon chaired, and she refused politely, only to have him call her right back and ask why.

She was furious. "Don't you know?" she demanded. "You had Jill rub my nose in it for—how did she put this?—chasing you to the opera!"

There was a long pause. "I asked Sherry to give you the ticket to the opera, since she couldn't use it," he confessed, to her surprise. "If anyone was chasing, it was me."

She felt her heart stop. "What?"

"You heard me," he said curtly. There was another pause. "Work with me on the committee. You'll enjoy it."

She would. But she was reluctant to get closer to him than a telephone receiver. "I don't know that I would," she said finally. "You're not yourself lately."

"I know that." He was feeling his way. "Can't we start again?"

She hesitated. "As what?" she asked bluntly.

"Co-workers. Friends. Whatever you like."

That was capitulation, of a sort, at least. Perhaps he was through trying to make her pay for John's untimely death. Whatever his reason, her life was empty without him, wasn't it? Surely friendship was better than nothing at all? She refused to think about how his kisses had felt.

"Is Jill on the committee?" she asked suddenly, wary of plots.

"No!"

That was definite enough. "All right, then," she said heavily. "I'll do it."

"Good! I'll pick you up for the meeting tomorrow night."

"No, you won't," she returned shortly. "I'll drive myself. Where is it?"

He told her. There was nothing in his voice to betray whether or not he was irritated by her stubborn refusal to ride with him. He was even more irritated by Jill's interference. He'd made a bad mistake there, taking out Tira's worst enemy. He'd been depressed and Jill was good company, but it would have to stop. Tira wasn't going to take kindly to having Jill antagonize her out of sheer rivalry.

Tira went to the meeting, finding several old friends serving on the committee. They worked for three hours on preparations for a party, complete with an elderly local man who had agreed to play Santa Claus for the children. Tira was to help serve and bring two cakes, having volunteered because she had no plans for Christmas Eve other than to lay a trap for that mouse in the kitchen. Another woman, a widow, also volunteered to help, and two of the men, including Simon.

He stopped her by her car after the meeting. "The boys are having a Christmas party Saturday night in Jacobsville. They'd like you to come."

"I don't…"

He put a big forefinger across her soft mouth, startling her. The intimacy was unfamiliar and worrisome.

"Charles can do without you for one Saturday night, can't he?" he asked curtly.

"I haven't seen Charles lately. His brother, Gene, is

in the hospital," she said, having forgotten whether or not she'd mentioned it to him. "Nessa isn't coping well at all, and Charles can't leave her alone."

"Nessa?"

"Gene's wife." She wanted to tell him about Nessa and Charles, but it wasn't her secret and letting him think she and Charles were close was the only shield she had at the moment. She couldn't let her guard down. She still didn't quite trust him. His new attitude toward her was puzzling and she didn't understand why he'd changed.

"I see."

"You don't, but it doesn't matter. I want to go home. I'm cold."

He searched her quiet face. "I could offer an alternative," he said in a soft, velvety tone.

She looked up at him with cool disdain. "I don't do casual affairs, Simon," she said bluntly. "Just in case the thought had crossed your mind lately."

He looked as if he'd been slapped. His jaw tautened. "Don't you? Then if your affair with Charles Percy isn't casual, why hasn't he married you?"

"I don't want to marry again," she said in a husky voice, averting her eyes. "Not ever."

He hesitated. He knew why she felt that way, that she'd been betrayed in the worst way. Her father-in-law had told him everything, but he was uncertain about whether or not to tell her that he knew.

She glanced at him warily. "Does Jill know that you're still grieving for your wife?" she asked, taking the fight right into the enemy camp. "Or is she just an occasional midnight snack?"

His eyebrows arched. "That's a hell of a comparison."

"Isn't it?" She smiled sweetly. "I'm going home."

"Come to Jacobsville with me."

"And into the jaws of death or kitchen slavery?" she taunted. "I know all about the biscuit mania. I'm not about to be captured by your loopy brothers."

"They won't come near you," he promised. "Corrigan's hired a new cook. She's redheaded and she can bake anything."

"She won't last two weeks before Leopold has her running for the border," she assured him.

It pleased him that she knew his brothers so well, that she took an interest in his family. She and Corrigan had been friends and occasionally had dated in the past, but there had been no spark between them. In fact, Charles Percy had always been in the way of any other man and Tira. Why hadn't he noticed that before?

"You've been going around with Charles ever since you left John," he recalled absently.

"Charles is my friend," she said.

"Friend," he scoffed, his eyes insulting. "Is that what it's called these days?"

"You should know," she returned. "What does Jill call it?"

His eyes narrowed angrily. "At least she's honest about what she wants from me," he replied. "And it isn't my money."

She shrugged. "To each his own."

He searched her face quietly. "You kissed me back the other night."

Her cheeks went ruddy and she looked away, clutching her purse. "I have to go."

He was right behind her. He didn't touch her, but she could feel the warm threat of him all down her spine, oddly comforting in the chilly December air.

"Stop running!"

Her eyes closed for an instant before she reached for the door handle. "We seemed to be friends once," she said in a husky tone. "But we weren't, not really. You only tolerated me. I'm amazed that I went through all those years so blind that I never saw the contempt you felt when you looked at me."

"Tira..."

She turned, holding up a hand. "I'm not accusing you. I just want you to know that I'm not carrying a torch for you or breaking my heart because you go around with Jill." Her eyes were lackluster and he realized with a start that she'd lost a lot of weight in the past few months. She looked fragile, breakable.

"What are you saying?" he asked.

"That I don't need you to pity me, Simon," she said with visible pride. "I don't really want a closer association with you, whatever Jill says or you think. I'm rearranging my life. I've started over. I don't want to go back to the way we were."

He felt those words like a knife. She meant them. It was in her whole expression.

"I see," he said quietly.

"No, you don't," she replied heavily. "You're sort of like a drug," she mused. "I was addicted to you and I've been cured, but even small doses are dangerous to my recovery."

His heart leaped. He caught her gaze and held it relentlessly. "What did you say?"

"You know what I mean," she returned. "I'm not going to let myself become addicted again. I have Charles and you have Jill. Let's go our separate ways and get on with our lives. I was serious about the pistol and the mouse, you know, it wasn't some face-saving excuse. I never meant to kill myself over you."

"Oh, hell, I knew that."

"Then why…"

"Yes?"

She turned her purse in her hands. "Why do you keep engineering situations where we'll be thrown together?" she asked. "It serves no purpose."

His hand came out of his pocket and lifted to touch, lightly, her upswept hair. She flinched and he dropped his hand with a long sigh.

"You can't forget, can you?" he asked slowly.

"I'm trying," she assured him. "But every time we're together, people speculate. The newspaper stories were pretty hard to live down, even for me. I don't really want to rekindle speculation."

"You never cared about gossip before."

"I was never publicly savaged before," she countered. "I've been made to look like some clinging, simpering nymph crying for a man who doesn't want her. My pride is in shreds!"

He was watching her narrowly. "How do you know that I don't want you, Tira?" he asked deliberately.

She stared at him without speaking, floored by the question.

"I'll pick you up at six on Saturday and drive you to Jacobsville," he said. "Wear something elegant. It's formal."

"I won't go," she said through her teeth.

"You'll go," he replied with chilling certainty.

He turned and walked to his own car with her glaring after him. Well, they'd just see about that! she told herself.

It was barely a week until Christmas. Tira had the party for the children to look forward to on Christmas

Eve, to help her feel some Christmas spirit. She had an artificial tree that she set up in her living room every year. She'd have loved a real one, with its own dirt ball so that it could be set out in the yard after the holidays, but she was violently allergic to fir trees of any kind. The expensive artificial tree was very authentic looking and once she decorated it, it could have fooled an expert at a distance.

She had a collection of faux gold-plated cherubs and elegant gold foil ribbons to use for decorations, along with gold and silver bead strands and fairy lights. For whimsy, there were a few mechanical ornaments scattered deep within the limbs, which could be activated by the touch of a finger. She had a red-and-white latch-hook rug that went around the base of the tree, and around that was a Lionel "O" scale train set—the one she'd seen in the window of the department store that day she'd come across Simon on the sidewalk. She'd gone back and bought the train, and now she enjoyed watching it run. It only lacked one or two little lighted buildings to go beside it. Those, she reasoned, she could add later.

She stood back and admired her handiwork. She was wearing a gold-and-white caftan that echoed the color scheme of the tree, especially with her hair loose. It was Saturday, but she wasn't going to the Hart party. In fact, when Simon rang the doorbell, he wasn't going to get into the house. She felt very smug about the ease with which she'd avoided him.

"Very nice," came a deep, amused voice from behind her.

She whirled and found Simon, in evening clothing, watching her from the doorway.

"*How…how did you get in?*" she gasped.

"Mrs. Lester kindly left the back door unlocked for me," he mused. "I told her that we were going out and that you'd probably forget. She's very obliging. A real romantic, Mrs. Lester."

"I'll fire her Monday the minute she gets back from her sister's!" she snarled.

"No, you won't. She's a treasure."

She swept back her hair. "I'm not going to Jacobsville!"

"You are," he said. "Either you get dressed, or I dress you."

"Ha!" She folded her arms across her chest and dared him to do his worst.

The prospect seemed to amuse him. He took her by the arm with his good hand and led her down the hall to her bedroom, opened the door, put her in and closed it behind them. He'd already been here, she could tell, because a white strapless evening gown was laid out on the bed, along with filmy underthings that matched it.

"You...you invaded my bedroom!" she raged.

"Yes, I did. It was very educational. You don't dress like a siren at all. Most of your wardrobe seems to consist of cotton underthings and jeans and tank tops." He glanced at her. "I like that caftan you're wearing, but it's not quite appropriate for tonight's festivities."

"I'm not putting on that dress."

He chuckled softly. "You are. Sooner or later."

She started toward the door and found herself swept up against him, held firmly by that damned prosthesis that seemed to work every bit as well as the arm it had replaced.

"I'm not going to hurt you," he promised softly. "But you're going."

"I will...what are you...doing?"

She'd forgotten the front zip that kept the caftan on her. He released it with a minimum of fuss and the whole thing dropped to the floor, leaving her in her bare feet and nude except for her serviceable white briefs.

She gaped at him. He looked at her body with the appreciation of an artist, noting the creamy soft rise of her breasts with their tight rosy nipples and the supple curve of her waist that flared to rounded hips and long, elegant legs.

"Don't you…look at me!" she gasped, trying to cover herself.

His eyes met hers quizzically. "Don't you want me to?" he asked softly.

The question surprised her. She only stared at him, watching his gaze fall again to her nudity and sweep over it with pure delight. She shivered at the feel of his gaze.

"It's all right," he said gently, surprised by the way she was reacting. "I'm not even going to touch you. I promise."

She drew in a shaky breath, held close by one arm while his other hand traced along her flushed cheek and down to the corner of her tremulous mouth.

What an unexpected creature she was, he thought with some confusion. She was embarrassed, shy, even a little ashamed to stand here this way. She blushed like a girl. He knew that she couldn't be totally innocent, but her reaction was nothing like that of an experienced woman.

His fingers traced over her mouth and down the curve of her pulsating throat to her collarbone. They hesitated there and his gaze fell to her mouth.

The silence in the bedroom was like the silence in the eye of a hurricane. If she breathed the wrong way, it would break the spell, and he'd draw away. His fingers, even now, were hesitating at her collarbone and his mouth hovered above hers as if he couldn't quite decide what to do next.

She shivered, her own eyes lingering helplessly on the long, wide curve of his mouth.

He moved, just slightly, so that her body was completely against his, and he let her feel the slow burgeoning of his arousal. It shocked her. He saw the flush spread all over her high cheekbones.

"Tira," he said roughly, "tell me what you want."

"I don't...know," she whispered brokenly, searching his pale, glittering eyes. "I don't know!"

He felt her hips move, just a fraction, felt her body shift so that she was faintly arched toward him. "Don't you?" he whispered back. "Your body does. Shall I show you what it's asking me to do?"

She couldn't manage words, but he didn't seem to need them. With a faint smile, he lifted his hand and spread it against her rib cage, slowly, torturously sliding it up until it was resting just at the underside of her taut breast. She shivered and caught her breath, her eyes wide and hungry and still frightened.

"It won't hurt," he whispered, and his hand moved up and over her nipple, softly caressing.

She clutched his shoulders and hid her face against him in a torment of shattered sensations, moaning sharply at the intimate touch.

He hesitated. "What's wrong?" he asked gently. His face nuzzled against her cheek, forcing her head back so that he could see her shocked, helpless submission. He touched her again, easing his fingers together over the hard nipple as he tugged at it gently. The look on her face made his whole body go rigid.

Her head went back. Her eyes closed. She shivered, biting her lip to keep from weeping, the pleasure was so overwhelming.

If she was shaken, so was he. It was relatively chaste love play, but she was already reacting as if his body was intimately moving on hers. Her response was as unexpected as it was flattering.

"Come here," he said with rough urgency, tugging her to the bed. He pulled her down with him on the coverlet beside her gown and shifted so that she was beneath him. His rapid heartbeat was causing him to shake even before he found her mouth with his and began to caress her intimately.

"Simon," she sobbed. But she was pulling, not pushing. Her mouth opened for him, her body rose as he caressed it with his hand and then with his open mouth. He suckled her, groaning when she shivered and cried out from the pleasure. He was in so deep that he couldn't have pulled back to save his own life. He'd never known an exchange so heated, so erotic. He wanted to do things to and with her that he'd never dreamed of doing to a woman in his life.

His mouth eased back onto hers and gentled her as his hand moved under the elastic at her hips and descended slowly. Her legs parted for him. She gasped as he began to touch her, sobbed, wept, clutched him. She was ready for him, and he'd barely begun.

Even while his head spun with delight, he knew that it was wrong. It was all wrong. He'd been too long without a woman and this was too fiery, too consuming, for a first time with her. He was going in headfirst and she wouldn't enjoy it. But he couldn't stop himself.

"Tira," he groaned at her ear. "Sweetheart, not now. Not like this. For God's sake, help me…!"

His hand stilled, his mouth lay hot and hard against her throat while he lay against her, his big body faintly tremulous as he tried to overcome his urgent, aching need for her.

Chapter Seven

Tira barely heard him. Her body was shivering with new sensations, with exquisite glimpses of the pleasure he could offer her. She felt him go heavy in her arms and slowly, breath by breath, she began to realize where they were and what they were doing.

She caught her breath sharply, aware that her hands were still tangled in the thick, cool darkness of his wavy hair. She was almost completely nude and he'd touched her....

"Simon!" she exclaimed, aghast.

"Shhh." His mouth turned against her throat. His hand withdrew to her waist and his head lifted. He was breathing as raggedly as she was. The turbulence of his eyes surprised her, because his usual impeccable control was completely gone. He saw her expression and managed a smile. "Are you shocked that we could be like this, together?" he asked gently.

"Yes."

"So am I. But I don't want you like this, not in a fever so high that I can't think past relief," he said quietly. He moved away from her with obvious reluctance and took one last, sweeping glance at her yielded body before he sat up with his back to her and leaned forward to breathe.

She tugged the coverlet over her heated flesh and

bit her swollen lips in an agony of shame and embarrassment. How in the world had *that* happened? If he hadn't stopped…!

He got to his feet, stretched hugely and then turned toward her. She lay with her glorious hair in a tangle around her white face, looking up at him almost fearfully.

"There's no need to look like that, Tira," he said softly, with eyes so tender that they confused her. He reached down and tugged the coverlet away, pulling her slowly to her feet. "The world won't end."

He reached for the strapless bra he'd taken from her bureau and using the prosthesis to anchor it, he looped it around her and held it in place.

"You'll have to fasten it," he said with a complete lack of self-consciousness. "I can't do operations that complex."

She obeyed him as if she were a puppet and he was pulling strings.

He held the half-slip and coaxed her to lean against him while she stepped into it. He pulled it up. He reached for the exquisite gown and deftly slid it over her head, watching while she tugged it into place. He turned her around and while she held up her hair, he zipped it into place.

He led her to the vanity and handed her a brush. She sat down obediently and put her unruly hair back into some sort of order, belatedly using a faint pink lipstick and a little powder. He stood behind her the whole while, watching.

When she finished, he drew her up again and held her in front of him.

"How long have we known each other?" he asked solemnly.

"A long time. Years." She couldn't meet his probing gaze. She felt as if she had absolutely no will of her own. The sheer vulnerability was new and frightening. She took a deep breath. "We should go."

He tilted her remorseful eyes up to his. "Don't be ashamed of what we did together," he said quietly.

She winced. "You don't even like me…!"

He drew her close and rocked her against his tall body, his cheek pressed to her hair as he stroked the silken length of it. "Shhh." He kissed her hair and then her cheek, working his way up to her wet eyes. He kissed the tears away gently and then lifted his head and looked down into the drowned green depths. He couldn't remember ever feeling so tender with a woman. He remembered how her soft skin felt against his mouth and his breathing became labored. He stepped back a little, so that she wouldn't notice how easily she aroused him now.

She sniffed inelegantly and reached on the vanity for a tissue. "My nose will be as red as my eyes," she commented, trying to break the tension.

"As red as the highlights in your glorious hair," he murmured, touching it. He sighed. "I want you with me tonight," he said softly. "But if you really don't want to go, I won't force you."

She looked up, puzzled by his phrasing. "You said you would."

He frowned slightly. "I don't like making you cry," he said bluntly. "Until now, I didn't know that I could. It's uncomfortable."

"I've had a long week," she said evasively.

"We both have. Come with me. No strings. You'll have fun."

She hesitated, but only for a minute. "All right."

He reached down and curled her small hand into his big one. The contact was thrilling, exciting. She looked up into eyes that confused her.

"Don't think," he said. "Come along."

He pulled her along with him, out of the bedroom, out the door. It was new to have Simon act possessively about her, to be tender with her. It hurt terribly, in a way, because now she knew exactly what she'd missed in her life. Simon would be all she'd ever need, but she cared too much to settle for a casual affair. Regardless of what he thought of her marriage to John, and she had no reason to believe that he'd changed his mind about it, she did believe in marriage. She didn't want to be anyone's one-night stand; not even Simon's.

The long drive down to Jacobsville wasn't as harrowing as she'd expected it to be. Simon talked about politics and began asking pointed questions about an upcoming fund-raiser.

She wasn't comfortable with the new relationship between them, so when he asked if she might like to help with some projects for the governor if he took on the attorney general's job, she immediately suspected that he was using her helpless attraction to him to win her support.

She looked down at the small white beaded evening bag in her lap. "If I have time," she said, stalling.

He glanced at her as they passed through the gaily decorated downtown section of Jacobsville, dressed like a Christmas tree for the holidays with bright colored lights and tinsel.

"What else have you got to do lately?" he asked pointedly.

She stared at her bag. "I might do another exhibit."

He didn't ask again, but he looked thoughtful.

The Hart ranch was impressive, sprawling for miles, with the white fence that surrounded the house and immediate grounds draped with green garlands and artificial poinsettias.

"They haven't done that before," she commented as they went down the long paved driveway to the house.

"Oh, they've made a number of improvements since Dorie married Corrigan last Christmas and moved into their new house next door to this one," he explained.

"Reluctant improvements, if I know Callaghan."

He chuckled. "Cag doesn't go in much for frills."

"Is he still not eating pork?"

He gave her a wry glance. "Not yet."

It was a family joke that the eldest bachelor brother wouldn't touch any part of a pig since he'd seen the movie about the one that talked, a box office smash.

"I can't say that I blame him," she murmured. "I saw the movie three times myself."

He chuckled. It was a rare sound these days and she glanced at him with a longing that she quickly concealed when his eyes darted toward her.

He pulled up in front of the sprawling ranch house and got out, noting that Tira did the same without waiting for him to open her door. Her independent spirit irritated him at times, but he respected her for it.

When she started up the steps ahead of him, he caught her hand and kept it in his as they reached the porch, where Corrigan and Dorie greeted them with warm hugs and smiles. Tira smiled automatically, so aware of Simon's big hand in hers that she was almost floating.

"You're just in time," Corrigan said. "Leopold spiked the punch and didn't tell Tess, and she got the wrong side of Evan Tremayne's tongue. She's in the kitchen giving Leo hell and swearing that he'll never get another biscuit."

"He must be in tears by now," Simon mused.

"He's on his knees, in fact, groveling." Corrigan grinned. "It suits him."

They went inside, where they met Evan and his wife, Anna, who was obviously and joyfully pregnant with their first child, and the Ballenger brothers, Calhoun and Justin, with their wives Abby and Shelby, all headed toward the front door together. They were all founding families in the area, with tremendous wealth and power locally. Tira knew of them, but it was the first time she'd met them face-to-face. It didn't surprise her that the brothers had such contacts. They made friends despite their sometimes reclusive tendencies. All the same, the party looked as if it had only just started, and it puzzled her that these people were leaving so soon. They didn't seem angry, but with those bland expressions, it was sometimes hard to tell if they were.

Tira looked around for Cag and Rey and just spotted them going through the swinging door of the kitchen. In the open doorway she caught a glimpse of Leopold on his knees in a prayerful stance with a thin young redhead standing over him looking outraged.

Tira chuckled. Simon, having seen the same thing, laughed out loud.

"This is too good to miss. Come on." He nodded at other people he knew as they wove their way through the crowd and reached the kitchen.

Stealthily Simon pushed open the door. The sight that met their eyes was pitiful. Leopold was still on his knees, with Cag verbally flaying him while Rey looked on approvingly.

They glanced toward the door when Simon and Tira entered. Leopold actually blushed as he scrambled to his feet.

Tess grimaced as she spotted Simon, one of the only two brothers who actively intimidated her. "I don't care what they say, I'm quitting!" she told him despite her nervousness. "He—" she pointed at Leopold "—poured two bottles of vodka in my special tropical punch, and Evan Tremayne didn't realize it was spiked until he'd had his second glass and fell over a chair." She blushed. "He said terrible things to me! And he—" she pointed at Leopold again "—thought it was funny!"

"Evan Tremayne falling over a chair would make most people in Jacobsville giggle," Tira stated, "knowing how he hates alcohol."

"It gets worse," Tess continued, brushing back a short strand of red hair, her blue eyes flashing. "Evan thought the punch was so good that he gave a glass of it to Justin Ballenger."

"Oh, God," Simon groaned. "Two of the most fanatical teetotalers in the county."

"Justin got a guitar and started singing some Spanish song. Shelby dragged the guitar out of his hands just in time," Tess explained. She put her face in her hands. "That was when Evan realized the punch was spiked and he said I should be strung up over the barn by my apron strings for doing such a nasty thing to your guests."

"I'll speak to Evan."

"Not now, you won't," Tira mentioned. "We just met the Tremaynes going out the front door, along with both Ballenger brothers and their wives."

"Oh, God!" Leo groaned again.

"I'll phone him and apologize," Rey promised. "I'll call them all and apologize. You can't leave!"

"Yes, I can. I quit." Tess had taken off her apron and thrown it at Leopold. "You'd better learn how to bake biscuits, is all I can say. They—" she pointed toward Cag and Rey "—will probably kill you when I leave, and I'm glad! I hope they throw you out in the corral and let the crows eat you! That would get rid of two evils, because the crows will die of food poisoning for sure!"

She stormed through the door and Leopold groaned out loud. Cag's quiet eyes followed her and his face tautened curiously.

"Leo, how could you?" Rey asked, aghast.

"It wasn't two bottles of vodka," he protested. "It was one. And I meant to give it to Tess, just to irritate her, but I got sidetracked and Evan and Justin…well, you know." He brightened. "At least Calhoun didn't get a taste of it!" he added, as if that made things all right. Calhoun, once a playboy, was as bad as his brother about liquor since his marriage.

"He left, just the same. But you've got problems closer to home. You'd better go after her," Simon pointed out.

"And fast!" Rey said through his teeth, black eyes flashing.

"Like a twister," Cag added with narrowed eyes. "If she leaves, you're going to get branded along with that stock I had shipped in today."

"I'm going, I'm going!" Leopold rushed out the back door after their housekeeper.

"Isn't she a little young for a housekeeper?" Simon asked his brothers. "She barely looks nineteen."

"She's twenty-two," Cag said. "Her dad was working for us when he dropped dead of a heart attack. There's no family and she can cook." His powerful shoulders lifted and fell. "It seemed an ideal solution. If we could just keep Leo away from her, things would be fine."

"Why does he have to torment the housekeepers all the time?" Rey asked miserably.

"He'll settle down one day," Cag murmured. He looked distracted, and he was glaring toward the back door. "He'd better not upset her again. In fact, I think I'll make sure he doesn't."

He nodded to the others and went after Leo and Tess.

"He's sweet on her," Rey said when the door closed behind him. "Not that he'll admit it. He thinks she's too young, and she's scared to death of him. She finds every sort of excuse to get out of the kitchen if he's the first one down in the mornings. It's sort of comical, in a way. I don't guess she knows that she could bring him to his knees with a smile."

"She's very young," Tira commented.

Rey glanced at her. "Yes, she is. Just what Cag needs, too, something to nurture. He's always bringing home stray kittens and puppies…just like her." He pointed to a small kitten curled up in a little bed in the corner of the kitchen. "She rescued the kitten from the highway. Cag bought the bed for it. They're a match made in heaven, but Leo's going to ruin everything. I think he's sweet on her, too, and trying to cut Cag out before she notices how much time he spends watching her."

"This is not our problem," Simon assured his brother. "But I'd send Leo off to cooking school if I were you. No woman is ever going to be stupid enough to marry him and if he learns to make biscuits, you can do without housekeepers."

"He made scrambled eggs one morning when Tess had to go to the eye doctor early to pick up her contacts," Rey said. "The dogs wouldn't even touch them!" He glared at Tira and Simon and shrugged. "Come on. We've still got a few guests who haven't gone home. I'll introduce you to them."

He led them into the other room and stopped suddenly, turning to look at them. "Wait a minute. Corrigan said you weren't speaking to each other after that newspaper stupidity."

Simon still had Tira's slender hand tight in his. "A slight misunderstanding. We made up. Didn't we?" he asked, looking down at Tira with an expression that made her face turn red.

Rey made a sound under his breath and quickly changed the subject.

Corrigan and Dorie joined them at the punch bowl, which had been refilled and dealcoholized. Dorie looked almost as pregnant as Anna Tremayne had, and she was radiant. Not even the thin scar on her delicate cheek could detract from her beauty.

"We'd almost given up hope," she murmured, laughing up at her adoring husband. "And then, wham!"

"We're over the moon," Corrigan said. The limp left over from his accident of years ago was much less noticeable now, he didn't even require a cane.

"I'm going to be an uncle," Simon murmured. "I might like that. I saw a terrific set of "O" scale electric trains in a San Antonio toy store a few days ago. Kids love trains."

"That's right, boys and girls alike," Tira murmured, not mentioning that she'd bought that train set for herself.

"Did you know that two of our local doctors, who are married to each other, have several layouts of them?" Corrigan murmured. "The doctors Coltrain. They invited kids from the local orphanage over for Christmas this year and have them set up and running. It's something of a local legend."

"I like trains," Simon said. "Remember that set Dad bought us?" he asked Corrigan.

"Yeah." The brothers shared a memory, not altogether a good one judging from their expression.

"This isn't spiked, anymore?" Tira asked, changing the subject as she stared at the punch bowl.

"I swear," Corrigan said, smiling affectionately at her. "Help yourself."

She did, filling one for Simon as well, and talk went to general subjects rather than personal ones.

The local live cowboy band played a slow, lazy tune and Simon pulled Tira onto the dance floor, wrapping her up tight in his arms.

The one with the prosthesis was a little uncomfortable and she moved imperceptibly.

"Too tight?" Simon asked softly, and let up on the pressure. "Sorry. I'm used to the damned thing, but I still can't quite judge how much pressure to use."

"It's all right. It didn't hurt."

He lifted his head and looked down into her eyes. "You're the only woman who's ever seen me without it," he mused. "In the hospital, when it was a stump—"

"You may have lost part of your arm, but you're alive," she interrupted. "If you hadn't been found for another hour, nothing would have saved you. As it was, you'd lost almost too much blood."

"You stayed with me," he recalled. "You made me fight. You made me live. I didn't want to."

She averted her eyes. "I know how much Melia meant to you, Simon. You don't have to remind me."

Secrets, he thought. There were so many secrets that he kept, that she didn't know about. Perhaps it kept the distance between them. It was time to shorten it.

"Melia had an abortion."

She didn't grasp what he was saying at first, and the lovely green eyes she lifted to his were curious. "What?"

"I made her pregnant and she ended it, and never told me," he said shortly. "She didn't want to ruin her figure. Of course, she wasn't positive that the baby was mine. It could have been by one of her other lovers."

She'd stopped dancing to stare up at him uncomprehendingly.

"She told me, the night of the accident," he continued. "That's why I lost control of the car in a curve, in the rain, and I remember thinking in the split second before it crashed that I didn't care to live with all my illusions dead."

"Illusions?" she echoed.

"That my marriage was perfect," he said. "That my beloved wife loved me equally, that she wanted my children and a lifetime with only me." He laughed coldly. "I married a cheap, selfish woman whose only concern was living in luxury and notching her bedpost. It excited her that she had men and I didn't know. She had them in my bed." His voice choked with anger, and he looked over her head. His arm had unconsciously tightened around Tira, and this time she didn't protest. She was shocked by what he was telling her. She'd thought, everyone had thought, that he'd buried his heart in Melia's grave and had mourned her for years.

"The child was what hurt the most," he said stiffly. "I believed her when she said she thought she was sterile. It was a lie. Everything she said was a lie, and I was too besotted to realize it. She made a fool of me."

"I'm so sorry for all the pain you've been through." Her eyes filled with tears. "It must have been awful."

He looked down at her, his eyes narrow and probing. "You were married to John when it happened. You came to the hospital every day. You held my hand, my good hand, and talked to me, forced me to get up, to try. I always felt that you left John because of me, and it made me feel guilty. I thought I'd broken up your marriage."

She dropped her gaze to his strong neck. "No," she said tersely. "You didn't break it up."

He curled her fingers into his and brought them to his chest, holding them there warmly. "Were you in love with him, at first?"

"I was attracted to him, very fond of him," she confessed softly. "And I wanted, badly, to make our marriage work." She shivered a little and he drew her closer. Her eyes closed. "I thought…I wasn't woman enough."

His indrawn breath was audible. He knew the truth about her marriage now, but he hesitated to bring up a painful subject again when things were going so well for them. His lips moved down to her eyes and kissed the eyelids with breathless tenderness.

"Don't cry," he said curtly. "You're more than woman enough. Come closer, and I'll prove it to you, right here."

"Simon…"

His arm slid down, unobtrusively, and drew her hips firmly against his. He shuddered as the touch of her body produced an immediate, violent effect.

She gasped, but he wouldn't let her step back.

"Do you feel how much I want you?" he whispered in her ear. "I've barely touched you and I'm capable."

"You're a man…"

"It doesn't, it never has, happened that fast with anyone else," he said through his teeth. "I want you so badly that it hurts like hell. Yes, Tira, you're woman enough for any man. I'm sorry that your husband didn't… No, that's a lie." He lifted his head and looked into her shocked eyes. "I'm glad he couldn't have you."

The words went right over her head because she was so shocked at what he was saying. She stared at him in evident confusion and embarrassment, her eyes darting around to see if anyone was watching. Nobody was.

"It doesn't show. There's no reason to be so tense." His arm moved back up to her waist and loosened a little.

She drew in steadying breaths, but she felt weak. Her head went to his chest and she made a plaintive little sound against it.

His fingers contracted around hers. "We opened Pandora's box together in your bedroom, on your bed," he whispered at her ear. "We want each other, Tira."

She swallowed. "I can't."

"Why not?"

She hesitated, but only for an instant. "I don't have affairs, Simon."

"Of course you do, darling," he drawled with barely concealed jealousy. "What else do you have with Charles Percy?"

Chapter Eight

Tira stopped dancing. She wasn't sure why she was upset, because Simon had made no bones about thinking she was sleeping with Charles. Apparently when he'd made light love to her earlier, he'd thought her responses were those of an experienced woman. She wondered what he'd think if he knew the truth, that she'd waited for him all these years, that she wanted no other man.

"Go ahead," he invited, a strange light in his eyes. "Deny it."

She let her gaze fall to his wide, firm mouth. "Think what you like," she invited. "You will anyway. And I'll remind you, Simon, that you have no right to question me about Charles."

"No right? After what you let me do to you?"

She flushed and her teeth clenched. "One weak moment..."

"Weak, the devil," he muttered quietly. "You were starving to death. Doesn't he make love to you anymore?"

"Simon, please don't," she pleaded. "Not tonight."

The hand holding hers contracted. "Were you thinking of him, then?"

"Heavens, no!" she burst out, aghast.

He searched her eyes for a long moment, until he saw her cheeks flush. His hand relaxed.

"I wasn't the only one who was starving," she murmured, a little embarrassed.

He coaxed her cheek onto his chest. "No, you weren't," he agreed. He closed his eyes as they moved to the music.

She was surprised that he could admit his own hunger. They were moving into a totally new relationship. She didn't know what to make of it, and she didn't quite trust him, either. But what she was feeling was so delicious that she couldn't fight it. She let her body go lax against him and breathed in the spicy scent of his cologne. Her hand moved gently against his shirt, feeling hair and hard, warm muscle under it. He stiffened and it delighted her that he could react so strongly to such an innocent caress.

"You'd better not," he whispered at her ear.

Her hand stilled. "Are you…hairy all over?" she whispered back.

He stiffened even more. "In places."

Her cheek moved against his chest and she sighed. "I'm sleepy," she murmured, closing her eyes as they moved lazily to the music.

"Want to go home?"

"We haven't been here very long."

"It doesn't matter. I've had a hard week, too." He let her move away. "Come on. We'll make our excuses and leave."

They found Corrigan and asked him to tell the others Merry Christmas for them.

"They're still trying to talk Tess out of leaving," he murmured dryly. "I hope they can. The smell of baking biscuits makes Dorie sick right now," he said, glancing down at his wife lovingly. "So they'll have to go without if they can't change her mind."

"I wish them luck," Simon said. "We enjoyed the party. Next year, maybe I'll throw one and you can all come up to San Antonio for it."

"I'll hold you to that," Corrigan replied. He glanced from one of them to the other. "Have you two given up combat?"

"For the moment," Tira agreed with a wan smile.

"For good," Simon added.

"We'll see about that," Tira returned, her eyes flashing at him even through her fatigue.

They said their goodbyes and Simon drove them back to San Antonio. But instead of taking her home, he took her to his apartment.

She wondered why she didn't protest, which she certainly should have. She was too curious about why he'd come here.

"No questions?" he asked when they stepped out of the elevator on the penthouse floor.

"I suppose you'll tell me when you're ready," she replied, but with a faintly wary gaze.

"No need to worry," he said as he unlocked his door. "You won't get seduced unless you want to."

She blushed again and hated her own naivete. She followed him inside.

She'd never seen his apartment before. This was one invitation she'd always hoped for and never got. Simon's private life was so private that even his brothers knew little of it.

The apartment was huge and furnished in browns and creams and oranges. He had large oil paintings, mostly of landscapes, on the walls, and the furniture had a vaguely Mediterranean look to it. It was heavy and old, and beautifully polished.

She ran her hand over the rosewood back of the

green velvet-covered sofa that graced the living room. "This is beautiful," she commented.

"I hoped you might think so."

There was a long pause, during which she became more and more uncomfortable. She glanced at Simon and found him watching her with quiet, unblinking silvery eyes.

"You're making me nervous," she laughed unsteadily.

"Why?"

She shrugged in the folds of her velvet wrap. "I'm not sure."

He moved toward her with a walk that was as blatant as if he'd been whispering seductive comments to her. He took the cloak from her shoulders and the evening bag from her hands, tossing both onto the sofa. His jacket followed it. He took her hands and lifted them to his tie.

She hesitated. His fingers pressed her hands closer.

With breath that was coming hard and fast into her throat, she unfastened the silk tie and tossed it onto the sofa. He guided her fingers back to the top buttons of his shirt.

The silence in the apartment was tense, like the set of Simon's handsome, lean face. He stood quietly before her, letting her unfasten the shirt. But when she started to push it away, he shook his head.

"Looking at the prosthesis doesn't bother me," she said huskily.

"Humor me."

He drew her close and, pressing her fingers into the thick hair that covered his broad, muscular chest, he bent to her mouth.

His lips were tender and slow. He kissed her with something akin to reverence, brushing her nose with his as he made light contacts that provoked a new and sweeping longing for more.

Her fingers contracted in the hair on his chest and she went on tiptoe to coax his mouth harder against her own.

She felt his good hand on the zipper that held up her gown. She didn't protest as he slid it down and let the dress fall to the floor. She didn't protest, either, when he undid the catches to her longline bra with just the fingers of one hand. That, too, fell away and his gaze dropped hungrily to her pretty, taut breasts.

She stepped out of her shoes and he took her hand, pulling her along with him to his bedroom. It was decorated in the same earth tones as the living room. The bed was king-size, overlaid with a cream-and-brown striped quilted bedspread and a matching dust ruffle.

He reached behind him and closed the door, locking it as well.

She looked into his eyes with mingled hunger and apprehension. She knew exactly what he was going to do. She wanted to tell him how inexperienced she was, but she couldn't quite get the words out.

He led her to the bed and eased her down onto it. His hand went to his belt. He let his slacks fall to the floor and, clad only in black silk boxer shorts, he sat down on the bed and removed his shoes and socks.

"Your shirt," she whispered.

He eased down beside her, levering himself just above her at an angle. "I don't think I can do this without the prosthesis," he said quietly. "But I'd rather you didn't see it. Do you mind?"

She shook her head. He was devastating at close range. She loved the look of him, the feel of his hand on her face, her throat, then suddenly whispering over her taut breasts.

She arched under even that light pressure and her hands clenched as she looked up at him.

"Are you going to let me take you?" he asked in a soft, blunt tone.

She bit her lower lip worriedly. "Simon, I'm not sure—"

"Yes, you are," he interrupted. "You want me every bit as badly as I want you."

She still hesitated, but then she spoke. "Yes, I do." that was all she said—she couldn't tell him her secret yet.

He touched the hard tip of her breast and watched her shiver. "You beautiful creature," he said half under his breath. "I only hope I can do you justice."

While she was searching for the right words to make her confession, his head bent and his mouth suddenly opened right on her breast.

She caught his head, her nails biting into his scalp.

He lifted himself just enough to see her worried eyes. "I'm only going to suckle you," he said with soft surprise, wondering what sort of lover Charles Percy must have been to make her so afraid. "I won't hurt you."

He bent again, and this time she didn't protest. She couldn't. It was so sweet that it made her head spin to feel his hot, hard, moist mouth closing over the tight nipple. She moaned under her breath and writhed with pleasure. He nibbled her for a long time, moving slowly from one breast to the other while his hand traced erotic patterns on her belly and the insides of her thighs.

She barely noticed when he removed her briefs and then his own. His practiced caresses overwhelmed her. She was so enthralled by them that she ached to know him completely.

A long, feverish few minutes later, he moved between her long legs and his mouth pushed hard against her lips as his hips eased down against hers and he penetrated her.

The sensation was shocking, frightening. She drifted from a euphoric tension to harsh pain. Her nails bit into his broad shoulders and she called his name. But he was in over his head, all too quickly. He groaned harshly and pushed harder, crying out as he felt her envelop him.

"Oh…!" she sobbed, pushing against his chest.

He stilled for an instant, shuddering, and lifted tortured eyes to hers. "I'm hurting you?" he whispered shakenly. "Dear God…no, sweetheart!…don't move like that…!"

She shifted her hips in an effort to avoid the pain, and her sharp movements took him right over the edge.

His face tautened. He pushed, hard, his body totally out of control. "Oh, God, Tira, I'm so sorry…!" he said through his teeth, his eyes closed, his body suddenly urgent on hers.

He whispered it constantly until he completed his possession of her, and seconds later, he arched and shuddered and cried out in a hoarse groan as completion left him exhausted and shivering on her damp body.

She felt him relax heavily onto her damp skin, so that she could barely breathe for the weight. She wept silently at the reality of intimacy. It wasn't glorious fireworks of ecstasy at all. It was just a painful way to give a man pleasure. She hated him. She hated herself more for giving in.

"Please," she choked. "Let me go."

There was a pause. He drew in a long breath. "Not on your life," he said huskily.

He lifted his head and stared into her eyes with an expression on his lean face that she couldn't begin to understand.

"Charles Percy," he said deliberately, "is definitely not your lover."

She swallowed and her face flamed. "I...I never said he was, not really," she stammered.

He supported himself on the prosthesis and looked down at what he could see of her damp, shivering body. He touched her delicately on her stomach and then trailed his hand down to her thighs. There was a smear of blood on them that seemed to capture his attention for a moment.

"Simon, it hurts," she whispered, embarrassed.

His eyes went back to hers. "I know," he replied gently. His hand moved gently between her long legs to where their bodies were still completely joined, and she caught his wrist, gasping.

"Shhh," he whispered. Ignoring her protests, he began to touch her.

Shocked at the sudden burst of unexpected pleasure, her wide eyes went homing to his. Her mouth opened as the breath came careening out of her. She caught his shoulders again, digging her nails in. This was...it was... Her eyes closed and she moaned harshly and shivered.

"That's it," he whispered, easing his mouth down onto hers as she shivered and shivered again. "This isn't going to hurt. Open your mouth. I want you to know me completely, in every way there is." His hips moved slowly, and he felt her whole body jump as his sensual caresses began to kindle a frightening sweet tension in her. "I'm going to teach you to feel pleasure."

She gripped his shoulders and held on, her eyes

closed as his mouth worked its way even deeper into her own. She moved her legs around his muscular thighs to help him, to bring him into even closer contact, and gasped when she felt his invasion of her grow even more powerful, more insistent. The pain was still there, but it didn't matter anymore, because there was such pleasure overlaying it. She wanted him!

She heard her own voice sobbing, pleading with him, as the frenzy of pleasure grew to unbearable proportions. She was beyond pride, beyond protest. He was giving her pleasure of a sort she'd never dreamed existed. She belonged to him, was part of him, owned by him.

His movements grew urgent, deep. He whispered something into her open mouth but she couldn't hear him anymore. She was focused on some dark, sweet goal, every muscle straining toward it, her heartbeat pulsing in time with it, her tense body lifting to meet his as she pleaded for it.

His hips shifted all at once in a violent, hard rhythm that brought the ecstasy rushing over her like a wave of white-hot sensation. She cried out endlessly as it swept her away, her body pressing to his in a convulsive arch as the pleasure went on and on and on and she couldn't get close enough…!

This time, she didn't feel the weight of him as he collapsed onto her exhausted body. She held him tightly, pulsing in the soft aftermath, her legs trembling as they curled around his. She could hear his ragged breathing as she heard her own.

A long time later, he lifted his head and looked down into her wide eyes. He smiled at the faint shock in them. "Yes," he whispered. "It was good, wasn't it?"

She made an embarrassed sound and hid her face against him.

He smiled against her hair. "I thought it would never stop," he whispered huskily, brushing damp strands of hair away from her lips, her eyes as he turned her toward him. "I've never been fulfilled so completely in all my life."

She searched his eyes, seeing such tenderness in them that she felt warm all over. She reached up and touched his damp face with pure wonder, from his thick eyebrows to his wide, firm mouth and his stubborn chin. She couldn't even speak.

"You must be the only twenty-eight-year-old virgin in Texas," he murmured, and he wasn't joking. His eyes were solemn. "Did you save it for me, all these years?"

She didn't want to admit that. He probably guessed that she had, but only a little pride remained in her arsenal.

She sighed quietly. "I never knew a man that I wanted enough," she confessed, averting a direct answer. She dropped her gaze to his broad, bare chest where the thick hair was damp with sweat. "I suppose you've lost count of all the women you've had in the past few years."

His finger traced her soft mouth. "I haven't had a woman since Melia died. I dated Jill, but we were never intimate."

Her surprise was all too evident as she met his rueful gaze. "What?"

His powerful shoulders rose and fell. "A one-armed man isn't a lover many women would choose. I've been sensitive about it, and perhaps a little standoffish when it came to invitations." He searched her eyes. "I've always been comfortable with you. I knew that if I fumbled, you wouldn't laugh at me."

"Never that," she agreed quietly. She looked at the way they were lying and flushed.

"Now you know," he murmured with a warm smile.

"Yes. Now I know."

"I'm sorry I had to hurt you." Regret was in his eyes as well as his tone. He traced her eyebrows. "It had been too long and I lost control. I couldn't pull away."

"I understood."

"You were tight," he said bluntly. "And very much a virgin. I apologize wholeheartedly for every nasty insinuation I've ever made about you."

She was uncomfortable. Was he apologizing for making love to her?

He tilted her face back up to his and kissed her tenderly. "I won't say I'm sorry," he whispered into her mouth. "You can't imagine how it felt, to know I was the first with you."

She frowned worriedly.

He lifted his head and saw her expression. "What's wrong?" he asked.

"You didn't use anything," she said.

"No. I assumed that you were on the pill," he replied. "That went along with the assumption that you were sleeping with Charles and you'd never gotten pregnant."

The very word made her flush even more. "Well, I'm not," she faltered.

An expression crossed his face that she couldn't understand. He looked down at her body pressed so closely, so intimately to his, and curiously, his big hand smoothed over her flat belly in a strangely protective caress.

"If I made you pregnant…"

He didn't have to finish the sentence. She always seemed to know what he was thinking. She reached up and put her cool fingers against his wide mouth.

"You know me," she whispered, anticipating the question he was afraid to ask.

He sighed and let the worry flow out of him. He bent to her mouth and traced it with his lips. "It would complicate things."

She only smiled. "Yes."

His mouth pressed down hard on hers all at once and his hips moved suggestively.

She cried out.

He stilled instantly, because it wasn't a cry of pleasure. "This is uncomfortable for you now," he said speculatively.

"It is," she confessed reluctantly. "I'm sorry."

"No, I'm sorry that I hurt you." He lifted his weight away and met her eyes. "It may be uncomfortable when I withdraw. I'll be as slow as I can."

The blunt remark made her cheeks go hot, but she watched him lift away from her with frank curiosity and a little awe.

"Oh, my," she whispered when he rolled over onto his back.

"Yes, isn't it shocking?" he whispered and pulled her gently against his side. "And now you know why it was so uncomfortable, don't you?" he teased softly.

She laid her cheek on his broad shoulder. "I have seen the occasional centerfold," she murmured, embarrassed. "Although I have to admit that they weren't in your class!"

He chuckled and took a deep, slow breath. "Your body will adjust to me."

That sounded as if he didn't mean tonight to be an isolated incident, and she frowned, because it worried her. She didn't want to be his mistress. Did he think that she'd agreed to some casual sexual relationship because she'd given in to his ardor?

His hand smoothed over her long, graceful fingers.

"When you heal a little, I'll teach you how to give it back," he murmured sleepily. "That was the first thing I noticed when I kissed you," he added. "You didn't fight me, but you didn't respond, either."

She sighed. "I didn't know how," she said honestly. Her wide eyes stared across his chest to the big, dark bureau against the wall. Her nails scraped through the thick hair on his chest and she felt him move sinuously, as if he enjoyed it.

His hand pressed hers closer and he stretched, shivering a little in the aftermath. "I'd forgotten how good it could be," he murmured. He tugged on a damp strand of red-gold hair. "I'm not taking you home."

She stiffened. "But I..."

"But, nothing. You're mine. I'm not letting you go."

That sounded possessive. Perhaps it was a sexual thing that men felt afterward. She knew so little about intimacy and how men reacted to it.

As if he sensed her concern, he eased her over onto her side so that he could see her face. It disturbed him to see her expression.

"This was a mistake," he said at once when he saw her eyes. "Probably my biggest in a long line of them." His big hand pressed hard against her stomach. "But we're going to make it right. If you've got my baby in here, there's no way you're raising it alone. We'll get married as soon as I can get a license."

She was even more shocked by that statement than if he'd asked her to live in sin with him.

She took a breath and hesitated.

His eyes held hers firmly. "Do you want my baby?"

The way he said it made delicious chills run down her spine. There was all the tenderness in the world in the soft question, and tears stung her eyes.

"Oh, yes," she whispered.

He looked at her until her breathing changed, his eyes solemn and possessive as they trailed down to her submissive body and her soft, pretty breasts. He touched them delicately.

"Then we won't use anything," he murmured, lifting his eyes back to hers.

Her lips parted. There were so many questions spinning around in her mind that she couldn't grasp one to single out.

His fingers went up to her lips and traced them very slowly. "Why did you give yourself to me?" he asked.

She stared at him worriedly. "I thought you knew."

"I hope I do." He looked worried now. "I really didn't have any intention of seducing you, in case you wondered. I was going to kiss you. Maybe a little more than just that," he added with a rueful smile. "But you came in here with me like a lamb," he said, as if it awed him that she'd yielded so easily. "You never protested once, until I hurt you." He grimaced and brought her hand to his mouth, kissing the palm hungrily. "I never thought it would hurt you so much!" he said, as if the memory itself was painful. "You cried and started moving, and I lost my head completely. I couldn't even stop..."

"But, it's...it's normal for it to be a little uncomfortable the first time," she said quickly, putting her fingers against his hard mouth. "Simon, some girls are just a little unlucky. I suppose I was one of them. It's all right."

He met her eyes. His were still turbulent. "I wouldn't have hurt you for the world," he whispered huskily. "I wanted you to feel what I was feeling. I wanted you to feel as if the sun had exploded inside you." His fingers tangled softly in her hair. "It was…never like that," he added in quiet wonder as he searched her eyes. "I never knew it could be." He bent and touched his mouth to hers with breathless tenderness. "Dear God, I wanted to cherish you, and I couldn't keep my head long enough! It should have been tender between us, as tender as I feel inside when I touch you. But it had been years, and I was like an animal. I thought you were experienced…!"

She drew his face down to hers and kissed his eyelids closed. Her lips touched softly all over his face, his cheeks, his nose, his hard mouth. She kissed him as if he needed comforting.

"You wanted me," she whispered against his ear as she held him to her. "I wanted you, too. It didn't hurt the second time."

His arms slid under her and he shivered. "It won't ever hurt again. I swear it."

Her legs curled into his and she smiled dreamily. He might not love her, but he felt something much more than physical desire for her. That long, stumbling speech had convinced her of one thing, at least. She would marry him. There was enough to build on.

"Simon?" she whispered.

"Hmmm?"

"I'll marry you."

His mouth turned against her warm throat. "Of course you will," he whispered tenderly.

She closed her eyes and linked her arms around him, her fingers encountering the leather strap of the prosthesis. "Why don't you take it off?" she murmured sleepily.

He lifted his head and frowned. "Tira…"

She sat up, proudly nude, and drew him up with her

so that she could push the shirt away. She watched his teeth clench as she undid the straps and eased the artificial appliance away, along with the sleeve that covered the rest of his missing arm.

She drew it softly to her breasts and held it there, watching the expression that bloomed on his lean, hard face at the gesture.

"Yes, you still have feeling in it, don't you?" she murmured with the first glint of humor she'd felt in a long time as she saw the desire kindle in his pale eyes.

"There, and other places," he said tautly. "And you're walking wounded. Don't torture me."

"Okay." She pushed him back down and curled up against him with absolute trust.

She looked like a fairy lying there next to him, as natural as rain or sun with his torn body. He looked at her with open curiosity.

"Doesn't it bother you, really?" he asked.

She nuzzled closer. "Simon, would it bother you if I was missing an arm?" she asked unexpectedly.

He thought about that for a minute. "No."

"Then that answers your question." She smiled. "I'm sleepy."

He laughed softly. "So am I."

He reached up and turned off the lamp, drowsily pulling the covers over them.

She stiffened and he held her closer.

"What is it?" he asked quickly.

"Simon, do you have a housekeeper?"

"Sure. She comes in on Tuesdays and Thursdays." His mouth brushed her forehead. "It's Saturday night," he reminded her. "And we're engaged."

"Okay."

His arm gathered her even closer. "We'll get the license first thing Monday morning and we'll be married Thursday. Who do you want to stand up with us?"

"I suppose it will have to be your brothers," she groaned.

He grinned. "Just thank your lucky stars you didn't refuse to marry me. Remember what happened to Dorie?"

She did. She closed her eyes. "I'm thankful." She drank in the spicy scent of him. "Simon, are you sure?"

"I'm sure." He drew her closer. "And so are you. Go to sleep."

Chapter Nine

They got up and showered and then made breakfast together. Tira was still shy with him, after what they'd done, and he seemed to find it enchanting. He watched her fry bacon and scramble eggs while he made coffee. She was wearing one of his shirts and he was wearing only a pair of slacks.

"We'll make an economical couple," he mused. "I like the way you look in my shirts. We'll have to try a few more on you."

"I like the way you look without your shirt," she murmured, casting soft glances at him.

He wasn't wearing the prosthesis and he frowned, as if he wasn't certain whether she was teasing.

She took up the eggs, slid them onto the plate with the bacon, turned the burner off and went to him.

"You're still Simon," she said simply. "It never mattered to me. It never will, except that I'm sorry it had to happen to you." She touched his chest with soft, tender hands. "I like looking at you," she told him honestly. "I wasn't teasing."

He looked at her in the morning light with eyes that puzzled her. He touched the glory of her long hair tenderly. "This is all wrong," he said quietly. "I should have taken you out, bought you roses and candy, called you at two in the morning just to talk. Then I should have bought a ring and asked you, very correctly, to marry me. I spoiled everything because I couldn't wait to get you into bed with me."

She was surprised that it worried him so much. She studied his hard face. "It's all right."

He drew in a harsh breath and bent to kiss her forehead tenderly. "I'm sorry, just the same."

She smiled and snuggled close to him. "I love you."

The words hit him right in the stomach. He drew in his breath as if he felt them. His hand tightened on her shoulder until it bruised. Inevitably he thought of all the wasted years when he'd kept her at a distance, treated her with contempt, ignored her.

"Hey." She laughed, wiggling.

He let go belatedly. His expression disturbed her. He didn't look like a happy prospective bridegroom. The eyes that met hers were oddly tortured.

He put her away from him with a forced smile that wouldn't have fooled a total stranger, much less Tira.

"Let's have breakfast."

"Of course."

They ate in silence, hardly speaking. He had a second cup of coffee and then excused himself while she put the breakfast things into the dishwasher.

She assumed that he was dressing and wanted her to do the same. She went back into the bedroom and quickly donned the clothing he'd removed the night before, having retrieved half of it from the living room. She didn't understand what was wrong with him, unless he really had lost his head and was now regretting everything including the marriage proposal. She knew from gossip that men often said things they didn't mean to make a woman go to bed with them. She must have been an easy mark, at that, so obviously in love with him that he knew she wouldn't resist him.

Last night it had seemed right and beautiful. This morning it seemed sordid and she felt cheap. Looking at herself in his mirror, she saw the new maturity in her face and eyes and mourned the hopeful young woman who'd come home with him.

He paused in the doorway, watching her. He was fully dressed, right down to the prosthesis.

"I'll take you home," he said quietly.

She turned, without looking at him. "That would be best."

He drove her there in a silence as profound as the one they'd shared over breakfast. When he pulled into her driveway, she held up a hand when he started to cut off the engine.

"You don't need to walk me to the door," she said formally. "I'll…see you."

She scrambled out of the car and slammed the door behind her, all but running for her front door.

The key wouldn't go in the first time, and she could hardly see the lock anyway for the tears.

She didn't realize that Simon had followed her until she felt his hand at her back, easing her inside the house.

"No, please…" she sobbed.

He pulled her into his arms and held her, rocked her, his lips in her hair.

"Sweetheart, don't," he whispered, his deep voice anguished. "It's all right! Don't cry!"

Which only made the tears fall faster. She cried until she was almost sick from crying, and when she finally lifted her head from his chest and saw his grim expression, it was all she could manage not to start again.

"I wish I could carry you," he murmured angrily,

catching her by the hand to pull her toward the living room. "It used to give me a distinct advantage at times like these to have two good arms."

He sat down on the sofa and pulled her down into his lap, easing her into the elbow that was part prosthesis so that he could mop up her tears with his handkerchief.

"I don't even have to ask what you're thinking," he muttered irritably as he dried her eyes and nose. "I saw it all in my mirror. Good God, don't you think I'm sorry, too?"

"I know you are," she choked. "It's all right. You don't have to feel guilty. I could have said no."

He stilled. "Guilty about what?"

"Seducing me!"

"I didn't."

Her eyes opened wide and she gaped at him. "You did!"

"You never once said you didn't want to," he reminded her. "In fact, I distinctly remember asking if you did."

She flushed. "Well?"

"I don't feel guilty about *that*," he said curtly.

Her eyebrows lifted. "Then what are you sorry about?"

"That you had to come home in your evening gown feeling like a woman I bought for the night," he replied irritably. He touched her disheveled hair. "You didn't even have a brush or makeup with you."

She searched his face curiously. He was constantly surprising her these days.

He touched her unvarnished lips with a wry finger. "Now you're home," he said. "Go put on some jeans and a shirt and we'll go to Jacobsville and ride horses and have a picnic."

She lost her train of thought somewhere. "You want to take me riding?"

He let his gaze slide down her body and back up and his lips drew up into a sardonic smile. "On second thought, I guess that isn't a very good idea."

She realized belatedly what he was saying and flushed. "Simon!"

"Well, why dance around it? You're sore, aren't you?" he asked bluntly.

She averted her eyes. "Yes."

"We'll have the picnic, but we'll go in a truck when we get to the ranch."

She lifted her face back to his and searched his pale eyes. He looked older today, but more relaxed and approachable than she'd ever seen him. There were faint streaks of silver at his temples now, and silver threads mixed in with the jet black of his hair. She reached up and touched them.

"I'm almost forty," he said.

She bit her lower lip, thinking how many years had passed when they could have been like this, younger and looking forward to children, to a life together.

He drew her face to his chest and smoothed over her hair. She was so very fragile, so breakable now. He'd seen her as a flamboyant, independent, spirited woman who was stubborn and hot tempered. And here she lay in his arms as if she were a child, trusting and gentle and so sweet that she made his heart ache.

He nuzzled his cheek against hers so that he could find her soft mouth, and he kissed it until a groan of anguish forced its way out of his throat. Oh, God, he thought, the years he'd wasted!

She heard the groan and drew back to look at him.

He was breathing roughly. His eyes, turbulent and

fierce, lanced down into hers. He started to speak, just as the doorbell rang.

They both jumped at the unexpected loudness of it.

"That's probably Mrs. Lester," she said worriedly.

"On a Sunday? I thought she spent weekends with her sister?"

She did. Tira climbed out of his arms with warning bells going off in her head. She had a sick feeling that when she opened that door, her whole life was going to change.

And it did.

Charles Percy stood there with both hands in his pockets, looking ten years older and sick at heart.

"Charles!" she exclaimed, speechless.

His eyes ran over her clothing and his eyebrows arched. "Isn't it early for evening gowns?" He scowled. "Surely you aren't just getting home?"

"As a matter of fact, she is," Simon said from the doorway of the living room, and he looked more dangerous than Tira had ever seen him.

He approached Charles with unblinking irritation. "Isn't it early for you to be calling?" he asked pointedly.

"I have to talk to Tira," Charles said, obviously not understanding the situation at all. "It's urgent."

Simon leaned against the doorjamb and waved a hand in invitation.

Charles glared at him. "Alone," he emphasized. His scowl deepened. "And what are you doing here, anyway?" he added, having been so occupied with Gene and Nessa that he still thought Simon and Tira were feuding. "After what you and your vicious girlfriend said to her at the charity ball, I'm amazed she'll even speak to you."

Jill had gone right out of Tira's mind in the past

twenty-four hours. Now she looked at Simon and remembered the other woman vividly, and a look of horror overtook her features.

Simon saw his life coming apart in those wide green eyes. Tira hadn't remembered Jill until now, thank God, but she was going to remember a lot more, thanks to Charles here. He glared at the man as if he'd have liked to punch him.

"Jill is part of the past," he said emphatically.

"Is she, really?" Charles asked haughtily. "That's funny. She's been hinting to all and sundry that you're about to pop the question."

Tira's face drained of color. She couldn't even look at Simon.

Simon called him a name that made her flush and caused Charles to stiffen his spine.

Charles opened the door wide. "I think this would be a good time to let Tira collect herself. Don't you?"

Simon didn't budge. "Tira, do you want me to leave?" he asked bluntly.

She still couldn't lift her eyes. "It might be best."

What a ghostly, thin little voice. The old Tira would have laid about him with a baseball bat. But he'd weakened her, and now she thought he'd betrayed her. Jill had lied. If Tira loved him, why couldn't she see that? Why was she so ready to believe Charles?

Unless… He glared at the other man. Did she love Charles? Had she given in to a purely physical desire the night before and now she was ashamed and using Jill as an excuse?

"Please go, Simon," Tira said when he hesitated. She couldn't bear the thought that he'd seduced her on a whim and everything he'd said since was a lie. But how could Jill make up something as serious as an engagement? She put a hand to her head. She couldn't think straight!

Simon shot a cold glare at Tira and another one at Charles. He didn't say a single word as he stalked out the door to his car.

Tira served coffee in the living room, having changed into jeans and a sweater. She didn't dare think about what had happened or she'd go mad. Simon and Jill. Simon and Jill…

"What happened?" Charles asked curtly.

"One minute we were engaged and the next minute he was gone," she said, trying to make light of it.

"*Engaged?*"

She nodded, refusing to meet his eyes.

He put the evening gown and Simon's fury together and groaned. "Oh, no. Please tell me I didn't put my foot in it again?"

She shrugged. "If Jill says he's proposed to her, I don't know what to think. I guess I've been an idiot."

"I shouldn't have come. I shouldn't have opened my mouth." He put his face in his hands. "I'm so sorry."

"Why did you come?" she asked suddenly.

He drew his hands over his face, down to his chin. "Gene died this morning," he said gruffly. "I've just left Nessa with a nurse and made the arrangements at the funeral home. I came by to ask if you could stay with her tonight. She doesn't want to be alone, and for obvious reasons, I can't stay in my own house with her right now."

"You want me to stay with her in your house?" she asked.

He nodded. "Can you?"

"Charles, of course I can," she said, putting aside her

own broken relationship for the moment. Charles's need was far greater. "I'll just pack a few things."

"I'll drive you over," he said. "You won't need your car until tomorrow. I'll bring you home then."

"Nessa can come with me," she said. "Mrs. Lester and I will take good care of her."

"That would be nice. But tonight, she doesn't need to be moved. She's sedated, and sleeping right now."

"Okay."

"Tira, do you want me to call Simon and explain, before we go?" he asked worriedly.

"No," she said. "It can wait."

Charles was the one in trouble right now. She refused to think about her own situation. She packed a bag, left a note for Mrs. Lester and locked the door behind them.

The next morning Mrs. Lester found only a hastily scribbled note saying that Tira had gone home with Charles—and not why. So when Simon called the next morning, she told him with obvious reluctance that apparently Tira had gone to spend the night at Charles's house and hadn't returned.

"I suppose it was his turn," he said with bridled fury, thanked her and hung up. He packed a bag without taking time to think things through and caught the next flight to Austin to see the governor about the job he'd been offered.

Gene's funeral was held on the Wednesday, and from the way Nessa clung to Charles, Tira knew that at least somebody's life was eventually going to work out. Having heard from Mrs. Lester that Simon had phoned and gone away furious having thought she spent the night with Charles, she had no hope at all for her own future.

She spent the next few days helping Nessa clear away Gene's things and get her life in some sort of order. Charles was more than willing to do what he could. By the time Christmas Eve rolled around, Tira was all by herself and so miserable that she felt like doing nothing but cry.

Nevertheless, she perked herself up, dressed in a neat red pantsuit and went to the orphans' Christmas party that she'd promised to attend.

She carried two cakes that she and Mrs. Lester had baked, along with all the paraphernalia that went with festive eats. Other people on the committee brought punch and cookies and candy, and there were plenty of gaily wrapped presents.

Tira hadn't expected to see Simon, and she didn't. But Jill, of all people, showed up with an armload of presents.

"Why, how lovely to see you, Tira," Jill exclaimed. She didn't get too close—she probably remembered the cup of coffee.

"Lovely to see you, too, Jill," Tira said with a noxious smile. "Do join the fun."

"Oh, I can't stay," she said quickly. "I'm filling in for Simon. Poor dear, he's got a raging headache and he couldn't make it."

"Simon doesn't have headaches," Tira said curtly, averting her eyes. "He gives them."

"I thought you knew he frequently gets them when he flies," Jill murmured condescendingly. "I've nursed him through several. Anyway, he just got back from Austin. He's accepted the appointment as attorney general, by the way." She sighed dramatically. "I'm to go with him to the governor's New Year's Ball! And I've got just the dress to wear, too!"

Tira wanted to go off and be sick. Her life had become a nightmare.

"Must run, dear," Jill said quickly. "I have to get home to Simon. Hope the party's a great success. See you!"

She was gone in the flash of an eye. Tira put on the best act she'd ever given for the orphans, handing out cake and presents with a smile that felt glued on. The media showed up to film the event for the eleven o'clock news, as a human interest story, and Tira managed to keep her back to the cameras. She didn't want Simon to gloat if he saw how she really looked.

After the party, she wrapped herself in her leather coat, went home and threw up for half an hour. The nausea was new. She never got sick. There could only be one reason for it, and it wasn't anything she'd eaten. Two weeks into her only pregnancy with Tira, her mother had said, the nausea had been immediately apparent long before the doctors could tell she was pregnant.

Tira went to bed and cried herself to sleep. She did want the child, that was no lie, but she was so mad at Simon that she could have shot him. Poor little baby, to have such a lying pig for a father!

Just as she opened her eyes, there was a scratching sound and she looked up in time to see the unwelcome mouse, who'd been delightfully absent for two weeks, return like a bad penny. He scurried down the hall and she cursed under her breath. Well, now she had a mission again. She was going to get that mouse. Then she was going to get Simon!

She fixed herself a small milk shake for Christmas dinner and carried it to her studio. She wasn't even dressed festively. She was wearing jeans and a sweater and socks, with her hair brushed but not styled and no makeup on. She felt lousy and the milk shake was the only thing she could look at without throwing up.

Charles and Nessa had offered to let her spend Christmas with them, but she declined. The last thing she felt like was company.

She wandered through the studio looking at her latest creations. She sat down at her sculpting table and stared at the lump of clay under the wet cloth that she'd only started that morning. She wasn't really in the mood to work, least of all on Christmas Day, but she didn't feel like doing anything else, either.

Why, oh, why, had she gone to Simon's apartment? Why hadn't she insisted that he take her home? In fact, why hadn't she left him strictly alone after John died? She couldn't blame anyone for the mess her life was in. She'd brought it on herself by chasing after a man who didn't want her. Well, he did now—but only in one way. And after he married Jill…

She placed a protective hand over her stomach and sighed. She had the baby. She knew that she was pregnant. She'd have the tests, but they really weren't necessary. Already she could feel the life inside her instinctively, and she wondered if the baby would look like her or like Simon.

There was a loud tap at the back door. She frowned. Most people rang the doorbell. It wasn't likely to be Charles and Nessa, and it was completely out of the question that it could be Simon. Perhaps a lost traveler?

She got up, milk shake in hand, and went to the back door, slipping the chain before she opened it.

Simon stared down at her with quiet, unreadable eyes. He had dark circles under his eyes and new lines in his face. "It's Christmas," he said. "Do I get to come in?"

He was wearing a suit and tie. He looked elegant, hardly a match for her today.

She shrugged. "Suit yourself," she said tautly. She looked pointedly past him to see if he was alone.

His jaw tautened. "Did you expect me to bring someone?"

"I thought Jill might be with you," she said.

He actually flinched.

She let out a long breath. "Sorry. Your private life is none of my business," she said as she closed the door.

When she turned around, it was to find his hand clenched hard at his side.

"Speaking of private lives, where's Charles?" he asked icily.

She stared at him blankly. "With Nessa, of course."

He scowled. "What's he still doing with her?"

"Gene died and Nessa needs Charles now more than ever." She frowned when he looked stunned. "Charles has been in love with Nessa for years. Gene tricked her into marrying him, hoping to inherit her father's real estate company. It went broke and he made Nessa his scapegoat. She wouldn't leave him because she knew he had a bad heart, and Charles almost went mad. Now that Gene's gone, they'll marry as soon as they can."

He looked puzzled. "You went home with him..."

"I went to his house to stay with Nessa, the night after Gene had died," she said flatly. "Charles said that it wouldn't look right for her to be there alone, and she wouldn't stay at her own house."

He averted his eyes. He couldn't look at her. Once again, it seemed, he'd gotten the whole thing upside down and made a mess of it.

"Why are you here?" she asked with some of her old hauteur. "In case you were wondering, I'm not going to shoot myself," she added sarcastically. "I'm through pining for you."

He shoved his hand into his pocket and glanced toward her, noticing her sock-clad feet and the milk shake in her hand. "What's that?" he asked suddenly.

"Lunch," she returned curtly.

His face changed. His eyes lifted to hers and he didn't miss her paleness or the way she quickly avoided meeting his searching gaze.

"No turkey and dressing?"

She shifted. "No appetite," she returned.

He lifted an eyebrow and his eyes began to twinkle as they dropped eloquently to her stomach. "Really?"

She threw the milk shake at him. He ducked, but it hit the kitchen cabinet in its plastic container and she groaned at the mess she was going to have to clean up later. Right now, though, it didn't matter.

"I hate you!" she raged. "You seduced me and then you ran like the yellow dog you are! You let Jill nurse you through headaches and spend Christmas Eve with you, and I hope you do marry her, you deserve each other, you… you…!"

She was sobbing by now, totally out of control, with tears streaming down her red face.

He drew her close to him and rocked her warmly, his hand smoothing her wild hair while she cried. "There, there," he whispered at her ear. "The first few months are hard, but it will get better. I'll buy you dill pickles and feed you ice cream and make dry toast and tea for you when you wake up in the morning feeling queasy."

She stilled against him. "W…what?"

"My baby, you're almost certainly pregnant," he

whispered huskily, holding her closer. "From the look of things, very, very pregnant, and I feel like dancing on the lawn!"

Chapter Ten

She looked up at him with confusion, torn between breaking his neck and kissing him.

"Wh...what makes you think I'm pregnant?" she asked haughtily.

He smiled lazily. "The milk shake."

She shifted. "It's barely been two weeks."

"Two long, lonely weeks," he said heavily. He touched her hair, her face, as if he'd ached for her as badly as she had for him. "I can't seem to stop putting my foot in my mouth."

She lowered her eyes to his tie. It was a nice tie, she thought absently, touching its silky red surface. "You had company."

He tilted her face up to his eyes. "Jill likes to hurt you, doesn't she?" he asked quietly. "Why are you so willing to believe everything she says? I've never had any inclination to marry her, in the past or now. And as for her nursing me through a headache, you, of all people, should know I don't get them, ever."

"She said...!"

"I came home from Austin miserable and alone and I got drunk for the first time since the wreck," he said flatly. "She got in past the doorman at the hotel and announced that she'd come to nurse me. I had her shown to the front door."

Her eyebrows arched. That wasn't what Jill had said.

His eyes searched over her wan face. "And you don't believe me, do you?" he asked with resignation. "I can't blame you. I've done nothing but make mistakes with you, from the very beginning. I've lived my whole life keeping to myself, keeping people at bay. I loved Melia, in my way, but even she was never allowed as close as you got. Especially," he added huskily, "in bed."

"I don't understand."

His fingers traced her full lower lip. "I never completely lost control with her," he said softly. "The first time with you, I went right over the edge. I hurt you because I couldn't hold anything back." He smiled gently. "You didn't realize, did you?"

"I don't know much about…that."

"So I discovered." His jaw tautened as he looked at her. "Married but untouched."

Something niggled at the back of her mind, something he'd said about John. She couldn't remember it.

He bent and brushed his mouth gently over her forehead. "We have to get married," he whispered. "I want to bring our baby into the world under my name."

"Simon…"

He drew her close and his lips slid gently over her half-open mouth. She could feel his heartbeat go wild the minute he touched her. His big body actually trembled.

She looked up at him with quiet curiosity, seeing the raging desire he wasn't bothering to conceal blazing in his eyes, and her whole body stilled.

"That's right," he murmured. "Take a good look. I've managed to hide it from you for years, but there's no need now."

"You wanted me, before?" she asked.

"I wanted you the first time I saw you," he said huskily. His lean hand moved from her neck down to the hard peak of her breast visible under the sweater, and he brushed over it with his fingers, watching her shiver. "You were the most gloriously beautiful creature I'd ever seen. But I was married and I imagined that it was nothing more than the sort of lust a man occasionally feels for a totally inappropriate sort of woman."

"You thought I was cheap."

"No. I thought you were experienced," he said, and there was regret in his eyes. "I threw you at John to save myself, without having the first idea what I was about to subject you to. I'm sorry, if it matters. I never used to think of myself as the sort of man to run from trouble, but I spent years running from you."

She lowered her gaze to his tie again. Her heart was racing. He'd never spoken to her this way in the past. She felt his hand in her hair, tangling in it as if he loved its very feel, and her eyes closed at the tenderness in the caress.

"I don't want to be vulnerable," he said through his teeth. "Not like this."

She let out a long sigh. She understood what he meant. "Neither did I, all those years ago," she said heavily. "Charles was kind to me. He knew how I felt about you, and he provided me with the same sort of camouflage I gave him for Nessa's sake. Everyone thought we were lovers."

"I suppose you know I thought you were experienced when I took you to bed?"

She nodded.

"Even when you cried out, the first time, I thought it was pleasure, not pain. I'll never forget how I felt when I realized how wrong I'd been about you." His hand tightened on her soft body unconsciously. "I know how bad it was. Are you…all right?"

"Yes."

He drew her forehead against him and held it there while he fought for the right words to heal some of the damage he'd done. His eyes closed as he bent over her. It was like coming home. He'd never known a feeling like it.

She sighed and slid her arms under his and around him, giving him her weight.

He actually shivered.

She lifted her head and looked up, curious. His face was tight, his eyes brilliant with feeling. She didn't need a crystal ball to understand why. His very vulnerability knocked down all the barriers. She knew how proud he was, how he hated having her see him this way. But it was part of loving, a part he had yet to learn.

She took his hand in hers. "Come on," she said softly. "I can fix what's wrong with you."

"How do you know what's wrong with me?" he taunted.

She tugged at his hand. "Don't be silly."

She pulled him along with her out of the kitchen to her bedroom and closed the door behind her. She was a little apprehensive. Despite the pleasure he'd given her, the memory of the pain was still very vivid.

He took a slow breath. "I'll always have to be careful with you," he said, as if he read the thoughts in her eyes. "I'm overendowed and you're pretty innocent, in spite of what we did together."

She blinked. "You…are?"

He scowled. "You said you'd seen centerfolds."

She colored wildly. "Not…of men…like that!"

"Well, well." He chuckled softly and moved closer to her. "I feel like a walking anatomy lab."

"Do you, really?" She drew his hand under her sweater and up to soft, warm skin, and shivered when he touched her. Her heart was in the eyes she lifted to his. "It won't hurt...?"

He drew her close and kissed her worried eyes shut. "No," he whispered tenderly. "I promise it won't!"

She let him undress her, still hesitant and shy with him, but obviously willing.

When she was down to her briefs, she began undressing him, to his amusement.

"This is new," he mused. "I've had to do it myself for a number of years."

She looked up, hesitating. "All that time," she said. "Didn't you want anyone?"

"I wanted you," he replied solemnly. "Sometimes, I wanted you desperately."

"You never even hinted...!"

"You know why," he said, as if it shamed him to remember. "I should have been shot."

She lowered her eyes to the bare, broad chest she'd uncovered. "That would have been a waste," she said with a husky note in her voice. Her fingers spread over the thick hair that covered him, and he groaned softly. She put her mouth against his breastbone. "I've missed you," she whispered, and her voice broke.

"I've missed you!"

He bent to her mouth and kissed her slowly, tenderly, while between them, they got the rest of the obstacles out of the way.

When she reached for the strap of the prosthesis, his fingers stayed her.

"We'll have to find out sometime if you can do without it," she said gently. Her eyes searched his. "You can always put it back on, if you have to."

He sighed heavily. "All right."

He let her take it off, the uncertainty plain in his dark face. It made him vulnerable somehow, and he felt vulnerable enough with his hunger for her blatantly clear.

She stretched out on the pale pink sheets and watched him come down to her with wide, curious eyes.

Amazingly he was able to balance, if a little heavily at first. But she helped him, her body stabilizing his as they kissed and touched in the most tender exchange of caresses they'd ever shared for long, achingly sweet minutes until the urgency began to break through.

It was tender even as he eased down against her and she felt him probing at her most secret place. She tensed, expecting pain, but it was easy now, if a little uncomfortable just at first.

He turned her face to his and made her watch his eyes as they moved together slowly. He pressed soft, quiet kisses against her mouth as the lazy tempo of his hips brought them into stark intimacy.

She gasped and pushed upward as the pleasure shot through her, but he shook his head, calming her.

"Wh…why?" she gasped.

"Because I want it to be intense," he whispered unsteadily, nuzzling her face with his as he fought for enough breath to speak. His teeth clenched as he felt the first deep bites of pleasure rippling through him. "I want it to take a long time. I want to…touch you…as deeply inside…as it's humanly possible!"

She felt him in every pore, every cell. Her fingers clenched behind his strong neck because he was even more potent now than he'd been their first time together. Her teeth worried her lower lip as she looked up at him, torn between pleasure and apprehension.

"Don't be afraid," he whispered brokenly. "Don't be afraid of me."

"It wasn't like this...before," she sobbed. Her eyes closed on a wave of pleasure so sharp that it stiffened her from head to toe. "Dear...God...Simon!"

"Baby," he choked at her ear. His body moved tenderly, even in its great urgency, from side to side, intensifying the pleasure, bringing her to the brink of some unbelievably deep chasm. She was going to fall...to fall...

She barely heard her own voice shattering into a thousand pieces as she reached up to him in an arc, sobbing, wanting more of him, more, ever more!

"Oh, God, don't...I'll hurt you!" he bit off as she pulled him down sharply to her.

"Never," she breathed. "Never! Oh, Simon...!"

She sobbed as the convulsions took her. It had never been this sweeping. Her eyes opened in the middle of the spasms and met his, and she saw in them the same helpless loss of control, the ecstasy that made a tight, agonized caricature of his face. It faded into a black oblivion as the pleasure became unbearable and she lost consciousness for a space of seconds.

"Tira? *Tira!*"

His hand was trembling as it touched her face, her neck where the pulse hammered.

"Oh, God, honey, open your eyes and look at me! Are you all right?"

She felt her eyelids part slowly. His face was above hers, worried, tormented, his eyes glittering with fear.

She smiled lazily. "Hello," she whispered, so exhausted that she could barely manage words. She moved and felt him deep in her body and moaned with pleasure.

"Good God, I thought I'd killed you!" he breathed, relaxing on her. He was heavy, and she loved his weight. She held him close, nuzzling her face into his cool, damp throat. "You fainted!"

"I couldn't help it," she murmured. "Oh, it was so good. So good, so good!"

He rolled over onto his back, carrying her with him. He shivered, too, as the movements kindled little swirls of pleasure.

She curled her legs into his and closed her eyes. "I love you," she whispered sleepily.

He drew in a shaky breath. "I noticed."

She kissed his neck lazily and sighed. "Simon, I think I really am pregnant."

"So do I."

She moved against him sinuously. "Are you sorry?"

"I'm overjoyed."

That sounded genuine, and reassuring.

"I'm sleepy."

He stretched under her. He'd used more muscles than he realized he had. "So am I."

It was the last thing she heard for a long time. When she woke again, she was under the sheet with her hair spread over the pillow. Simon was wearing everything but his jacket, and he was sitting on the edge of the bed just looking at her.

She opened her eyes and stared up at him. She'd never seen that expression on his face before. It wasn't one she could understand.

"Is something wrong?" she asked.

His hand went to her flat stomach over the sheet. "You don't think we hurt the baby?"

She smiled sleepily. "No. We didn't hurt the baby."

He wasn't quite convinced. "The way we loved this time..."

"Oh, that sounds nice," she murmured, smiling up at him with quiet, dreamy eyes.

His hand moved to hers and entangled with it. "What? That we loved?"

She nodded.

He drew their clasped hands to his broad thigh and studied them. "I've been thinking."

"What about?"

"It shouldn't be a quick ceremony in a justice of the peace's office," he said. He shrugged. "It should be in a church, with you in white satin."

"White? But..."

He lifted his eyes. They glittered at her. "White."

She swallowed. "Okay."

He relaxed a little. "I don't want people talking about you, as if we'd done something to be ashamed of—even though we have."

Her eyes opened wide. "What?"

"I used to go to church. I haven't forgotten how things are supposed to be done. We jumped the gun, twice, and I'm not very proud of it. But considering the circumstances, and this," he added gently, touching her belly with a curious little smile, "I think we're not quite beyond redemption."

"Of course we're not," she said softly. "God is a lot more understanding than most people are."

"And it isn't as if we aren't going to get married and give our baby a settled home and parents who love him," he continued. "So with all that in mind, I've put the wheels in motion."

"Wheels?"

He cleared his throat. "I phoned my brothers."

She sat straight up in bed with eyes like an owl's. "*Them?* You didn't! Simon, you couldn't!"

"There, there," he soothed her, "it won't be so bad. They're old hands at weddings. Look what a wonderful one they arranged for Corrigan. You went. So did I. It was great."

"They arranged Corrigan's wedding without any encouragement from Dorie at all! They kidnapped her and wrapped her in ribbons and carried her home to Corrigan for Christmas, for heaven's sake! I know all about those hooligans, and I can arrange my own wedding!" she burst out.

Just as she said that, the back door—the one they'd forgotten to lock—opened and they heard footsteps along with voices in the corridor.

The bedroom door flew open, and there they were, all of them except Corrigan. They stopped dead at the sight that met their eyes.

Cag glared at Simon. "You cad!" he snarled. "No wonder you needed us to arrange a wedding! How could you do that to a nice girl like her?"

"Disgraceful," Leopold added, with a rakish grin. "Doesn't she look pretty like that?"

"Don't leer at your future sister-in-law," Rey muttered, hitting him with his Stetson. He put half a hand over his eyes. "Simon, we'd better do this quick."

"All we need is a dress size," Leopold said.

"I am not giving you my dress size, you hooligans!" Tira raged, embarrassed.

"Better get it one size larger, she's pregnant," Simon offered.

"Oh, thank you very much!" Tira exclaimed, horrified.

"You're welcome." He grinned, unrepentant.

"*Pregnant?*" three voices echoed.

The insults were even worse now, and Leopold began flogging Simon with that huge white Stetson.

"Oh, Lord!" Tira groaned, hiding her head in the hands propped on her upbent knees.

"It's a size ten," Rey called from the closet, where he'd been inspecting Tira's dresses. "We'd better make it a twelve. Lots of lace, too. We can get the same minister that married Corrigan and Dorie. And it had better be no later than three weeks," he added with a black glare at Simon. "Considering her condition!"

"It isn't a condition," Simon informed him curtly, "it's a baby!"

"And we thought they weren't speaking." Leopold grinned.

"We don't know yet that it's a baby," Tira said with a glare.

"She was having a milk shake for Christmas dinner," Simon told them.

"We saw it. Goes well with the cabinets, I thought," Rey commented.

"Don't worry, the mouse will eat it," Tira muttered.

"Mouse?" Cag asked.

"He can't be trapped or run out or baited," she sighed. "I've had three exterminators in. They've all given up. The mouse is still here."

"I'll bring Herman over," Cag said.

The others looked at him wide-eyed. "No!" they chorused.

"About the service," Simon diverted them, "we need to invite the governor and his staff—Wally said he'd give her away," he added, glancing at Tira.

"The governor is going to give me away? Our governor? The governor of our state?" Tira asked, aghast.

"Well, we've only got one." He grimaced. "Forgot to tell you, didn't I? I've accepted the attorney general slot. I hope you won't mind living in Austin."

"Austin."

She looked confused. Simon glanced at his brothers and waved his hand toward them. "Get busy, we haven't got a lot of time," he said. "And don't forget the media. It never hurts any political party to have coverage of a sentimental event."

"There he goes again, being a politician," Cag muttered.

"Well, he is, isn't he?" Rey chuckled. "Okay, boys, let's go. We've got a busy day ahead of us tomorrow. See you."

Cag hesitated as they went out the door. "This wasn't done properly," he told his brother. "Shame on you."

Simon actually blushed. "One day," he told the other man, "you'll understand."

"Don't count on it."

Cag closed the door, leaving two quiet people behind.

"He's never been in love," Simon murmured, staring at his feet. "He doesn't have a clue what it's like to want someone so bad that it makes you sick."

She stared at him curiously. "Is that how it was for you, today?"

"Today, and the first time," he said, turning his face to her. He searched her eyes quietly. "But in case you've been wondering, I'm not marrying you for sex."

"Oh."

He glowered. "Or for the baby. I want him very much, but I would have married you if there wasn't going to be one."

She was really confused now. Did this mean what it sounded like? No, it had to have something to do with politics. It certainly wouldn't hurt his standing in the political arena to have a pregnant, pretty, capable wife beside him, especially when there was controversy.

That was when the reality of their situation hit her. She was going to marry a public official, not a local attorney. He was going to be appointed attorney general to fill the present unexpired term, but he'd have to run for the office the following year. They'd live in a goldfish bowl.

She stared at him with horror in every single line of her face as the implications hit her like a ton of bricks. She sat straight up in bed, with the sheet clutched to her breasts, and stared at Simon horrified. He didn't know about John. Despite the enlightened times, some revelations could be extremely damaging, and not only to her and, consequently, Simon. There was John's father, a successful businessman. How in the world would it affect him to have the whole state know that John had been gay?

The fear was a living, breathing thing. Simon had no idea about all this. He hadn't spoken of John or what he thought now that he knew Tira wasn't a murderess, but the truth could hurt him badly. It might hurt the governor as well; the whole political party, in fact.

She bit her lip almost through and lowered her eyes to the bed. "Simon, I can't marry you," she whispered in a ghostly tone.

"You what?"

"You heard me. I can't marry you. I'm sorry."

He moved closer, and tilted her face up to his quiet eyes. "Why not?"

"Because..." She hesitated. She didn't want to ever

have to tell him the truth about his best friend. "Because I don't want to live in a goldfish bowl," she lied.

He knew her now. He knew her right down to her soul. He sighed and smiled at her warmly. "You mean, you don't want to marry me because you're afraid the truth about John will come to light and hurt me when I run for office next year."

Chapter Eleven

She was so astonished that she couldn't even speak. "You…know?" she whispered.

He nodded. "I've known since that night at the gallery, when I spoke to your ex-father-in-law," he replied quietly. "He told me everything." His face hardened. "That was when I knew what I'd done to you, and to myself. That was when I hit rock bottom."

"But you never said a word…" Things came flying back into her mind. "Yes, you did," she contradicted herself. "You said that you were glad John couldn't have me…you knew then!"

He nodded. "It must have been sheer hell for you."

"I was fond of him," she said. "I would have tried to be a good wife. But I married him because I couldn't have you and it didn't really matter anymore." Her eyes were sad as they met his. "You loved Melia."

"I thought I did," he replied. "I loved an illusion, a woman who only existed in my imagination. The reality was horrible." He reached out and touched her belly lightly, and she knew he was remembering.

Her fingers covered his. "You don't even have to ask how I feel about the baby, do you?"

He chuckled. "I never would have. You love kids."

He grimaced. "I hated missing the Christmas Eve party. I watched you on television. I even knew why you kept your back to the camera. It was eloquent."

"Jill has been a pain," she muttered.

"Not only for you," he agreed. He sighed softly. "Tira, I hope you know that there hasn't been anyone else."

"It would have been hard to miss today," she said, and flushed a little.

He drew her across him and into the crook of his arm, studying her pretty face. "It doesn't bother you at all that I'm crippled, does it?"

"Crippled?" she asked, as if the thought had never occurred to her.

That surprise was genuine. He leaned closer. "Sweetheart, I'm missing half my left arm," he said pointedly.

"Are you, really?" She drew his head down to hers and kissed him warmly on his hard mouth. "You didn't need the prosthesis, either, did you?"

He chuckled against her lips. "Apparently not." His eyes shone warmly into hers. "How can you still love me after all I've put you through?" he asked solemnly.

She let the sheet fall away from her high, pretty breasts and laid back against his arm to let him look. "Because you make love so nicely?"

He shook his head. "No, that's not it." He touched her breasts, enjoying their immediate reaction. "Habit, perhaps. God knows, I don't deserve you."

She searched his face quietly. "I never knew you were vulnerable at all," she said, "that you could be tender, that you could laugh without being cynical. I never knew you at all."

"I didn't know you, either." He bent and kissed her softly. "What a lot of secrets we kept from each other."

She snuggled close. "What about John?" she asked worriedly. "If it comes out, it can hurt you and the party, it could even hurt John's father."

"You worry entirely too much," he said. "So what if it does? It's ancient history. I expect to be an exemplary attorney general—again—and what sort of pond scum would attack a beautiful pregnant woman?"

"I won't always be pregnant."

He lifted his head and gave her a wicked look. "No?"

She hit his chest. "I don't want to be the mother of a football team!"

"You'd love it," he returned, smiling at the radiance of her face. He chuckled. "I can see you already, letting them tackle you in mud puddles."

"They can tackle you. I'll carry the ball."

He glanced ruefully at the arm that was supporting her. "You might have to."

She touched his shoulder gently. "Does it really worry you so much?"

"It used to," he said honestly. "Until the first time you let me make love to you." He drew in a long breath. "You can't imagine how afraid I was to let you see the prosthesis. Then I was afraid to take it off, because I thought I might not be able to function as a man without using it for balance."

"We'd have found a way," she said simply. "People do."

He frowned slightly. "You make everything so easy."

She lifted her fingers and smoothed away the frown. "Not everything. You don't feel trapped?"

He caught her hand and pulled the soft palm to his lips, kissing it with breathless tenderness. "I feel as if I've got the world in my arms," he returned huskily.

She smiled. "So do I."

He looked as if he wanted to say something more, but he brought her close and wrapped her up against him instead.

The arrangements were complicated. Instead of a wedding, they seemed to be planning a political coup as well. The governor sent his private secretary and the brothers ended up in a furious fight with her over control of the event. It almost came to blows before Simon stepped in and reminded them that they couldn't plan the wedding without assistance. They informed him haughtily that they'd done it before. He threw up his hand and left them to it.

Tira had coffee with him in her living room in the midst of wedding invitations that she was hand signing. There must have been five hundred.

"I'm being buried," she said pointedly, gesturing toward the overflowing coffee table. "And that mouse is getting to me," she added. "I found *him* under one of the envelopes earlier!"

"Cag will take care of him while we're on our honeymoon. We can stay here until we find a house in Austin in a neighborhood you like."

"One you like, too," she said.

"If you like it, so will I."

It bothered her that he was letting her make all these decisions. She knew she was being cosseted, but she wasn't sure why.

"The brothers haven't been by today."

"They're in a meeting with Miss Chase, slugging it out," he replied. "When I left, she was reaching for a vase."

"Oh, dear."

"She's a tough little bird. She's not going to let them turn our wedding into a circus."

"They have fairly good taste," she admitted.

"They called Nashville to see how many country music stars they could hire to appear at the reception."

"Oh, good Lord!" she burst out.

"That isn't what Miss Chase said. She really needs to watch her language," he murmured. "Rey was turning red in the face when I ran for my life."

"You don't run."

"Only on occasion. Rey has the worst temper of the lot."

"I'd put five dollars on Miss Chase," she giggled.

He watched her lift the cup to her lips. "Should you be drinking coffee?"

"It's decaf, darling," she teased.

The endearment caught him off guard. His breath caught in his throat.

The reaction surprised her, because he usually seemed so unassailable. She wasn't quite sure of herself even now. "If you don't like it, I won't..." she began.

"Oh, I like it," he said huskily. "I'm not used to endearments, that's all."

"Yes, I know. You don't use them often."

"Only when I make love to you," he returned.

She lowered her eyes. He hadn't done that since the day they got engaged, when the brothers had burst into their lives again. She'd wondered why, but she was too shy to ask him.

"Hey," he said softly, coaxing her eyes up. "It isn't lack of interest. It's a lack of privacy."

She smiled wanly. "I wondered." She shrugged. "You haven't been around much."

"I've been trying to put together an office staff before I'm sworn in the first of January," he reminded her. "It's been a rush job."

"Of course. I know how much pressure you're under. If you'd like, we could postpone the wedding," she offered.

"Do you really want to be married in a maternity dress?" he teased.

Her reply was unexpected. She started crying.

He got up and pulled her up, wrapping her close. "It's nerves," he whispered. "They'll pass."

She didn't stop. The tears were worse.

"Tira?"

"I started," she sobbed.

"What?"

She looked up at him. Her eyes were swimming and red. "I'm not pregnant." She sounded as if the world had ended.

He pulled out a handkerchief and dried the tears. "I'm sorry," he whispered, and looked it. "I really am."

She took the handkerchief and made a better job of her face, pressing her cheek against his chest. "I didn't know how to tell you. But now you know. So if you don't want to go through with it..."

He stiffened. His head lifted and he looked at her as if he thought she was possessed. "Why wouldn't I want to go through with it?" he burst out.

"Well, I'm not pregnant, Simon," she repeated.

He let out the breath he was holding. "I told you I wasn't marrying you because of the baby. But you weren't completely convinced, were you?"

She looked sheepish. "I had my doubts."

He searched her wet eyes slowly. He held her cheek in his big, warm hand and traced her mouth with his thumb. "I'm sorry that you aren't pregnant. I want a baby very much with you. But I'm marrying you because I love you. I thought you knew."

Her heart jumped into her throat. "You never said."

"Some words come harder than others for me," he replied. He drew in a long breath. "I thought, I hoped, you'd know by the way we were in bed together. I couldn't have been so out of control the first time or so tender the next if I hadn't loved you to distraction."

"I don't know much about intimacy."

"You'll learn a lot more pretty soon," he murmured dryly. He frowned quizzically. "You were going to marry me, thinking I only wanted you for the baby?"

"I love you," she said simply. "I thought, when the baby came, you might learn to love me." Her face dissolved again into tears. "And then…then I knew there wasn't going to be a baby."

He kissed her tenderly, sipping the tears from her wet eyes, smiling. "There will be," he whispered. "One day, I promise you, there will be. Right now, I only want to marry you and live with you and love you. The rest will fall into place all by itself."

She looked into his eyes and felt the glory of it all the way to her soul. "I love you," she sobbed. "More than my life."

"That," he whispered as he bent to her mouth, "is exactly the way I feel about you!"

The wedding, despite the warring camps of its organizers, came off perfectly. It was a media event, at the ranch in Jacobsville, with all the leading families of the town in attendance and Tira glorious in a trailing white gown as she walked down the red carpet to the rose arbor where Simon and all his brothers and the minister waited. Dorie Hart was her matron of honor and the other Hart boys were best men.

The service was brief but eloquent, and when Simon placed the ring on her finger and then lifted her veil and kissed her, it was with such tenderness that she couldn't even manage to speak afterward. They went back down the aisle in a shower of rice and rose petals, laughing all the way.

The reception didn't have singers from Nashville. Instead the whole Jacobsville Symphony Orchestra turned out to play, and the food was flown in from San Antonio. It was a gala event and there were plenty of people present to enjoy it.

Tira hid a yawn and smiled apologetically at her new husband. "Sorry! I'm so tired and sleepy I can hardly stand up. I don't know what's wrong with me!"

"A nice Jamaican honeymoon is going to cure you of wanting sleep at all," he promised in a slow, deep drawl. "You are the most beautiful bride who ever walked down an aisle, and I'm the luckiest man alive."

She reached a hand up to his cheek and smiled lovingly at him. "I'm the luckiest woman."

He kissed her palm. "I wish we were ten years

younger, Tira," he said with genuine regret. "I've wasted all that time."

"It wasn't wasted. It only made what we have so much better," she assured him.

"I hope we have fifty years," he said, and meant it.

They flew out late that night for their Caribbean destination. Cag, who hadn't forgotten the mouse, asked for the key to Tira's house and assured her that the mouse would be a memory when they returned. She had a prick of conscience, because in a way the mouse had brought her and Simon together. But it was for the best, she told herself. They couldn't go on living with a mouse! Although she did wonder what plan Cag had in mind that hadn't already been tried.

The Jamaican hotel where they stayed was right on the beach at Montego Bay, but they spent little time on the sand. Simon was ardent and inexhaustible, having kept his distance until the wedding.

He lay beside her, barely breathing after a marathon of passion that had left them both drenched in sweat and too tired to move.

"You need to take more vitamins," he teased, watching her yawn yet again. "You aren't keeping up with me."

She chuckled and rolled against him with a loving sigh. "It's the wedding and all the preparations," she whispered. "I'm just worn-out. Not that worn-out, though," she added, kissing his bare shoulder softly. "I love you, Simon."

He pulled her close. "I love you, Mrs. Hart. Very, very much."

She trailed her fingers across his broad, hair-roughened chest and wanted to say something else, but she fell asleep in the middle of it.

A short, blissful week later, they arrived back at her house with colorful T-shirts and wonderful memories.

"I could use some coffee," Simon said. "Want me to make it?"

"I'll do it, if you'll take the cases into the bedroom," she replied, heading for the kitchen.

She opened the cupboard to get out the coffee and came face-to-face with the biggest snake she'd ever seen in her life.

Simon heard a noise in the kitchen, put down the suitcases and went to see what had happened.

His heart jumped into his throat when he immediately connected the open cupboard, the huge snake and his new wife lying unconscious on the floor.

He bent, lifting her against his chest. "Tira, sweetheart, are you all right?" he asked softly, smoothing back her hair. "Can you hear me?"

She moved. Her eyelids fluttered and she opened her eyes, saw Simon, and immediately remembered why she was on the floor.

"Simon, there's a...a...*ssssssnake!*"

"Herman."

She stared at him. "There's a snake in the cupboard," she repeated.

"Herman," he repeated. "It's Cag's albino python."

"It's in *our* cupboard," she stated.

"Yes, I know. He brought it over to catch the mouse. Herman's a great mouser," he added. "Hell of a barrier to Cag's social life, but a really good mousetrap. We won't have a mouse now. Looks healthy, doesn't he?" he added, nodding toward the cupboard.

While they were staring at the huge snake, the back door suddenly opened and Cag came in with a gunnysack. He saw Tira and Simon on the floor and groaned.

"Oh, God, I'm too late!" he said heartily. "I'm sorry, Tira, I let the time slip away from me. I forgot all about Herman until I remembered the date, and you'd already left the airport when I tried to catch you." He sighed worriedly. "I haven't killed you, have I?"

"Not at all," Tira assured him with grim humor. "I've been tired a lot lately, too. I guess I'm getting fragile in my old age."

Simon helped her to her feet, but he was watching her with a curious intensity. She made coffee while Cag got his scaly friend into a bag and assured her that she'd have no more mouse problems. Tira offered him coffee, but he declined, saying that he had to get Herman home before the big python got irritable. He was shedding, which was always a bad time to handle him.

"Any time would be a bad time for me," Tira told her husband when their guest had gone.

"You fainted," he said.

"Yes, I know. I was frightened."

"You've been overly tired and sleeping a lot, and I notice that you don't eat breakfast anymore." He caught her hand and pulled her down onto his lap. "You were sure you weren't pregnant. I'm sure you are. I want you to see a doctor."

"But I started," she tried to explain.

"I want you to see a doctor."

She nuzzled her face into his throat. "Okay," she said, and kissed him. "But I'm not getting my hopes up. It's probably just some female dysfunction."

The telephone rang in Simon's office, where he was winding up his partnership before getting ready to move into the state government office that had been provided for him.

"Hello," he murmured, only half listening.

"Mr. Hart, your wife's here," his secretary murmured with unusual dryness.

"Okay, Mrs. Mack, send her in."

"I, uh, think you should come out, sir."

"What? Oh. Very well."

His mind was still on the brief he'd been preparing, so when he opened the door he wasn't expecting the surprise he got.

Tira was standing there in a very becoming maternity dress, and had an ear-to-ear smile on her face.

"It's weeks too early, but I don't care. The doctor says I'm pregnant and I'm wearing it," she told him.

He went forward in a daze and scooped her close, bending over her with eyes that were suspiciously bright. "I knew it," he whispered huskily. "I knew!"

"I wish I had!" she exclaimed, hugging him hard. "All that wailing and gnashing of teeth, and for nothing!"

He chuckled. "What a nice surprise!"

"I thought so. Will you take me to lunch?" she added. "I want dill pickles and strawberry ice cream."

"Yuuuck!" Mrs. Mack said theatrically.

"Never you mind, Mrs. Mack, I'll take her home

and feed her," Simon said placatingly. He glanced at his wife with a beaming smile. "We'll have Mrs. Lester fix us something. I want to enjoy looking at you in that outfit while we eat."

She held his hand out the door and felt as if she had the world.

Later, after they arrived home, Mrs. Lester seated them at the dining-room table and brought in a nice lunch of cold cuts and omelets with decaffeinated coffee for Tira. She was smiling, too, because she was going with them to Austin.

"A baby and a husband who loves me, a terrific cook and housekeeper, and a mouseless house to leave behind," Tira said. "What more could a woman ask?"

"Mouseless?" Mrs. Lester asked.

"Yes, don't you remember?" Tira asked gleefully. "Cag got rid of the mouse while we were on our honeymoon and you were at your sister's."

Mrs. Lester nodded. "Got rid of the mouse. Mmm-hmm." She went and opened the kitchen door and invited them to look at the cabinet. They peered in the door and there he was, the mouse, sitting on the counter with a cracker in his paws, blatantly nibbling away.

"I don't believe it!" Tira burst out.

It got worse. Mrs. Lester went into the kitchen, held out her hand, and the mouse climbed into it.

"He's domesticated," she said proudly. "I came in here the other morning and he was sitting on the cabinet. He didn't even try to run, so I held out my hand and he climbed into it. I had a suspicion, so I put him in a box and took him to the vet. The vet says that he isn't a wild mouse at all, he's somebody's pet mouse that got left behind and had to fend for himself. Obviously he belonged to the previous owners of this house. So I thought, if you don't mind, of course," she added kindly, "I'd keep him. He can come with us to Austin."

Tira looked at Simon and burst out laughing. The mouse, who had no interest whatsoever in human conversation, continued to nibble his cracker contentedly, safe in the hands of his new owner.

* * * * *

CALLAGHAN'S BRIDE

Chapter One

The kitchen cat twirled around Tess's legs and almost tripped her on her way to the oven. She smiled at it ruefully and made time to pour it a bowl of cat food. The cat was always hungry, it seemed. Probably it was still afraid of starving, because it had been a stray when Tess took it in.

It was the bane of Tess Brady's existence that she couldn't resist stray or hurt animals. Most of her young life had been spent around rodeos with her father, twice the world champion calf roper. She hadn't had a lot to do with animals, which might have explained why she loved them. Now that her father was gone, and she was truly on her own, she enjoyed having little things to take care of. Her charges ranged from birds with broken wings to sick calves. There was an unbroken procession.

This cat was her latest acquisition. It had come to the back door as a kitten just after Thanksgiving, squalling in the dark, rainy night. Tess had taken it in, despite the grumbling from two of her three bosses. The big boss, the one who didn't like her, had been her only ally in letting the cat stay.

That surprised her. Callaghan Hart was one tough hombre. He'd been a captain in the Green Berets and had seen action in Operation Desert Storm. He was the next-to-eldest of the five Hart brothers who owned the sweeping Hart Ranch Properties, a conglomerate of ranches and feedlots located in several western states. The headquarter ranch was in Jacobsville, Texas. Simon, the eldest brother, was an attorney in San Antonio. Corrigan, who was four years younger than Simon, had married over a year and a half ago. He and his wife Dorie had a new baby son. There were three other Hart bachelors left in Jacobsville: Reynard, the youngest, Leopold, the second youngest, and Callaghan who was just two years younger than Simon. They all lived on the Jacobsville property.

Tess's father had worked for the Hart brothers for a little over six months when he dropped dead in the corral of a heart attack. It had been devastating for Tess, whose mother had run out on them when she was little. Cray Brady, her father, was an only child. There wasn't any other family that she knew of. The Harts had also known that. When their housekeeper had expressed a desire to retire, Tess had seemed the perfect replacement because she could cook and keep house. She could also ride like a cowboy and shoot like an expert and curse in fluent Spanish, but the Hart boys didn't know about those skills because she'd never had occasion to display them. Her talents these days were confined to making the fluffy biscuits the brothers couldn't live without and producing basic but hearty meals. Everything except sweets because none of the brothers seemed to like them.

It would have been the perfect job, even with Leopold's endless pranks, except that she was afraid of Callaghan. It showed, which made things even worse.

He watched her all the time, from her curly red-gold hair and pale blue eyes to her small feet, as if he was just waiting for her to make a mistake so that he could fire her. Over breakfast, those black Spanish eyes would cut into her averted face like a diamond. They were set in a lean, dark face with a broad forehead and a heavy, jutting brow. He had a big nose and big ears and big feet, but his long, chiseled mouth was perfect and he had thick, straight hair as black as a raven. He wasn't handsome, but he was commanding and arrogant and frightening even to other men. Leopold had once told her that the brothers tried to step in if Cag ever lost his temper enough to get physical. He had an extensive background in combat, but even his size alone made him dangerous. It was fortunate that he rarely let his temper get the best of him.

Tess had never been able to understand why Cag disliked her so much. He hadn't said a word of protest when the others decided to offer her the job of housekeeper and cook after her father's sudden death. And he was the one who made Leopold apologize after a particularly unpleasant prank at a party. But he never stopped cutting at Tess or finding ways to get at her.

Like this morning. She'd always put strawberry preserves on the table for breakfast, because the brothers preferred them. But this morning Cag had wanted apple butter and she couldn't find any. He'd been scathing about her lack of organization and stomped off without a second biscuit or another cup of coffee.

"His birthday is a week from Saturday," Leopold had explained ruefully. "He hates getting older."

Reynard agreed. "Last year, he went away for a week around this time of the year. Nobody knew where he was, either." He shook his head. "Poor old Cag."

"Why do you call him that?" Tess asked curiously.

"I don't know," Rey said, smiling thoughtfully. "I guess because, of all of us, he's the most alone."

She hadn't thought of it that way, but Rey was right. Cag was alone. He didn't date, and he didn't go out "with the boys," as many other men did. He kept to himself. When he wasn't working—which was rarely—he was reading history books. It had surprised Tess during her first weeks as housekeeper to find that he read Spanish colonial history, in Spanish. She hadn't known that he was bilingual, although she found it out later when two of the Hispanic cowboys got into a no-holds-barred fight with a Texas cowboy who'd been deliberately baiting them. The Texas cowboy had been fired and the two Latinos had been quietly and efficiently cursed within an inch of their lives in the coldest, most bitingly perfect Spanish Tess had ever heard. She herself was bilingual, having spent most of her youth in the Southwest.

Cag didn't know she spoke Spanish. It was one of many accomplishments she was too shy to share with him. She kept to herself most of the time, except when Dorie came with Corrigan to the ranch to visit. They lived in a house of their own several miles away—although it was still on the Hart ranch. Dorie was sweet and kind, and Tess adored her. Now that the baby was here, Tess looked forward to the visits even more. She adored children.

What she didn't adore was Herman. Although she was truly an animal lover, her affection didn't extend to snakes. The great albino python with his yellow-patterned white skin and red eyes terrified her. He lived in an enormous aquarium against one wall of Cag's room, and he had a nasty habit of escaping. Tess had found him in a variety of unlikely spots, including the washing machine. He wasn't dangerous because Cag kept him well fed, and he was always closely watched for a day or so after he ate—which wasn't very often. Eventually she learned not to scream. Like measles and colds, Herman was a force of nature that simply had to be accepted. Cag loved the vile reptile. It seemed to be the only thing that he really cared about.

Well, maybe he liked the cat, too. She'd seen him playing with it once, with a long piece of string. He didn't know that. When he wasn't aware anyone was watching, he seemed to be a different person. And nobody had forgotten about what happened after he saw what was subsequently referred to as the "pig" movie. Rey had sworn that his older brother was all but in tears during one of the scenes in the touching, funny motion picture. Cag saw it three times in the theater and later bought a copy of his own.

Since the movie, Cag didn't eat pork anymore, not ham nor sausage nor bacon. And he made everyone who did feel uncomfortable. It was one of many paradoxes about this complicated man. He wasn't afraid of anything on this earth, but apparently he had a soft heart hidden deep inside. Tess had never been privileged to see it, because Cag didn't like her. She wished that she wasn't so uneasy around him. But then, most people were.

Christmas Eve came later in the week, and Tess served an evening meal fit for royalty, complete with all the trimmings. The married Harts were starting their own tradition for Christmas Day, so the family celebration was on Christmas Eve.

Tess ate with them, because all four brothers had looked outraged when she started to set a place for herself in the kitchen with widowed Mrs. Lewis, who came almost every day to do the mopping and waxing and general cleaning that Tess didn't have time for. It was very democratic of them, she supposed, and it did feel nice to at least appear to be part of a family—even if it wasn't her own. Mrs. Lewis went home to her visiting children, anyway, so Tess would have been in the kitchen alone.

She was wearing the best dress she had—a nice red plaid one, but it was cheap and it looked it when compared to the dress that Dorie Hart was wearing. They went out of their way to make her feel secure, though, and by the time they started on the pumpkin and pecan pies and the huge dark fruitcake, she wasn't worried about her dress anymore. Everyone included her in the conversation. Except for Cag's silence, it would have been perfect. But he didn't even look at her. She tried not to care.

She got presents, another unexpected treat, in return for her homemade gifts. She'd crocheted elegant trim for two pillowcases that she'd embroidered for the Harts, matching them to the color schemes in their individual bedrooms—something she'd asked Dorie to conspire with her about. She did elegant crochet work. She was making things for Dorie's baby boy in her spare time, a labor of love.

The gifts she received weren't handmade, but she loved them just the same. The brothers chipped in to buy her a winter coat. It was a black leather one with big cuffs and a sash. She'd never seen anything so beautiful in all her life, and she cried over it. The women gave her presents, too. She had a delicious floral perfume from Dorie and a designer scarf in just the right shades of blue from Mrs. Lewis. She felt on top of the world as she cleared away the dinner dishes and got to work in the kitchen.

Leo paused by the counter and tugged at her apron strings with a mischievous grin.

"Don't you dare," she warned him. She smiled, though, before she turned her attention back to the dishes.

"Cag didn't say a word," he remarked. "He's gone off to ride the fence line near the river with Mack before it gets dark." Mack was the cattle foreman, a man even more silent than Cag. The ranch was so big that there were foremen over every aspect of it: the cattle, the horses, the mechanical crew, the office crew, the salesmen—there was even a veterinarian on retainer. Tess's father had been the livestock foreman for the brief time he spent at the Hart ranch before his untimely death. Tess's mother had left them when Tess was still a little girl, sick of the nomadic life that her husband loved. In recent years Tess hadn't heard a word from her. She was glad. She hoped she never had to see her mother again.

"Oh." She put a plate in the dishwasher. "Because of me?" she added quietly.

He hesitated. "I don't know." He toyed with a knife on the counter. "He hasn't been himself lately. Well," he amended with a wry smile, "he has, but he's been worse than usual."

"I haven't done anything, have I?" she asked, and turned worried eyes up to his.

She was so young, he mused, watching all the uncertainties rush across her smooth, lightly freckled face.

She wasn't pretty, but she wasn't plain, either. She had an inner light that seemed to radiate from her when she was happy. He liked hearing her sing when she mopped and swept, when she went out to feed the few chickens they kept for egg production. Despite the fairly recent tragedy in her life, she was a happy person.

"No," he said belatedly. "You haven't done a thing. You'll get used to Cag's moods. He doesn't have them too often. Just at Christmas, his birthday and sometimes in the summer."

"Why?" she asked.

He hesitated, then shrugged. "He went overseas in Operation Desert Storm," he said. "He never talks about it. Whatever he did was classified. But he was in some tight corners and he came home wounded. While he was recuperating in West Germany, his fiancée married somebody else. Christmas and July remind him, and he gets broody."

She grimaced. "He doesn't seem the sort of man who would ask a woman to marry him unless he was serious."

"He isn't. It hurt him, really bad. He hasn't had much time for women since." He smiled gently. "It gets sort of funny when we go to conventions. There's Cag in black tie, standing out like a beacon, and women just follow him around like pet calves. He never seems to notice."

"I guess he's still healing," she said, and relaxed a little. At least it wasn't just her that set him off.

"I don't know that he ever will," he replied. He pursed his lips, watching her work. "You're very domestic, aren't you?"

She poured detergent into the dishwasher with a smile and turned it on. "I've always had to be. My mother left us when I was little, although she came back to visit just once, when I was sixteen. We never saw her again." She shivered inwardly at the memory. "Anyway, I learned to cook and clean for Daddy at an early age."

"No brothers or sisters?"

She shook her head. "Just us. I wanted to get a job or go on to college after high school, to help out. But he needed me, and I just kept putting it off. I'm glad I did, now." Her eyes clouded a little. "I loved him to death. I kept thinking though, what if we'd known about his heart in time, could anything have been done?"

"You can't do that to yourself," he stated. "Things happen. Bad things, sometimes. You have to realize that you can't control life."

"That's a hard lesson."

He nodded. "But it's one we all have to learn." He frowned slightly. "Just how old are you—twenty or so?"

She looked taken aback. "I'm twenty-one. I'll be twenty-two in March."

Now he looked taken aback. "You don't seem that old."

She chuckled. "Is that a compliment or an insult?"

He cocked an amused eyebrow. "I suppose you'll see it as the latter."

She wiped an imaginary spot on the counter with a cloth. "Callaghan's the oldest, isn't he?"

"Simon," he corrected. "Cag's going to be thirty-eight on Saturday."

She averted her eyes, as if she didn't want him to see whatever was in them. "He took a long time to get engaged."

"Herman doesn't exactly make for lasting relationships," he told her with a grin.

She understood that. Tess always had Cag put a cover over the albino python's tank before she cleaned his room. That had been the first of many strikes against her. She had a mortal terror of snakes from childhood, having been almost bitten by rattlesnakes several times before her father realized she couldn't see three feet in front of her. Glasses had followed, but the minute she was old enough to protest, she insisted on getting contact lenses.

"Love me, love my enormous terrifying snake, hmm?" she commented. "Well, at least he found someone who was willing to, at first."

"She didn't like Herman, either," he replied. "She told Cag that she wasn't sharing him with a snake. When they got married, he was going to give him to a man who breeds albinos."

"I see." It was telling that Cag would give in to a woman. She'd never seen him give in to anyone in the months she and her father had been at the ranch.

"He gives with both hands," he said quietly. "If he didn't come across as a holy terror, he wouldn't have a shirt left. Nobody sees him as the soft touch he really is."

"He's the last man in the world I'd think of as a giver."

"You don't know him," Leo said.

"No, of course I don't," she returned.

"He's another generation from you," he mused, watching her color. "Now, I'm young and handsome and rich and I know how to show a girl a good time without making an issue of it."

Her eyebrows rose. "You're modest, too!"

He grinned. "You bet I am! It's my middle name." He leaned against the counter, looking rakish. He was really the handsomest of the brothers, tall and big with blond-streaked brown hair and dark eyes. He didn't date a lot, but there were always hopeful women hanging around. Tess thought privately that he was probably something of a rake. But she was out of the running. Or so she thought. It came as a shock when he added, "So how about dinner and a movie Friday night?"

She didn't accept at once. She looked worried. "Look, I'm the hired help," she said. "I wouldn't feel comfortable."

Both eyebrows went up in an arch. "Are we despots?"

She smiled. "Of course not. I just don't think it's a good idea, that's all."

"You have your own quarters over the garage," he said pointedly. "You aren't living under the roof with us in sin, and nobody's going to talk if you go out with one of us."

"I know."

"But you still don't want to go."

She smiled worriedly. "You're very nice."

He looked perplexed. "I am?"

"Yes."

He took a slow breath and smiled wistfully. "Well, I'm glad you think so." Accepting defeat, he moved away from the counter. "Dinner was excellent, by the way. You're a terrific cook."

"Thanks. I enjoy it."

"How about making another pot of coffee? I've got to help Cag with the books and I hate it. I'll need a jolt of caffeine to get me through the night."

"He's going to come home and work through Christmas Eve, too?" she exclaimed.

"Cag always works, as you'll find out. In a way it substitutes for all that he hasn't got. He doesn't think of it as work, though. He likes business."

"To each his own," she murmured.

"Amen." He tweaked her curly red-gold hair. "Don't spend the night in the kitchen. You can watch one of the new movies on pay-per-view in the living room, if you like. Rey's going to visit one of his friends who's in town for the holidays, and Cag and I won't hear the television from the study."

"Have the others gone?"

"Cag wouldn't say where he was going, but Corrigan's taken Dorie home for their own celebration." He smiled. "I never thought I'd see my big brother happily married. It's nice."

"So are they."

He hesitated at the door and glanced back at her. "Is Cag nice?"

She shifted. "I don't know."

A light flickered in his eyes and went out. She wasn't all that young, but she was innocent. She didn't realize that she'd classed him with the married brother. No woman who found him attractive was going to refer to him as "nice." It killed his hopes, but it started him thinking in other directions. Cag was openly hostile to Tess, and she backed away whenever she saw him coming. It was unusual for Cag to be that antagonistic, especially to someone like Tess, who was sensitive and sweet.

Cag was locked tight inside himself. The defection of his fiancée had left Cag wounded and twice shy of women, even of little Tess who didn't have a sophisticated repertoire to try on him. His bad humor had started just about the time she'd come into the house to work, and it hadn't stopped. He had moods during the months that reminded him of when he went off to war and when his engagement had been broken. But they didn't usually last more than a day. This one was lasting all too long. For Tess's sake, he hoped it didn't go on indefinitely.

Christmas Day was quiet. Not surprisingly, Cag worked through it, too, and the rest of the week that followed. Simon and Tira married, a delightful event.

Callaghan's birthday was the one they didn't celebrate. The brothers said that he hated parties, cakes and surprises, in that order. But Tess couldn't believe that the big man wanted people to forget such a special occasion. So Saturday morning after breakfast, she baked a birthday cake, a chocolate one because she'd noticed him having a slice of one that Dorie had baked a few weeks ago. None of the Hart boys were keen on sweets, which they rarely ate. She'd heard from the former cook, Mrs. Culbertson, that it was probably because their own mother never baked. She'd left the boys with their father. It gave Tess something in common with them, because her mother had deserted her, too.

She iced the cake and put Happy Birthday on the top. She put on just one candle instead of thirty-eight. She left it on the table and went out to the mailbox, with the cat trailing behind her, to put a few letters that the brothers' male secretary had left on the hall table in the morning mail.

She hadn't thought any of the brothers would be in until the evening meal, because a sudden arctic wave had come south to promote an unseasonal freeze. All the hands were out checking on pregnant cows and examining water heaters in the cattle troughs to make sure they were working. Rey had said they probably wouldn't stop for lunch.

But when she got back to the kitchen, her new leather coat tight around her body, she found Callaghan in the kitchen and the remains of her cake, her beautiful cake, on the floor below a huge chocolate spot on the kitchen wall.

He turned, outraged beyond all proportion, looking broader than usual in his shepherd's coat. His black eyes glittered at her from under his wide-brimmed Stetson. "I don't need reminding that I'm thirty-eight," he said in a soft, dangerous tone. "And I don't want a cake, or a party, or presents. I want nothing from you! Do you understand?"

The very softness of his voice was frightening. She noticed that, of all the brothers, he was the one who never yelled or shouted. But his eyes were even more intimidating than his cold tone.

"Sorry," she said in a choked whisper.

"You can't find a damned jar of apple butter for the biscuits, but you've got time to waste on things like...that!" he snapped, jerking his head toward the ruin of her cake lying shattered on the pale yellow linoleum.

She bit her lower lip and stood just looking at him, her blue eyes huge in her white face, where freckles stood out like flecks of butter in churned milk.

"What the hell possessed you? Didn't they tell you I hate birthdays, damn it?"

His voice cut her like a whip. His eyes alone were enough to make her knees wobble, burning into her like black flames. She swallowed. Her mouth was so dry she wondered why her tongue didn't stick to the roof of it. "Sorry," she said again.

Her lack of response made him wild. He glared at her as if he hated her.

He took a step toward her, a violent, quick movement, and she backed up at once, getting behind the chopping block near the wall.

Her whole posture was one of fear. He stopped in his tracks and stared at her, scowling.

Her hands gripped the edge of the block and she looked young and hunted. She bit her lower lip, waiting for the rest of the explosion that she knew was coming. She'd only wanted to do something nice for him. Maybe she'd also wanted to make friends. It had been a horrible mistake. It was blatantly obvious that he didn't want her for a friend.

"Hey, Cag, could you—" Rey stopped dead in his tracks as he opened the kitchen door and took in the scene with a glance. Tess, white-faced, all but shivering and not from the cold. Cag, with his big hands curled into fists at his sides, his black eyes blazing. The cake, shattered against a wall.

Cag seemed to jerk as if his brother's appearance had jolted him out of the frozen rage that had held him captive.

"Here, now," Rey said, talking quietly, because he knew his brother in these flash-fire tempers. "Don't do this. Cag, look at her. Come on, look at her, Cag."

He seemed to come to his senses when he caught the bright glimmer of unshed tears in those blue, blue eyes. She was shaking, visibly frightened.

He let out a breath and his fists unclenched. Tess was swallowing, as if to keep her fear hidden, and her hands were pushed deep into the pockets of her coat. She was shaking and she could barely get a breath of air.

"We have to get those culls ready to ship." Rey was still speaking softly. "Cag, are you coming? We can't find the manifest and the trucks are here for the cattle."

"The manifest." Cag took a long breath. "It's in the second drawer of the desk, in the folder. I forgot to put it back in the file. Go ahead. I'll be right with you."

Rey didn't budge. Couldn't Cag see that the girl was terrified of him?

He eased around his brother and went to the chopping block, getting between the two of them.

"You need to get out of that coat. It's hot in here!" Rey said, forcing a laugh that he didn't feel. "Come on, pilgrim, shed the coat."

He untied it and she let him remove it, her eyes going to his chest and resting there, as if she'd found refuge.

Cag hesitated, but only for an instant. He said something filthy in elegant Spanish, turned on his heel and went out, slamming the door behind him.

Tess slumped, a convulsive shudder leaving her sick. She wiped unobtrusively at her eyes.

"Thanks for saving me," she said huskily.

"He's funny about birthdays," he said quietly. "I don't guess we made it clear enough for you, but at least he didn't throw the cake *at* you," he added with a grin. "Old Charlie Greer used to bake for us before we found Mrs. Culbertson, whom you replaced. Charlie made a cake for Cag's birthday and ended up wearing it."

"Why?" she asked curiously.

"Nobody knows. Except maybe Simon," he amended. "They were older than the rest of us. I guess it goes back a long way. We don't talk about it, but I'm sure you've heard some of the gossip about our mother."

She nodded jerkily.

"Simon and Corrigan got past the bad memories and made good marriages. Cag..." He shook his head. "He was like this even when he got engaged. And we all thought that it was more a physical infatuation than a need to marry. She was, if you'll pardon the expression, the world's best tease. A totally warped woman. Thank God she had enough rope to hang herself before he ended up with her around his neck like an albatross."

She was still getting her breath back. She took the coat that Rey was holding. "I'll put it up. Thanks."

"He'll apologize eventually," he said slowly.

"It won't help." She smoothed over the surface of the leather coat. She looked up, anger beginning to replace fear and hurt. "I'm leaving. I'm sorry, but I can't stay here and worry about any other little quirks like that. He's scary."

He looked shocked. "He wouldn't have hit you," he said softly, grimacing when he saw quick tears film her eyes. "Tess, he'd never! He has rages. None of us really understand them, because he won't talk about what's happened to him, ever. But he's not a maniac."

"No, of course not. He just doesn't like me."

Rey wished he could dispute that. It was true, Cag was overtly antagonistic toward her, for reasons that none of the brothers understood.

"I hope you can find someone to replace me," she said with shaky pride. "Because I'm going as soon as I get packed."

"Tess, not like this. Give it a few days."

"No." She went to hang up her coat. She'd had enough of Callaghan Hart. She wouldn't ever get over what he'd said, the way he'd looked at her. He'd frightened her badly and she wasn't going to work for a man who could go berserk over a cake.

Chapter Two

Rey went out to the corral where the culls—the non-producing second-year heifers and cows—were being held, along with the young steers fattened and ready for market. Both groups were ready to be loaded into trucks and taken away to their various buyers. A few more steers than usual had been sold because drought had limited the size of the summer corn and hay crop. Buying feed for the winter was not cost-productive. Not even an operation the size of the Harts's could afford deadweight in these hard economic times.

Cag was staring at the milling cattle absently, his heavy brows drawn down in thought, his whole posture stiff and unapproachable.

Rey came up beside him, half a head shorter, lither and more rawboned than the bigger man.

"Well, she's packing," he said bluntly.

Cag's eyes glanced off his brother's and went back to the corral. His jaw clenched. "I hate birthdays! I know she was told."

"Sure she was, but she didn't realize that breaking the rule was going to be life-threatening."

"Hell!" Cag exploded, turning with black-eyed fury. "I never raised a hand to her! I wouldn't, no matter how mad I got."

"Would you need to?" his brother asked solemnly. "Damn it, Cag, she was shaking like a leaf. She's just a kid, and it's been a rough few months for her. She hasn't even got over losing her dad yet."

"Lay it on," Cag said under his breath, moving restlessly.

"Where's she going to go?" he persisted. "She hasn't seen her mother since she was sixteen years old. She has no family, no friends. Even cooking jobs aren't that thick on the ground this time of year, not in Jacobsville."

Cag took off his hat and wiped his forehead on his sleeve before he replaced it. He'd been helping run the steers down the chute into the loading corral and he was sweating, despite the cold. He didn't say a word.

Leo came up with a rope in his hand, watching his brothers curiously.

"What's going on?" he asked.

"Oh, nothing," Rey muttered, thoroughly disgusted. "Tess made him a birthday cake and he destroyed it. She's packing."

Leo let out a rough sigh and turned his eyes toward the house. "I can't say I blame her. I got her into trouble at the Christmas party by spiking the holiday punch, and now this. I guess she thinks we're all lunatics and she's better off without us."

"No doubt." Rey shrugged. "Well, let's get the cattle loaded."

"You aren't going to try to stop her?" Leo asked.

"What would be the point?" Rey asked solemnly. His face hardened. "If you'd seen her, you wouldn't want to stop her." He glared at Cag. "Nice work, pal. I hope she can pack with her hands shaking that badly!"

Rey stormed off toward the truck. Leo gave his older brother a speaking glance and followed.

Cag, feeling two inches high and sick with himself, turned reluctantly and went back toward the house.

Tess had her suitcases neatly loaded. She closed the big one, making one last sweep around the bedroom that had been hers for the past few weeks. It was a wrench to leave, but she couldn't handle scenes like that. She'd settle for harder work in more peaceful surroundings. At least, Cag wouldn't be around to make her life hell.

She picked up her father's world champion gold belt buckle and smoothed her fingers over it. She took it everywhere with her, like a lucky talisman to ward off evil. It hadn't worked today, but it usually did. She put it gently into the small suitcase and carefully closed the lid, snapping the latches shut.

A sound behind her caught her attention and she turned around, going white in the face when she saw who had opened the door.

She moved around the bed and behind the wing chair that stood near the window, her eyes wide and unblinking.

He was bareheaded. He didn't speak. His black eyes slid over her pale features and he took a long, deep breath.

"You don't have anywhere to go," he began.

It wasn't the best of opening gambits. Her chin went up. "I'll sleep at a Salvation Army shelter," she said coldly. "Dad and I spent a lot of nights there when we were on the road and he didn't win any events."

He scowled. "What?"

She hated having admitted that, to him of all people. Her face closed up. "Will you let one of the hands drive me to town? I can catch a bus up to Victoria."

He shoved his hands into the pockets of his close-fitting jeans, straining the fabric against his powerful thighs. He stared at her broodingly.

"Never mind," she said heavily. "I'll walk or hitch a ride."

She picked up her old coat, the threadbare tweed one she'd had for years, and slipped it on.

"Where's your new coat?" he asked shortly.

"In the hall closet. Don't worry, I'm not taking anything that doesn't belong to me."

She said it so matter-of-factly that he was wounded right through. "We gave it to you," he said.

Her eyes met his squarely. "I don't want it, or a job, or anything else you gave me out of pity."

He was shocked. He'd never realized she thought of it like that. "You needed a job and we needed a cook," he said flatly. "It wasn't pity."

She shrugged and seemed to slouch. "All right, have it any way you like. It doesn't matter."

She slipped her shoulder bag over her arm and picked up her worn suitcases, one big one and an overnight bag, part of a matched set of vinyl luggage that she and her father had won in a raffle.

But when she reached the door, Cag didn't move out of the way. She couldn't get around him, either. She stopped an arm's length away and stared at him.

He was trying to think of a way to keep her without sacrificing his pride. Rey was right; she was just a kid and he'd been unreasonable. He shocked himself lately. He was a sucker for helpless things, for little things, but he'd been brutal to this child and he didn't know why.

"Can I get by, please?" she asked through stiff lips.

He scowled. A muscle jumped beside his mouth. He moved closer, smiling coldly with self-contempt when she backed up. He pushed the door shut.

She backed up again, her eyes widening at the unexpected action, but he didn't come any closer.

"When I was six," he said with cold black eyes, "I wanted a birthday cake like the other kids had. A cake and a party. Simon had gone to town with Dad and Corrigan. It was before Rey was born. Leo was asleep and my mother and I were in the kitchen alone. She made some pert remark about spoiled brats thinking they deserved treats when they were nothing but nuisances. She had a cake on the counter, one that a neighbor had sent home with Dad. She smashed the cake into my face," he recalled, his eyes darker than ever, "and started hitting me. I don't think she would have stopped, except that Leo woke up and started squalling. She sent me to my room and locked me in. I don't know what she told my father, but I got a hell of a spanking from him." He searched her shocked eyes. "I never asked for another cake."

She put the suitcases down slowly and shocked him by walking right up to him and touching him lightly on the chest with a shy, nervous little hand. It didn't occur to him that he'd never confessed that particular incident to anyone, not even his brothers. She seemed to know it, just the same.

"My father couldn't cook. He opened cans," she said quietly. "I learned to cook when I was eleven, in self-defense. My mother wouldn't have baked me a cake, either, even if she'd stayed with us. She didn't want me, but Dad did, and he put her into a position where she had to marry him. She never forgave either of us for it. She left before I started school."

"Where is she now?"

She didn't meet his eyes. "I don't know. I don't care."

His chest rose and fell roughly. She made him uncomfortable. He moved back, so that her disturbing hand fell away from his chest.

She didn't question why he didn't like her to touch him. It had been an impulse and now she knew not to do it again. She lifted her face and searched his dark eyes. "I know you don't like me," she said. "It's better if I get a job somewhere else. I'm almost twenty-two. I can take care of myself."

His eyes averted to the window. "Wait until spring," he said stiffly. "You'll have an easier time finding work then."

She hesitated. She didn't really want to go, but she couldn't stay here with such unbridled resentment as he felt for her.

He glanced down at her with something odd glittering in his black eyes. "My brothers will drown me if I let you walk out that door," he said curtly. "Neither of them is speaking to me."

They both knew that he didn't care in the least what his brothers thought of him. It was a peace initiative.

She moved restlessly. "Dorie's had the baby. She can make biscuits again."

"She won't," he said curtly. "She's too busy worshiping the baby."

Her gaze dropped to the floor. "It's a sweet baby."

A wave of heat ran through his body. He turned and

started back toward the door. "Do what you please," he said.

She still hesitated.

He opened the door and turned before he went through it, looking dark as thunder and almost as intimidating. "Too afraid of me to stay?" he drawled, hitting her right in her pride with deadly accuracy.

She drew herself up with smoldering fury. "I am *not* afraid of you!"

His eyebrows arched. "Sure you are. That's why you're running away like a scared kid."

"I wasn't running! I'm not a scared kid, either!"

That was more like it. He could manage if she fought back. He couldn't live with the image of her white and shaking and backing away from him. It had hurt like the very devil.

He pulled his Stetson low over his eyes. "Suit yourself. But if you stay, you'd damned sure better not lose the apple butter again," he said with biting sarcasm.

"Next time, you'll get it right between the eyes," she muttered to herself.

"I heard that."

She glared at him. "And if you ever, ever, throw another cake at me…!"

"I didn't throw it at you," he said pointedly. "I threw it at the wall."

Her face was growing redder by the second. "I spent two hours making the damned thing!"

"Lost apple butter, cursed cake, damned women…" He was still muttering as he stomped off down the hall with the faint, musical jingle of spurs following him.

Tess stood unsteadily by the bed for several seconds before she snapped out of her trance and put her suitcases back on the bed to unpack them. She needed her head read for agreeing to stay, but she didn't really have anywhere else to go. And what he'd told her reached that part of her that was unbearably touched by small, wounded things.

She could see a little Cag with his face covered in cake, being brutally hit by an uncaring woman, trying not to cry. Amazingly it excused every harsh word, every violent action. She wondered how many other childhood scars were hiding behind that hard, expressionless face.

Cag was coldly formal with her after that, as if he regretted having shared one of his deeper secrets with her. But there weren't any more violent outbursts. He kept out of her way and she kept out of his. The winter months passed into a routine sameness. Without the rush and excitement of the holidays, Tess found herself with plenty of time on her hands when she was finished with her chores. The brothers worked all hours, even when they weren't bothered with birthing cattle and roundup, as they were in the warmer months of spring.

But there were fences to mend, outbuildings to repair, upkeep on the machinery that was used to process feed. There were sick animals to treat and corrals to build and vehicles to overhaul. It never seemed to end. And in between all that, there were conferences and conventions and business trips.

It was rare, Tess found, to have all three bachelor brothers at the table at the same time. More often than not, she set places only for Rey and Leo, because Cag spent more and more time away. They assured her that she wasn't to blame, that it was just pressing business, but she wondered just the same. She knew that Cag only tolerated her for the sake of her domestic skills, that he hated the very sight of her. But the other brothers were so kind that it almost made up for Cag. And the ever-present Mrs. Lewis, doing the rough chores, was a fountain of information about the history of the Hart ranch and the surrounding area. Tess, a history buff, learned a lot about the wild old days and stored the information away almost greedily. The lazy, pleasant days indoors seemed to drag and she was grateful for any interesting tidbits that Mrs. Lewis sent her way.

Then spring arrived and the ranch became a madhouse. Tess had to learn to answer the extension phone in the living room while the two secretaries in the separate office complex started processing calving information into the brothers' huge mainframe computer. The sheer volume of it was shocking to Tess, who'd spent her whole life on ranches.

The only modern idea, besides the computers, that the brothers had adapted to their operation was the implantation of computer chips under the skin of the individual cattle. This was not only to identify them with a handheld computer, but also to tag them in case of rustling—a sad practice that had continued unabashed into the computer age.

On the Hart ranch, there were no hormone implants, no artificial insemination, no unnecessary antibiotics or pesticides. The brothers didn't even use pesticides on their crops, having found ways to encourage the development of superior strains of forage and the survival of good insects that kept away the bad ones. It was all very ecological and fascinating, and it was even profitable. One of the local ranchers, J. D.

Langley, worked hand in glove with them on these renegade methods. They shared ideas and investment strategies and went together as a solid front to cattlemen's meetings. Tess found J. D. "Donavan" Langley intimidating, but his wife and nephew had softened him, or so people said. She shuddered to think how he'd been before he mellowed.

The volume of business the brothers did was overwhelming. The telephone rang constantly. So did the fax machine. Tess was press-ganged into learning how to operate that, and the computer, so that she could help send and receive urgent e-mail messages to various beef producers and feedlots and buyers.

"But I'm not trained!" she wailed to Leo and Rey.

They only grinned. "There, there, you're doing a fine job," Leo told her encouragingly.

"But I won't have time to cook proper meals," she continued.

"As long as we have enough biscuits and strawberry preserves and apple butter, that's no problem at all," Rey assured her. "And if things get too hectic, we'll order out."

They did, frequently, in the coming weeks. One night two pizza delivery trucks drove up and unloaded enough pizzas for the entire secretarial and sales staff and the cowboys, not to mention the brothers. They worked long hours and they were demanding bosses, but they never forgot the loyalty and sacrifice of the people who worked for them. They paid good wages, too.

"Why don't you ever spend any money on yourself?" Leo asked Tess one night when, bleary-eyed from the computer, she was ready to go to bed.

"What?"

"You're wearing the same clothes you had last year," he said pointedly. "Don't you want some new jeans, at least, and some new tops?"

"I hadn't thought about it," she confessed. "I've just been putting my wages into the bank and forgetting about them. I suppose I should go shopping."

"Yes, you should." He leaned down toward her. "The very minute we get caught up!"

She groaned. "We'll never get caught up! I heard old Fred saying that he'd had to learn how to use a handheld computer so he could scan the cattle in the low pasture, and he was almost in tears."

"We hired more help," he stated.

"Yes, but there was more work after that! It's never going to end," she wailed. "If those stupid cows don't stop having calves…!"

"Bite your tongue, woman, that's profit you're scoffing at!"

"I know, but—"

"We're all tired," he assured her. "And any day now, it's going to slack off. We're doing compilation figures for five ranches, you know," he added. "It isn't just this one. We have to record each new calf along with its history, we have to revise lists for cattle that have died or been culled, cattle that we traded, new cattle that we've bought. Besides that, we have to have birth weights, weight gain ratios, average daily weight gain and feeding data. All that information has to be kept current or it's no use to us."

"I know. But we'll all get sick of pizzas and I'll forget how to make biscuits!"

"God forbid," he said, taking off his hat and holding it to his heart.

She was too tired to laugh, but she did smile. She worked her way down the long hall toward her room over the garage, feeling as drained as she looked.

She met Cag coming from the general direction of the garage, dressed in a neat gray suit with a subdued burgundy tie and a cream-colored Stetson. He was just back from a trustee meeting in Dallas, and he looked expensive and sophisticated and unapproachable.

She nodded in a cool greeting, and averted her eyes as she passed him.

He stepped in front of her, blocking her path. One big, lean hand tilted her chin up. He looked at her without smiling, his dark eyes glittering with disapproval.

"What have they been doing to you?" he asked curtly.

The comment shocked her, but she didn't read anything into it. Cag would never be concerned about her and she knew it. "We're all putting herd records into the computer, even old Fred," she said wearily. "We're tired."

"Yes, I know. It's a nightmare every year about this time. Are you getting enough sleep?"

She nodded. "I don't know much about computers and it's hard, that's all. I don't mind the work."

His hand hesitated for just an instant before he dropped it. He looked tougher than ever. "You'll be back to your old duties in no time. God forbid that we should drag you kicking and screaming out of the kitchen and into the twentieth century."

That was sarcastic, and she wished she had enough energy to hit him. He was always mocking her, picking at her.

"You haven't complained about the biscuits yet," she reminded him curtly.

His black eyes swept over her disparagingly. "You look about ten," he chided. "All big eyes. And you wear that damned rig or those black jeans and that pink shirt all the time. Don't you have any clothes?"

She couldn't believe her ears. First the brothers had talked about her lack of new clothes, and now he was going to harp on it! "Now, look here, you can't tell me what to wear!"

"If you want to get married, you'll never manage it like that," he scoffed. "No man is going to look twice at a woman who can't be bothered to even brush her hair!"

She actually gasped. She hadn't expected a frontal attack when he'd just walked in the door. "Well, excuse me!" she snapped, well aware that her curly head was untidy. She put a hand to it defensively. "I haven't had time to brush my hair. I've been too busy listing what bull sired what calf!"

He searched over her wan face and he relented, just a little. "Go to bed," he said stiffly. "You look like the walking dead."

"What a nice compliment," she muttered. "Thanks awfully."

She started to walk away, but he caught her arm and pulled her back around. He reached into his pocket, took something out, and handed it to her.

It was a jewelry box, square and velvet-covered. She looked at him and he nodded toward the box, indicating that he wanted her to open it.

She began to, with shaking hands. It was unexpected that he should buy her anything. She lifted the lid to find that there, nestled on a bed of gray satin, was a beautiful faceted sapphire pendant surrounded by tiny diamonds on a thin gold chain. She'd never seen anything so beautiful in her life. It was like a piece of summer sky caught in stone. It sparkled even in the dim shine of the security lights around the house and garage.

"Oh!" she exclaimed, shocked and touched by the unexpected gift. Then she looked up, warily, wondering if she'd been presumptuous and it wasn't a gift at all. She held it out to him. "Oh, I see. You just wanted to show it to me..."

He closed her fingers around the box. His big hands were warm and strong. They felt nice.

"I bought it for you," he said, and looked briefly uncomfortable.

She was totally at sea, and looked it. She glanced down at the pretty thing in her hand and back up at him with a perplexed expression.

"Belated birthday present," he said gruffly, not meeting her eyes.

"But...my birthday was the first of March," she said, her voice terse, "and I never mentioned it."

"Never mentioned it," he agreed, searching her tired face intently. "Never had a cake, a present, even a card."

She averted her eyes.

"Hell!"

The curse, and the look on his face, surprised her.

He couldn't tell her that he felt guilty about her birthday. He hadn't even known that it had gone by until Leo told him two weeks ago. She could have had a cake and little presents, and cards. But she'd kept it to herself because of the way he'd acted about the cake she'd made for him. He knew without a word being spoken that he'd spoiled birthdays for her just as his mother had spoiled them for him. His conscience beat him to death over it. It was why he'd spent so much time away, that guilt, and it was why he'd gone into a jewelers, impulsively, when he never did anything on impulse, and bought the little necklace for her.

"Thanks," she murmured, curling her fingers around the box. But she wouldn't look at him.

There was something else, he thought, watching her posture stiffen. Something…

"What is it?" he asked abruptly.

She took a slow breath. "When do you want me to leave?" she asked bravely.

He scowled. "When do I what?"

"You said, that day I baked the cake, that I could go in the spring," she reminded him, because she'd never been able to forget. "It's spring."

He scowled more and stuck one hand into his pocket, thinking fast. "How could we do without you during roundup?" he asked reasonably. "Stay until summer."

She felt the box against her palms, warm from his body where it had lain in his pocket. It was sort of like a link between them, even if he hadn't meant it that way. She'd never had a present from a man before, except the coat the brothers had given her. But that hadn't been personal like this. She wasn't sure how it was intended, as a sort of conscience-reliever or a genuinely warm gesture.

"We'll talk about it another time," he said after a minute. "I'm tired and I've still got things to do."

He turned and walked past her without looking back. She found herself watching him helplessly with the jewelery box held like a priceless treasure in her two hands.

As if he felt her eyes he stopped suddenly, at the back door, and only his head pivoted. His black eyes met hers in the distance between them, and it was suddenly as if lightning had struck. She felt her knees quivering under her, her heart racing. He was only looking, but she couldn't get her breath at all.

He didn't glance away, and neither did she. In that instant, she lost her heart. She felt him fight to break the contact of their eyes, and win. He moved away quickly, into the house, and she ground her teeth together at this unexpected complication.

Of all the men in the world to become infatuated with, Cag Hart was the very last she should have picked. But knowing it didn't stop the way she felt. With a weary sigh, she turned and went back toward her room. She knew she wouldn't sleep, no matter how tired she was. She linked the necklace around her neck and admired it in the mirror, worrying briefly about the expense, because she'd seen on the clasp that it was 14K gold—not a trifle at all. But it would have been equally precious to her if it had been gold-tone metal, and she was sure Cag knew it. She went to sleep, wearing it.

Chapter Three

Everything would have been absolutely fine, except that she forgot to take the necklace off the next morning and the brothers gave her a hard time over breakfast. That, in turn, embarrassed Cag, who stomped out without his second cup of coffee, glaring at Tess as if she'd been responsible for the whole thing.

They apologized when they realized that they'd just made a bad situation worse. But as the day wore on, she wondered if she shouldn't have left the necklace in its box in her chest of drawers. It had seemed to irritate Cag that she wanted to wear it. The beautiful thing was so special that she could hardly get past mirrors. She loved just looking at it.

Her mind was so preoccupied with her present that she didn't pay close attention to the big aquarium in Cag's room when she went to make the bed. And that was a mistake. She was bending over to pull up the multicolored Navajo patterned comforter on the big four-postered bed when she heard a faint noise. The next thing she knew, she was wearing Herman the python around her neck.

The weight of the huge reptile buckled her knees. Herman weighed more than she did by about ten pounds. She screamed and wrestled, and the harder she struggled the harder an equally frightened Herman held on, certain that he was going to hit the floor bouncing if he relaxed his clinch one bit!

Leo came running, but he stopped at the doorway. No snake-lover, he hadn't the faintest idea how to extricate their housekeeper from the scaly embrace she was being subjected to.

"Get Cag!" she squeaked, pulling at Herman's coils. "Hurry, before he eats me!"

"He won't eat you," Leo promised from a pale face. "He only eats freeze-dried dead things with fur, honest! Cag's at the corral. We were just going to ride out to the line camp. Back in a jiffy!"

Stomping feet ran down the hall. Torturous minutes later, heavier stomping feet ran back again.

Tess was kneeling with the huge reptile wrapped around her, his head arched over hers so that she looked as if she might be wearing a snaky headdress.

"Herman, for Pete's sake!" Cag raged. "How did you get out *this* time?"

"Could you possibly question him later, *after* you've got him off me?" she urged. "He weighs a ton!"

"There, there," he said gently, because he knew how frightened she was of Herman. He approached them slowly, careful not to spook his pet. He smoothed his big hand under the snake's chin and stroked him gently, soothing him as he spoke softly, all the time gently unwinding him from Tess's stooped shoulders.

When he had him completely free, he walked back to the aquarium and scowled as he peered at the lid, which was ajar.

"Maybe he's got a crowbar in there," he murmured, shifting Herman's formidable weight until he could release the other catches enough to lift the lid from the tank. "I don't know why he keeps climbing out."

"How would you like to live in a room three times your size with no playmates?" she muttered, rubbing her aching shoulders. "He's sprained both my shoulders and probably cracked part of my spine. He fell on me!"

He put Herman in the tank and locked the lid before he turned. "Fell?" He scowled. "From where?"

"There!"

She gestured toward one of the wide, tall sculptured posts that graced his king-size bed.

He whistled. "He hasn't gone climbing in a while." He moved a little closer to her and his black eyes narrowed. "You okay?"

"I told you," she mumbled, "I've got fractured bones everywhere!"

He smiled gently. "Sore muscles, more likely." His eyes were quizzical, soft. "You weren't really scared, were you?"

She hesitated. Then she smiled back, just faintly. "Well, no, not really. I've sort of got used to him." She shrugged. "He feels nice. Like a thick silk scarf."

Cag didn't say a word. He just stood there, looking at her, with a sort of funny smile.

"I thought they were slimy."

The smile widened. "Most people do, until they touch one. Snakes are clean. They aren't generally violent unless they're provoked, or unless they're shedding or they've just eaten. Half the work is knowing when not to pick them up." He took off his hat and ran a hand through his thick hair. "I've had Herman for twelve years," he added. "He's like family, although most people don't understand that you can have affection for a snake."

She studied his hard face, remembering that his former fiancée had insisted that he get rid of Herman. Even if he loved a woman, it would be hard for him to give up a much-loved pet.

"I used to have an iguana," she said, "when I was about twelve. One of the guys at the rodeo had it with him, and he was going off to college. He asked would I like him." She smiled reminiscently. "He was green and huge, like some prehistoric creature, like a real live dragon. He liked shredded squash and bananas and he'd let you hold him. When you petted him on the head he'd close his eyes and raise his chin. I had him for three years."

"What happened?"

"He just died," she said. "I never knew why. The vet said that he couldn't see a thing wrong with him, and that I'd done everything right by the book to keep him healthy. We could have had him autopsied, but Dad didn't have the money to pay for it. He was pretty old when I got him. I like to think it was just his time, and not anything I did wrong."

"Sometimes pets do just die." He was looking at Herman, coiled up happily in his tank and looking angelic, in his snaky fashion. "Look at him," he muttered. "Doesn't look like he's ever thought of escaping, does he?"

"I still remember when I opened up the washing machine to do clothes and found him coiled inside. I almost quit on the spot."

"You've come a long way since then," he had to admit. His eyes went to the blue and white sparkle of the necklace and he stared at it.

"I'm sorry," she mumbled, wrapping her hand around it guiltily. "I never should have worn it around your brothers. But it's so lovely. It's like wearing a piece of the sky around my neck."

"I'm glad you like it," he said gruffly. "Wear it all you like. They'll find something else to harp on in a day or so."

"I didn't think they'd notice."

He cocked an eyebrow. "I haven't bought a present for a woman in almost seven years," he said shortly. "It's noteworthy around here, despite my intentions."

Her face colored. "Oh, I know it was just for my birthday," she said quickly.

"You work hard enough to deserve a treat now and again," he returned impatiently. "You're sure you're okay?"

She nodded. "A little thing like a broken back won't slow me down."

He glowered at her. "He only weighs a hundred and ten pounds."

"Yeah? Well, I only weigh a hundred!"

His eyes went over her suddenly. "You've lost weight."

"You said that before, but I haven't. I've always been thin."

"Eat more."

Her eyebrows arched. "I'll eat what I like, thank you."

He made a rough sound in his throat. "And where are those new clothes we've been trying to get you to buy?"

"I don't want any more clothes. I have plenty of clothes."

"Plenty, the devil," he muttered angrily. "You'll go into town tomorrow and get some new jeans and shirts. Got that?"

She lifted her chin stubbornly. "I will not! Listen here, I may work for you, but you don't tell me what I can wear!"

He stared at her for a minute with narrowed eyes. "On second thought," he muttered, moving toward her, "why wait until tomorrow? And like hell I can't tell you what to wear!"

"Callaghan!" she shrieked, protesting.

By the time she got his name out of her shocked mouth, he had her over his shoulder in a fireman's lift. He walked right down the hall with her, passing Leo, who was just on his way back in to see what had happened.

"Oh, my gosh, did Herman bite her?" he gasped. "Is she killed?"

"No, of course he didn't bite her!" Cag huffed and kept walking.

"Then where are you taking her?"

"To the nearest department store."

"To the…you are? Good man!"

"Turncoat!" Tess called back to him.

"Get her a dress!" Leo added.

"I hate dresses!"

"In that case, get her two dresses!"

"You shut up, Leo!" she groaned.

Rey was standing at the back door when Cag approached it with his burden.

"Going out?" Rey asked pleasantly, and opened the door with a flourish. "Have fun, now."

"Rescue me!" Tess called to him.

"Say, wasn't there a song about that?" Rey asked Leo, who joined him on the porch.

"There sure was. It went like this… 'Rescue me!'" he sang.

The two of them were still singing it, arm in arm, off-key, at the top of their lungs, when Cag drove away in the ranch truck with a furious Tess at his side.

"I don't want new clothes!" she raged.

He glanced toward her red face and grinned. "Too late. We're already halfway to town."

This strangely jubilant mood of his surprised her. Cag, of all the brothers, never seemed to play. Of course, neither did Simon, but he was rarely around. Leo and Rey, she'd been told, had once been just as taciturn as the older Harts. But since Dorie came back into Corrigan's life, they were always up to their necks in something. All Cag did was work. It was completely unlike him to take any personal interest in her welfare.

"Leo could have taken me," she muttered, folding her arms over her chest.

"He's too polite to carry you out the door," he replied. "And Rey's too much a gentleman. Most of the time, anyway."

"These jeans just got broke in good."

"They've got holes in them," he said pointedly.

"It's fashionable."

"Most fashionable jeans have holes in them when you buy them. Those—" he gestured toward the worn knees "—got like that from hard work. I've seen you on your knees scrubbing the kitchen floor. Which reminds me, we bought you one of those little floor cleaners that's specially made for linoleum. They're sending it out with the butane and lumber we ordered at the same time."

"A floor cleaner?" she asked, stunned.

"It will make things a little easier for you."

She was delighted that he was concerned about her chores. She didn't say another word, but she couldn't quite stop smiling.

Minutes later, he pulled up in front of the downtown department store and led her inside to the women's section. He stopped in front of Mrs. Bellamy, the saleslady who'd practically come with the store.

He tilted his hat respectfully. "Mrs. Bellamy, can you fit her out with jeans and shirts and new boots and a dress or two?" he asked, nodding toward Tess, who was feeling more and more like a mannequin. "We can't have our housekeeper looking like *that!*" He gestured toward her faded shirt and holey jeans.

"My goodness, no, Mr. Hart," Mrs. Bellamy agreed at once. She frowned thoughtfully. "And we just received such a nice shipment of summer things, too! You come right along with me, Miss Tess, and we'll fix you up!" She took Tess's arm and waved her hand at Cag. "Shoo, now, Mr. Hart," she murmured absently, and Tess had to stifle a giggle at his expression. "She'll be ready to pick up in about an hour."

I'm a parcel, Tess thought, and Cag's a fly. She put a hand over her wobbly mouth as she went meekly along with the older woman. Hysterical laughter would not save her now.

Cag watched her go with an amused smile. So she didn't want new clothes, huh? They'd see about that! Mrs. Bellamy wasn't going to let a potential commission walk away from her!

An hour later, Cag went back for Tess and found her trying on a royal blue and white full-skirted dress with spaghetti straps and a shirred bodice. Against her white skin the sapphire-and-diamond necklace was brilliant. With her freckled white shoulders bare and the creamy tops of her breasts showing, she took his breath away.

"Isn't that dress just the thing, Tess?" Mrs. Bellamy was murmuring. "You wait right here. I want to show you one more! Oh, hello, Mr. Hart!" she called as she passed him. She waved a hand toward Tess. "What do you think? Isn't it cute? Now where did I see that pretty black lacy thing…"

Tess turned as Cag joined her. His face gave nothing away, but his black eyes glittered over the soft skin left bare by the dress. It certainly made her eyes bluer.

"Is it…too revealing?" Tess asked nervously, because of the way he was watching her.

He shook his head. "It suits you. It even matches the necklace." His voice sounded deep and husky. He moved closer and one big, lean hand lifted involuntarily to her throat where the small sapphire lay in its bed of diamonds and gold. His hand rested there for an instant before it moved restlessly over the thin strap of the dress. His fingertips absently traced over her soft skin as he studied her, noticing its silky warmth.

Her breath caught in her throat. She felt her heartbeat shaking the dress even as she noticed his black eyes lowering to the flesh left bare by the shirred bodice.

His fingers contracted on her shoulder and her intake of breath was suddenly audible.

He met her eyes relentlessly, looking for hidden signs that she couldn't keep from him.

"This is the sort of dress," he said gruffly, "that makes a man want to pull the bodice down."

"Mr.…Hart!" she exclaimed.

He scowled faintly as he searched her shocked eyes. "Don't you know anything about dresses and the effect they have on men?" he wanted to know.

Her trembling hands went to tug the bodice up even

more. "I do not! But I know that I won't have it if it makes you…makes a man think…such things!"

His hand jerked suddenly, as if her skin had burned it. "I was teasing!" he lied sharply, moving away. "It's fine. You look fine. And yes," he added firmly, "you'll have it, all right!"

She didn't know what to think. He was acting very strangely, and now he wouldn't look at her at all. Teasing? Then why was he so stiff and uncomfortable looking if he was teasing? And why keep his back to her and Mrs. Bellamy, who'd just rejoined them.

"Here, Tess, try on this one. I'll box that one while you're dressing." She rushed the girl off before she could say anything to Cag.

That was just as well. He was fighting a raging arousal that had shocked him senseless. Tess was beginning to have a very noticeable effect on him, and he was quite sorry that he'd insisted on bringing her here. If she wore that dress around him, it was going to cause some major problems.

He stood breathing deliberately until his rebellious body was back under control. He noticed that Tess didn't show him the black dress she'd tried on. But she shook her head when Mrs. Bellamy asked her about it. She was trying to refuse the blue one, too. He wasn't having that. She looked so beautiful in it. That was one she had to have.

"You're not turning that blue one back in," he said firmly. "You'll need something to wear if you're asked out anywhere." He hated thinking about her in that dress with another man. But she didn't date. It shouldn't worry him. "Did you get some jeans and blouses, and how about those boots?"

After Mrs. Bellamy rattled off an inventory, he produced a credit card and watched her ring up a total. He wouldn't let Tess see it. She looked worried enough already.

He took the two large bags and the dress bag from Mrs. Bellamy with thanks and hustled Tess back out to the double-cabbed truck. He put the purchases on the back seat and loaded Tess into the passenger seat.

She sat without fastening her belt until he got in beside her.

"You spent too much," she said nervously, her big blue eyes echoing her mood. "I won't be able to pay you back for months, even if you take so much a week out of my salary."

"Think of the clothes as a uniform," he said gently. "You can't walk around in what you've been wearing. What will people think of us?"

"Nobody ever comes to see you."

"Visiting cattlemen do. Politicians do. We even have the occasional cookout. People notice these things. And you'll look neater in new stuff."

She shrugged and sighed with defeat. "Okay, then. Thanks."

He didn't crank the truck. He threw a long arm over the back of the seat and looked at her openly. Her barely contained excitement over the clothes began to make sense to him. "You've never had new things," he said suddenly.

She flushed. "On the rodeo circuit, when you lose, you don't make much. Dad and I bought most of our stuff from yard sales, or were given hand-me-downs by other rodeo people." She glanced at him nervously. "I used to compete in barrel racing, and I won third place a few times, but I didn't have a good enough horse to go higher. We had to sell him just before Dad gave up and came here to work."

"Why, Tess," he said softly. "I never knew you could ride at all!"

"I haven't had much chance to."

"I'll take you out with me one morning. Can you ride a quarter horse?"

She smiled. "If he's well trained, sure I can!"

He chuckled. "We'll see, after the biggest part of the roundup's over. We'd never get much done with all the cowboys showing off for you."

She flushed. "Nobody looks at me. I'm too skinny."

"But you're not," he protested. His eyes narrowed. "You're slender, but nobody could mistake you for a boy."

"Thanks."

He reached out unexpectedly and tugged a short reddish-gold curl, bringing her face around so that he could search it. He wasn't smiling. His eyes narrowed as his gaze slid lazily over her eyes, cheekbones and down to her mouth.

"The blue dress suited you," he said. "How did the black one look?"

She shifted restlessly. "It was too low."

"Low what?"

She swallowed. "It was cut almost to the waist. I could never wear something like that in public!"

His gaze fell lower, to the quick rise and fall of her small breasts. "A lot of women couldn't get away with it," he murmured. "But you could. You're small enough that you wouldn't need to wear a bra with it."

"Mr. Hart!" she exclaimed, jerking back.

His eyebrows arched. "I've been Callaghan for

months and today I've already been Mr. Hart twice. What did I say?"

Her face was a flaming red. "You…you know what you said!"

He did, all at once, and he chuckled helplessly. He shook his head as he reached for the ignition and switched it on. "And I thought Mrs. Lewis was old-fashioned. You make her look like a hippie!"

She wrapped her arms over her chest, still shaken by the remark. "You mustn't go around saying things like that. It's indecent!"

He had to force himself not to laugh again. She was serious. He shouldn't tease her, but it was irresistible. She made him feel warm inside, when he'd been empty for years. He should have realized that he was walking slowly toward an abyss, but he didn't notice. He enjoyed having her around, spoiling her a little. He glanced sideways at her. "Put your belt on, honey."

Honey! She fumbled it into the lock at her side, glancing at him uncertainly. He never used endearments and she didn't like them. But that deep, rough voice made her toes curl. She could almost imagine him whispering that word under his breath as he kissed a woman.

She went scarlet. Why had she thought of that? And if the thought wasn't bad enough, her eyes went suddenly to his hard mouth and lingered there in spite of her resolve. She wondered if that mouth could wreak the devastation she thought it could. She'd only been kissed a time or two, and never by anybody who knew how. Callaghan would know how, she was sure of it.

He caught her looking at him and one eyebrow went up. "And what sort of scandalous thoughts are going through that prudish mind now?" he taunted.

She caught her breath. "I don't know what you mean!"

"No?"

"No! And I do not have a prudish mind!"

"You could have fooled me," he said under his breath, and actually grinned.

"Hold your breath until you get any more apple butter with your biscuits," she muttered back. "And wait until you get another biscuit, too!"

"You can't starve me," he said smugly. "Rey and Leo will protect me."

"Oh, right, like they protected me! How could you do that? Carrying me out like a package, and them standing there singing like fools. I don't know why I ever agreed to work for such a loopy family!"

"Loopy? Us?"

"You! You're all crazy."

"What does that make you?" he murmured dryly. "You work for us."

"I need my head read!"

"I'll get somebody on it first thing."

She glanced at him sourly. "I thought you wanted me to quit."

"I already told you, not during roundup!" he reminded her. "Maybe when summer comes, if you're determined."

"I'm not determined. You're determined. You don't like me."

He pursed his lips, staring straight ahead. "I don't, do I?" he said absently. "But you're a fine housekeeper and a terrific cook. If I fired you, the others would stick me in a horse trough and hold me under."

"You destroyed the cake I baked for you," she recalled uneasily. "And you let your snake fall on me."

"That was Herman's own idea," he assured her. His face hardened. "The cake—you know why."

"I know now." She relented. "I'm sorry. I don't know what nice mothers are like, either, because I never had one. But if I had little kids, I'd make their birthdays so special," she said almost to herself, smiling. "I'd bake cakes and give them parties, and make ice cream. And they'd have lots and lots of presents." Her hand went involuntarily to the necklace he'd given her.

He saw that, and something warm kindled in his chest. "You like kids?" he asked without wanting to.

"Very much. Do you?"

"I haven't had much to do with them. I like Mack's toddler, though," he added. The foreman had a little boy two years old who always ran to Cag to be picked up. He always took something over for the child when he went to see Mack and his wife. Tess knew, although he never mentioned it.

She looked out the window. "I don't suppose I'll ever have kids of my own."

He scowled. "Why do you say that?"

She wrapped her arms around her chest. "I don't like...the sort of thing that you have to do to get them."

He stepped on the brakes so hard that the seat belt jerked tight and stared at her intently.

She flushed. "Well, some women are cold!"

"How do you know that you are?" he snapped, hating himself for even asking.

She averted her gaze out the window. "I can't stand to have a man touch me."

"Really?" he drawled. "Then why did you gasp and stand there with your heartbeat shaking you when I slid my hand over your shoulder in the dress shop?"

Her body jerked. "I never!"

"You most certainly did," he retorted, and felt a wave of delight wash over him at the memory of her soft skin under his hands. It had flattered him, touched him, that she was vulnerable with him.

"It was...I mean, I was surprised. That's all!" she added belligerently.

His fingers tapped on the steering wheel as he contemplated her with narrowed eyes. "Something happened to you. What?"

She stared at him, stunned.

"Come on. You know I don't gossip."

She did. She moved restlessly against the seat. "One of my mother's lovers made a heavy pass at me," she muttered. "I was sixteen and grass green, and he scared me to death."

"And now you're twenty-two," he added. He stared at her even harder. "There aren't any twenty-two-year-old virgins left in America."

"Says who?" she shot at him, and then flushed as she felt herself fall right into the trap.

His lips pursed, and he smiled so faintly that she almost missed it.

"That being the case," he said in a soft, mocking tone, "how do you know that you're frigid?"

She was going to choke to death trying to answer that. She drew in an exasperated breath. "Can't we go home?"

She made the word sound soft, mysterious, enticing. He'd lived in houses all his life. She made him want a home. But it wasn't a thing he was going to admit just yet, even to himself.

"Sure," he said after a minute. "We can go home."

He took his foot off the brake, put the truck in gear and sent it flying down the road.

It never occurred to him that taking her shopping had been the last thing on his mind this morning, or that his pleasure in her company was unusual. He was reclusive these days, stoic and unapproachable; except when Tess came close. She was vulnerable in so many ways, like the kitten they'd both adopted. Surely it was just her youth that appealed to him. It was like giving treats to a deprived child and enjoying its reactions.

Except that she trembled under his hands and he'd been years on his own. He liked touching her and she liked letting him. It was something he was going to have to watch. The whole situation was explosive. But he was sure he could handle it. She was a sweet kid. It wouldn't hurt if he spoiled her just a little. Of course it wouldn't.

Chapter Four

The brothers, like Tess and the rest of the staff, were worn to a frazzle by the time roundup was almost over.

Tess hadn't thought Cag meant it when he'd invited her to ride with him while he gathered strays, but early one morning after breakfast, he sent her to change into jeans and boots. He was waiting for her at the stable when she joined him there.

"Listen, I'm a little rusty," Tess began as she stared dubiously toward two saddled horses, one of whom was a sleek black gelding who pranced in place.

"Don't worry. I wouldn't put you on Black Diamond even if you asked. He's mine. This is Whirlwind," he said, nodding toward a pretty little red mare. "She's a registered quarter horse and smart as a whip. She'll take care of you." He summed her up with a glance, smiling at the blue windbreaker that matched her eyes and the Atlanta Braves baseball cap perched atop her red-gold curls.

"You look about ten," he mused, determined to put an invisible Off Limits sign on her mentally.

"And you look about—" she began.

He cut her off in midsentence. "Hop aboard and let's get started."

She vaulted easily into the saddle and gathered the reins loosely in her hands, smiling at the pleasure of being on a horse again. She hadn't ridden since her father's death.

He tilted his tan Stetson over his eyes and turned his mount expertly. "We'll go out this way," he directed, taking the lead toward the grassy path that wound toward the line camp in the distance. "Catch up."

She patted the horse's neck gently and whispered to her. She trotted up next to Cag's mount and kept the pace.

"We do most of this with light aircraft, but there are always a few mavericks who aren't intimidated by flying machines. They get into the brush and hide. So we have to go after those on horseback." He glanced at her jean-clad legs and frowned. "I should have dug you out some chaps," he murmured, and she noticed that he was wearing his own—bat-wing chaps with stains and scratches from this sort of work. "Don't ride into the brush like that," he added firmly. "You'll rip your legs open on the thorns."

"Okay," she said easily.

He set the pace and she followed, feeling oddly happy and at peace. It was nice riding with him like this across the wide, flat plain. She felt as if they were the only two people on earth. There was a delicious silence out here, broken only by the wind and the soft snorting of the horses and occasionally a distant sound of a car or airplane.

They worked through several acres of scrubland, flushing cows and calves and steers from their hiding places and herding them toward the distant holding pens. The men had erected several stockades in which to place the separated cattle, and they'd brought in a tilt-tray, so that the calves could be branded and ear-tagged.

The cows, identified with the handheld computer by

the computer chips embedded in their tough hides, were either culled and placed in a second corral to be shipped out, or driven toward another pasture. The calves would be shipped to auction. The steers, already under contract, would go to their buyers. Even so far away from the ranch, there was tremendous organization in the operation.

Tess took off her Braves cap and wiped her sweating forehead on her sleeve.

Hardy, one of the older hands, grinned as he fetched up beside her on his own horse. "Still betting on them Braves, are you? They lost the pennant again last fall…that's two years in a row."

"Oh, yeah? Well, they won it once already," she reminded him with a smug grin. "Who needs two?"

He chuckled, shook his head and rode off.

"Baseball fanatic," Cag murmured dryly as he joined her.

"I'll bet you watched the playoffs last fall, too," she accused.

He didn't reply. "Hungry?" he asked. "We can get coffee and some stew over at the chuck wagon."

"I thought only those big outfits up in the Rockies still packed out a chuck wagon."

"If we didn't, we'd all go hungry here," he told her. "This ranch is a lot bigger than it looks."

"I saw it on the map in your office," she replied. "It sure covers a lot of land."

"You should see our spread in Montana," he mused. "It's the biggest of the lot. And the one that kept us all so busy a few weeks ago, trying to get the records on the computer."

She glanced back to where two of the men were

working handheld computers. "Do all your cowboys know how to use those things?" she asked.

"Most of them. You'd be amazed how many college boys we get here between exams and new classes. We had an aeronautical engineer last summer and a professor of archaeology the year before that."

"Archaeology!"

He grinned. "He spent more time digging than he spent working cattle, but he taught us how to date projectile points and pottery."

"How interesting." She stretched her aching back. "I guess you've been to college."

"I got my degree in business from Harvard."

She glanced at him warily. "And I barely finished high school."

"You've got years left to go to college, if you want to."

"Slim chance of that," she said carelessly. "I can't work and go to school at the same time."

"You can do what our cowboys do—work a quarter and go to school a quarter." He fingered the reins gently. "In fact, we could arrange it so that you could do that, if you like. Jacobsville has a community college. You could commute."

The breath left her in a rush. "You'd let me?" she asked.

"Sure, if you want to."

"Oh, my goodness." She thought about it with growing delight. She could study botany. She loved to grow things. She might even learn how to cultivate roses and do grafting. Her eyes sparkled.

"Well?"

"I could study botany," she said absently. "I could learn to grow roses."

He frowned. "Horticulture?"

"Yes." She glanced at him. "Isn't that what college teaches you?"

"It does, certainly. But if you want horticulture, the vocational school offers a diploma in it."

Her face became radiant at the thought. "Oh, how wonderful!"

"What an expression," he mused, surprised at the pleasure it gave him. "Is that what you want to do, learn to grow plants?"

"Not just plants," she said. "*Roses!*"

"We've got dozens of them out back."

"No, not just old-fashioned roses. Tea roses. I want to do grafts. I want to…to create new hybrids."

He shook his head. "That's over my head."

"It's over mine, too. That's why I want to learn it."

"No ambition to be a professional of some sort?" he persisted. "A teacher, a lawyer, a doctor, a journalist?"

She hesitated, frowning as she studied his hard face. "I like flowers," she said slowly. "Is there something wrong with that? I mean, should I want to study something else?"

He didn't know how to answer that. "Most women do, these days."

"Sure, but most women don't want jobs working in a kitchen and keeping house and growing flowers, do they?" She bit her lip. "I don't know that I'd be smart enough to do horticulture…"

"Of course you would, if you want to do it," he said impatiently. His good humor seemed to evaporate as he stared at her. "Do you want to spend your life working in somebody else's kitchen?"

She shifted. "I guess I will," she said. "I don't want to get married, and I don't really see myself teaching kids or practicing medicine. I enjoy cooking and keeping house. And I love growing things." She glanced at him belligerently. "What's wrong with that?"

"Nothing. Not a damned thing."

"Now I've made you mad."

His hand wrapped around the reins. He didn't look at her as he urged his mount ahead, toward the chuck wagon where several cowboys were holding full plates.

He couldn't tell her that it wasn't her lack of ambition that disturbed him. It was the picture he had of her, surrounded by little redheaded kids digging in the rose garden. It upset him, unsettled him. He couldn't start thinking like that. Tess was just a kid, despite her age, and he'd better keep that in mind. She hadn't even started to live yet. She'd never known intimacy with a man. She was likely to fall headlong in love with the first man who touched her. He thought about that, about being the first, and it rocked him to the soles of his feet. He had to get his mind on something else!

They had a brief lunch with several of the cowboys. Tess let Cag do most of the talking. She ate her stew with a biscuit, drank a cup of coffee and tried not to notice the speculative glances she was getting. She didn't know that it was unusual for Cag to be seen in the company of a woman, even the ranch housekeeper. Certainly he'd never brought anyone female out to a roundup before. It aroused the men's curiosity.

Cag ignored the looks. He knew that having Tess along was innocent, so what did it matter what anyone else thought? It wasn't as if he was planning to drag her off into the brush and make love to her. Even as he thought it, he pictured it. His whole body went hot.

"We'd better get going," he said abruptly, rising to his feet.

Tess thanked the cook for her lunch, and followed Cag back to the horses.

They rode off toward the far pastures without a word being spoken. She wondered what she'd done to make Cag mad, but she didn't want to say anything. It might only make matters worse. She wondered if he was mad because she wanted to go back to school.

They left the camp behind and rode in a tense silence. Her eyes kept going to his tall, powerful body. He seemed part of the horse he rode, so comfortable and careless that he might have been born in the saddle. He had powerful broad shoulders and lean hips, with long legs that were sensuously outlined by the tight-fitting jeans he wore under the chaps. She'd seen plenty of rodeo cowboys in her young life, but none of them would have held a candle to Cag. He looked elegant even in old clothes.

He turned his head and caught her staring, then frowned when she blushed.

"Did you ever go rodeoing?" she asked to cover her confusion.

He shook his head. "Never had much use for it," he said honestly. "I didn't need the money, and I always had enough to do here, or on one of the other ranches in the combine."

"Dad couldn't seem to stay in one place for very long," she murmured thoughtfully. "He loved the rodeo circuit, but he didn't win very often."

"It wasn't much of a life for you, was it?" he asked. "It must have been hard to go to school at all."

She smiled. "My education was hit-and-miss, if that's

what you mean. But there were these correspondence courses I took so I could get my high school diploma." She flushed deeper and glanced at him. "I know I'm not very educated."

He reined in at a small stream that crossed the wooded path, in the shade of a big oak tree, and let his horse drink, motioning her to follow suit. "It wasn't a criticism," he said. "Maybe I'm too blunt sometimes, but people always know where they stand with me."

"I noticed."

A corner of his mouth quirked. "You aren't shy about expressing your own opinions," he recalled. "It's refreshing."

"Oh, I learned to fight back early," she murmured. "Rodeo's a tough game, and some of the other kids I met were pretty physical when they got mad. I may not be big, but I can kick like a mule."

"I don't doubt it." He drew one long leg up and hooked it over the pommel while he studied her. "But despite all that male company, you don't know much about men."

This was disturbing territory. She averted her gaze to the bubbling stream at their feet. "So you said, when we went to the store." She remembered suddenly the feel of his hard fingers on her soft skin and her heart began to race.

His black eyes narrowed. "Didn't you ever go out on dates?"

Her lithe body shifted in the saddle. "These days, most girls don't care what they do and they're clued up about how to take care of themselves." She glanced at him and away. "It makes it rough for the few of us who don't think it's decent to behave that way. Men seem to expect a girl to give out on the first date and they get mad when she won't."

He traced a cut on his chaps. "So you stopped going out."

She nodded. "It seemed the best way. Besides," she murmured uncomfortably, "I told you. I don't like… that."

"*That?*"

He was going to worry the subject to death. "That," she emphasized. "You know, being grabbed and forcibly fondled and having a man try to stick his tongue down your throat!"

He chuckled helplessly.

"Oh, you don't understand!"

"In fact, I do," he replied, and the smile on his lips was full of worldly knowledge and indulgent amusement. "You were lucky that your would-be suitors didn't know any more than you did."

She frowned because she didn't understand.

His black eyes searched her face. "Tess, an experienced man doesn't grab. Ever. He doesn't have to. And French kisses need to be worked up to, very slowly."

Her heart was really going now. It shook the cotton blouse she was wearing. She stared at the chaps where Cag's long fingers were resting, and remembered the feel of his lean, strong hands.

"Embarrassed?" he asked softly.

She hesitated. Then she nodded.

His heart jumped wildly as he stared at her, unblinking. "And curious?" he added in a deep, slow drawl.

After a few seconds, she nodded again, but she couldn't make herself meet his eyes.

His hand clenched on the pommel of his saddle as

he fought the hunger he felt to teach her those things, to satisfy her curiosity. His gaze fell to her soft mouth and he wanted it. It was crazy, what he was thinking. He couldn't afford a lapse like that. She was just a kid and she worked for him…

She heard the creak of leather as he swung down out of the saddle. After a minute, she felt his lean hands hard on her waist. He lifted her down from the horse abruptly and left the horses to drink their fill.

The sun filtered down to the ground in patterns through the oak leaves there, in the middle of nowhere, in the shelter of the trees where thick grass grew on the shallow banks of the stream and open pasture beyond the spot. The wind whipped around, but Tess couldn't hear it or the gurgle of the stream above the sound of her own heart.

His hands felt rough against her skin. They felt as if he wasn't quite in control, and when she looked up at him, she realized that he wasn't. His face was like steel. The only thing alive in it was those black Spanish eyes, the legacy of a noble Madrid ancestry.

She felt her knees wobble because of the way he was looking at her, his eyes bold on her body, as if he knew exactly what was under her clothing.

The thought of Callaghan Hart's mouth on her lips made her breath catch in her throat. She'd always been a little afraid of him, not because she thought he might hurt her, but because late at night she lay wondering how it would feel if he kissed her. She'd thought about it a lot lately, to her shame. He was mature, experienced, confident, all the things she wasn't. She knew she couldn't handle an affair with him. She was equally sure that he wouldn't have any amorous interest in a novice like her. She'd *been* sure, she amended. Because he was looking at her now in a way he'd never looked at her before.

Her cold hands pressed nervously into the soft cotton of his shirt, feeling the warmth and strength of his chest under it.

"Callaghan," she whispered uncertainly.

His hard lips parted. "Nobody else calls me that," he said tersely, dropping his gaze to her mouth. He liked the way she made his name sound, as if it had a sort of magic.

Her fingers spread. She liked the feel of warm muscle under the shirt, and the soft, spongy feel of thick hair behind the buttons. He was hairy there, she suspected.

He wasn't breathing normally. She could feel his heartbeat against her skin. Her hands pressed gingerly against him, to explore, hesitantly, the hardness of his chest.

He stiffened. His hands on her waist contracted. His breathing changed.

Her hands stilled immediately. She looked up into glittery black eyes. She didn't understand his reactions, never having experienced them before.

"You don't know anything at all, do you?" he asked tersely, and it sounded as if he was talking to himself. He looked down at her short-nailed, capable little hands resting so nervously on top of his shirt. "Why did you stop?"

"You got stiff," she said.

He lifted an eyebrow. "Stiff?"

He looked as if he was trying not to smile, despite the tautness of his face and body.

"You know," she murmured. "Tense. Like you didn't want me to touch you."

He let out a slow breath. His hands moved from her

waist to cover her cold fingers and press them closer. They felt warm and cozy, almost comforting. They flattened her hands so that she could feel his body in every cell.

She moved her fingers experimentally where the buttons ran down toward his belt.

"Don't get ambitious," he said, stilling her hands. "I'm not taking off my shirt for you."

"As if I would *ever…!*" she burst out, embarrassed.

He smiled indulgently, studying her flushed face, her wide, bright eyes. "I don't care whether you would, ever, you're not going to. Lift your face."

"Why?" she expelled on a choked breath.

"You know why."

She bit her lip, hard, studying his face with worried eyes. "You don't like me."

"Liking doesn't have anything to do with this." He let go of her hands and gripped her elbows, lifting her easily within reach of his mouth. His gaze fell to it and his chest rose and fell roughly. "You said you were curious," he murmured at her lips. "I'm going to do something about it."

Her hands gripped his shirt, wrinkling it, as his mouth came closer. She could taste the coffee on his warm breath and she felt as if the whole world had stopped spinning, as if the wind had stopped blowing, while she hung there, waiting.

His hard lips just barely touched hers, brushing lightly over the sensitive flesh to savor it. Her eyes closed and she held herself perfectly still, so that he wouldn't stop.

He lifted his head fractionally. She looked as if she couldn't bear to have him draw back. Whatever she felt, it wasn't fear.

He bent again. His top lip nudged under hers, and then down to toy with her lower lip. He felt her gasp. Apparently the kisses she'd had from other men hadn't been arousing. He felt her hands tighten on his shirt with a sense of pure arrogant pleasure.

He brought both lips down slowly over her bottom one, letting his tongue slide softly against the silky, moist inner tissue. She gasped and her mouth opened.

"Yes," he whispered as his own mouth opened to meet it, press into it, parting her lips wide so that he could cover them completely.

She made a tiny sound and her body stiffened, but he ignored the faint involuntary protest. His arms reached down, enclosing, lifting, so that she was completely off the ground in a hungry, warm embrace that seemed to swallow her whole.

The kiss was hard, slow, insistent and delicious. She clasped her hands at the back of Cag's neck and clung to it, her mouth accepting his, loving the hard crush of it. When she felt his tongue slipping past her lips, she didn't protest. She opened her mouth for him, met the slow, velvety thrust with a husky little moan, and closed her eyes even tighter as the intimacy of the kiss made her whole body clench with pleasure.

It seemed a long time before he lifted his head and watched her dazed, misty eyes open.

He searched them in the heady silence of the glade. Nearby a horse whinnied, but he didn't hear it. His heart was beating in time with Tess's, in a feverish rush. He was feeling sensations he'd almost forgotten how to feel. His body was swelling, aching, against hers. He watched her face color and knew that she felt it and understood it.

He eased her back down onto her feet and let her move away a few inches. His eyes never left hers and he didn't let her go completely.

She looked as stunned as he felt. He searched her eyes as his big hand lifted and his fingers traced a blatant path down her breast to the hard tip.

She gasped, but she didn't try to stop him. She couldn't, and he knew it.

His hand returned to her waist.

She leaned her forehead against him while she got her breath back. She wondered if she should be embarrassed. She felt hot all over and oddly swollen. Her mouth was sore, but she wished his hard lips were still covering it. The sensations curling through her body were new and exciting and a little frightening.

"Was it just…a lesson?" she whispered, because she wanted to know.

His hands smoothed gently over her curly head. He stared past it, toward the stream where the horses were still drinking. "No."

"Then, why?"

His fingers slid into her curls. He sighed heavily. "I don't know."

Her eyes closed. She stood against him with the wind blowing all around them and thought that she'd never been so happy, or felt so complete.

He was feeling something comparable, but it disturbed him and made him angry. He hadn't wanted it to come to this. He'd always known, at some level, that it would be devastating to kiss her. This little redhead with her pert manner and fiery temper. She could bring him to his knees. Did she know that?

He lifted his head and looked down at her. She

wasn't smiling, flirting, teasing, or pert. She looked as shattered as he felt.

He put her away from him, still holding her a little too tightly by the arms.

"Don't read anything into it," he said shortly.

Her breath was jerky. "I won't."

"It was just proximity," he explained. "And abstinence."

"Sure."

She wasn't humoring him. She really believed him. He was amazed that she didn't know how completely he'd lost control, how violently his body reacted to her. He frowned.

She shifted uneasily and moved back. His hands fell away. Her eyes met his and her thin brows wrinkled. "You won't…you won't tell the brothers?" she asked. She moved a shoulder. "I wouldn't want them to think I was, well, trying to… I mean, that I was flirting or chasing you or…anything."

"I don't think you're even real," he murmured half-absently as he studied her. "I don't gossip. I told you that. As if I'd start telling tales about you, to my own damned brothers, just because a kiss got a little out of hand!"

She went scarlet. She whirled away from him and stumbled down the bank to catch the mare's reins. She mounted after the second try, irritated that he was already comfortably in the saddle by then, watching her.

"As for the rest of it," he continued, as if there hadn't been any pause between words, "you weren't chasing me. I invited you out here."

She nodded, but she couldn't meet his eyes. What she was feeling was far too explosive, and she was afraid it might show in her eyes.

Her embarrassment was almost tangible. He sighed and rode closer, putting out a hand to tilt up her chin.

"Don't make such heavy weather of a kiss, Tess," he said quietly. "It's no big deal. Okay?"

"Okay." She almost choked on the word. The most earthshaking event of her life, and it was no big deal. Probably to him it hadn't been. The way he kissed, he'd probably worked for years perfecting his technique. But she'd never been kissed like that, and she was shattered. Still, he wasn't going to know it. He didn't even like her, he'd said as much. It had been an impulse, and obviously it was one he already regretted.

"Where do we go next?" she asked with a forced smile.

He scowled. She was upset. He should never have touched her, but it had been irresistible. It had been pure delight to kiss her. Now he had to forget that he ever had.

"The next pasture," he said curtly. "We'll roust out whatever cattle wildlife we find and then call it a day. You're drooping."

"I guess I am, a little," she confessed. "It's hot."

In more ways than one, he thought, but he didn't dare say it aloud. "Let's go, then."

He rode off, leaving her to follow. Neither of them mentioned what had happened. By the end of the day, they only spoke when they had to. And by the next morning, Cag was glaring at her as if she were the reason for global warming. Everything was back to normal.

Chapter Five

Spring turned to summer. Cag didn't invite Tess to go riding again, but he did have Leo speak to her about starting horticulture classes in the fall.

"I'd really like to," she told Leo. "But will I still be here then?" she added on a nervous laugh. "Cag's worse than ever lately. Any day now, he's going to fire me."

"That isn't likely," Leo assured her, secretly positive that Cag would never let her leave despite his antagonism, because the older man cared too much about her. Oddly Tess was the only person who didn't seem to realize that.

"If I'm still here," she said. "I'd love to go to school."

"We'll take care of it. Cheer up, will you?" he added gently. "You look depressed lately."

"Oh, I'm not," she assured him, lying through her teeth. "I feel just fine, really!"

She didn't tell him that she wasn't sleeping well, because she laid awake nights remembering the way Cag had kissed her. But if she'd hoped for a repeat of that afternoon, it had never come. Cag was all but hostile to her since, complaining about everything from the way she dusted to the way she fastened his socks together in the drawers. Nothing she did pleased him.

Mrs. Lewis remarked dryly that he acted lovesick,

and Tess began to agonize about some shadowy woman that he might be seeing on those long evenings when he left the ranch and didn't come home until midnight. He never talked about a woman, but then, he didn't gossip. And even his brothers knew very little about his private life. It worried Tess so badly that even her appetite suffered. How would she survive if Cag married? She didn't like thinking about him with another woman. In fact, she hated it. When she realized why, she felt even worse. How in the world was it that she'd managed to fall in love with a man who couldn't stand to be around her, a man who thought of her only as a cook and housekeeper?

What was she going to do about it? She was terrified that it might show, although she saw no signs of it in her mirror. Cag paid her no more attention than he paid the housecleaning. He seemed to find her presence irritating, though, most especially at mealtimes. She began to find reasons to eat early or late, so that she didn't have to sit at the table with him glaring at her.

Oddly that made things worse. He started picking at her, and not in any teasing way. It got so bad that Leo and Rey took him aside and called him on it. He thought Tess had put them up to it, and blamed her. She withdrew into herself and sat alone in her room at night crocheting an afghan while she watched old black-and-white movies on the little television set her father had given her for Christmas four years ago. She spent less time with the brothers than ever, out of self-defense. But Cag's attitude hurt. She wondered if he was trying to make her quit, even though it was his idea to get her into school in the fall quarter. Perhaps, she thought miserably, he meant her to live in at the school dormitory and quit her job. The thought brought tears to her eyes and made her misery complete.

It was a beautiful summer day when haying got underway on the ranch to provide winter forage for the cattle. It hadn't rained for over a week and a half, and while the danger of drought was ever present, this was a necessary dry spell. The hay would rot in the field if it rained. Besides, it was a comfortable heat, unseasonably cool. Even so, it was hot enough for shorts.

Tess had on a pair of denim cutoffs that she'd made from a torn pair of jeans, and she was wearing socks and sneakers and a gray tank top. She looked young and fresh and full of energy, bouncing across the hayfield with the small red cooler in her hands. She hadn't wanted to go near Cag, but Leo had persuaded her that his older brother would be dying of thirst out there in the blazing sun with nothing to drink. He sent a reluctant Tess out to him with a cooler full of supplies.

Cag, driving the tractor that was scooping the hay into huge round bales, stopped and let the engine idle when he saw her coming toward him. He was alone in the field, having sent two other men into adjacent fields to bale hay in the same fashion. It was blazing hot in the sun, despite his wide-brimmed straw hat. He was bare-chested and still pouring sweat. He'd forgotten to bring anything along to drink, and he hadn't really expected anyone to think about sending him something. He smiled ruefully to himself, certain that Tess wouldn't have thought of it on her own. She was still too nervous of him to come this close willingly, especially considering the way he'd treated her since that unfortunate kiss in the pasture.

It wasn't that he disliked her. It was that he liked her far too much. He ached every time he looked at her, especially since he'd kissed her. He found himself thinking about it all the time. She was years younger, another generation. Some nice boy would come along and she'd go head over heels. He had to remember that and not let a few minutes of remembered pleasure blind him to reality. Tess was too young for him. Period.

He cut off the tractor and jumped down as she approached him. Her eyes seemed to flicker as they brushed his sweaty chest, thick with black hair that ran down into his close-fitting jeans.

He wiped his hand on a work cloth. "Brought survival gear, did you?" he asked.

"Just a couple of cans of beer and two sandwiches," she said tautly. "Leo asked me to."

"Naturally," he drawled sarcastically. "I'd hardly expect you to volunteer."

She bit her lower lip to keep from arguing with him. She was keenly aware of his dislike. She offered the cooler.

He took it from her, noticing how she avoided touching him as it changed hands.

"Go back along the path," he said, irritated by his own concern for her. "I've seen two big rattlesnakes since I started. They won't like the sun, so they'll be in a cool place. And that—" he indicated her shorts and sneakers "—is stupid gear to wear in a pasture. You should have on thick jeans and boots. Good God, you weren't even looking where your feet were!"

"I was watching the ravens," she said defensively, indicating two of them lighting and flying away in the field.

"They're after field mice." His narrowed black eyes cut

into her flushed, averted face. "You're all but shaking. What the hell's wrong with you today?" he demanded.

Her eyes shot back up to his and she stepped back. "Nothing. I should go."

He realized belatedly that the sight of him without his shirt was affecting her. He didn't have to ask why. He already knew. Her hands had been shyly exploring his chest, even through the shirt, the day he'd kissed her, and she'd wanted to unfasten it. But she'd acted as if she couldn't bear to be near him ever since. She avoided him and it made him furious.

"Why don't you run along home?" he asked curtly. "You've done your duty, after all."

"I didn't mind."

"Hell!" He put the cooler down. "You can't be bothered to come within five feet of me unless somebody orders you to." He bit off the words, glaring at her. He was being unreasonable, but he couldn't help himself. "You won't bring me coffee in the office when I'm working unless the door's open and one of my brothers is within shouting distance. What do you expect, you scrawny little redhead, that the sight of you maddens me with such passion that I'm likely to ravish you on the floor? You don't even have a woman's body yet!" he muttered, his eyes on her small, pert breasts under the tank top.

She saw where he was looking and it wounded her. The whiplash of his voice hit her like a brick. She stared at him uncomprehendingly, her eyes wounded. "I never… never said…" she stammered.

"As if you could make me lose my head," he continued coldly, his voice like a sharp blade as his eyes went over her disparagingly.

Her face flamed and the eyes that met his were suddenly clouded not with anger, but with pain. Tears flooded them and she whirled with a sob, running in the direction from which she'd come.

She hated him! *Hated* him! He was the enemy. He'd never wanted her here and now he was telling her that she didn't even attract him. How obvious it was now that he'd only been playing with her when he kissed her. He didn't want her, or need her, or even like her, and she was dying of love for him! She felt sick inside. She couldn't control her tears or the sobs that broke from her lips as she ran blindly into the small sweep of thick hay that he hadn't yet cut.

She heard his voice, yelling something, but she was too upset to hear him. Suddenly her foot hit something that gave and she stopped dead, whirling at a sound like frying bacon that came from the ground beside her.

The ugly flat, venomous head reared as the tail that shot up from the coil rattled its deadly warning. A rattler—five feet long at least—and she'd stepped on it! Its head drew back ominiously and she was frozen with fear, too confused to act. If she moved it would strike. If she didn't move it would strike. She could already feel the pain in her leg where the fangs would penetrate….

She was vaguely aware of a drumming sound like running, heavy footsteps. Through her tears she saw the sudden flash of something metallic go past her. The snake and its head abruptly parted company, and then long, powerful arms were around her, under her, lifting her to a sweat-glistening hard chest that was under her cheek.

"God!"

Cag's arms contracted. He was hurting her and she didn't care. Her arms tightened around his neck and she sobbed convulsively. He curled her against him in an ardent fever of need, feeling her soft breasts press hard into his bare, sweaty, hair-roughened chest as his face burrowed into her throat. She thought he trembled, but surely she imagined it. The terror came full force now that the threat was over, and she gave way to her misery.

They clung to each other in the hot sunlight with the sultry breeze wafting around them, oblivious to the man running toward them. Tess felt the warm, hard muscles in his back strain as she touched them, felt Cag's breath in her ear, against her hair. His cheek drew across hers and her nails dug into him. His indrawn breath was audible. His arms contracted again, and this time it wasn't comfort, it was a deep, dragging hunger that found an immediate response in her.

His face moved against hers jerkily, dragging down from her cheek, so that his lower lip slowly, achingly, began to draw itself right across her soft, parted mouth. Her breath drew in sharply at the exquisite feel of it. She wanted his lips on hers, the way they had been that spring day by the stream. She wanted to kiss him until her young body stopped aching.

He hesitated. His hand was resting at the edge of her breast and even as the embrace became hungry, she stopped breathing altogether as she felt his hard lips suddenly part and search for hers, felt the caressing pressure of those lean fingers begin to move up....

On the edge of the abyss, a barely glimpsed movement in the distance brought Cag's dark head up and he saw Leo running toward them. He was almost trembling with the need to take Tess's soft mouth, but he forced himself to breathe normally. All the hot emotion slowly drained out of his face, and he stared at his young brother as if he didn't recognize him for the first few seconds.

"What was it, a rattler?" Leo asked, panting for breath as he came up beside them.

Cag nodded his head toward the snake. It lay in two pieces, one writhing like mad in the hot sun. Between the two pieces was the big hunting knife that Cag always carried when he was working alone in the fields.

"Whew!" Leo whistled, shaking his head. "Pretty accurate, for a man who was running when he threw it. I saw you from the south field," he added.

"I've killed a few snakes in my time," Cag replied, and averted his eyes before Leo could ask if any of them had had two legs. "Here," he murmured to Tess, his voice unconsciously tender. "Are you all right?"

She sniffed and wiped her red eyes and nodded. She was embarrassed, because at the last, it hadn't been comfort that had brought them so close together. It was staggering after the things he said, the harshness of his manner before she'd stepped on the snake.

Cag put her down gingerly and moved back, but his turbulent eyes never left her.

"It didn't strike you?" he asked belatedly, and went on one knee to search over her legs.

"No," she faltered. The feel of those hard fingers on her skin made her weak. "No, I'm fine." She was looking down at him with eyes full of emotion. He was beautiful, she thought dazedly, and when he started to stand up again, her eyes lingered helplessly on that broad, sexy chest with its fine covering of hair. Her hand had touched it just as he put her down, and her fingers still tingled.

"Heavens, Tess!" Leo breathed, taking off his hat to

wipe the sweat from his brow. "You don't run across a hayfield like that, without looking where you're going! When we cut hay, we always find half a dozen of the damned things!"

"It's not her fault," Cag said in a surprisingly calm voice. "I upset her."

She didn't look at Cag. She couldn't. She turned to Leo with a wan smile. "Could you walk me back, just to the track that leads up to the house?" she asked. "I'm a little shaky."

"Sure," he said gently. "I'll carry you, if you like."

"No, I can walk." She turned away. With her back to Cag she added carefully, "Thanks for what you did. I've never seen anybody use a knife like that. It would have had me just a second later."

Cag didn't say anything. He turned away and retrieved his knife, wiping it on his jeans before he stuck it back into the sheath on his belt. He stalked back toward the tractor. He never looked back.

"What did he do to upset you?" Leo asked when they were out of earshot.

"The usual things," she said with resignation in her voice. "I can't imagine why he doesn't fire me," she added. "First he said I could go in the spring, but we got too busy, then he said I could go in the summer. But here it is, and I'm still here."

He didn't mention that he had his own suspicions about that. Cag was in deep, and quite obviously fighting a defensive battle where Tess was concerned. But he'd seen the look on Cag's face when he was holding her, and dislike was not what it looked like to him.

"Did you see him throw the knife?" she asked, still

awed by the skill of it. "Dad used to have a throwing knife and he could never quite get the hang of hitting the target. Neither could I. It's a lot harder than it looks. He did it running."

"He's a combat veteran," he said. "He's still in the reserves. Nothing about Cag surprises us anymore."

She glanced at him with twinkling eyes. "Did you really hit Turkey Sanders to keep Cag from doing it?"

"Dorie told you!" He chuckled.

"Yes. She said you don't let Cag get into fights."

"We don't dare. He doesn't lose his temper much, but when he does, it's best to get out of the line of fire."

"Yes, I know," she said uneasily, still remembering the birthday cake.

He glanced at her. "You've had a hard time."

"With him?" She shrugged. "He's not so bad. Not as bad as he was around Christmas," she added. "I guess I'm getting used to sarcasm and insults. They bounce off these days."

He made a rough sound under his breath. "Maybe he'll calm down eventually."

"It doesn't matter. I like my job. It pays well."

He laughed, sliding a friendly arm around her shoulders as they walked. "At least there are compensations."

Neither of them saw a pair of black eyes across the field glaring after them hotly. Cag didn't like that arm around Tess, not one bit. He was going to have something to say to Leo about it later.

Blissfully unaware, Leo stopped at the trail that led back to the house. "Okay now?" he asked Tess.

"Yes, thanks."

He studied her quietly. "It may get worse before it gets better, especially now," he said with some concern.

"What do you mean?"

"Never you mind," he replied, and his eyes held a secret amusement.

That evening, after the brothers cleaned up and had supper, Cag motioned Leo into the study and closed the door.

"Something wrong?" Leo asked, puzzled by his brother's taciturn silence since the afternoon.

Cag perched himself on the edge of his desk and stared, unblinking, at the younger man.

"Something," he agreed. Now that he was facing the subject, he didn't want to talk about it. He looked as disturbed as he felt.

"It's Tess, isn't it?" Leo asked quietly.

"She's twenty-two," Cag said evenly, staring hard at his brother. "And green as spring hay. Don't hit on her."

It was the last thing Leo expected the older man to say. "Don't *what?*" he asked, just to make sure he wasn't hearing things.

Cag looked mildly uncomfortable. "You had your arm around her on the way out of the field."

Leo's dark eyes twinkled. "Yes, I did, didn't I?" He pursed his lips and glanced at his brother with pure calculation. "She's a soft little thing, like a kitten."

Cag's face hardened and his eyes became dangerous. "She's off limits. Got that?"

Leo lifted both eyebrows. "Why?"

"Because she's a virgin," Cag said through his teeth. "And she works for us."

"I'm glad you remembered those things this afternoon," Leo returned. "But it's a shame you'd forgotten all about them until you saw me coming toward you.

Or are you going to try and convince me that you weren't about to kiss the breath out of her?"

Cag's teeth ground together. "I was comforting her!"

"Is *that* what you call it?" came the wry response. "Son of a gun. I'm glad I have you to tell me these things."

"I wasn't hitting on her!"

Leo held up both hands. "Of course not!"

"If she's too young for you, she's damned sure too young for me."

"Was I arguing?"

Cag unruffled a little. "Anyway, she wants to go to school and study horticulture in the fall. She may not want to stay on here, once she gets a taste of younger men."

Why, he really believed that, Leo thought, his attention diverted. Didn't he see the way Tess looked at him, the way she acted around him lately? Or was he trying not to see it?

"She won't have to wait for that to happen," Leo murmured. "We hired a new assistant sales manager last week, remember? Sandy Gaines?"

Cag scowled. "The skinny blond fellow?"

"Skinny, sure, but he seems to have plenty of charm when it comes to our Tess. He brought her a teddy bear from his last trip to St. Louis, and he keeps asking her out. So far she won't go."

Cag didn't want to think about Tess with another man, especially the new salesman. "She could do worse, I guess," he said despite his misgivings.

"You might ask her out yourself," Leo suggested carelessly.

Cag's dark eyes held a world of cynicism. "I'm thirty-eight and she works for me."

Leo only smiled.

Cag turned away to the fireplace and stared down at the gas logs with resignation. "Does it show?" he asked after a minute.

That he cared for her, he meant. Leo smiled affectionately. "Only to someone who knows you pretty well. She doesn't. You won't let her close enough," Leo added.

Broad shoulders rose and fell. His eyes lifted to the huge painting of a running herd of horses tearing across a stormy plain. A great-uncle had painted it. Its wildness appealed to the brothers.

"She's grass green," Cag said quietly. "Anybody could turn her head right now. But it wouldn't last. She's too immature for anything…serious." He turned and met his brother's curious eyes. "The thing is," he said curtly, "that I can't keep my head if I touch her."

"So you keep her carefully at a distance to avoid complications."

Cag hesitated. Then he nodded. He stuffed his hands into the pockets of his jeans and paced. "I don't know what else to do. Maybe if we get her into school this fall, it will help. I was thinking we might even get her a job somewhere else."

"I noticed," Leo said dryly. "And then you tell her to wait one more season. She's waited two already."

Cag's black eyes cut into him. "I haven't been serious about a woman since I was sent to the Middle East," he said through his teeth. "I've been pretty bitter. I haven't wanted my heart twisted out of my chest again. Then, she came along." He nodded in the general direction of the kitchen. "With her curly red hair and big blue eyes and that pert little boyish figure." He shook his head as if to clear the image from it. "Damn it, I ache just looking at her!" He whirled. "I've got to get her out of here before I do something about it!"

Leo studied his hand. "Are you sure you don't want to do something about it?" he asked softly. "Because she wants you to. She was shaking when you put her down."

Cag glared at him. "The snake scared her."

"*You* scared her," came the wry response. "Have you forgotten how to tell when a woman's aroused?"

"No, I haven't forgotten," he replied grimly. "And that's why she's got to go. Right now."

"Just hold on. There's no need to go rushing into anything," Leo counseled.

"Oh, for God's sake, it's just a matter of time, don't you see?" Cag groaned. "You can't hold back an avalanche!"

"Like that, is it?"

"Worse." Cag lowered his head with a hard sigh. "Never like this. Never."

Leo, who'd never felt what passed for love in the world, stared at his brother with compassion but no real understanding of what he was going through.

"She fits in around here," Leo murmured.

"Sure she does. But I'm not going to marry her!"

Leo's eyebrows lifted. "Why not? Don't you want kids?"

"Corrigan's got one."

"Kids of your own," Leo persisted with a grin. "Little boys with big feet and curly red hair."

Cag lifted a paperweight from the desk and tossed it deliberately in one hand.

Leo held up both hands in a defensive gesture. "Don't throw it. I'm reformed. I won't say another word."

The paperweight was replaced on the desk. "Like I said before, I'm too old for her. After all the other considerations have been taken into account, that one remains. Sixteen years is too much."

"Do you know Ted Regan?"

Cag scowled. "Sure. Why?"

"Do you know how much older he is than Coreen?"

Cag swallowed. "Theirs is a different relationship."

"Calhoun Ballenger and Abby?"

Cag glared at him.

"Evan and Anna Tremayne?"

The glare became a black scowl.

Leo shrugged. "Dig your own grave, then. You should hear Ted groan about the wasted years he spent keeping Coreen at bay. They've got a child of their own now and they're talking about another one in the near future. Silver hair and all, Ted's the happiest fellow I know. Coreen keeps him young."

"I'll bet people talked."

"Of course people talked. But they didn't care."

That grin was irritating. Cag turned away from him. He didn't dare think about kids with curly red hair. He was already in over his head and having enough trouble trying to breathe.

"One day, a young man will come along and sweep her off her feet."

"You've already done that, several times," Leo said pointedly. "Carrying her off to the store to buy new clothes, and just today, out of the path of a rattler."

"She doesn't weigh as much as a good sack of potatoes."

"She needs feeding up. She's all nerves lately. Especially when you're around."

Cag's big hands clenched in his pockets. "I want to move the heifers into the west pasture tomorrow. What do you think?"

"I think it's a week too soon."

The broad shoulders shrugged. "Then we'll wait one more week. How about the pastures on the bottoms?"

"We haven't had rain, but we will. If they flood, we'll have every cowboy on the place out pulling cows out of mud." His eyes narrowed. "You know all that better than I do."

"I'm changing the subject."

Leo threw up his hands. "All right. Don't listen to me. But Sandy Gaines means business. He's flirting with her, hard. He's young and personable and educated, and he wears nice suits and drives a red Corvette."

Cag glared at him. "She can see through clothes and a car, even a nice car."

"She's had digs and sarcasm and insults from you," Leo said and he was serious. "A man who tells her she's pretty and treats her gently might walk up on her blind side. She's warming to him a little. I don't like it. I've heard things about him."

"What sort of things?" Cag asked without wanting to.

"That he's fine until he gets his hands on a bottle of liquor, and then he's every woman's worst nightmare. You and I both know the type. We don't want our Tess getting into a situation she can't handle."

"She wouldn't tolerate that sort of behavior from a man," he said stiffly.

"Of course not, but she barely weighs a hundred pounds sopping wet! Or have you forgotten that she couldn't even get away from Herman, and he only outweighs her by ten pounds? Gaines is almost your size!"

Cag's teeth clenched. "She won't go out with him," he said doggedly. "She's got better sense."

* * *

That impression only lasted two more days. Sandy Gaines, a dark-haired, blue-eyed charmer, came by to discuss a new advertising campaign with the brothers and waylaid Tess in the hall. He asked her to a dance at the Jacobsville dance hall that Friday night and she, frustrated and hurt by Cag's sarcasm and coldness, accepted without hesitation.

Chapter Six

Sandy picked her up early for the dance in his low-slung used red Corvette. Cag was nearby and he watched them with cold eyes, so eaten up with jealousy that he could hardly bear it. She was wearing their dress, to top it all, the blue dress he'd helped her pick out when he'd taken her shopping. How could she wear it for that city dude?

"Get her home by midnight," he told Sandy, and he didn't smile.

"Sure thing, Mr. Hart!"

Sandy put Tess into the car quickly and drove off. Tess didn't even look at Cag. She was uncomfortably aware of the dress she had on, and why Cag glared at her. But he didn't want to take her anywhere, after all, so why should he object to her going out on a date? He didn't even like her!

"What's he, your dad?" Sandy drawled, driving far too fast.

"They all look out for me," she said stiffly.

Sandy laughed cynically. "Yeah? Well, he acts like you're his private stock." He glanced at her. "Are you?"

"Not at all," she replied with deliberate carelessness.

"Good." He reached for her hand and pressed it. "We're going to have a nice time. I've looked forward to this all week. You're a pretty little thing."

She smiled. "Thanks."

"Now you just enjoy yourself and don't worry about heavy-handed surrogate parents, okay?"

"Okay."

But it didn't work out that way. The first two dances were fun, and she enjoyed the music. But very quickly, Sandy found his way to the bar. After his second whiskey sour, he became another man. He held her too closely and his hands wandered. When he tried to kiss her, she struggled.

"Oh, no, you don't," he muttered when she tried to sidestep him. He caught her hand and pulled her out of the big structure by a side door. Seconds later, he pushed her roughly up against the wall in the dim light.

Before she could get a hand up, he was kissing her—horrible wet, invasive kisses that made her gag. She tasted the whiskey on his breath and it sickened her even further. His hands grasped her small breasts roughly, hurting, twisting. She cried out and fought him, trying to get away, but his hips levered down over hers with an obscene motion as he laughed, enjoying her struggles as she tried valiantly to kick him.

It was like that other time, when she was sixteen and she'd been at the mercy of another lecherous man. The memories further weakened her, made her sick. She tried to get her knee up, but she only gave him an opening that brought them even more intimately together and frightened her further. She was beating at his chest, raging at him, and his hand was in the neckline of her dress, popping buttons off in his drunken haste, when she felt the pressure against her body suddenly lessen.

There were muffled curses that stopped when Sandy was suddenly pushed up against the wall himself with one arm behind him and a mercilessly efficient hand at his neck, the thumb hard under his ear. Cag looked violent as Tess had rarely seen him. The hold was more than dangerous, it was professional. She didn't have the slightest doubt that he could drop the other man instantly if it became necessary.

"Move, and I'll break your neck," Cag said in a voice like hot steel. His black eyes cut to Tess and took in her disheveled clothing, her torn bodice. He jerked his head toward the ranch pickup that was parked just at the edge of the grass. "It's unlocked. Go and get inside."

She hesitated, sick and wobbly and afraid.

"Go on," Cag said softly.

She turned. She might have pleaded for Sandy, except that she didn't think he deserved having her plead for him. He might have…God only knew what he might have done if Cag hadn't shown up! She resisted the urge to kick him while Cag had him powerless, and she wobbled off toward the truck.

She was aware of dull thuds behind her, but she didn't turn. She went to the truck, climbed in and sat shivering until a cold, taciturn Cag joined her.

Before he got into the cab, he pulled off the denim shirt he was wearing over a black T-shirt and put it over her shoulders the wrong way. He didn't attempt to touch her, probably aware that she was sick enough of being touched at the moment.

"Get into that," he said as he fastened his seat belt, "and fasten your belt."

He reached for the ignition and she noticed that his knuckles were bleeding. As she struggled into the shoulder harness she glanced toward the barn and saw Sandy leaning against the wall, looking very weak.

"I couldn't make him stop," she said in a thin voice. "I didn't expect him to…to get drunk. He seemed so nice. I never go out with big men usually—" Her voice broke. "Damn him! Oh, damn him! I never dreamed he'd be like *that!* He seemed like such a nice man!"

He glanced toward her with a face like black thunder, but he didn't speak. He put the truck in gear and drove her home.

The others were out for the evening. They were alone in the house. She started to go down the hall toward her room, but he turned her into the study and closed the door.

He seated her on the big black antique leather divan that graced the corner near the picture window and went to pour brandy into a snifter.

He came back and sat beside her, easing her cold, trembling hands around the bowl and offering it at her swollen lips. It stung and she hesitated, but he tilted it up again.

She let out a single sob and quickly controlled herself. "Sorry," she said.

"Why did you go out with him?"

"He flattered me," she said with pure self-disgust. "He was sweet to me and he seemed sort of boyish. I thought…I thought he'd be a perfect gentleman, the sort of man I'd never have to fight off. But he was different when we were alone. And then he started drinking."

"You're grass green," he muttered. "You can't size up men even now, can you?"

"I haven't dated much."

"I noticed."

She glanced up at his set features and then down into the brandy.

"Why haven't you?" he persisted.

She tried not to notice how sexy he looked in that black T-shirt that clung to every muscle he had. He was big, lean, all powerful muscle and bristling vitality. It made her weak to look at him, and she averted her eyes.

"My mother came to see us one day, when I was sixteen," she said uneasily. "She wanted to see how much I'd grown up, she said." She shifted. "She brought her latest lover. He was a playboy with lots of money and apparently he saw that it irritated her when he paid me some attention, so he put on the charm and kept it up all day. After supper, she was miffed enough to take my dad off into another room. Dad was crazy about her, even then." She swallowed. "It made her lover furious and vengeful. He closed the door and before I knew what was happening, he locked it and threw me down onto the sofa. He tore my clothes and touched me…." She closed her eyes at the horrible memory. "It was like tonight, only worse. He was a big man and strong. I couldn't get away, no matter how hard I fought, and in the end I just screamed. My father broke in the door to get to him. I'll never forget what he said to that man, and my mother, before he threw them off the place. I never saw her again. Or wanted to."

Cag let out the breath he'd been holding. So many things made sense now. He searched her wan little face with feelings of possession. She'd had so much pain and fear from men. She probably had no idea that tenderness even existed.

"You're tied up in bad memories, aren't you, little one?" he asked quietly. "Maybe they need to be replaced with better ones."

"Do they?" Her voice was sad, resigned. She finished the brandy and Cag put the snifter on the table.

She started to get up, only to find him blocking her way. He eased her back down onto the wide divan and slid down alongside her.

She gasped, wondering if she'd gotten out of the frying pan only to fall into the fire. She frantically put her hands against his broad chest and opened her mouth to protest, but his fingers touched it lightly as he laid beside her and arched over her prone body resting his formidable weight on his forearm.

"There's nothing to be afraid of, Tess," he said quietly. "Whatever disagreements we've had, you know that I'd never hurt you physically. Especially after the ordeal you've just been through."

She knew, but she was still nervous of him. He was even more powerfully built than Sandy, and in this way, in an intimate way, he was also an unknown quantity.

While she was thinking, worrying, he bent and she felt the warm threat of his big body as his mouth drew softly over her eyes, closing the lids. It moved to her temples, her eyebrows. He kissed her closed eyes, his tongue lightly skimming the lashes. She jerked, and his lean hand eased under her nape, soothing her, calming her.

She had little experience, but she wasn't so naive that she couldn't recognize his. Every touch, every caress, was expert. He eased down so slowly that she only realized how close he really was when she moved and felt his warm, hard chest move with her. By then, she was a prisoner of her own sensual curiosity, sedated by the exquisite pleasure his mouth was giving her as it explored her face.

By the time he reached her lips, the feel and smell of him were already familiar. When his hard mouth eased her lips apart and moved into them, she felt the increased pressure of his chest against her breasts, and she stiffened with real fear.

He lifted away immediately, but only a breath. His black eyes searched her blue ones slowly.

"You still don't know me like this," he murmured, as if he were talking to himself as he studied her flushed face, understanding the fear he read in it. "You're afraid, aren't you?"

She swallowed. Her mouth felt dry as she looked at him. "I think I am," she whispered.

He smiled lazily and traced her lips with a lean forefinger. "Will you relax if I promise to go so far and stop?" he whispered.

"So…far?" she asked in a hushed tone, searching his black eyes curiously.

He nodded. He teased her lips apart and touched the inside of her lower lip with the tip of his finger. "We'll make a little love," he whispered as he bent. "And then you'll go to bed. Your own, not mine," he added with dry mischief.

Her fingers clenched and unclenched on the soft fabric of his undershirt, like a kitten kneading a new place to lay. She could hear her own breath sighing out against his mouth as it came closer.

"You don't like me," she breathed.

His thumb rubbed quite roughly over her mouth. "Are you sure? You must know that I want you!" he said, and it came out almost as a growl. "Taunting you was the only way I knew to keep you at arm's length, to protect you. I was a fool! I'm too old for you, but at least I'm not like that damned idiot who took you out tonight!"

Nothing got into her sluggish brain except those first three feverish words. "You want me?" she whispered as if it was some dark secret. She looked up at him with wonder and saw the muted ferocity in his eyes.

His hand was on her waist now and it contracted until it all but bruised. "Yes, Tess. Is it shocking to hear me say it?" His gaze fell to her mouth and lower, to the two little peaks that formed suddenly against the torn bodice of her dress and were revealed even under the thick fabric of his concealing shirt. "You want me, too," he whispered, bending. "I can see it...."

She wanted to ask how he knew, but the taste of his breath against her lips weakened her. She wanted him to kiss her. She wanted nothing more in the world. Her nails curled into his powerful chest and she felt him shiver again just as his mouth slowly, tenderly, eased down on her parted lips.

He drew back almost at once, only to ease down again as his lips toyed with hers, brushing lightly from the upper lip to the lower one, teasing and lifting away in a silence that smoldered. She felt the warm pressure increase from second to second, and the leisure of his movements reassured her. She began to relax. Her body lost its rigor and softened against him. After a few seconds of the lazy, tender pressure, her lips opened eagerly for him. She heard a soft intake of breath as he accepted the unspoken invitation with increasingly intimate movements of his hard mouth.

The spicy fragrance of his cologne surrounded her. She knew that as long as she lived, every time she smelled it, it would invoke these images of Cag lying against her on the leather divan in the muted light of the study. She would hear the soft creak of the leather as his body moved closer to her own; she would hear the faint ticking of the old-fashioned grandfather clock near the desk. Most of all, she would feel the hard warmth of Cag's mouth and the slow caress of his lean hands up and down her rib cage, making her body ache with new pleasures.

His head lifted and he looked at her again, this time reading with pinpoint accuracy the sultry look of her eyes, the faint pulse in her throat, the hard tips of her breasts rising against the slip that her half-open bodice revealed. Somewhere along the way, he'd unbuttoned his shirt that she was wearing and it was lying back away from her torn dress.

He traced the ragged edge of the fabric with returning anger. "Did it have to be this dress?" he groaned.

She winced. "You never seemed to look at me," she defended herself. "He wanted to take me out, and it was the nicest thing I had in my closet."

He sighed heavily. "Yes, I know." He smiled wryly. "I didn't think I could risk taking you out. But look what happened because I didn't."

"He was so drunk," she whispered hoarsely. "He would have forced me…"

"Not while there was a breath in my body," he returned intently.

"How did you know?" she asked suddenly.

He pushed a stray curl away from her cheek. "I don't know," he said, frowning as if it disturbed him. "Something I'd heard about Gaines bothered me. One of the men said that he was fine as long as there wasn't a bottle anywhere nearby, and another one mentioned a threatened lawsuit over a disastrous date. I remembered that you'd gone to the dance at the bar." He shrugged.

"Maybe it was a premonition. Thank God I paid attention to it."

"Yes." A thick strand of jet black hair had fallen onto his broad forehead. Hesitantly she reached up and pushed it back, her fingers lingering on its coolness.

He smiled because it was the first time that she'd voluntarily touched him.

She sought his eyes, sought permission. As if he understood the new feelings that were flaring up inside her, he drew her hand down to his chest and opened her fingers, pressing them there, firmly.

Her hand moved experimentally, pressing down and then curling into the thick hair she could feel under the soft fabric of his shirt.

Impatiently he lifted himself and peeled off the T-shirt, tossing it to the floor. He lay back down again beside her, curling his leg into hers as he guided her hand back to his chest.

She hesitated again. This was another step, an even bigger one.

"Even teenagers do this," he mused, smiling gently at her inhibitions. "It's perfectly permissible."

"Is it?" Her fingers touched him as if she expected them to be burned. But then they pressed into the thick pelt of hair and explored, fascinated by the size and breadth of his chest, the warmth and strength of it.

He arched with pure pleasure and laughed delightedly at the sensations she aroused. It had been a long time since a woman had touched him like that.

She smiled shyly, fascinated by his reaction. He seemed so stoic, so reserved, that this lack of inhibition was surprising.

"Men are like cats," he murmured. "We love to be stroked."

"Oh." She studied him as if he were an exhibit in a museum, curious about every single cell of his body.

"Feeling more secure now?" he asked softly. "More adventurous?"

"I'm not sure." She looked up at him, quizzically.

"Nothing heavy," he promised. His black eyes were softer than she'd ever seen them. "It's no news to me that you're a rank beginner."

"What are you…going to do?" she stammered, wide-eyed.

"Kiss you," he breathed, letting his gaze fall to her bare breasts.

"Th…there?" she gasped.

He touched her lightly, smiling at the expression on her taut face. "There," he whispered. He bent and drew his cheek softly over the bruised flesh, careful not to hurt her with the light pressure.

While she was trying to cope with so many new and shocking sensations, his mouth smoothed back over the soft, silky flesh and she felt it open. He tasted her flushed skin in a heated fever of need. Her hands curled up into his thick hair and she held him to her, whimpering softly with pleasure as she found herself drawing his face hungrily to where the flesh was very taut and sensitive.

"Here?" he whispered, hesitating.

"Oh…yes!" she choked.

His mouth opened obediently and he drew the hard nipple into it with a faint, soft suction that brought a sharp cry from her dry lips.

She thought she felt him tremble, and then he was

moving onto his back, breathing roughly as he carried her with him. He held her at his side, their legs intimately entangled, while he fought to get his breath back.

His skin was cool against her hot breasts where they were pressed together above the waist. Her cheek was against the hard muscle of his upper arm and she caught again that elusive spicy scent that clung to him.

Her hand eased onto the thick hair at his chest, but he caught it and held it a little roughly at her side.

"No," he whispered.

She didn't understand what she'd done wrong. A minute later, he got to his feet and bent to retrieve his undershirt. While he shrugged into it, she tugged up her bodice and tried to fasten it.

But when she would have gotten to her feet, he pressed her back down.

"Stay put," he said quietly. He turned and left the room.

She'd barely gotten her breathing calm when he was back, sitting down beside her with a cold can of beer in his hand.

He popped it open and took a sip before he pulled her up beside him and held it to her lips.

"I don't like beer," she murmured dazedly.

"I'm going to taste of it," he replied matter-of-factly. "If you swallow some, you won't find the taste so unpleasant when I kiss you."

Her heart jumped wildly.

He met her surprised expression with a smile. "Did you think we were finished?" he asked softly.

She blushed.

"I was getting too aroused," he murmured dryly. "And so were you. I'm not going to let it go that far."

She searched his hard face with open curiosity.

"What does it feel like to you, when you kiss me like that?" she asked quickly, before she lost her nerve.

"How does it feel when I do it?"

"I don't know. Shivery. Hot. I never felt anything like that before."

He took a sip of the beer and looked down at her hungrily. "Neither did I," he said tersely. His eyes seemed to possess her as they ran like caressing hands all over her. "Your breasts are freckled," he said with an intimate smile and chuckled when she blushed. He held her face up to his and kissed her nose. "I'm not going to rush out to the nearest bar and gossip about it," he whispered when he saw the faint apprehension in her wide eyes. "It's a lover's secret; a thing we don't share with other people. Like the scar on my belly."

She frowned slightly. He tugged down the waistband of his jeans and drew her hand against him where a long, thick scar was just visible above his belt.

"It runs down to my groin," he said solemnly. "Fortunately, it missed the more…vital areas. But it was touch and go for a few days and the scar is never going to go away."

Her fingers lingered there. "I'm sorry you were hurt."

He held her hand to him and smiled. "This is something I haven't shown to anyone else," he told her. "Except my brothers."

It made sense then. She looked up into his eyes. "A…lover's secret," she whispered, amazed that she could think of him like that, so easily.

He nodded. He wasn't smiling. "Like the freckles on your breasts, just around the nipples."

She felt her breath gathering speed, like an old-time steam engine. Her breasts felt tight, and not because of Sandy's rough handling. She frowned a little because it was uncomfortable and she still didn't quite understand it.

"We swell, both of us, when we're aroused," he said quietly, glancing at the small hand that had come up to rest a little gingerly against one taut nipple. "It's uncomfortable, isn't it?"

"Just…just a little." She felt like a child in a candy store, breathless with delight as she looked at him. "I liked…what you did," she whispered.

"So did I. Have a few sips of this and I'll do it again."

Her breath caught. She sipped and wrinkled her nose. He took two more huge swallows before he put the can on the table and came back to her.

He stretched out beside her and this time when he slid his leg in between both of hers, it wasn't shocking or frightening. It felt natural, right. His hands slid under her as he bent again to her mouth. Now the kisses weren't tentative and seeking. They were slow and insistent and arousing. They were passionate kisses, meant to drag a response from the most unwilling partner.

Tess found herself clinging to him as if she might drown, her nails biting into his nape, and every kiss was more intimate than the last, more demanding, more arousing, more complete.

When his powerful body eased completely down over hers, she didn't protest at all. Her arms slid around his waist, her legs parted immediately, and she melted into the leather under them, welcoming the hard crush of him, the sudden heat and swelling that betrayed his hunger.

"You can feel it, can't you?" he whispered intimately at her ear and moved a little, just to make sure she could.

"Cag…!"

"I want you so badly, Tess!" he whispered, and his mouth slid over her cheek and onto her lips. He bit at them with a new and staggering intimacy that set her body on fire. When his tongue eased into her mouth, she opened her lips to accept it. When he pressed her legs further apart so that he could settle intimately between them, she arched into him. When he groaned and his hands found her breasts, she gave everything that she was into his keeping. He never thought he could draw back in time. He shook convulsively with the effort. He dragged his hips away and turned, lying on his back with Tess settled close against his side while he fought his own need, and hers.

"Don't…move!" he stated when she turned closer to him.

She stilled at once, half-heard bits of advice from a parade of motherly women coming back to her and making sudden sense.

She could feel Cag's powerful body vibrating with the hunger the kisses had built in it. He was like corded wood, breathing harshly. It fascinated her that he'd wanted her that much, when she was a rank beginner. He certainly wasn't!

When she felt him begin to relax, she let out a sigh of relief. She hadn't known what to do or say. Men in that condition were a mystery to her.

She felt his hand in her curly hair, holding her cheek to his chest. Under it, she heard the heavy, hard beat of his heart, like a fast drum.

"I haven't touched a woman since my fiancée threw me over," he said in a harsh tone.

Years ago. He didn't say it, but Tess knew that was

what he was implying. She lifted her head and raised up, resting her hand on his shoulder to steady her as she searched his face. There was a hard flush along his high cheekbones, but his eyes were quiet, soft, full of mystery as they met hers.

"You want to know why I drew back."

She nodded.

He let go of her hair and touched her soft, swollen mouth with his. "You're a virgin."

He sounded so certain of it that she didn't bother to argue. It would have been pretty pointless at the moment, anyway.

"Oh. I see." She didn't, but it sounded mature.

He chuckled gently. "You don't know beans," he corrected. He moved suddenly, turning her over so that his body half covered hers and his eyes were inches from her own. His big hand caught her hip and curved it up into his intimately. The reaction of his body was fierce and immediate; and very stark. She flushed.

"I don't date anymore," he said, watching her mouth. "I don't have anything to do with women. This—" he moved her subtly against that part of him that was most obvious "—is delicious and heady and even a little shocking. I haven't felt it in a very long time."

Curiosity warred with embarrassment. "But I'm not experienced," she said.

He nodded. "And you think it should take an experienced woman to arouse me this much."

"Well, yes."

He bent and drew his lips over her open mouth in a shivery little caress that made her breath catch. "It happens every time I touch you," he whispered into her lips. "An experienced woman would have realized immediately why I was so hostile and antagonistic toward you. It's taken you months."

He covered her mouth with his, kissing her almost violently as his hand slid back inside her dress and played havoc with her self-control. But it only lasted seconds. He got up abruptly and pulled her up with him, holding her a few inches away from him with steely hands at her waist.

"You have to go to bed. Alone. Right now," he said emphatically.

Her breath came in soft spurts as she looked up at him with her heart in her eyes.

He actually groaned and pulled her close, into a bearish embrace. He stood holding her, shivering as they pressed together.

"Dear God," he whispered poignantly, and it sounded reverent, almost a plea for divine assistance. "Tess, do you know how old I am?" he groaned at her ear. "We're almost a generation apart!"

Her eyes were closed. She was dreaming. It had all been a dream, a sweet, sensuous dream that she never wanted to end.

"I can still feel your mouth on my breasts when I close my eyes," she whispered.

He made another rough sound and his arms tightened almost to pain. He didn't know how he was going to let her go.

"Baby," he whispered, "this is getting dangerous."

"You never called me 'baby' before," she murmured.

"I was never this close to being your lover before," he whispered gruffly. His head lifted and his black eyes glittered down into her pale blue ones. "Not like this, Tess," he said roughly. "Not in a fever, because you've had a bad experience."

"You made love to me," she said, still dazed by the realization of how much their turbulent relationship had changed in the space of a few minutes.

"You wanted me to," he returned.

"Oh, yes," she confessed softly. Her lips parted and she watched, fascinated at the expression on his face when he looked down at them.

She reached up to him on tiptoe, amazed that it took such a tiny little tug to bring his hard mouth crashing passionately down onto her parted lips. He actually lifted her off the floor in his ardor, groaning as the kiss went on endlessly.

She felt swollen all over when he eased her back down onto her feet.

"This won't do," he said unsteadily. He held her by the shoulders, firmly. "Are you listening?"

"I'm trying to," she agreed, searching his eyes as if they held the key to paradise. His hands contracted. "I want you, honey," he said curtly. "Want you badly enough to seduce you, do you understand?" His gaze fell to her waist and lingered there with the beginnings of shock. All at once, he was thinking with real hunger of little boys with curly red hair....

Chapter Seven

"Why are you looking at me like that?" Tess asked softly.

His hands contracted on her waist for an instant before he suddenly came to his senses and realized what he was thinking and how impossible it was. He closed his eyes and breathed slowly, until he got back the control he'd almost lost.

He put her away from him with an odd tenderness. "You're very young," he said. "I only meant to comfort you. Things just…got out of hand. I'm sorry."

She searched his eyes and knew that what they'd shared hadn't made a whit of difference to their turbulent relationship. He wanted her, all right, but there was guilt in his face. He thought she was too young for anything permanent. Or perhaps that was the excuse he had to use to conceal the real one—that he was afraid to get involved with a woman again because he'd been so badly hurt by one.

She dropped her gaze to his broad chest, watching its jerky rise and fall curiously. He wasn't unaffected by her. That was oddly comforting.

"Thanks for getting rid of the bad memory, anyway," she said in a subdued tone.

He hesitated before he spoke, choosing his words.

"Tess, it wasn't only that," he said softly. "But you have to realize how things are. I've been alone for a long time. I let you go to my head." He took a long, harsh breath. "I'm not a marrying man. Not anymore. But you're a marrying woman."

She ground her teeth together. Well, that was plain enough. She looked up at him, red-cheeked. "I didn't propose! And don't get your hopes up, because I won't. Ever. So there."

He cocked his head, and for an instant something twinkled deep in his eyes. "Never? I'm devastated."

The humor was unexpected and it eased the pain of the awkward situation a little. She peeked up at him. "You're very attractive," she continued, "but it takes more than looks to make a marriage. You can't cook and you don't know which end of a broom to use. Besides that, you throw cakes at people."

He couldn't deny that. His firm mouth, still swollen from the hot kisses they'd shared, tugged up at the corners. "I missed you by a mile. In fact," he reminded her, "you weren't even in the room when I threw it."

She held up a hand. "I'm sorry. It's too late for excuses. You're right off my list of marriage prospects. I hope you can stand the shock."

He chuckled softly. "So do I." She was still flushed, but she looked less tormented than she had. "Are you all right now?" he asked gently.

She nodded and then said, "Yes. Thank you," she added, her voice softer then she intended it to be.

He only smiled. "He won't be back, in case you're worried about that," he added. "I fired him on the spot."

She drew in a breath. "I can't say I'm sorry about that. He wasn't what he seemed."

"Most men aren't. And the next time you accept a date, I want to know first."

She stared at him. "I beg your pardon?"

"You heard me. You may not consider me good husband material," he murmured, "but I'm going to look out for your interests just the same." He studied her seriously for a moment. "If I can't seduce you, nobody else can, either."

"Well, talk about sour grapes!" she accused.

"Count on it," he agreed.

"And what if I want to be seduced?" she continued.

"Not this week," he returned dryly. "I'll have to look at my calendar."

"I didn't mean you!"

His black eyes slid up and down her body in the torn dress that she'd covered with his shirt. "You did earlier," he murmured with a tender smile. "And I wanted to."

She sighed. "So did I. But I won't propose, even if you beg."

He shrugged powerful shoulders. "My heart's broken."

She chuckled in spite of herself. "Sure it is."

She turned and reached for the doorknob.

"Tess."

She glanced back at him. "Yes?"

His face was solemn, no longer teasing. "They told you about her, didn't they?"

He meant his brothers had told her about his doomed engagement. She didn't pretend ignorance. "Yes, they did," she replied.

"It was a long time ago, but it took me years to get over it. She was young, too, and she thought I was just what she wanted. But the minute I was out of sight, she found somebody else."

"And you think I would, too, because I'm not mature enough to be serious," she guessed.

His broad chest rose and fell. "That's about the size of it. You're pretty green, honey. It might be nothing more concrete than a good case of repressed lust."

"If that's my excuse, what's yours?" she asked with pursed lips. "Abstinence?"

"That's my story and I'm sticking to it like glue."

She laughed softly. "Coward."

He lifted one eyebrow. "You can write a check on that. I've been burned and I've got the scars to prove it."

"And I'm too young to be in love with you."

His heart jerked in his chest. The thought of Tess being in love with him made his head spin, but he had to hold on to his common sense. "That's right." His gaze went homing to her soft mouth and he could taste it all over again. He folded his arms over his broad chest and looked at her openly, without amusement or mockery. "Years too young."

"Okay. Just checking." She opened the door. A crash of thunder rumbled into the silence that followed. Seconds later, the bushes outside his window scratched against the glass as the wind raged.

"Are you afraid of storms?" he asked.

She shook her head. "Are you?"

"I'll tell you tomorrow."

She looked puzzled.

"You've spent enough time around livestock to know that thunderstorms play hell with cattle from time to time. We'll have to go out and check on ours if this keeps up. You can lie in your nice, soft dry bed and think about all of us getting soaked to the skin."

She thought about how bad summer colds could be. "Wear a raincoat," she told him.

He smiled at that affectionate concern, and it was in his eyes this time, too. "Okay, boss."

She grinned. "That'll be the day."

He lifted an eyebrow. "You're big on songs these days," he murmured. "That was one of Buddy Holly's. Want me to sing it to you?"

She realized belatedly which song he was talking about, and she shook her head. "No, thanks. It would upset the neighbors' dogs."

He glowered at her. "I have a good voice."

"Sure you do, as long as you don't use it for singing," she agreed. "Good night, Callaghan. Thanks again for rescuing me."

"I can't let anything happen to the family biscuit chef," he said casually. "We'd all starve."

She let him get away with that. He might not believe in marriage, but he was different after their ardent interlude. He'd never picked at her, teased her, before. Come to think of it, she'd never teased him. She'd been too afraid. That was ancient history now. She gave him one last shy, smiling glance and went out the door.

He stood where she left him, his eyes narrowed, his body still singing with the pleasure she'd given him. She was too young. His mind knew it. If he could only convince the rest of him…

Surprisingly Tess slept that night, despite the storms that rippled by, one after another. The memory of Cag's tender passion had all but blotted out the bad memories Gaines had given her. If only Cag wanted her on a permanent basis. At least they'd gotten past the awkwardness that followed that physical explosion of pleasure. It would make things easier for both of them.

She made breakfast the following morning and there was nobody to eat it. One of the men, wet and bedraggled looking, came to the back door to explain why breakfast went untouched.

It seemed that the high winds combined with drenching rain had brought down some huge old oak trees, right through several fences. While she slept soundly, in the outer pastures, cattle had gotten loose and had to be rounded up again, and the broken fences had to be mended. Half the outfit was soaked and all but frozen from the effort. The brothers had dragged in about daylight and fallen asleep, too tired even for their beloved biscuits.

It was almost noon before they came wandering into the kitchen. Breakfast had gone to the ranch dogs and the chickens, but she had beef and potatoes in a thick stew—with biscuits—waiting.

Rey and Leo smiled at her. To her astonishment, Cag gave her an openly affectionate glance as he sat down at the head of the table and reached for the coffeepot.

"It amazes me how you always keep food hot," Leo remarked. "Thanks, Tess. We were dead on our feet when we finally got back this morning."

"It was a rough night, I gather," she murmured as she ferried butter and jam to the table.

Leo watched her curiously. "We heard that you had one of your own," he said, regretting the careless remark when he saw her flush. "I'm sorry we didn't get our hands on Gaines before he ran for the border," he added, and the familiar, funny man she'd come to know suddenly became someone else.

"That goes double for me," Rey added grimly.

"Well, he had plenty of attention without counting on either of you," Cag remarked pleasantly. "I understand that he left tire marks on his way out in the early hours of the morning. The sniveling little weasel," he added.

"Amazing, isn't it, that Gaines actually walked away under his own steam," Leo told Rey.

Rey nodded. "And here we've been wasting our time saving people from him—" he indicated Cag "—for years."

"People don't need saving from me," Cag offered. "I'm not a homicidal maniac. I can control my temper," he added.

Leo pursed his lips. "Say, Tess, did the chocolate icing stain ever come completely off the wall...?"

She was fumbling with a lid that wouldn't come off, flustered from the whole conversation and wishing she could sink through the floor.

"Here, give me that," Cag said softly.

She gave it to him. Their hands touched and they looked at each other for just a second too long, something the brothers picked up on immediately.

Cag opened the jar and put it on the table while she went to get spoons.

"At least he's stopped throwing cakes at people," Rey remarked.

Cag lifted the jar of apple butter and looked at his brother intently.

Rey held up a hand and grinned sheepishly as he fell to eating his stew.

"If it's all right, I thought I'd go ahead and apply to the local technical school," Tess said quickly, before she lost her nerve. "For fall classes in horticulture, you know."

"Sure," Leo said. "Go ahead."

Cag lifted his gaze to her slender body and remembered how sweet it had been to hold in the silence of the study. He let his gaze fall back to his plate. He couldn't deter her. She didn't belong to him. She did need an occupation, something that would support her. He didn't like the idea of her keeping house for anyone else. She was safe here; she might not be in some other household. And if she went as a commuter, she could still work for the brothers.

"I could...live in the dormitory, if you want," she continued doggedly.

That brought Cag's head up. "Live in the dormitory? What the hell for?" he exclaimed.

His surprise took some of the gloom out of her heart. She clasped her hands tight in front of her, against her new jeans. "Well, you only said I could stay until summer," she said reasonably. "It's summer now. You didn't say anything about staying until fall."

Cag looked hunted. "You won't find another job easily in the fall, with all the high school seniors out grabbing them," he said curtly. He glanced back at his plate. "Stay until winter."

She wondered why Rey and Leo were strangling on their coffee.

"Is it too strong?" she asked worriedly, nodding toward the cups.

"Just...right." Leo chocked, coughing. "I think I caught cold last night. Sorry. I need a tissue..."

"Me, too!" Rey exploded.

They almost knocked over their chairs in their rush to get out of the room. Muffled laughter floated back even after the door had been closed.

"Idiots," Cag muttered. He looked up at Tess, and something brushed against his heart, as softly as a butterfly. He could hardly breathe.

She looked at him with eyes that loved him, and hated the very feeling. He wanted her to go, she knew he did, but he kept putting it off because he was sorry for her. She was so tired of being pitied by him.

"I don't mind living in the dormitory at school, if you want me to leave here," she repeated softly.

He got up from his chair and moved toward her. His big, lean hands rested on her shoulders and he looked down from his great height with quiet, wondering eyes. She was already like part of him. She made him bubble inside, as if he'd had champagne. The touch of her, the taste of her, were suddenly all too familiar.

"How would you manage to support yourself, with no job?" he asked realistically.

"I could get something part-time, at the school."

"And who'll bake biscuits for us?" he asked softly. "And worry about us when we're tired? Who'll remember to set the alarm clocks and remind me to clean Herman's cage? Who'll fuss if I don't wear my raincoat?" he added affectionately.

She shrugged. His hands felt nice. She loved their warmth and strength, their tenderness.

He tilted her chin up and searched her quiet eyes. Fires kindled deep in his body and made him hungry. He couldn't afford to indulge what he was feeling. Especially not here, in the kitchen, where his brothers could walk in any minute.

But while he was thinking it, his rebellious hands slid up to frame her face and he bent, brushing his mouth tenderly over her soft lips.

"You shouldn't let me do this," he whispered.

"Oh, I'm not," she assured him softly. "I'm resisting you like crazy." She reached up to link her arms around his neck.

"Are you?" He smiled as he coaxed her lips under his and kissed her slowly.

She smiled against his mouth, lifting toward him. "Yes. I'm fighting like mad. Can't you tell?"

"I love the way you fight me…!"

The kiss became possessive, insistent, feverish, all in the space of seconds. He lifted her against him and groaned at the fierce passion she kindled in him so effortlessly.

Only the sound of booted feet heading their way broke them apart. He set her down gently and struggled to get back in his chair and breathe normally. He managed it, just.

Tess kept her back to the brothers until she could regain her own composure. But she didn't realize that her mouth was swollen and the softness in her eyes was an equally vivid giveaway.

Cag was cursing himself and circumstances under his breath for all he was worth. Having her here was going to be an unbearable temptation. Why hadn't he agreed to letting her live in at the school?

Because he ached for her, that was why. He was alive as he hadn't been in seven long years and the thought of going back into his shell was painful.

His black eyes settled on Tess and he wondered how he could ever have lived from day to day without looking at her at least once. He was getting a fixation on red curly hair and pale freckled skin. She was too young for him. He knew that, but he couldn't seem to keep his hands off her. He didn't know what he was going to do. If he didn't find something to occupy him, and quickly, he was going to end up seducing her. That would be the end of the world. The absolute end.

Tess borrowed one of the ranch trucks the next morning after breakfast and drove herself to the campus of the Jacobsville Vocational-Technical School. The admissions office was easy to find. She was given forms to fill out, a course schedule for the fall quarter, and advice on financial assistance. From there, she went to the financial office and filled out more forms. It took until lunch to finally finish, but she had a sense of accomplishment by the time she left the campus.

On her way back to the ranch, she stopped in at the local café and had coffee and a sandwich while she did some thinking about her situation.

Cag said he didn't want her to move out, but did he really mean it, or was he just sorry for her? He liked kissing her, but he didn't want to keep doing it. He seemed not to be able to stop. Maybe, she thought, that was the whole problem. She made him forget all the reasons why he shouldn't get involved with her, every time he came close.

If she was gone, of course, he wouldn't get close enough to have his scruples damaged. But he'd said that he didn't want her to leave. It was a puzzle she couldn't seem to solve.

The sandwich tasted flat, although it was roast beef, one of her favorites. She put it down and stared at it without seeing.

"Thinking of giving it its freedom, huh?" Leo asked with a grin, and sat down across from her. He took off his hat, laid it on the chair beside him and gestured toward the sandwich. "I hate to tell you this, but there's absolutely no way known to science that a roast beef sandwich can be rejuvenated." He leaned forward conspiratorially. "Take it from a beef expert."

She chuckled despite her sadness. "Oh, Leo, you're just impossible," she choked.

"It runs in the family." He held up a hand and when the waitress came to see what he wanted, he ordered coffee.

"No lunch?" Tess asked.

He shook his head. "No time. I'm due at the Brewsters's in forty-five minutes for a business meeting over lunch. Rubber chicken and overdone potatoes, like last time," he muttered. He glanced at her. "I wish you were cooking for it instead of Brewster's daughter. She's pretty as a picture and I hear tell she had operatic aspirations, but she couldn't make canned soup taste good."

He sounded so disgusted that Tess smiled in spite of herself. "Are you going by yourself, or are the brothers going, too?"

"Just Cag and me. Rey escaped on a morning flight to Tulsa to close a land deal up there."

She lowered her eyes to the half-finished sandwich. "Does Cag like her...Miss Brewster?"

He hesitated. "Cag doesn't like women, period. I thought you knew."

"You said she was pretty."

"Like half a dozen other women who have fathers in the cattle business," he agreed. "Some of them can even cook. But as you know Cag gave up on women when he was thrown over for a younger man. Hell, the guy was only three years younger than him, at that. She used his age as an excuse. It wasn't, really. She just didn't want him. The other guy had money, too, and she did want him."

"I see."

He sipped coffee and pursed his lips thoughtfully. "I've told you before how Cag reacts to women most of the time," he reminded her. "He runs." He smiled. "Of course, he's been doing his best to run from you since last Christmas."

She looked at him with her heart in her eyes. "He has?" she asked.

"Sure! He wants you to go off to school so you'll remove temptation from his path. But he also wants you to stay at the ranch while you go to school, in case you run into any handsome eligible bachelors there. I think he plans to save you from them, if you do."

She was confused and it showed.

"He said," he related, "that you shouldn't be exposed to potential seducers without us to protect you."

She didn't know whether to laugh or cry.

He held up a hand when she started to speak. "He thinks you should commute."

"But he doesn't want me at the ranch, don't you see?" she asked miserably, running a hand through her short, curly hair. "He keeps leaving to get away from me!"

"Why would he leave if you weren't getting to him?" he asked reasonably.

"It's still a rotten way to live," she said pointedly. "Maybe if I go to school I'll meet somebody who'll think I'm old enough for them."

"Oh, that's just sour grapes," he murmured dryly.

"You have no idea *how* sour," she replied. "I give up. I can't spend the rest of my life hoping that he'll change his mind about me. He's had almost a year, and he hasn't changed a thing."

"He stopped throwing cakes," he said.

"Because I stopped baking them!"

He checked his watch and grimaced. "I'd love to stay here and talk recipes with you, but I'm late." He got up and smiled at her. "Don't brood, okay? I have a feeling that things are going to work out just fine."

That wasn't what she thought, but he was gone before she could put the thought into words.

Chapter Eight

It was inevitable that Leo would bring up the matter of the Brewster girl's cooking the next day. Breakfast was too much of a rush, and they didn't get to come home for lunch. But when two of the three brothers and Tess sat down to supper, Leo let it fly with both barrels.

"That Janie Brewster isn't too bad-looking, is she?" Leo murmured between bites of perfectly cooked barbecued chicken. "Of course, she can ruin a chicken."

Cag glanced at him quickly, as if the remark puzzled him. Then he glanced at Tess's studiously down bent head and understood immediately what Leo was trying to do.

He took a forkful of chicken and ate it before he replied, "She'll never make a cook. Or even much of a wife," he added deliberately. "She knows everything."

"She does have a university degree."

"In psychology," Cag reminded him. "I got psychoanalyzed over every bite of food." He glanced at Tess. "It seems that I have repressed feelings of inadequacy because I keep a giant reptile," he related with a twinkle in his black eyes.

Tess's own eyes widened. "You do?"

He nodded. "And I won't eat carrots because I have some deep-seated need to defy my mother."

She put a napkin to her mouth, trying to ward off laughter.

"You forgot the remark she made about the asparagus," Leo prompted.

Cag looked uncomfortable. "We can forget that one."

"But it's the best one!" Leo turned to Tess. "She said that he won't eat asparagus because of associations with impo—"

"Shut up!" Cag roared.

Leo, who never meant to repeat the blatant sexual remark, only grinned. "Okay."

Tess guessed, quite correctly, that the word Cag had cut off was "impotence." And she was in a perfect position to tell Leo that it certainly didn't apply to his older brother, but she wouldn't have dared.

As it was, her eyes met Cag's across the table, and she flushed at the absolutely wicked glitter in those black eyes, and almost upset her coffee.

Leo, watching the byplay, was affectionately amused at the two of them trying so hard not to react. There was a sort of intimate merriment between them, despite Cag's attempts to ward off intimacy. Apparently he hadn't been wholly successful.

"I've got a week's worth of paperwork to get through," Cag said after a minute, getting up.

"But I made dessert," Tess said.

He turned, surprised. "I don't eat sweets. You know that."

She smiled secretively. "You'll like this one. It isn't really a conventional dessert."

He pushed in his chair. "Okay," he said. "But you'll have to bring it to me in the office. How about some coffee, too?"

"Sure."

Leo put down his napkin. "Well, you do the hard stuff. I'm going down to Shea's Bar to see if I can find Billy Telford. He promised me faithfully that he was going to give me a price on that Salers bull we're after. He's holding us up hoping that he can get more from the Tremaynes."

"The Tremaynes don't run Salers cattle," Cag said, frowning.

"Yes, but that's because Billy's only just been deluging them with facts on the advantages of diversification." He shrugged. "I don't think they'll buy it, but Billy does. I'm going to see if I can't get him dru…I mean," he amended immediately, "get him to give me a price."

"Don't you dare," Cag warned. "I'm not bailing you out again. I mean it."

"You drink from time to time," Leo said indignantly.

"With good reason, and I'm quiet about it. You aren't. None of us have forgotten the last time you cut loose in Jacobsville."

"I'd just gotten my degree," Leo said curtly. "It was a great reason to celebrate."

"To celebrate, yes. Not to wreck the bar. And several customers."

"As I recall, Corrigan and Rey helped."

"You bad boys," Tess murmured under her breath.

Cag glanced at her. "I never drink to excess anymore."

"Neither do I. And I didn't say that I was going to get drunk," Leo persisted. "I said I was going to get *Billy* drunk. He's much more malleable when he's not sober."

Cag shook a finger at him. "Nothing he signs inebriated will be legal. You remember that."

Leo threw up both hands. "For heaven's sake!"

"We can do without that bull."

"We can't! He's a grand champion," Leo said with pure, naked hunger in his tone. "I never saw such a beautiful animal. He's lean and healthy and glossy, like silk. He's a sire worthy of a foundation herd. I want him!"

Cag exchanged an amused glance with Tess. "It's love, I reckon," he drawled.

"With all due respect to women," Leo sighed, "there is nothing in the world more beautiful than a pedigree bull in his prime."

"No wonder you aren't married, you pervert," Cag said.

Leo glared at him. "I don't want to marry the bull, I just want to own him! Listen, your breeding program is standing still. I have ideas. Good ideas. But I need that bull." He slammed his hat down on his head. "And one way or another, Billy's going to sell him to me!"

He turned and strode out the door, looking formidable and determined.

"Is it really that good a bull?" Tess asked.

Cag chuckled. "I suppose it is." He shook his head. "But I think Leo has ulterior motives."

"Such as?"

"Never you mind." He studied her warmly for a minute, approving of her chambray shirt and jeans. She always looked neat and feminine, even if she didn't go in for seductive dresses and tight-fitting clothes. "Bring your mysterious dessert on into the office when you get it ready. Don't forget the coffee."

"Not me, boss," she replied with a pert smile.

She put the finishing touches on the elegant dessert and placed it on a tray with the cup of coffee Cag liked after supper. She carried the whole caboodle into the study, where he was hunched over his desk with a pencil in one hand and his head in the other, going over what looked like reams of figure-studded pages of paper.

He got up when she entered and took the tray from her, placing it on the very edge of the desk. He scowled.

"What is it?" he asked, nodding toward a saucer of what looked like white foam rubber with whipped cream on top.

"It's a miniature Pavlova," she explained. "It's a hard meringue with a soft center, filled with fresh fruit and whipped cream. It takes a long time to make, but it's pretty good. At least, I think it is."

He picked up the dessert fork she'd provided and drew it down through the dessert. It made a faint crunching sound. Intrigued, he lifted a forkful of the frothy-looking substance to his mouth and tasted it. It melted on his tongue.

His face softened. "Why, this is good," he said, surprised.

"I thought you might like it," she said, beaming. "It isn't really a sweet dessert. It's like eating a cloud."

He chuckled. "That's a pretty good description." He sat down in the big leather swivel chair behind his desk with the saucer in his hand. But he didn't start eating again.

He lifted his chin. "Come here."

"Who, me?" she asked.

"Yes, you."

She edged closer. "You said that I mustn't let you do things to me."

"Did I say that?" he asked in mock surprise.

"Yes, you did."

He held out the arm that wasn't holding the

saucer. "Well, ignore me. I'm sure I was out of my mind at the time."

She chuckled softly, moving to the chair. He pulled her down onto his lap so that she rested against his broad chest, with his shoulder supporting her back. He dipped out a forkful of her dessert and held it to her lips.

"It's not bad, is it?" she asked, smiling.

He took a bite of his own. "It's unique. I'll bet the others would love it, too." He glanced down at her expression and lifted an eyebrow. "Mm-hmm," he murmured thoughtfully. "So you made it just for me, did you?"

She shifted closer. "You work harder than everybody else. I thought you deserved something special."

He smiled warmly at her. "I'm not the only hard worker around here. Who scrubbed the kitchen floor on her hands and knees after I bought her a machine that does it?"

She flushed. "It's a very nice machine. I really appreciate it. But it's better if you do it with a toothbrush. I mean, the dirt in the linoleum pattern just doesn't come up any other way. And I do like a nice kitchen."

He grimaced. "What am I going to do with you? A modern woman isn't supposed to scrub floors on her hands and knees. She's supposed to get a degree and take a corporate presidency away from some good old boy in Houston."

She snuggled close to him and closed her eyes, loving his warm strength against her. Her hand smoothed over his shirt just at the pocket, feeling its softness.

"I don't want a degree. I'd like to grow roses."

"So you said." He fed her another bite of the dessert,

which left one for himself. Then he sat up to put the saucer on the desk and reach for the coffee.

"I'll get it." She slid off his lap and fixed the coffee the way he liked it.

He took it from her and coaxed her back onto his lap. It felt good to hold her like that, in the pleasant silence of the office. He shared the coffee with her, too.

Her hand rested on his while she sipped the hot liquid, staring up into eyes that seemed fascinated by her. She wondered at their sudden closeness, when they'd been at odds for such a long time.

He was feeling something similar. He liked holding her, touching her. She filled an empty place in him with joy and delight. He wasn't lonely when she was close to him.

"Why roses?" he asked when they finished the coffee and he put the cup back on the desk.

"They're old," she said, settling back down against his chest. "They have a nobility, a history. For instance, did you know that Napoleon's Empress Josephine was famous for her rose garden, and that despite the war with England, she managed to get her roses shipped through enemy lines?"

He chuckled. "Now how did you know about that?"

"It was in one of my gardening magazines. Roses are prehistoric," she continued. "They're one of the oldest living plants. I like the hybrids, too, though. Dad bought me a beautiful tea rose the last year we lived in Victoria. I guess it's still where I planted it. But the house was rented, and we weren't likely to have a permanent home after that, so I didn't want to uproot my rosebush."

He smoothed his fingers over her small, soft hand

where it pressed over his pocket. His fingers explored her neat, short nails while his breath sighed out at her forehead, ruffling her hair.

"I never had much use for flowers. Our mother wasn't much of a gardener, either."

She leaned back against his shoulder so that she could see his face. He looked bitter.

Her fingers went up to his mouth and traced his hard, firm lips. "You mustn't try to live in the past," she said. "There's a whole world out there waiting to be seen and touched and lived in."

"How can you be so optimistic, after the life you've had?" he wanted to know.

"I'm an incurable optimist, I guess," she said. "I've seen so much of the ugly side of life that I never take any nice thing for granted. It's been great, living here, being part of a family, even though I just work for you."

His lips pursed against her exploring fingers. He caught them and nibbled absently at their tips while he looked down into her eyes. "I like the way you cook."

"I'm not pretty, though," she mused, "and I can't psychoanalyze you over the vegetables."

"Thank God."

She chuckled.

He tugged at a lock of her hair and searched her eyes. "Cute of Leo to bring up the asparagus." His eyes narrowed and his smile faded as he looked down at her with kindling desire. "You knew what he was going to say, didn't you?"

She nodded. Her heart was racing too fast to allow for speech.

"Well, it was interesting, having asparagus signify impotence," he murmured dryly, smiling at her blush.

"But we could have told Miss Brewster that the asparagus lied, couldn't we, Tess?" he drawled.

She hid her hot face against him, feeling his laughter as his chest rippled with it.

"Sorry," he said at her ear, bending to gather her even closer against him. "I shouldn't tease you. It's irresistible. I love the way you blush." His arms tightened and his face nuzzled against hers, coaxing it around so that his lips could find her soft mouth. "I love…so much about you, Tess," he growled against her lips.

She reached up to hold him while the kiss grew and grew, like a spark being fanned into a bonfire.

He lifted away from her for an instant, to search her eyes and look down at her soft, yielding body.

Without the slightest hesitation, his hand smoothed over the chambray shirt she was wearing and went right to her small breast, covering it boldly, teasing the nipple to immediate hardness with his thumb.

Her lips parted with the excitement he aroused, and he bent and took her soft sigh right into his mouth.

She didn't have the experience to know how rare this mutual delight was, but he did. It was pleasurable with some women, but with Tess, it was like walking through fireworks. He enjoyed every single thing about her, from the way she curled into him when he touched her to the way her mouth opened eagerly for his. It made him feel vaguely invincible.

He made a rough sound in his throat as his hand edged between them, feeling blindly for her shirt buttons. She wasn't coy about that, either. She lay submissively in his arms, letting him open the shirt, letting him unclip her bra and push it away.

She didn't have to tell him that she liked his gazing

on her body. It was even in the way her breath caught and fluttered.

He touched her delicately, lifting his gaze to her face to watch the way she reacted to it.

It occurred to him that she might love him, must love him, to let him be so familiar with her body, which he knew instinctively was innocent.

His heart jumped up into his throat as he traced around one tight little pink nipple.

"What did you do for experience before I came along?" he murmured half-teasingly.

"I watched movies on cable," she said, her own voice breathless. She shivered and her short nails dug into his shoulder. "Callaghan, is it supposed to…do that?" she whispered.

"What?"

She bit her lip and couldn't quite look at him.

He bent to her mouth and liberated her lower lip with a soft, searching kiss. "It's supposed to make your body swell," he whispered into her lips. "Does it?"

She swallowed hard. "All over?"

"All over."

She nuzzled her face into his hot throat while his hands worked magic on her. "It makes me ache."

"It's supposed to do that, too."

He had the weight of her in one big palm and he bent his head to put his mouth, open, on the nipple.

She shivered again and he heard a tight sob pass her lips. He knew he was going to get in over his head, and it didn't seem to matter anymore.

With a rough curse, he suddenly got to his feet and stripped her out of the shirt and bra before he lifted her and, with his mouth hard on hers, carried her to the divan.

He stretched her out on it, yielding and openly hungry, and came down beside her, one long leg inserted boldly between both of hers.

"Do you have any idea how dangerous this is?" he ground out against her breasts.

Her hands were fumbling for buttons. "It isn't, because we aren't…doing anything," she whispered with deathbed humor as she forced the stubborn shirt buttons apart and pushed the fabric away from hard, warm, hair-covered muscles. "You are…so beautiful," she added in a hushed, rapt whisper as she touched him and felt him go tense.

His teeth clenched. "Tess…" He made her name sound like a plea for mercy.

"Oh, come here. Please!" She drew him down on her, so that her bare breasts merged with his hard chest. She held him close while they kissed hungrily, feeling his long legs suddenly shift so that he was between them, pressing against her in a new and urgent way.

He lifted his head and looked into her eyes. His own were coal black, glittering with desire, his face drawn and taut.

She watched him openly, all too aware of his capability, and that he could lose his head right here and she wouldn't care.

He shifted against her deliberately, and his head spun with pleasure. He laughed, but without humor.

"If I'd ever imagined that a virgin—" he stressed the word in a harsh, choked tone "—could make an utter fool of me!"

Her hands had been sliding up and down the hard muscles of his back with pure wonder. Now they stilled, uncertain. "A…fool?" she whispered.

"Tess, have you gone numb from the waist down?" he asked through his teeth. "Can't you feel what's happened to me?"

"Well…yes," she said hesitantly. "Isn't it normal?"

He laughed in spite of the stabbing ache she'd given him. "Baby, you haven't got a clue, have you?"

"Did I do something wrong?"

"No!" He eased down again, giving in to his need, and hers, but careful not to give her too much of his formidable weight. His mouth moved lazily over her forehead, down to close her wide, wounded eyes. "You haven't done anything wrong. I want you," he whispered tenderly.

"I want you, too," she whispered back shyly.

He sighed as if he had the weight of the world on him. One big, lean hand slid under her hips and lifted them slowly, sensually into the hard thrust of him, and held her there.

She stiffened suddenly and a tiny little cry crawled out of her tight throat as she registered the heat and power of him in such stark intimacy.

"When it gets this bad," he whispered at her ear, "a man will lie, cheat, steal, kill to get rid of it! If I had just a little less honor, I'd tell you anything that would get those jeans off you in the least possible time."

"Get my jeans off…!"

The shock in her voice broke the tension. He lifted his head and burst out laughing despite the urgency in his body when he saw her face.

"You don't imagine that we could make love *through* them?" he asked.

She was scarlet. And he was laughing, the animal! She hit his shoulder angrily. "You stop that!"

He chuckled helplessly, shifting suddenly to lie beside her on the wide leather divan. He pulled her against him and lay there fighting for breath and control, deliciously aware of her bare breasts pressing warmly against his rib cage.

"Just when I think I'll go mad, you act your age."

"I'm not a kid!" she protested.

He smoothed her ruffled hair lazily and his chest rose and fell in a long sigh while the urgency slowly passed out of his body. "Yes, you are," he contradicted, his voice soft and affectionate. "And if we keep doing this, eventually, blushes or not, you're coming out of those jeans."

"As if I'd let you!"

"You'd help me," he returned. "Tess, I haven't really tried to seduce you," he added quietly. "You're as hungry for me as I am for you, and I know tricks I haven't used yet."

She drank in the male smell of his body with pleasure. "Such as?"

"You really want to know?" He drew her close and whispered in her ear.

"Callaghan!"

He kissed her shocked face, closing her open mouth with warm, tender kisses. "You've got a lot to learn, and I ache to teach it to you," he said after a minute. "But you aren't geared for an affair, and I have far too many principles to seduce a woman who works for me." He sighed wearily and drew her closer, wrapping her up against him. "Good God, Tess, how did we ever get into this situation?"

"You insisted that I sit on your lap while you ate dessert," she replied reasonably.

"It happened long before that. Months ago. I fought you like mad to keep you at arm's length."

"It didn't work," she informed him.

"So I noticed."

He didn't speak again and neither did she for a long time. They lay in each other's arms in the silence of the study, listening to the muted sounds of the night outside the window.

"Do you want me to go?" she asked finally.

His arms contracted. "Sure," he replied facetiously. "Like I want to give up breathing."

That was reassuring. She felt the same way. But he still wasn't mentioning anything permanent. Even through the euphoria of lying half nude against him, she did realize that.

Finally he let go of her and got up from the divan, careful not to look at her as he fetched her shirt and bra and put them beside her.

"You'd better..." He gestured, not putting it into words.

She dressed quickly, watching his long back as he stood beside the desk, idly touching the papers on it.

She got to her feet at last and after a minute she went around him to get the tray.

"I'll take this back to the kitchen."

He nodded without speaking. He was too choked with conflicting emotions to put a single one of them into words.

But when she went to pick up the tray, his hand covered the back of hers, briefly.

"I've put off a conference that I meant to attend in Kansas City," he said quietly. "I'm going to go. Rey will be back in the morning before I leave, and Leo will be here."

She looked up at him with wide, soft eyes in a face that made his heart ache.

He cursed softly. "Tess, it wouldn't work," he said through his teeth. "You know it wouldn't!"

She made a motion with her shoulders and lowered her revealing eyes so that he couldn't read what was in them. "Okay."

"You'll like school," he forced himself to say. "There will be boys your own age, nice boys, not like some of the toughs you meet on the rodeo circuit."

"Sure."

"You can commute," he added after a minute. "None of us want you to give up your job while you're going to school. And I'll make sure we aren't alone again, like this."

She swallowed the lump in her throat and even forced a smile. "Okay."

He watched her pick up the tray and go out of the room. When he finally closed the door behind her, it was like putting the finishing touches on a high wall. He actually winced.

Chapter Nine

Cag was dressed in a lightweight gray vested suit the next morning when he came in to breakfast. His suitcase was packed and waiting by the front door, along with his silver belly Stetson. He looked elegant when he dressed up. Tess had to force herself not to stare at him too closely while she served the meal.

Rey had walked in, still dressed in a suit himself, just as Tess started to put breakfast down on the table. He, like Callaghan, would never win any beauty contests, but he paid for dressing. He looked elegant and faintly dangerous, in a sexy sort of way. Tess was glad she was immune to him, and wondered vaguely if there had ever been a special woman in his life.

"I feel like Cinderella before the ball," Leo muttered, glancing from one of his brothers to the other. He was in jeans and a blue-checked shirt and boots, his blond-streaked brown hair shining like gold in the ceiling light.

Cag didn't react, but Rey took him up on it, peering deliberately under the table to see if Leo was wearing a dress.

"Cute, cute," Leo drawled. He picked up his fork and stabbed the air toward his brother. "I meant figuratively speaking. I don't wear dresses."

"Good thing, with your hairy legs," Rey retorted. He glanced toward Cag. "You leaving?"

Cag nodded as he finished a mouthful of eggs and washed it down with coffee. "I'm going to that legislative cattlemen's conference in Kansas City. I decided that I'd better go. The journals don't keep us completely up-to-date on pending legislation, and I've heard some rumors I don't like about new regulations."

"I've heard those same rumors," Leo remarked.

"We have to start policing our own industry better," Cag said. "All the rules and regulations and laws in the world won't work without better enforcement." He looked up. "You should have kept your seat on the legislative committee at the state cattlemen's association."

"Hindsight is a fine thing," Leo agreed. "I had too much to do at the time."

"If they ask you again, take it."

"You bet I will." He glanced at Cag. "Why don't you do it?"

Cag smiled. "I've got more than I can do already, as you'll discover when you look at the paperwork in the study. I only got half the figures keyed into the computer. You'll need to take the rest down to Margie in the office and get her to finish."

"Sure."

Neither Leo nor Rey noticed that Tess had turned away to the sink deliberately, because she knew why Cag hadn't finished that paperwork. She didn't want the other two brothers to see her flush.

Cag noticed. He didn't look at her, though, because he'd become more readable lately where she was concerned. He finished his coffee and got up.

"Well, I'm off. I'll try to be back by next weekend.

You can reach me at the Airport Hilton in Kansas City if you need me."

"We won't," Leo said with a grin. "Have a good time."

Cag glanced involuntarily at Tess, thinking how empty life without her was going to be, even for a few days. He'd grown all too fond of that red curly head of hair and those heavenly blue eyes.

"Take care of Tess while I'm gone," he said, trying to make a joke of it and failing miserably.

"I'll take care of myself, thanks very much," she shot right back and forced a smile, so that he'd think it wasn't killing her to watch him walk out the door.

"You never told us how your application went," Leo said suddenly.

"Oh, I was accepted on the spot," Tess said. "They've scheduled me for three classes when fall quarter begins. I went to the financial aid office and applied for tuition, which they say I can get, and it will pay for my books."

Cag frowned. "You've already applied?"

"Yes," she said with determined brightness. "I start in three weeks. I can hardly wait."

"So I see." Cag finished his goodbyes, added a few things for his brothers to take care of while he was away and left without another word.

Tess wondered why he was irritated that she'd applied for admission to the vocational school, when he'd already said he wanted her to do it. She knew he hadn't changed his mind. His behavior was puzzling.

Cag was thinking the same thing as he slammed his hat on his head, picked up his suitcase, and went out the front door. He'd known she was applying, but now it was definite. He thought of her in his arms the night before, hungry for his kisses, and then he thought of all the young men she'd meet when she started classes. She might meet a young man who liked roses, too. He had visions of her youthful crush on him melting quickly away in the heat of a new romance, and it made him vaguely sick.

He'd tried not to get in over his head, but it looked as if he was only fooling himself. Tess had wormed her way under his skin, right where his heart was. He wondered how he'd ever imagined that he could make a little love to her and walk away. He'd never been quite so confused or worried in his life. He wanted Tess as he'd never wanted anything. But he was afraid that she was in love with love, not him, because he was the first man who'd ever been intimate with her even in a slight way. He couldn't forget the fiancée who'd dropped him for someone younger. He couldn't bear to go through that a second time.

He got into the ranch truck and drove toward the airport, but his heart wasn't in it. Tess was going to go away to school, and he was going to lose her. But not right away, he comforted himself. She'd still be living at the ranch. He'd have time to get himself sorted out. And it wasn't as if she was going to meet someone else at once. He had plenty of time. The thought comforted him, and he put that worry aside.

Cag wouldn't have been quite so comforted if he'd seen the big black limousine that drew up in front of the Hart ranch house barely two hours after he'd left.

Rey and Leo had already gone out with the men to look over a new batch of bulls when someone rang the doorbell.

Tess wiped her hands on a kitchen towel and left the pots she'd been scrubbing in the sink when she went to answer it.

A tall, taciturn man in a suit, carrying a briefcase, was standing there.

"Miss Theresa Brady?" the man asked politely.

It was a shock to hear her given name. She'd been called Tess for so long that she'd all but forgotten that it was a contraction of Theresa.

"Yes," she said hesitantly.

He held out a hand. "I'm Clint Matherson," he said, shaking hands. "Your late mother's attorney."

Her hand went limp in his. "My...*late*...mother?"

"I'm sorry to tell you that your mother passed away almost a month ago in Singapore. It wasn't possible to get word to you until now. I found you through a detective agency, but I've been out of town and the message only reached me a week ago. I'm very sorry," he said belatedly.

She hadn't thought of her mother in years, and only then with regret. It might have been sad to lose her if she'd ever shown the slightest affection for her only child, but she hadn't.

"I didn't know where she was," Tess said honestly. "We hadn't communicated since I was sixteen."

"Yes, she, uh, made me aware of that. She left you a portfolio of stocks in a trading company out of Singapore," he added. "If we could sit down and discuss her will?"

"I'm sorry. Of course. Come into the living room, please."

He sat down in an armchair and laid out the documents on the spotless oak coffee table, moving her flower arrangement aside to make room for them.

"I can't tell you much about this company. Frankly the stocks are as much a surprise to you as they are to me. She didn't ask my advice before she sank her money into them. You did know that she married a wealthy Singapore importer six years ago?"

"No," Tess said stiffly. "As I said, we haven't corresponded."

"A pity," he replied. "She gave up drinking and led a fairly admirable life in her last years. She was widowed about the time she contracted cancer. Her illness perhaps changed her outlook somewhat. I understand that she had plans to ask you to come out and visit with her, but she never carried them out." He smiled thinly. "She told me she was ashamed of the way she'd treated you, Miss Brady, and not too hopeful of making amends."

Tess clasped her hands together on the knees of her jeans. "I would have listened, if she'd wanted to talk to me."

He shrugged. "Perhaps it's just as well. But time is a great healer." He indicated the documents. "I'll have these stocks checked out by the end of the week. I should be able to give you some idea of their current worth on the Asian market then. You can decide whether you'd rather keep them or sell them. There are a few odds and ends, like her jewelry, which will be sent on to me and I'll forward them to you."

The thought of having something, anything, of her mother's made her uneasy. "Wasn't there any other relative?"

"A stepdaughter who still lives in Singapore. But she was already provided for by her father's will."

"Wouldn't she like the jewelry?"

He was surprised. "Well, she was fond of your mother,

I understand. They were good friends. Yes, I imagine she would like it. But it's yours, Miss Brady. You were a blood relative."

"I never felt like one," she replied stiffly. "I'd like the daughter to have the jewelry and the other...personal things." She glanced at him and away. "It's hard to put into words, but I don't really want anything of hers. Not even the stock."

"Ah, but you have no choice about that," he said, surprising her. "There's no provision if you don't accept it. There must be some goal you've set in life that it would help you achieve. I understand that you work as a housekeeper here since your father's untimely death. Wouldn't you like to be financially independent?"

That remark changed her life. If she had a little money of her own, Callaghan wouldn't have to keep her on here because he was sorry for her. It would give her some measure of independence, even if leaving Callaghan broke her heart.

"Yes, I would," she answered the lawyer. "And I'll accept the stock. Thank you."

He indicated the places her signature was required, closed the documents up in his briefcase, shook hands and promised to be in touch soon about the stock.

"How much do you think it could be worth?" she asked hesitantly when he was on the verge of leaving.

"Hard to tell. It was bought for eighty dollars a share, but that was last year."

"And how much was bought?"

He smiled musingly. "About a million dollars worth."

She was pale. Her hand found the door and held on for support. "Oh."

"So you see, you won't be dependent on other people for your livelihood. Your mother may have neglected you in life, but she didn't forget you at the end. That must be some comfort."

It wasn't, but she smiled and pretended that it was. She closed the door and leaned back against it. Everything had changed in the course of a few minutes. She was a woman of means. She could do what she pleased. But it would be without Callaghan Hart, and that was the hardest pill of all to swallow.

She told the brothers about her visitor at the supper table.

They were silent after she related the size of the inheritance, glancing at each other as if communicating in some mysterious fashion.

"I can still go to school, but I'll be able to support myself now," she told them. "And I guess," she added reluctantly, "I won't need to work. I'm sorry to leave, but we've known for a long time that Callaghan really would prefer to have another cook."

"Why don't you ever call him Cag, like we do?" Leo asked gently.

She stared at her coffee cup. "It never seemed comfortable, I guess."

They exchanged another mysterious glance.

"Well, we'll advertise as soon as Cag comes home and we have time to discuss what we want to do," Rey said. "We'll miss you, Tess. Especially your biscuits."

"Amen to that. A good biscuit chef is really hard to find in these liberated times. I guess we'll be eating them out of tins from now on."

"Now, now," Tess chided, "Dorie can bake biscuits and even real bread. I'll bet she won't mind keeping you supplied. But you'll find a cook. I know you will."

They looked at her silently. "She won't be you," Leo said, and he smiled wistfully.

Tess got used to the idea of leaving in the days that followed. She was almost reconciled to it when Cag showed up late the next Friday afternoon. He looked tired and worn and unhappy until he saw Tess. His black eyes began to light up at once, and her heart ached, because it could have been so different if he'd loved her. She stood quietly in the kitchen when she wanted to fling herself into his arms and kiss him to death.

"Missed me?" he drawled.

She nodded, but she wouldn't look at him. "I've got to gather eggs. I forgot this morning. Welcome home," she said belatedly as she carried a small wicker basket out the back door.

"There you are!" Leo called, joining his brother in the kitchen. He clapped a hand on the taller man's shoulder. "How'd it go?"

"Fine. What's wrong with Tess?"

"What do you mean?"

Cag's eyes darkened. "She wouldn't look at me."

"Oh. Well, she's been unsettled since the lawyer came," Leo replied, carefully choosing his words. "Sudden wealth would do that to most people."

Cag's face lost a few shades of color. "Wealth?"

"Her mother died and left her a small fortune in stocks," he told the older man, watching with compassion the effect it had on him. "She says she'll be leaving as soon as we can hire a replacement. No need for her to work with a million dollars worth of stock, is there?"

Cag went to the sink and poured himself a glass of water

that he didn't want, just to keep from groaning aloud. Tess had money. She was quitting. He'd thought he had time to work out his own feelings, and suddenly it was all up. She was leaving and he'd never see her again. She'd find somebody younger and get married and have babies. Tess would love having children of her own....

He put the glass down with a thud. "I've got things to do. How about those new bulls?"

"They came in, and I got Billy to sell me that Salers bull," he added smugly. "I've put him in a pasture all to himself with his own salt lick and a nice clean stall to keep him out of bad weather when it comes."

Cag didn't rise to the occasion which he would have only days before. He looked thoughtful and worried. Very worried.

"It won't be the same without Tess, will it?" Leo prompted gently.

Cag's face closed up completely. "I'll change and get back to the paperwork."

"Aren't you going to tell me how the conference went?"

"Later," Cag said absently. He walked out of the room without a backward glance.

He acted oddly for the rest of the day. And he wasn't at the supper table.

"Said he had to go into town, God knows what for," Rey murmured as he buttered a flaky biscuit. "They pull in the sidewalks at six. He knows that."

"Maybe he's got something on his mind," Leo mused, watching Tess fuss over the chicken dish she was putting into a serving bowl.

Rey sighed. "Something big. He wasn't going toward Jacobsville," he added. "He was headed toward Shea's."

That brought Leo's head up. "He was?"

Tess finished putting food on the table, so preoccupied by Cag's reappearance that she couldn't put two thoughts together in any sort of order. It was much harder to leave than she'd even anticipated.

She missed the comment about Shea's Bar entirely, and she barely touched her own food. She cleaned up the kitchen, blind to the brothers' troubled glances, and went to bed early. She felt like it was the end of the world.

So did Cag, who sat quietly at a corner table at Shea's Bar, drinking one whiskey highball after another until he was pleasantly numb and barely coherent.

No fool, he left the truck locked at the bar and took a cab back to the ranch. If the driver wondered at the identity of his overly-quiet passenger, he didn't ask. He took the bills that were fumbled out of the cowhide wallet and drove away.

Cag managed to get through the living room without falling over anything, amazing considering the amount of whiskey he'd imbibed. He made it to his own room and even into the shower, an undertaking of mammoth proportions.

With his hair still damp and only a short robe covering his nudity, it occurred to him that he should ask Tess why the rush to get away from the ranch. That it was three in the morning didn't seem to matter. If she was asleep, why, she could just wake up and answer him.

He knocked at her door, but there was no answer. He opened it and walked in, bumping into a chair and the side table before he ever reached the bed.

He sat down on the side of it and noticed how hot the room was. She hadn't turned on the air conditioner, and then he remembered that his brothers had told him they'd shut the unit off temporarily while it was being worked on. No wonder it was so hot.

He reached out and pushed gently at Tess's shoulder under the cover. She moaned and kicked the cover away and he caught his breath. She was lying there just in her briefs, without any other covering, her beautiful little breasts bare and firm in the muted light of the security lamp outside her window.

He couldn't help himself. He reached out and traced those pretty breasts with the tips of his fingers, smiling when she arched and they went hard-tipped at once.

It seemed the most natural thing in the world to slide out of his robe and into bed beside her.

He turned her against his nude body, feeling her quiver softly and then ease closer to him. She felt like heaven in his arms. The feel of her soft, warm skin so intimately kindled a raging arousal in him.

He moved her onto her back and slid over her, his mouth gently smoothing across her lips until they parted and responded despite the sharp tang of whiskey on his breath.

Half-asleep, and sure that she was dreaming, her arms went under his and around him, her legs moved to admit him into an intimacy that made his head spin. He moved against her blindly, hungrily, urgently, his mouth insistent on her mouth as he felt surges of pleasure breaking like waves inside him.

"Ca...Callaghan? Callaghan?" she whimpered.

"Yes, Tess...!" He caught her mouth again and his hand went to her thigh, pulling her even closer, straining against the thin nylon barrier that was all that separated them.

She didn't fight his seduction. If this was what he wanted, it was what she wanted, too. She relaxed and gave in to the sweet, fierce sensations that came from the intimate contact with his powerful body.

But even as his fingers sought her hips in a fierce urgency, the liquor finally caught up with him. He gave a soft, explosive sigh and a curse and suddenly went limp on her, the full weight of his body pressing her hard into the sheets.

She lay dazed, wondering exactly what had happened. Cag had no clothes on. She was wearing briefs, but nothing more. Not being totally stupid, she realized that sex involved a little more contact than this, but it was blatant intimacy, all the same. She shifted experimentally, but nothing happened. He'd been very aroused, but now he was relaxed all over.

She eased away a little and pushed. He went over onto his back in a liquid sprawl and with a long sigh.

Curious, she sat up in bed and looked at him, surprised at how much she enjoyed the sight of him like that. He might have been a warm statue for all the movement in him, but he was a delight even to her innocent eyes. She smiled secretively as she studied him unashamedly, thinking that for tonight he belonged to her, even if he didn't want to. After all, she hadn't coaxed him in here. He'd come of his own free will. He had to feel something for her, if he'd had to go out and get himself drunk to express what he really wanted.

While she looked at him she weighed her options. She could leave him here and shoo him out first thing in the morning—unless, of course, he awoke in the same condition he'd just been in except sober. In which case, her innocence was really going to be gone. Or she could try to get him back to his room. That would be impossible. He was deadweight. She could call the brothers to help her—but that would create a scandal.

In the end, she curled up beside him, pulled the sheet over both of them and went to sleep in his arms. Let tomorrow take care of itself, she mused while she enjoyed the feel of all that latent strength so close against her nudity. She loved him. If this was all she could ever have, she was going to have this one night. Even if he never knew about it.

Cag felt little hammers at either side of his head. He couldn't seem to open his eyes to discover what was the sound that had disturbed him. He remembered drinking a glass of bourbon whiskey. Several glasses. He remembered taking a shower and falling into bed. He remembered....

His eyes flew open and he sat straight up. But instead of looking at the bare back beside him, covered just decently by a sheet, he scanned his own nudity to the door, where Rey and Leo were standing frozen in place.

He jerked the sheet over his hips, held his throbbing head and said, predictably, "How did I get in here?"

"You bounder," Leo murmured, so delighted by his brother's predicament that he had to bite his tongue to keep from smiling. Finally he'd got Cag just where he wanted him!

"That goes double for me," Rey said, acting disgusted as he glanced toward Tess's prone figure barely covered by the sheet. "And she works for us!"

"Not anymore," Leo said with pure confidence as he

folded his arms over his chest. "Guess who's getting married?" He raised his voice, despite Cag's outraged look. "Tess? Tess! Wake up!"

She forced her eyes open, glanced at Cag and froze. As she pulled up the sheet to her chin, she turned and saw the brothers standing poker-faced in the doorway.

Then she did what any sane woman might do under the circumstances. She screamed.

Chapter Ten

An awkward few minutes later, a cold sober and poleaxed Cag jerked into his robe and Tess retreated under the sheet until he left. He never looked at her, or spoke. She huddled into the sheet and wished she could disappear.

She felt terrible. Even though it wasn't her fault, any of it. She hadn't gone and climbed into bed with him, after all, and she certainly hadn't invited him into bed with her! When she'd dozed off, she'd been almost convinced that the whole episode had been a dream. Now it was more like a nightmare.

Tess went into the kitchen to make the breakfast that the brothers had found missing at its usual time. That was why they'd come looking for her, and how they knew Cag was in bed with her. She groaned as she realized what she was going to have to endure around the table. She decided beforehand that she'd eat her breakfast after they finished and keep busy in another part of the house until they were gone.

The meal was on the table when three subdued men walked into the kitchen and sat down. Tess couldn't look at any of them. She mumbled something about dusting the living room and escaped.

Not ten minutes later, Leo came looking for her.

She was cleaning a window that she'd done twice already. She couldn't meet his eyes.

"Was everything okay? I'm sorry if the bacon was a little overdone…."

"Nobody's blaming you for anything," he said, interrupting her quietly. "And Cag's going to do the right thing."

She turned, red-faced. "But he didn't do anything, Leo," she said huskily. "He was drunk and he got into the wrong bed, that's all. Nothing, absolutely nothing, went on!"

He held up a hand. "Cag doesn't know that nothing went on," he said, lowering his voice. "And you aren't going to tell him. Listen to me," he emphasized when she tried to interrupt, "you're the only thing that's going to save him from drying into dust and blowing away, Tess. He's alone and he's going to stay that way. He'll never get married voluntarily. This is the only way it will ever happen, and you know it."

She lifted her head proudly. "I won't trick him into marriage," she said curtly.

"I'm not asking you to. *We'll* trick him into it. You just go along."

"I won't," she said stubbornly. "He shouldn't have to marry me for something he didn't do!"

"Well, he remembers some of it. And he's afraid of what he can't remember, so he's willing to get married."

She was still staring at him with her eyes unblinking. "I love him!" she said miserably. "How can I ever expect him to forgive me if I let him marry me when he doesn't want to!"

"He does want to. At least, he wants to right now.

Rey's gone for the license, you both go to the doctor in thirty minutes for a blood test and you get married Friday in the probate judge's office." He put a gentle hand on her shoulder. "Tess, if you love him, you have to save him from himself. He cares about you. It's so obvious to us that it's blatant. But he won't do anything about it. This is the only way he has a chance at happiness, and we're not letting him throw it away on half-baked fears of failure. So I'm sorry, but you're sort of the fall guy here. It's a gamble. But I'd bet on it."

"What about when he remembers, if he does, and we're already married?" she asked plaintively.

"That's a bridge you can cross when you have to." He gave her a wicked grin. "Besides, you need an insurance policy against anything that might...happen."

"Nothing's going to happen!" she growled, her fists clenched at her side.

"That's what you think," he murmured under his breath, smiling—but only after he'd closed the door between them. He rubbed his hands together with gleeful satisfaction and went to find his sibling.

It was like lightning striking. Everything happened too fast for Tess's protests to make any difference. She wanted to tell Cag the truth, because she hadn't been drunk and she remembered what had gone on. But somehow she couldn't get him to herself for five minutes in the three days that followed. Before she knew what was happening, she and Cag were in the probate judge's office with Corrigan and Dorie, Simon and Tira, Leo and Rey behind them, cheering them on.

Tess was wearing a white off-the-shoulder cotton dress with a sprig of lily of the valley in her hair in lieu of a veil, and carrying a small nosegay of flowers. They were pronounced man and wife and Cag leaned down to kiss her—on the cheek, perfunctorily, even reluctantly. He looked more like a man facing an incurable illness than a happy bridegroom, and Tess felt more guilty by the minute.

They all went to a restaurant to have lunch, which Tess didn't taste. Afterward, Leo and Rey went on a hastily arranged business trip to California while Corrigan and Simon and their respective wives went to their own homes.

Cag put Tess into the Mercedes, which he drove for special occasions, and took her back to the ranch.

She wanted to tell him the truth, but the look on his face didn't invite confidences, and she was certain that it would only make things worse and get his brothers into big trouble if she confessed now.

She knew that nothing had happened that night, but if she slept with Cag, he was going to know it, too. Besides, sleeping with him would eliminate any ideas of an annulment. She'd been thinking about that all day, that she could give him his freedom before any more damage was done. She had to talk to him before tonight, before their wedding night.

It was almost time to put on dinner and she'd just started changing out of her wedding dress when the door opened and Cag came in, closing the door deliberately behind him.

In nothing but a bra and half-slip, she turned, brush in hand, to stare at him as if he were an apparition. He was wearing his jeans and nothing else. His broad chest was bare and there was a look in his black eyes that she didn't like.

"Cag, I have to tell you...."

Before she could get the rest of the sentence out, he had her up in his arms and he was kissing her. It wasn't like other kisses they'd shared, which had an affectionate, teasing quality to them even in passion. These were rough, insistent, arousing kisses that were a prelude to out-and-out seduction.

Tess didn't have the experience to save herself. A few feverish minutes later, she was twisting under him on the cover of the bed trying to help him get rid of the last little bit of fabric that concealed her from his eyes.

He was out of his jeans by then, and his mouth was all over her yielding body. He touched and tasted her in ways she'd never experienced, until she was writhing with hunger.

By the time he slid between her legs and began to possess her, she was so eager that the tiny flash of pain went almost unnoticed.

But not by Cag. He stopped at once when he felt the barrier give and lifted his head. His arms trembled slightly with the effort as he arched over her and put a rein on his desire long enough to search her wide, dazed eyes.

"I tried...to tell you," she stammered shakily when she realized why he was hesitating.

"If I could stop, I swear to God...I would!" he said in a hoarse, harsh whisper. He shuddered and bent to her mouth. "But it's too late! I'd rather die than stop!"

He kissed her hungrily as his body eased down and found a slow, sweet rhythm that brought gasps from the mouth he was invading. He felt her nails biting into his hips, pulling him, pleading, her whole body one long aching plea for satisfaction. She sobbed into his mouth as he gave her what she wanted in waves of sweet, hot ecstasy that built into a frightening crescendo just at the last.

She cried out and felt him shiver above her with the same exquisite delight she was feeling. Seconds later, he collapsed in her arms and she took the weight of him with joy, clinging as he fought to get his breath. His heartbeat shook both of them in the damp, lazy aftermath.

She felt his breath at her ear, jerky and hot. "Did I hurt you?" he asked.

"No. Oh, no," she breathed, burrowing closer.

Her body moved just slightly and his own clenched. It had been years. He'd ached for Tess, for the fulfillment she'd just given him. It was too soon, and he wasn't going to get over this subterfuge that had made him her husband, but just now his mind wasn't the part of his body that was in control.

He moved experimentally and heard her breath catch even as sharp pleasure rippled up his spine. No, he thought as he pulled her under him again, it wasn't too soon. It wasn't too soon at all!

It was dark when he got out of bed and pulled his jeans back on. Tess was lying in a damp, limp, spent sprawl on the cover where he'd left her. She looked up at him with dazed blue eyes, her face rosy in the aftermath of passion, her body faintly marked where his hands and his mouth had explored her. She was his. She belonged to him. His head lifted with unconscious, arrogant pride of possession.

"How was it?" he asked.

She couldn't believe he'd said anything so blatant to her after the lovemaking that had been nothing short of a revelation. She hadn't dreamed that her body was capable of such sensations as she'd been feeling. And he asked her that question with the same interest he'd have shown about a weather report.

She stared at him, confused.

"Was it worth a sham wedding?" he continued, wounded by her silence that had made him feel obliged to go through with a wedding he didn't want. She'd trapped him and he felt like a fool, no matter how sweet the bait had been.

She drew the cover back over her nudity, ashamed because of the way he was looking at her. He made her feel as if she'd done something terrible.

"You knew nothing happened that night," he continued quietly. "I didn't. I was too drunk to care what I did, but I remembered all too well that I lost my head the minute I touched you. For all I knew, I might have gone through with it. But you knew better, and you let me marry you in spite of it, knowing it wasn't necessary."

She clutched the coverlet. "I tried to tell you, but I couldn't seem to get you alone for five minutes," she murmured defeatedly.

"Of course you couldn't," he returned. His voice was as cold as his eyes. "I wasn't going to make matters worse by seducing you a second time."

"I thought it was your brothers...."

She didn't finish, but her face gave the game away. His eyes positively glittered. "My brothers? Of course. My brothers!" He glared down at her. "They were in on it, too, weren't they? No wonder they did their best to make me feel like a heel! Did you convince them to go along with the lie?"

She wanted to tell him that it had been Leo's idea in the first place, but what good would it do now? He was making it clear that he'd married her against his will and blamed her for making it necessary. Nothing she could say would be much of a defense.

Her silence only made him madder. He turned toward the door.

"Where…are you going? Do you want supper?"

He looked at her over one broad, bare shoulder. "I've had all I want. Of everything."

He went through the doorway and slammed the door behind him.

Tess dissolved into tears of misery. Well, she was married, but at what cost? If Cag had ever been close to loving her, he wasn't anymore. He hated her; she'd seen it in his eyes. She'd trapped him and he hated her.

She got up, feeling unusually stiff and sore in odd places, and went to take a shower. The sooner she could get back to normal, or nearly normal, the better.

She bathed and dressed in a neat flowered shirtwaist dress, combed her freshly washed and dried curly hair and went to the kitchen to make supper. But even as she went into the room, she heard one of the ranch trucks crank up and roar away in a fury.

Curious, she searched the house for Cag, even braving his own bedroom. His closet was still open and she caught a whiff of aftershave. She leaned against the doorjamb with a long sigh. So he'd run out, on their wedding night. Well, what did she expect, that he'd stay home and play the part of the loving husband? Fat chance, after the things he'd said.

She fixed herself a sandwich with some cold roast beef and drank a glass of milk. Then she waited for Cag to come home.

When he hadn't come back by midnight, she went to her room and crawled into bed. She was certain that she lay awake for an hour, but she never heard him come in. She slept alone and miserable, still tingling with the memories of the past few hours. If only he'd loved her, just a little, she might have had hope. She had none, now.

By morning, she knew what she had to do. She went looking for Cag, to tell him she was leaving. She had the promise of her mother's legacy and a small savings account, plus last week's salary that she hadn't spent. She could afford a bus ticket and a cheap apartment somewhere, anywhere, out of Jacobsville.

It might have been just as well that Cag still hadn't come home. His room was empty, his bed hadn't been slept in. The brothers were still out of town and Mrs. Lewis wasn't coming again until the next week. Nobody would be here to say goodbye to her. But what did it matter? Cag had made his disgust and contempt very clear indeed. He wouldn't care if she left. She could get the divorce herself and have the papers sent to him. He didn't love her, so what reason was there to stay here and eat her heart out over a man who didn't want her?

She blushed a little as her mind provided vivid proof that it wasn't a case of his not wanting her physically. He'd been insatiable, inexhaustible. Perhaps that was why he left. Perhaps he was ashamed of how hungry he'd been for her, of letting her see that hunger. Her own inexperience had been her worst drawback, because she had no real knowledge of how men behaved after they'd soothed an ache. She didn't think a man in love would insult his new bride and leave her alone all night. Apparently he was still furious with her and in no mood to forgive what he saw as a betrayal of the worst kind.

Well, he needn't expect her to be sitting at home mourning his loss! She'd had enough of being alternately scorned, rejected and passionately kissed. He could find another object for his desires, like the noncooking Miss Brewster! And she wished the woman joy of him. Such a narrow-minded, hard-nosed man deserved a woman who'd lead him around by the ear!

Tess packed, took a long last look around the first real home she'd ever known and called a cab. She thought about leaving a note. But, after all, Cag hadn't left her one when he'd stayed out all night. He must have known that she'd be worried, but he hadn't cared about her feelings. Why should she care about his? Now it was her turn. But she was staying out much longer than a night.

She took the cab to the airport and walked into the terminal, staying only until the cab pulled away. She hailed another cab, climbed in and went to the bus station, just in case Cag tried to trace her. She wasn't going to make it easy for him! She bought a ticket for St. Louis and sat down to wait for the bus.

A plane ticket would have been nice, but she couldn't afford the luxury. She had to conserve her small store of cash. It would be enough to keep her for at least a week or two. After that, she could worry about getting enough to eat. But if she ran out of luck, there was always the shelter. Every city had one, full of compassionate people willing to help the down and out. If I ever get rich, she thought, I'll donate like crazy to keep those shelters open!

She *was* rich, she remembered suddenly, and bit her lip as she realized that she hadn't left the lawyer a forwarding address. She went to the nearest phone and, taking his card from her wallet, phoned and told his secretary that she was going out of town and would be in touch in a week or so. That business accomplished, she sat back down on one of the long benches and waited for the bus to arrive.

St. Louis was huge. Tess noticed barges going down the wide Mississippi and thought how much fun it would be to live in a river town. She'd lived inland all her life, it seemed.

She found a small efficiency apartment and paid a week's rent in advance. Then she bought a newspaper and got a sandwich from a nearby deli and went back to her room to read and eat.

There weren't a lot of jobs available. She could wait, of course, and hope for something she could do that paid a nice salary. But her skills were limited, and cooking was her best one. It seemed like kindly providence that there was a cooking job available at a local restaurant; and it was nearby!

She went the very next morning just after daylight to apply. The woman who interviewed her was dubious when Tess told her how old she was, but Tess promised she could do the job, which turned out to be that of a pastry chef.

The woman, still skeptical but desperate to fill the position, gave Tess a probationary job. Delighted, she got into the apron and cap and got started.

By the end of the day, her employer was quite impressed and Tess was hired unconditionally.

She went back to her apartment tired but satisfied that things had worked out for her so quickly. She spared a thought for Cag. If he'd come home, he probably wondered where she was. She didn't dare expand on that theme or she'd be in tears.

Running away had seemed the answer to all her problems yesterday, but it wasn't so cut-and-dried today. She was in a strange city where she had no family or friends, in a lonely apartment, and all she had to show for it was a job. She thought of the brothers waiting patiently for their breakfast and nobody there to fix it. She thought of Cag and how happy she'd felt that night she'd taken him the special dessert in his study. Things had been magical and for those few minutes, they'd belonged together. But how soon it had all fallen apart, through no real fault of her own.

"I should have stayed," she said, thinking aloud. "I should have made him listen."

But she hadn't. Now she had to live with the consequences. She hoped they wouldn't be too bad.

Callaghan dragged back into the house a day and a half after he'd left it with his misery so visible that it shocked his brothers, who'd come back from their business trip to an ominously empty house.

They surged forward when he walked through the door.

"Well?" Leo prompted impatiently, looking past Cag to the door. "Where is she?"

Cag's tired mind took a minute to work that question out. "Where is she? What do you mean, where is she? She isn't here?" he exploded.

Rey and Leo exchanged worried glances as Cag pushed past them and rushed down the hall to Tess's room. It was empty. Her suitcase was gone, her clothes were gone, her shoes were gone. He looked over her dresser and on the bed, but there was no note. She hadn't left a trace. Cag's heart turned over twice as he realized what she'd done. She'd run away. She'd left him.

His big fists clenched by his sides. His first thought was that he was glad she'd gone; his life could get back to normal. But his second thought was that he felt as if half his body were missing. He was empty inside. Cold. Alone, as he'd never been.

He heard his brothers come up behind him.

"Her things are gone," he said without any expression in his voice.

"No note?" Leo asked.

Cag shook his head.

"Surely she left a note," Rey murmured. "I'll check the office."

He went back down the hall. Leo leaned against the wall and stared unblinking at his big brother.

"Gave her hell, did you?" he asked pointedly.

Cag didn't look at him. His eyes were on the open closet door. "She lied. She tricked me into marriage." He turned his black eyes on Leo. "You helped her do it."

"Helped her? It was my idea," he said quietly. "You'd never have married her if it was left up to you. You'd have gone through life getting older and more alone, and Tess would have suffered for it. She loved you enough to risk it. I'd hoped you loved her enough to forgive it. Apparently I was wrong right down the line. I'm sorry. I never meant to cause this."

Cag was staring at him. "It was your idea, not hers?"

Leo shrugged. "She didn't want any part of it. She said if you didn't want to marry her, she wasn't going to do anything that would force you to. I talked her into keeping quiet and then Rey and I made sure you didn't have much time to talk to each other before the wedding." His eyes narrowed. "All of us care about you, God knows why, you're the blooming idiot of the family. A girl like that, a sweet, kind girl with no guile about her, wants to love you and you kick her out the door." He shook his head sadly. "I guess you and Herman belong together, like a pair of reptiles. I hope you'll be very happy."

He turned and went back down the hall to find Rey.

Cag wiped his forehead with his sleeve and stared blindly into space. Tess was self-sufficient, but she was young. And on top of all his other mistakes, he'd made one that caused the others to look like minor fumbles. He hadn't used anything during that long, sweet loving. Tess could be pregnant, and he didn't know where she was.

Chapter Eleven

Tess was enjoying her job. The owner gave her carte blanche to be creative, and she used it. Despite the aching hurt that Cag had dealt her, she took pride in her craft. She did a good job, didn't watch the clock and performed beautifully under pressure. By the end of the second week, they were already discussing giving her a raise.

She liked her success, but she wondered if Cag had worried about her. He was protective toward her, whatever his other feelings, and she was sorry she'd made things difficult for him. She really should call that lawyer and find out about her stock, so that she wouldn't have to depend on her job for all her necessities. And she could ask him to phone the brothers and tell them that she was okay. He'd never know where she was because she wasn't going to tell him.

She did telephone Clint Matherson, the lawyer, who was relieved to hear from her because he had, indeed, checked out those stocks her mother had left her.

"I don't know quite how to tell you this," he said heavily. "Your mother invested in a very dubious new company, which had poor management and little operating capital from the very start. The owner was apparently a friend of hers. To get to the point, the stock is worthless. Absolutely worthless. The company has just recently gone into receivership."

Tess let out a long breath and smiled wistfully. "Well, it was nice while it lasted, to think that she did remember me, that I was independently wealthy," she told the lawyer. "But I didn't count on it, if you see what I mean. I have a job as a pastry chef in a restaurant, and I'm doing very well. If you, uh, speak to the Hart brothers...."

"*Speak* to them!" he exclaimed. "How I'd love to have the chance! Callaghan Hart had me on the carpet for thirty minutes in my own office, and I never got one word out. He left his phone number, reminded me that his brother was acting attorney general of our state and left here certain that I'd call him if I had any news of you."

Her heart leaped into her throat. Callaghan was looking for her? She'd wondered if he cared enough. It could be hurt pride, that she'd walked out on him. It could be a lot of things, none of which concerned missing her because he loved her.

"Did you tell him about the stock?" she asked.

"As I said, Miss Brady, I never got the opportunity to speak."

"I see." She saw a lot, including the fact that the attorney didn't know she was married. Her spirits fell. If Callaghan hadn't even mentioned it, it must not matter to him. "Well, you can tell them that I'm okay. But I'm not telling you where I am, Mr. Matherson. So Callaghan can make a good guess."

"There are still papers to be signed..." he began.

"Then I'll find a way to let you send them to me, through someone else," she said, thinking up ways and means of concealing her whereabouts. "Thanks, Mr. Matherson. I'll get back to you."

She hung up, secure in her anonymity. It was a big country. He'd never find her.

Even as she was thinking those comforting thoughts, Clint Matherson was reading her telephone number, which he'd received automatically on his Caller ID box and copied down while they were speaking. He thought what a good thing it was that Miss Brady didn't know how to disable that function, if she even suspected that he had it. He didn't smirk, because intelligent, successful attorneys didn't do that. But he smiled.

Callaghan hadn't smiled for weeks. Leo and Rey walked wide around him, too, because he looked ready to deck anybody who set him off. The brothers had asked, just once, if Cag knew why Tess had left so abruptly and without leaving a note. They didn't dare ask again.

Even Mrs. Lewis was nervous. She was standing in for Tess as part-time cook as well as doing the heavy housework, but she was in awe of Callaghan in his black mood. She wasn't sure which scared her more, Cag or his scaly pet, she told Leo when Cag was out working on the ranch.

Always a hard worker, Cag had set new records for it since Tess's disappearance. He'd hired one private detective agency after another, with no results to date. A cabdriver with one of Jacobsville's two cab companies had been found who remembered taking her to the airport. But if she'd flown out of town, she'd done it under an assumed name and paid cash. It was impossible to find a clerk who remembered selling her a ticket.

Jacobsville had been thoroughly searched, too, but she wasn't here, or in nearby Victoria.

Callaghan could hardly tell his brothers the real reason that Tess had gone. His pride wouldn't let him. But he was bitterly sorry for the things he'd said to her, for the callous way he'd treated her. It had been a last-ditch stand to keep from giving in to the love and need that ate at him night and day. He wanted her more than he wanted his own life. He was willing to do anything to make amends. But Tess was gone and he couldn't find her. Some nights he thought he might go mad from the memories alone. She loved him, and he could treat her in such a way. It didn't bear thinking about. So he'd been maneuvered into marriage, so what? He loved her! Did it matter why they were married, if they could make it work?

But weeks passed with no word of her, and he had nightmares about the possibilities. She could have been kidnapped, murdered, raped, starving. Then he remembered her mother's legacy. She'd have that because surely she'd been in touch with…the lawyer! He could have kicked himself for not thinking of it sooner, but he'd been too upset to think straight.

Cag went to Matherson's office and made threats that would have taken the skin off a lesser man. She'd have to contact Matherson to get her inheritance. And when she did, he'd have her!

Sure enough, a few days after his visit there, the attorney phoned him.

He'd just come in from the stock pens, dirty and tired and worn to a nub.

"Hart," he said curtly as he answered the phone in his office.

"Matherson," came the reply. "I thought you might like to know that Miss Brady phoned me today."

Cag stood up, breathless, stiff with relief. "Yes? Where is she?"

"Well, I have Caller ID, so I got her number from the unit on my desk. But when I had the number checked out, it was a pay phone."

"Where?"

"In St. Louis, Missouri," came the reply. "And there's one other bit of helpful news. She's working as a pastry chef in a restaurant."

"I'll never forget you for this," Cag said with genuine gratitude. "And if you're ever in need of work, come see me. Good day, Mr. Matherson."

Cag picked up the phone and called the last detective agency he'd hired. By the end of the day, they had the name of the restaurant and the address of Tess's apartment.

Unwilling to wait for a flight out, Cag had a company Learjet pick him up at the Jacobsville airport and fly him straight to St. Louis.

It was the dinner hour by the time Cag checked into a hotel and changed into a nice suit. He had dinner at the restaurant where Tess worked and ordered biscuits.

The waiter gave him an odd look, but Cag refused to be swayed by offers of delicate pastries. The waiter gave in, shrugged and took the order.

"With apple butter," Cag added politely. He had experience enough of good restaurants to know that money could buy breakfast at odd hours if a wealthy customer wanted it and was willing to pay for the extra trouble.

The waiter relayed the order to Tess, who went pale and had to hold on to the counter for support.

"Describe the customer to me," she asked curtly.

The waiter, surprised, obliged her and saw the pale face go quite red with temper.

"He found me, did he? And now he thinks I'll cook him biscuits at this hour of the night!"

The assistant manager, hearing Tess's raised voice, came quickly over to hush her.

"The customer at table six wants biscuits and apple butter," the waiter said with resignation. "Miss Brady is unsettled."

"Table six?" The assistant manager frowned. "Yes, I saw him. He's dressed very expensively. If the man wants biscuits, bake him biscuits," he told Tess. "If he's influential, he could bring in more business."

Tess took off her chef's hat and put it on the counter. "Thank you for giving me the opportunity to work here, but I have to leave now. I make biscuits for breakfast. I don't make them for supper."

She turned and walked out the back door, to the astonishment of the staff.

The waiter was forced to relay the information to Cag, whose eyes twinkled.

"Well, in that case, I'll have to go and find her," he said, rising. "Nobody makes biscuits like Tess."

He left the man there, gaping, and went back to his hired car. With luck, he could beat Tess to her apartment.

And he did, with only seconds to spare as she got off the downtown bus and walked up the steps to her second-floor apartment.

Cag was standing there, leaning against the door. He looked worn and very tired, but his eyes weren't hostile at all. They were…strange.

He studied her closely, not missing the new lines in her face and the thinner contours of her body.

"You aren't cut out for restaurant work," he said quietly.

"Well, I'm not doing it anymore, thanks to you. I just quit!" she said belligerently, but her heart was racing madly at the sight of him. She'd missed him so badly that her eyes ached to look at him. But he'd hurt her. The wound was still fresh, and the sight of him rubbed salt in it. "Why are you here?" she continued curtly. "You said you'd had enough of me, didn't you?" she added, referring to what he'd said that hurt most.

He actually winced. "I said a lot of stupid things," he replied slowly. "I won't expect you to overlook them, and I'll apologize for every one, if you'll give me a chance to."

She seemed to droop. "Oh, what's the point, Callaghan?" she asked wearily. "I left. You've got what you wanted all along, a house without me in it. Why don't you go home?"

He sighed. He'd known it wouldn't be easy. He leaned his forearm against the wall and momentarily rested his head there while he tried to think of a single reason that would get Tess back on the ranch.

"Mrs. Lewis can't make biscuits," he said. He glanced at her. "We're all starving to death on what passes for her cooking. The roses are dying," he added, playing every card he had.

"It's been so dry," she murmured. Blue eyes met his. "Haven't you watered them?"

He made a rough sound. "I don't know anything about roses."

"But they'll die," she said, sounding plaintive. "Two of them are old roses. Antiques. They're precious, and not because of the cost."

"*Wellll,*" he drawled, "if you want to save them, you better come home."

"Not with you there!" she said haughtily.

He smiled with pure self-condemnation. "I was afraid you'd feel that way."

"I don't want to come back."

"Too rich to bother with work that's beneath your new station?" he asked sarcastically, because he was losing and he couldn't bear to.

She grimaced. "Well, there isn't going to be any money, actually," she said. "The stocks are worthless. My mother made a bad investment and lost a million dollars." She laughed but it sounded hollow. "I'll always have to work for my living. But, then, I always expected to. I never really thought she'd leave anything to me. She hated me."

"Maybe she hated herself for having deserted you, did you think of that?" he asked gently. "She couldn't love you without having to face what she'd done, and live with it. Some people would rather be alone, than admit fault."

"Maybe," she said. "But what difference does it make now? She's dead. I'll never know what she felt."

"Would you like to know what I feel?" he asked in a different tone.

She searched his eyes coolly. "I already know. I'm much too young for you. Besides, I'm a weakness that you can't tolerate. And I lie," she added shortly. "You said so."

He stuck his hands deep into his pockets and stared at her with regret. "Leo told me the wedding was all his idea."

"Of course you'd believe your brother. You just wouldn't believe me."

His chest rose and fell. "Yes, that's how it was," he admitted, not bothering to lie about it. "I made you run away. Then I couldn't find you." His black eyes glittered. "You'll never know how that felt."

"Sure I know," she returned grimly. "It felt just the same as when you walked out the door and didn't come back all night!"

He leaned against the wall wearily. He'd avoided the subject, walked around it, worried it to death. Now here it was. He lifted his gaze to her face. "I wanted you too badly to come home," he said. "I couldn't have kept my hands off you. So I spent the night in the bunkhouse."

"Gee, thanks for saving me," she muttered.

He stood erect with one of those lightning moves that once had intimidated her. "I should have come home and ravished you!" he said shortly. "At least you'd still be there now. You'd have been too weak to walk when I got through with you!"

She caught her breath. "Well!"

He moved forward and took her by the shoulders. He shook her gently. "Listen, redhead, I love you!" he said through his teeth, and never had a man looked less loverlike. "I want you, I need you and you're going home with me or I'll..."

Her breath was suspended somewhere south of her collarbone. "Or you'll what?" she asked.

He eased her back against the door and bent to her mouth. "Or you'll get what you escaped when I left you that night."

She lifted her mouth to his, relaxing under his weight as he pinned her there and kissed her so hungrily that she moaned. She clung to him. The past weeks had been so empty, so lonely. Cag was here, in her arms, saying that he loved her, and it wasn't a dream!

After a few feverish seconds, he forced himself to lift away from her.

"Let's go inside," he said in a tortured voice.

She only nodded. She fumbled her key into the lock and apparently he closed and locked it behind them. He didn't even turn on a light. He picked her up, purse and all, and carried her straight into the bedroom.

"Amazing how you found this room so easily when you've never been in here before," she whispered shakily as he laid her on the bed and began to remove everything that was in the way of his hands.

"Nesting instinct," he whispered, his hands urgent.

"Is that what it is?" She reached up, pushing at his jacket.

"First things first," he murmured, resisting her hands. When he had her out of her clothes, he started on his own.

Minutes later, he was beside her in the bed, but he did nothing about it, except to pull her completely against him and wrap her up under the covers.

"Oh, dear God," he groaned reverently as he held her close. "Tess, I was so afraid that I'd lost you! I couldn't have borne it."

She melted into him, aware of the stark arousal of his body. But he wasn't doing anything about it.

"I don't like being alone," she replied, nuzzling her face against his warm, bare chest.

"You won't be, ever again." His hands smoothed over her back. One eased between them to lie gently against her stomach. "How are you feeling?" he asked suddenly.

She knew what he was asking. "I don't think I'm pregnant," she answered the question he hadn't put into words. "I'm tired a lot, but that could be work stress."

"But you could be."

She smiled against him. If this was a dream, she hoped she didn't wake up too soon. "I guess so." She sighed. "Why? Nesting instinct?"

He chuckled. "Yes. I'm thirty-eight. I'd love kids. So would you. You could grow them along with your precious roses."

She stiffened. "My roses! Oh, Cag...!"

His intake of breath was audible. "That's the first time you've ever shortened my name."

"You didn't belong to me before," she said shyly.

His arms tightened. "And now I do?"

She hesitated. "I hope so."

"I know so. And you belong to me." He moved so that she was on her back. "I've been rough with you. Even the first time. Tonight, it's going to be so slow and silky sweet that you won't know your name by the time

I've satisfied you." He bent and touched his mouth with exquisite tenderness to her parted lips.

"How conceited," she teased daringly.

He chuckled with a worldliness she couldn't match. "And we'll see about that…."

It was unexpectedly tender this time, a feast of exquisite touches and rhythms that progressed far too slowly for the heat he roused in her slim young body. She arched toward him and he retreated. He touched her and just as she trembled on the brink of ecstasy, he stopped touching her and calmed her. Then he started again.

On and on it went, so that time seemed to hang, suspended, around them. He taught her how to touch him, how to build the need and then deny it. She moaned with frustration, and he chuckled with pure joy.

When he heard her sob under the insistent pressure of his mouth, he gave in to the hunger. But even then, he resisted her clinging hands, her whispered pleadings.

"Make it last," he whispered at her open mouth, lazily moving against her. "Make it last as long as you can. When it happens, you'll understand why I won't let you be impatient."

She was shuddering already, throbbing. She met the downward motion of his hips with upward movements of her own, her body one long plea for satisfaction.

"It's so…good," she whispered, her words pulsing with the rhythm of his body, the same throb in her voice that was in her limbs. "So good…!"

"It gets better," he breathed. He moved sinuously against her, a new movement that was so arousing that she cried out and clung to him with bruising fingers. "There?" he whispered. "Yes. There. And here…."

She was sobbing audibly. Her whole body ached. It was expanding, tense, fearsome, frightening. She was never going to live through it. She was blind, deaf, dumb, so much a part of him that she breathed only through him.

He felt her frantic motions, heard the shuddering desire in her voice as she begged him not to stop. He obliged her with smooth, quick, deep motions that were like stabs of pure pleasure. She closed her eyes and her teeth ground together as the tension suddenly built to unbearable heights and she arched up to him with her last ounce of strength.

"Yes. Now. Now, finally, now!" he said tightly.

There was no time. She went over some intangible edge and fell, throbbing with pleasure, burning with it, so oblivious to her surroundings that she had no idea where she was. She felt the urge deep in her body, growing, swelling, exploding. At some level she was aware of a harsh groan from the man above her, of the fierce convulsion of his body that mirrored what was happening to hers.

She lost consciousness for a few precious seconds of unbearable pleasure, and then sobbed fiercely as she lost it even as it began.

He held her, comforted her. His mouth touched her eyes, her cheeks, her open mouth. Her body was still locked closely into his, and when she was able to open her eyes, she saw his pupils dilated, glittering with the remnants of passion.

"Do you know that I love you, after that," he whispered unsteadily, "or would you like to hear it a few dozen more times?"

She managed to shake her head. "I…felt it," she whispered back, and blushed as she realized just how close they were. "I love you, too. But you knew that already."

"Yes," he replied tenderly, brushing back her damp, curly hair. "I knew it the first time you let me touch you." He smiled softly at her surprise. "You were so very innocent, Tess. Not at all the sort of girl who'd permit liberties like that to just any man. It had to be love for you."

"It wasn't for you," she said quietly. "Not at first."

"Oh, yes, it was," he denied. His fingers lingered near her ear. "I started fighting you the day you walked into the kitchen. I wanted you so badly that I ached every time I looked at you." He smiled ruefully. "I was so afraid that you'd realize it."

"Why didn't you say so?" she asked.

His fingers contracted. "Because of the bad experience I had with a younger woman who threw me over because she thought I was too old for her." His shoulders moved. "You were even younger than she was at the time." His eyes were dark, concerned. "I was in over my head almost at once, and I thought I'd never be enough for you…"

"Are you nuts?" she gasped. "Enough for me? You're too *much* for me, most of the time! I can't match you. Especially like this. I don't know anything!"

"You're learning fast," he mused, looking down their joined bodies in the light from the night-light. "And you love like a poem," he whispered. "I love the way you feel in my arms like this. You make me feel like the best lover in the world."

"You are," she said shyly.

"Oh, no," he argued. "It's only because you don't have anyone to compare me with."

"It wouldn't matter," she said.

He touched her cheek gently. "I don't guess it would," he said then. "Because it's like the first time, every time I'm with you. I can't remember other women."

She hit him. "You'd better not!"

He grinned. "Love me?"

She pressed close. "Desperately."

"Try to get away again," he invited. "You're my wife. You'll never get past the first fence."

She traced a path on his shoulder and frowned. "I just thought of something. Where are your brothers?"

"Leo and Rey are in Denver."

"What are they doing in Denver?" she asked.

He sighed. "Getting away from me. I've been sort of hard to get along with."

"You don't say! And that's unusual?"

He pinched her lightly, making her squeal. "I'll be a model of courtesy starting the minute we get home. I promise."

Her arms curled around his neck. "When are we going home?"

He chuckled and moved closer, sensuous movements that began to have noticeable results. "Not right now…."

It was two days later when they got back to the Hart ranch. And they still hadn't stopped smiling.

Tess had decided not to pursue her horticulture education just yet, because she couldn't leave Cag when she'd only just really found him. That could wait. So she had only one last tiny worry, about sleeping in the same room with an escaping Herman, although she loved Cag more than enough to tolerate his pet—in another bedroom.

But when she opened the door to Cag's room, which she would now share, the big aquarium was gone. She turned to Cag with a worried expression.

He put his arms around her and drew her close, glad that his brothers and Mrs. Lewis hadn't arrived just yet.

"Listen," he said softly, "remember that nesting instinct I told you I had?"

She nodded.

"Well, even the nicest birds don't keep a snake in the nest, where the babies are," he said, and his whole face smiled tenderly as he said it.

She caught her breath. "But you love him!"

"I love you more," he said simply. "I gave him to a friend of mine, who, coincidentally, has a female albino python. Speaking from experience, I can tell you that deep down any bachelor is far happier with a female of his own species than with any pet, no matter how cherished it is."

She touched his cheek lovingly. "Thank you."

He shrugged and smiled down at her. "I built the nest," he reminded her. "Now it's your turn."

"Want me to fill it, huh?"

He grinned.

She hugged him close and smiled against his broad chest. "I'll do my very best." Her heart felt full unto bursting. "Cag, I'm so happy."

"So am I, sweetheart." He bent and kissed her gently. "And now, there's just one more thing I need to make me the most contented man on earth."

She looked up at him expectantly, with a wicked gleam in her blue eyes. "Is there? What is it?" she asked suggestively.

"A pan of biscuits!" he burst out. "A great, big pan of biscuits! With apple butter!"

"You fraud! You charlatan! Luring me back here because of your stomach instead of your…Cag!"

He was laughing like a devil as he picked her up and tossed her gently onto the bed.

"I never said I wouldn't sing for my supper," he murmured dryly, and his hands went to his shirt buttons as he stood over her.

She felt breathless, joyful, absolutely gloriously loved. "In that case," she whispered, "you can have *two* pansful!"

By the time the brothers arrived that evening, Cag had already gone through half a panful. However, he seemed more interested in Tess than the food, anyway, so the brothers finally got their fill of biscuits after a long, dry spell.

"What are you two going to do when I build Tess a house like Dorie's got?" Cag asked them.

They looked horrified. Just horrified.

Rey put down his half-eaten biscuit and stared at Leo. "Doesn't that just beat all? Every time we find a good biscuit-maker, somebody goes and marries her and takes her away! First Corrigan, now him!"

"Well, they had good taste, you have to admit," Leo continued. "Besides, Tira can't bake at all, and Simon married her!"

"Simon isn't all that crazy about biscuits."

"Well, you do have a point there," Leo conceded.

Rey stared at Tess, who was sitting blatantly on her husband's lap feeding him a biscuit. He sighed. He'd been alone a long time, too.

"I'm not marrying anybody to get a biscuit," he said doggedly.

"Me, neither," Leo agreed, stuffing another one into his mouth. "Tell you what—" he pointed his apple butter spoon at Rey "—he can put up his house in the daytime and we'll take it down at night."

"You can try," Cag said good-naturedly.

"With our luck, we'll never find wives. Or if we do," Leo added dolefully, "they won't be able to cook at all."

"This is a great time to find a veteran housekeeper who can make bread," Cag stated. "Somebody who can take care of both of you when we move out."

"I can take care of myself," Rey muttered.

"So can I," Leo agreed.

"Be stubborn," Cag said. "But you'll change your tune one day."

"In a pig's eye!" they both said at once.

Later, lying in Tess's soft arms, Cag remembered when he'd said the same things his brothers just had.

"They'll fall like kingpins one day," he told Tess as he smoothed her hair.

"If they're lucky," she agreed.

He looked down into her gentle eyes and he wasn't smiling. "If they're very lucky," he whispered. "Was I worth all the trouble, Tess?"

She nodded. "Was I?"

"You were never any trouble." He kissed her tenderly. "I'm sorry I gave you such a hard time."

"You're making up for it," she returned, pulling him down to her. "I'd rather have you than that million dollars, Cag," she breathed into his lips. "I'd rather have you than the whole world!"

If Cag hadn't been so busy following his newly acquired nesting instinct, he could have told her the same thing. But he was certain that she knew it already.

* * * * *

Turn the page for a preview
of New York Times *bestselling author*
Diana Palmer's
newest hardcover for HQN books

Before Sunrise

Available this July at your favorite book outlet

Chapter One

Knoxville, Tennessee, May 1994

THE CROWD WAS DENSE, but he stood out. He was taller than most of the other spectators and looked elegant in his expensive, tailored gray-vested suit. He had a lean, dark face, faintly scarred, with large, almond-shaped black eyes and short eyelashes. His mouth was wide and thin-lipped, his chin stubbornly jutted. His thick, jet-black hair was gathered into a neat ponytail that fell almost to his waist in back. Several other men in the stands wore their hair that way. But they were white. Cortez was Comanche. He had the background to wear the unconventional hairstyle. On him, it looked sensual and wild and even a little dangerous.

Another ponytailed man, a redhead with a receding hairline and thick glasses, grinned and gave him the victory sign. Cortez shrugged, unimpressed, and turned his attention toward the graduation ceremonies. He was here against his will and the last thing he felt like was being friendly. If he'd followed his instincts, he'd still be in Washington going over a backlog of federal cases he was due to prosecute in court.

The dean of the university was announcing the names of the graduates. He'd reached the Ks, and on the program, Phoebe Margaret Keller was the second name under that heading.

It was a beautiful spring day at the University of Tennessee at Knoxville, so the commencement ceremony was being held outside. Phoebe was recognizable by the long platinum blond braid trailing down the back of her dark gown as she accepted her diploma with one hand and shook hands with the dean with the other. She moved past the podium and switched her tassel to the other side of her cap. Cortez could see the grin from where he was standing.

He'd met Phoebe a year earlier, while he was investigating some environmental sabotage in Charleston, South Carolina. Phoebe, an anthropology major, had helped him track down a toxic waste site. He'd found her more than attractive, despite her tomboyish appearance, but time and work pressure had been against them. He'd promised to come and see her graduate, and here he was. But the age difference was still pretty formidable, because he was thirty-six and she was twenty-three. He did know Phoebe's aunt Derrie, from having worked with her during the Kane Lombard pollution case. If he needed a reason for showing up at the graduation, Phoebe was Derrie's late brother's child and he was almost a friend of the family.

The dean's voice droned on, and graduate after graduate accepted a diploma. In no time at all, the exercises were over and whoops of joy and congratulations rang in the clear Tennessee air.

No longer drawing attention as the exuberant crowd moved toward the graduates, Cortez hung back, watching. His black eyes narrowed as a thought occurred to him. Phoebe wasn't one for crowds. Like himself, she was a loner. If she was going to work her way around the people to find her aunt Derrie, she'd do it away from the crowd. So he started looking for alternate routes from the stadium to the parking lot. Minutes later, he found her, easing around the side of the building, almost losing her balance as she struggled with the too-long gown, muttering to herself about people who couldn't measure people properly for gowns.

"Still talking to yourself, I see," he mused, leaning against the wall with his arms folded across his chest.

She looked up and saw him. With no time to prepare, her delight swept over her even features with a radiance that took his breath. Her pale blue eyes sparkled and her mouth, devoid of lipstick, opened on a sharply indrawn breath.

"Cortez!" she exclaimed.

She looked as if she'd run straight into his arms with the least invitation, and he smiled indulgently as he gave it to her. He levered away from the wall and opened his arms.

She went into them without any hesitation whatsoever, nestling close as he enfolded her tightly.

"You came," she murmured happily into his shoulder.

"I said I would," he reminded her. He chuckled at her unbridled enthusiasm. One lean hand tilted up her chin so that he could search her eyes. "Four years of hard work paid off, I see."

"So it did. I'm a graduate," she said, grinning.

"Certifiable," he agreed. His gaze fell to her soft pink mouth and darkened. He wanted to bend those few inches and kiss her, but there were too many reasons why he shouldn't. His hand was on her upper arm and, because he was fighting his instincts so hard, his grip began to tighten.

She tugged against his hold. “You’re crushing me,” she protested gently.

“Sorry.” He let her go with an apologetic smile. “That training at Quantico dies hard,” he added on a light note, alluding to his service with the FBI.

“No kiss, huh?” she chided with a loud sigh, searching his dark eyes.

One eye narrowed amusedly. “You’re an anthropology major. Tell me why I won’t kiss you,” he challenged.

“Native Americans,” she began smugly, “especially Native American men, rarely show their feelings in public. Kissing me in a crowd would be as distasteful to you as undressing in front of it.”

His eyes softened as they searched her face. “Whoever taught you anthropology did a very good job.”

She sighed. “Too good. What am I going to use it for in Charleston? I’ll end up teaching…”

“No, you won’t,” he corrected. “One of the reasons I came was to tell you about a job opportunity.”

Her eyes widened, brightened. “A job?”

“In D.C.,” he added. “Interested?”

“Am I ever!” A movement caught her eye. “Oh, there’s Aunt Derrie!” she said, and called to her aunt. “Aunt Derrie! Look, I graduated, I have proof!” She held up her diploma as she ran to hug her aunt and then shake hands with U.S. Senator Clayton Seymour, who’d been her aunt’s boss for years before they became engaged.

“We’re both very happy for you,” Derrie said warmly. “Hi, Cortez!” she beamed. “You know Clayton, don’t you?”

“Not directly,” Cortez said, but he shook hands anyway.

Clayton’s firm lips tugged into a smile. “I’ve heard a

lot about you from my brother-in-law, Kane Lombard. He and my sister Nikki wanted to come today, but their twins were sick. If you're going to be in town tonight, we'd love to have you join us for supper," he told Cortez. "We're taking Phoebe out for a graduation celebration."

"I wish I had time," he said quietly. "I have to go back tonight."

"Of course. Then we'll see you again sometime, in D.C.," Derrie said, puzzled by the strong vibes she sensed between her niece and Cortez.

"I've got something to discuss with Phoebe," he said, turning to Derrie and Clayton. "I need to borrow her for an hour or so."

"Go right ahead," Derrie said. "We'll go back to the hotel and have coffee and pie and rest until about six. Then we'll pick you up for supper, Phoebe."

"Thanks," she said. "Oh, my cap and gown…!" She stripped it off, along with her hat, and handed them to Derrie.

"Wait, Phoebe, weren't the honor graduates invited to a luncheon at the dean's house?" Derrie protested suddenly.

Phoebe didn't hesitate. "They'll never miss me," she said, and waved as she joined Cortez.

"An honor graduate, too," he mused as they walked back through the crowd toward his rental car. "Why doesn't that surprise me?"

"Anthropology is my life," she said simply, pausing to exchange congratulations with one of her friends on the way. She was so happy that she was walking on air.

"Nice touch, Phoebe," the girl's companion murmured with a dry glance at Cortez as they moved along, "bringing your anthropology homework along to graduation."

"Bill!" the girl cried, hitting him.

Phoebe had to stifle a giggle. Cortez wasn't smiling. On the other hand, he didn't explode, either. He gave Phoebe a stern look.

"Sorry," she murmured. "It's sort of a squirrelly day."

He shrugged. "No need to apologize. I remember what it's like on graduation day."

"Your degree would be in law, right?"

He nodded.

"Did your family come to your graduation?" she asked curiously.

He didn't answer her. It was a deliberate snub, and it should have made her uncomfortable, but she never held back with him.

"Another case of instant foot-in-mouth disease," she said immediately. "And I thought I was cured!"

He chuckled reluctantly. "You're as incorrigible as I remember you."

"I'm amazed that you did remember me, or that you took the trouble to find out when and where I was graduating so that you could be here," she said. "I couldn't send you an invitation," she added sheepishly, "because I didn't have your address. I didn't really expect you, either. We only spent an hour or two together last year."

"They were memorable ones. I don't like women very much," he said as they reached the unobtrusive rental car, a gray American-made car of recent vintage. He turned and looked down at her solemnly. "In fact," he added evenly, "I don't like being on public display very much."

She lifted both eyebrows. "Then why are you here?"

He stuck his hands deep into his pockets. "Because I like you," he said. His dark eyes narrowed. "And I don't want to."

"Thanks a lot!" she said, exasperated.

He stared at her. "I like honesty in a relationship."

"Are we having one?" she asked innocently. "I didn't notice."

His mouth pulled down at one corner. "If we were, you'd know," he said softly. "But I came because I promised that I would. And the offer of the job opportunity is genuine. Although," he added, "it's rather an unorthodox one."

"I'm not being asked to take over the archives at the Smithsonian, then? What a disappointment!"

Laughter bubbled out of his throat. "Funny girl." He opened the passenger door with exaggerated patience and he smiled faintly. "You bubble, don't you?" he remarked. "I've never known anyone so animated."

"Yes, well, that's because you're suffering from sensory deprivation resulting from too much time spent with your long nose stuck in law books. Dull, dry, boring things."

"The law is not boring," he returned.

"It depends which side you're sitting on." She frowned. "This job you're telling me about wouldn't have to do with anything legal, would it? Because I only had one course in government and a few hours of history, but..."

"I don't need a law clerk," he returned.

"Then what do you need?"

"You wouldn't be working for me," he corrected. "I have ties to a group that fights for sovereignty for the Native American tribes. They have a staff of attorneys. I thought you might fit in very well, with your background in anthropology. I've pulled some strings to get you an interview."

She didn't speak for a minute. "I think you're forgetting something. My major is anthropology. Most of it is forensic anthropology. Bones."

He glanced at her. "You wouldn't be doing that for them."

"What would I be doing?"

"It's a desk job," he admitted. "But a good one."

"I appreciate your thinking of me," she said carefully. "But I can't give up fieldwork. That's why I've applied at the Smithsonian for a position with the anthropology section."

He was quiet for a long moment. "Do you know how indigenous people feel about archaeology? We don't like having people dig up our sacred sites and our relatives, however old they are."

"I just graduated," she reminded him. "Of course I do. But there's a lot more to archaeology than digging up skeletons!"

His eyes were cold. "And it doesn't stop you from wanting to get a job doing something that resembles grave-digging?"

She gasped. "It is not grave-digging! For heaven's sake…"

He held up a hand. "We can agree to disagree, Phoebe," he told her. "You won't change my mind any more than I'll change yours. I'm sorry about the job, though. You'd have been an asset to them."

She unbent a little. "Thanks for recommending me, but I don't want a desk job. Besides, I may go on to graduate school after I've had a few months to get over the past four years. They've been pretty hectic."

"Yes, I remember."

"Why did you recommend me for that job? There must be a line of people who'd love to have it—people better qualified than I am."

He turned his head and looked directly into her eyes. There was something that he wasn't telling her, something deep inside him.

"Maybe I'm lonely," he said shortly. "There aren't

many people who aren't afraid to come close to me these days."

"Does that matter? You don't like people close," she said.

She searched his arrogant profile. There were new lines in that lean face, lines she hadn't seen last year, despite the solemnity of the time they'd spent together. "Something's upset you," she said out of the blue. "Or you're worried about something."

Both dark eyebrows went up. "I beg your pardon?" he asked curtly.

The hauteur went right over her head. "Not something to do with work, either," she continued, reasoning aloud. "It's something very personal…"

"Stop right there," he said shortly. "I invited you out to talk about a job, not about my private life."

"Ah. A closed door. Intriguing." She stared at him. "Not a woman?"

"You're the only woman in my life."

She laughed unexpectedly. "That's a good one."

"I'm not kidding. I don't have affairs or relationships." He glanced at her as he merged into traffic again and turned at the next corner. "I might make an exception for you, but don't get your hopes up. A man has his reputation to consider."

She grinned. "I'll remember that you said that."